ARROWS
OF
FIRE

ARROWS

OF

FIRE

MARLEN SUYAPA BODDEN

ROATAN
HALL
PRESS

This is a work of fiction. All of the characters, organizations, and events portrayed in this novel either are products of the author's imagination or are used fictitiously.

Dedicated in loving memory of my dear brother,
The Reverend Edsel Bodden, who, when I was a student,
took me to the Maya ruins at Copán and inspired me
to write this story.

THE MEXICA: MOCTEZOMA

Invaders, mostly white men, some black men, and even a few women, people who look nothing like any visitor we have ever had, come from across the sea on ships and are now on the way to Tenochtitlan. These strangers have increased their ranks with warriors and slaves taken during their march from the coast and approach with more than two thousand fighters, chiefly Tlaxcalans, our long-standing enemy, but now the ally of these bearded men. Some of the newcomers mount enormous beasts never seen in our land and carry weapons that breathe fire and swords made from a metal that neither breaks nor bends; others control large, ferocious dogs not used for food but for battle.

They insist on coming here despite my warnings. I have tried, but failed, to dissuade them, with significant quantities of valuable gems and what they crave most, the informants say: gold. More precisely, they seek information on the locations throughout my empire where my predecessors and I have amassed gold over the centuries. The Supreme Council of Elders urges me to stand and fight them, but I reject their counsel and will not attack them, for reasons to be explained.

Our Supreme Lord, Huitzilopochtli, God of the Sun and God of War, mandated how to deal with the bearded foreigners, and now I must command the senior scribe and an artist to help me complete the history of my empire that we began writing eighteen years ago, when I ascended to the role of Supreme Ruler and Speaker, Chief Priest, and Master Judge. They will hide it in the depths of the Main Temple for my successor so that, if I am executed and the victors appoint a puppet, he will know how to preserve our ways.

The knowledge that these strangers have departed Cholula and soon will arrive in Tenochtitlan renders me incapable of performing many of my duties; thus, I have given over the majority of them to my brother, except praying and offering sacrifices to the gods. I even have a covenant with Huitzilopochtli that, as long as I offer Him what I value most, a young woman named Treasured Flower of My Heart, he guarantees these invaders will not annihilate us.

Book One

THE RESURRECTION OF COYOLXAUHQUI

Chapter One

THE XOCHIMILCA: FLOWER

At the Tenochtitlan and Tlatelolco markets, so they would not try to escape, dealers pierced the noses of the slave men and women and connected them by threading a long, thin cord through the holes in each person's nostrils; then, one guard held each end, and if a captive were to cry, the traders would pull the cord. The young ones they would control by putting small wooden yokes around their necks and linking their harnesses together with a rope.

Papa said people usually became slaves because they could not pay their debts or were condemned criminals, and fathers who did not earn enough money sometimes sold their wives, children, or themselves into bondage. Whenever we passed the place where they held them, I tried not to look, but most times I could not help it, and tears came to my eyes.

My memories of our lives before the dreadful days are happy and center on our work as farmers. At the markets, which we reached by sailing from our home in Xochimilco, Papa and I sold flowers, beans, squashes, chilies, tomatoes, avocados, limes, and mangoes we grew in our field.

He had chosen me to work with him when I was ten because he had no sons, and I was the only one of his daughters who knew her basic numbers and could read and write all the words necessary for being a merchant. When I turned eleven, Papa paid a builder to make a small boat for me that carried only flowers, because they were not as heavy as vegetables and fruits.

We covered our goods in cool, wet cloths to keep them moist and left early in the morning, when the sun was not hot. I loved being on the water, even though, in the beginning, it was difficult, and I was slow, but Papa said that, in time, it was going to be easier, when I was stronger, and he was correct. Once we arrived at a canal dock, Papa hired porters to help us unload and carry everything to a stall we rented from the government of Tenochtitlan or Tlatelolco.

By the time I was twelve, my grandparents said I was strong like Papa but looked like Mama. I chopped wood for Mama's stove and helped her care for the little ones by feeding them and changing their clothes. I also joined Mama and other women and girls in our neighborhood when we washed our laundry in the stream and hung it to dry on rocks. Once a week, she made my favorite meal, flat corn cakes and turkey stew with vegetables. Sometimes, when Papa and I arrived home, Mama would know if I was more tired than usual.

"Daughter, how are you feeling?"

"Mama, my feet hurt."

"Get some water in a pail ready so my girl can soak her feet," Mama asked my sister Dahlia.

After I had washed and dried my feet, Mama would apply sap from the maguey plant to soothe my skin and let me rest until dinner was ready.

Papa, who was stocky and had wide shoulders and muscular arms, said I was the only girl he knew who could sail, as he touched my head—I think to let me know he was proud of me. He also said I was going to make a fine farmer and merchant one day and was sure he could get permission from Grandpa to leave the field to me when Papa passed away. Even though in most families only boys were allowed to take property, two women in our village had owned their land and sold their products at the markets ever since their young husbands had died at war.

"But I don't want the field if it means you have to die, Papa."

"Aaah, Daughter, you know better than to let the gods hear you say that, aaah, no one lives forever in the Middleworld, and aaah, the gods don't want us to fear death because it has to happen. The old have to make way for the young."

That was as much as he said about that topic. Papa did not like to discuss anything that had to do with feelings.

I went with him when we had to pay tribute to Moctezoma at a building in Tenochtitlan every two weeks with fruits and vegetables during harvest. When the flowers bloomed, we delivered the goods the same way we went to the market. We sailed our boats, which were docked at the back of our field, north on Lake Xochimilco to Lake Tezcoco, where Tenochtitlan was located. When we arrived at the coast of the city, we entered a canal and proceeded to a marina near the market, where we tied our boats to poles. Officials always accepted payments of flowers first so they would not wilt and become worthless to the collectors.

Sometimes, if there was a religious ceremony that was going to happen soon, a messenger from Tenochtitlan told Papa and other gardeners the day before to go directly to the Main Temple and arrive before the sun rose. To be on time, we had to be at our field, cut and load the flowers, and then leave when it was still dark.

We used torches at the field, but when we sailed, it was by moonlight, which I liked because it was peaceful, unlike during the day, when the lake and canals were crowded and noisy. In the early morning, I liked the rhythmic sounds the water made when the boats glided on the water as Papa and I used oars and long poles to dig into the soil underneath and steer and push. We left as soon as the officials accepted our payments, so I never got to witness a ceremony at that or any other temple.

There were so many people in the market at Tlatelolco that we had to walk slowly. Most spoke Nahuatl, but others conversed in languages I did not understand. Papa said people came from all over the world and had to hire interpreters. Merchants from Tlatelolco and Tenochtitlan also went to other towns and faraway parts, he said, and I asked him if we, too, could go to the other places.

"Aaah, no, not us, our flowers and vegetables would rot before we got there. Besides, the professional merchants are the ones who go everywhere to sell their goods, but they're not farmers. They usually trade metals, jewelry, pearls, precious stones, cottons, feathers, and cacao beans, things like that."

The market at Tlatelolco had about twenty thousand people on any given day, Papa said. Both cities had goods for sale he could never afford to buy, but that did not matter, he explained, because there were laws forbidding us to use most of them anyway, as they were for rulers and nobles. The items included gold, silver, crowns, miters, fine jewelry, and sculptures.

To protect everyone, the government paid armed warriors to stand stationed throughout the markets, and some, Papa said, were unseen because they did not wear uniforms. Inspectors walked around to ensure everything was high quality, and there was a building in one of the squares where judges sat to hear and resolve conflicts that originated in the markets.

The areas I found delightful were the streets where they sold spices and herbs and those that had colorful items for sale—not just flowers, but also completed manuscripts, paints and brushes, writing paper, and musical instruments such as drums, flutes, and rattles.

Vendors also sold breads and pastries, and customers could buy food like turkey, dog, deer, duck, rabbit, iguana, weasel, rattlesnake, maguey worm, grasshopper, and other insects. There also were pens located near the slaves where one could buy live animals.

The merchants not only sold goods, but some provided services where customers could be treated for medical problems; tailors, where one could order clothing or buy it made; painters and scribes, to have documents read or written on one's behalf; booths leased by stargazers and soothsayers, who helped customers interpret their dreams or predict their futures; and porters to carry packages.

But what I loved most of all in Tenochtitlan, even though we were not allowed to go inside it, was Moctezoma's private animal park located at the end of the market. He went there at least once a week, Papa said, or when he showed it to visiting rulers and noblemen, but I never saw him. There was a tall gate at the entrance guarded by four men, and on each side was a black jaguar in a large cage next to high trees with eagles perched on their branches.

Often, when we were done for the day and had packed our sacks and baskets and sold or traded all our goods, Papa would take me to the gate of the animal park and let me go near the shiny black jaguars, and, at times, they stopped pacing to stare at people. On sunny days, their light eyes looked like yellow fire, and one could see the honeycomb pattern in their fur. When their mouths were open, long pink tongues hanging out and incisors on display, I would stand close to Papa, excited but afraid they would break out.

I tried to look beyond the gate at the other animals but could not see anything else. Papa said the ruler had many other creatures from all over the world, including cougars, panthers, mountain lions, small wildcats, wolves, bears, monkeys, alligators, hawks, falcons, and snakes as big as boats, and he even had a House of Birds and a butterfly garden.

When we went to the markets in Tenochtitlan and Tlatelolco, it was two days at Tlatelolco and one at Tenochtitlan, and, even though it was hard work, they were my favorite parts of the week. When I turned twelve, we went to Tlatelolco four days and Tenochtitlan one day, but if it was after harvest and we had nothing to trade, I spent almost all my time with Mama and my sisters, taking care of our field or making elaborate cotton capes, decorated with fine feathers, the currency that was accepted for expensive items, or helping Papa make obsidian blades he traded with vendors at the market. The capes took a long time and were costly to make, but they fetched the highest prices.

At the markets, I helped Papa by counting the number of flowers, vegetables, or pieces of fruit the customers wanted. He accepted goods in trade, usually something he or Mama needed at home, but sometimes he collected payment in cacao beans, the currency we used for small purchases, and he carefully examined each bean to make sure it was genuine, rubbing the shell to see if it fell apart. He had to be cautious because counterfeiters sometimes dug out the contents of a bean, refilled the shell with soil, and glued the original shell back into one piece. At times, there was a commotion at the marketplace when a bean was found to be fake and a vendor had summoned an official, who arrested the thief.

Papa was a prosperous farmer and merchant and for that reason was not required by the government to work for any nobleman or serve in the military. He had inherited the field from his father and, with our family, had done such a good job he earned much more than Grandpa ever had. Papa's burden, like every other commoner's, however, was that he had to deliver a substantial part of his income in taxes to the ruler of Xochimilco and to Moctezoma, because Xochimilco was a tributary to Tenochtitlan.

Some years when Tenochtitlan had more wars than usual, Papa had to pay in the form of cotton warriors' uniforms, and that meant Papa had to obtain supplies from the market, and Mama and the girls had to spend time away from the field making them. But I never heard Papa complain that he did not have sons to help him work, and at home, we teased him by saying he was Supreme Ruler and Speaker of his palace. Papa was good to all of us, and I have nothing but lovely memories about my life and family before the bad times.

We lived in a village on the shore of Lake Xochimilco, where the houses, made of adobe or stone, were small, but the fields, facing canals and located behind each farmer's house, were large, and because we had so much farming land, we produced a significant quantity of goods.

Our terror began the year I turned twelve, after harvest, when we had finished selling all our goods for the season and the temperature was turning cold. Each day, Papa left home after our evening meal and did not return until late at night, but I never heard Mama complain, probably because it was not her place to tell him what to do. We had work to do at our field, but he was too tired to get up in the morning. The rest of us went to the field after we had finished our chores at home, and he joined us later in the afternoon.

My oldest sister, Blossom, was seventeen and had just been married to a boy in another village who was a farmer and so had moved to live with his family. Dahlia was fifteen, Sage fourteen, and the little ones, Jade, ten, Rose (named after our mother), eight, Calliandra, six, and the baby, Turquoise, three. My true name is Treasured Flower of My Heart, but my parents addressed me only as "Daughter," and my sisters called me "Sister."

I loved all my sisters, but I was closest to Blossom and Dahlia, and I cried the first night Blossom was gone to her new home. Dahlia, in her role as the new big sister, held me.

"Stop crying, Sister—you know we'll see Blossom soon! She doesn't live far away."

The next day, after dinner, Dahlia gave me a pink blouse with blue embroidered flowers she had been making for herself.

"Tell her, Mama, tell her," she said.

"A young man who lives in Blossom's village came today with a message from your sister. She misses us, so they are coming to visit in two weeks."

My sisters and I jumped up and down and laughed, and Papa smiled.

It was a week after men at the Tenochtitlan market had started pausing at our stall and looking at me that Papa started leaving us at night. One man wore the uniform of a government officer, and the other was a priest with long hair covered in dried blood and his face and hands painted black, the same color as his garments.

I tried to control my trembling hands, and several times I dropped fruit I was about to put in a customer's bag. Papa stood by me and, barely moving his lips, whispered not to say anything. When we were on our way home from the canal, I asked him who were those men staring at me.

"Aaah, Daughter, it's best not to ask anything about the ruler's representatives, aaah, just pretend you don't see them and when you see anybody who looks like he works in the government, or is a priest or priestess, don't say anything to him or her because they could take it as a sign that you're questioning the ruler. And, aaah, the ruler has the right to send his officials or priests to talk to us or, aaah, even just to look at us, anytime he wants to."

"Well, I thought it was because I'm the only girl on our street at the market who helps her father."

Papa did not reply.

The men returned twice the next week, and once the following one—different officials, but the same priest, I think—to stand in front of our stall and watch me. Each time I was more fearful, my legs unsteady as we walked to the dock afterward.

"Don't you think it's really strange they did this more than once, just stood there looking at me?"

Papa stopped, shifted his feet, and gazed at the ground.

"Aaah, Daughter, I guess you don't know you're a very pretty girl, aaah, well, you are. You haven't noticed that lots of people look at you?"

I shrugged my shoulders.

"No, but, Papa, why would the ruler send someone to do that, even if I am pretty?"

"Aaah, girl, I'm just a farmer. I don't know why the ruler does anything, aaah, all I know is that we have to obey him, just like my father and grandfather, and our people before them, for a long time back."

"But, Papa . . ."

"Sh-sh-sh. Be quiet, girl! Aaah, what if someone hears you?"

He almost never spoke to us harshly, so I knew to stop asking him about those men.

One morning, about a week after the official and the priest had last been to the market, Papa told Mama to take my sisters to the field but to leave me to take care of him because he was sick and I should make him soup and tea. Mama obeyed and instructed me to cook Papa's food, and I took a large pail and went with her and my sisters until they turned onto a path and I continued to a stream near us to get water.

Turning the corner back onto our road, I spotted something I had never seen in my neighborhood: litters. There were two outside our house; each rested on the shoulders of four enslaved men standing in two rows. The litters were made from a light-brown plain maguey fabric with no openings and looked like large boxes with wooden frames over which the heavy and opaque cloth was nailed. My heart pounded.

I walked slowly and near home heard Papa's voice mingling with those I did not recognize. I did not go in.

"Stop saying you haven't been fucking whores and drinking *iztac octli*," a man said.

My father spoke loudly. "Officer, that's not true."

"I can smell the damn drink from your mouth even now, you damn drunk!"

"No, no, sir, I—"

"That's it, dog. We had enough. Shut your stupid mouth. We're taking you to the judge, and you'll get the death penalty, you dumb fool. We told you, just give the Supreme Ruler the girl, and we won't report you for drinking *iztac octli* and fucking whores."

My heart knocked faster.

"No, no, please, not my little girl, no. I can pay. I can pay you for the fine. Please, no, don't take my baby girl. Like I said, she's only ten years old."

"You're sure she's only ten? She's kind of big."

"Yes, Officer, she's growing fast. Please, I beg you, not my girl."

Papa was screaming, and I did not know why he was saying I was only ten, but I figured he had to have a reason. So I decided that, whatever happened, if those men did take me away, I was going to say I was ten. I trembled.

"She's not your girl. She belongs to the Supreme Ruler now. Anyway, if you don't turn her over to us, we're going to arrest you."

"But why, aaah, why do they want her?"

"That's none of your damn business. So, tell us, now, where is she?"

"Aaah, she's, she's . . ."

"Now, that's it. I had enough. We're taking you in."

I dropped the pail, and water splashed my legs; I hid behind a bush in the backyard but still heard them because they were yelling, and Papa was even louder than before and crying.

"All right, all right, aaah. She's down at the field, with my wife."

"We told you last night to have her ready this morning," they said.

I heard them hit him. He screamed.

"Aaah, I'm sorry. I forgot."

"You didn't forget, you drunken fool, and she better be there. You, stay with him. We'll go to the field."

I do not know how long I sat under that bush, but I was tired and afraid when Mama and my sisters arrived at the house; I wanted to run to them. Calliandra was weeping so much that, at times, she seemed to be choking. When she was upset, she used to wrap her arms around Mama's leg, and Mama would make cooing sounds, but now I heard Mama only cry.

"You, get out here and help us find her," a man said. "The mother said she went to get water. She's got to be back and hiding around here somewhere."

They found me and pulled me out; one took me by the wrist and led me to the front of the house. My family was standing outside, and everyone was weeping—even Papa. All my sisters were holding on to Mama, who was looking at me. She tried to disentangle the girls, but they would not let her go, until they noticed I was there. My parents and the girls tried to come to me, but the men pushed them so hard they knocked the little ones to the ground.

I tried to run, but another man grabbed and held on to me, and, as I screamed, he dragged me to the road, next to a litter.

I was crying and jumping. He held and examined my hands, running a finger on calluses that had formed over the years since I had begun working. Then he lifted and pushed me inside the litter. There were two mats in there, and I landed on the one farthest from the opening in the fabric that covered the litter. I tried to leave, but the man who had thrown me in was standing outside. He shoved me again and put a hand on my shoulder so I could not move.

I heard the men beat Papa again, and one said that that was for lying to them. The one who had put me in the litter was tall and fat, much larger than Papa. He smelled rank and had a greasy and scarred face. He released me, came inside the litter, and sat by me on the other mat.

I tried to hit him, but he grabbed my wrists and yelled to the slaves not to move; then he exited and pulled me out. "Get me the yoke—this little bitch is wild."

"No, no, no. I'm sorry. Please, sir. I won't fight. Don't—please don't put that thing on me," I said.

I heard my family crying, and one of the men told them to stop making noise or he would take one of my sisters. They became silent.

"All right, good. I see you're afraid of the yoke," the man said to me. "I think you'll behave good now, and I'll be nice to you; I don't want to hurt your pretty little neck. You'll be good if I don't put it on you? Get back inside."

I obeyed but could not stop weeping. I wanted to ask him why and where they were taking me but was incapable of forming even a basic sentence. He entered the litter and sat next to me again. When he hit the floor with a cane, the slaves moved us.

"Damn it, bitch, that crying is making me crazy. I swear, I swear I'll put the yoke on you."

I did my best, but tears continued to fall. I could not see my house anymore because there was no way to look outside the litter. I smelled stale sweat from the bondsmen running beneath us. It did not take us long to arrive at the canal. The man held my wrists, pulled me out, led me to a boat similar to Papa's, and told me to board. The other men who had been at the house were already there with the other litter and slaves.

I was afraid of getting on, so I tried to run, but the man who was guarding me put his hand around my neck and squeezed.

"Want me to tie you?"

"No, no, sir. No, sir."

One of the men on the boat held up a yoke and smiled.

"So, we got to put it on you?"

I boarded, and they told me to sit on a bench and hold on to the side of the boat. I lied when the man who was my guard asked if I knew how to swim, but I cannot say why I did so; perhaps it was because I wanted to keep something special about myself from them.

"No."

I knew how to swim and dive, as did everyone who worked a raised field. Papa and Mama had taught my sisters and me, because we sometimes had to stay under water for a while, using long tubular reeds to breathe air from above in order to inspect and cut decayed roots.

"All right," the man said. "I'll stay close to you in case the boat turns over or something, but that won't happen. The slaves know how to take care of it."

At first, we traveled the same way Papa and I did to go to the markets in Tlatelolco and Tenochtitlan, northwest. I had stopped crying, and even though I was sad and afraid and still thinking about my family, I was also paying attention to the route we were taking. We sailed for some time; it became hot, and I perspired. No one spoke.

I observed details I had not seen before, such as small islands and craggy hills in the distance. I looked back on my life to see if there was a sign, something in my past that could show why this was happening to me.

All the girls in our village were raised the same way; we had to learn how to work in our families' fields and at home by helping our mothers with domestic tasks. When I was old enough to pay attention, I participated in our morning religious rituals, as we prayed and burned incense before the altar at home that Mama had taught us to maintain to our most important gods, the God of Rain and the Goddess of Agriculture. We went to the temple in our village only on special occasions, such as for festivals dedicated to particular gods or goddesses of agriculture. We never went to any ceremonies at the Main Temple in Tenochtitlan, as those required a special invitation. Mama and Papa never said bad things about priests, only that there was no reason to spend time around them when we could worship at home.

When we reached the causeway that began at Coyoacán, we went underneath it and continued in a northerly direction, as Papa and I normally did to get to the markets, and then northeast until we arrived at what I later learned was the southeastern part of Tenochtitlan, where we docked at the edge of a thick forest.

Everyone disembarked, and the slaves removed the litters from the boat. My guard helped me into one, and we left. We seemed to go west on a straight road, the only one I had seen, and I did not feel that we made any turns. Of course, I was trying to memorize our route.

All the time since they had taken me, I had been wondering what my family was doing and if they had stopped crying and gone to the field to work. I also tried to figure out the connection between the government officials and priests who had stared at me at the marketplace and what was happening to me now. It was not clear why one of the men who abducted me told Papa I belonged to the ruler, and I was not sure what "fucking a whore" meant, but I knew from overhearing adults that it was forbidden by the government to drink *iztac octli*.

If only Papa had given me more information about those men at the market, I thought, *or maybe if he had warned me they were coming for me, I could have run away and hid.* But that was not fair to him because I had nowhere to go, as Moctezoma—even we children knew because our parents had told us—had numerous spies and

officials everywhere; he ordered men in our village arrested even
if he only *suspected* them of saying anything critical about him.

The litter stopped, and my guard stuck his head out to say he
had a girl for the senior priestess; someone gave him permission
to enter. My captor told me it was almost time to get out.

"We're at your new home. I'm going to give you some advice,
because you seem like a nice girl, and I got girls of my own. Now,
don't make no trouble, or the priestesses will hurt you and do some
real bad things to you. Just be a good girl—do everything they say,
and you'll be all right."

"If you really want to help me, take me back home. Please,
please, sir—take me home." I cried.

He cleared his throat, but his voice cracked when he spoke. "All
right, fine. Go ahead—don't listen to me. Keep on thinking you
can cry or talk your way out of this. See what's going to happen
to you, real soon."

"Well, I wouldn't be here so people could hurt me if you hadn't
brought me here, would I?"

"All right. I see it's true what they said—you're a smart one.
You think that's going to help you?"

I heard what sounded like a gate opening, and we moved again.
As the litter stopped and my guard went out and reached in to grab
my arm, I leaned away from him and curled my body. He grunted
and yanked me out, hurting my shoulder, and now, standing outside, I saw we were in a courtyard.

The only people there were four priestesses, all dressed in black,
with dried blood on their long hair and on their faces, and two men
standing by a litter. One of the women had wrinkled skin, and her
hair was gray. She approached me and smelled so bad I wanted to
vomit. When she tried to touch me, I jumped backward.

"Come, child. Don't be afraid. This is your new home, you'll—"

"Don't you or any of you touch me! I'm not your child, and this is not my new home. I have only one home, and I'm going back to it."

I turned to run, but the men seized me again. Followed by the priestesses, they took me to the entrance of a building and dragged me through an open door and into a room with no windows that had a pallet on the floor. I cried and said I wanted my mama and papa. There were torches placed on stands, and the room was bright and hot. Drops of perspiration formed on my forehead and on my upper lip. The men forced me down on the mattress until two priestesses replaced them. Then the men left, and all the women worked together to hold me down.

"Get off me!" I screamed. "Get off me! Stop touching me! Why, why're you taking off my clothes?"

I continued to yell, but they ignored me. When I was naked, the old one examined me with her hands, just about everywhere— my breasts, face, hands, behind my ears, and nostrils—but what frightened me more than anything was when two of them spread my legs and restrained me by the shoulders, thighs, and ankles. The old priestess pressed my stomach with one hand and stuck her finger inside me.

"Stop, stop! Take your nasty finger out of me! Take it out—take it out! Please, take it out!"

She could not go far and pulled it out. She nodded, and they let me go. I stood and tried to escape, but two of the priestesses caught me and made me stand in front of the old one. I was shaking.

"Tell me, now, are you going to stop trying to run, and will you be obedient?"

"No, I won't ever obey you—you dirty, nasty people!"

Someone handed her a stick. I was still naked.

"No, no, no! What're, what're you going to do with that stick? I'm sorry about what I said. I'm so sorry! Please, I will—I will obey you. Please, please—don't put that stick in me."

My body went limp, and I fell to my knees. Tears were dripping down my face and onto my neck and chest, and I repeated I was sorry. My heart was beating fiercely. I squeezed my legs together.

"Oh, that's a good girl, but you've already put us through too much. You still have to be punished for that, so you'll learn your lesson and never misbehave again," the old woman said.

She told the others to get me dressed, and I was relieved, actually ecstatic, that the priestess did not put that stick in me. I wiped tears away with my hands and was glad to have my clothes back on.

"Now, come with us."

I did, back bent and head down, and they took me to the same courtyard. I shivered. They led me to a long wooden cage on its side, with an opening on one end, and ordered me in. I hesitated, and the old priestess, still holding the stick, shook her head.

I entered, and they turned the cage so my head was down and my feet were sticking out at the top and they tied each ankle to the sides of the cage. My head ached against the bars of the cage, so I held on to its sides to relieve the pressure on my skull, but splinters on the wood were painful on my hands.

"Oh, no! Oh, no—what're you going to do to me? What're you going to do with that stick?"

I screamed.

"I'm sorry. I swear—I promise. I'll never disobey you again. Please, please don't hurt me."

I sobbed, but no one replied. All the priestesses took turns, until each was tired, it seemed, hitting me with that stick on the soles of my feet, and I begged for mercy countless times, but they did not stop until all had beaten the soles, and only the soles, of my feet. At one point, I fainted, and when I woke up, I thought they had set me on fire.

My clothes and hair were wet and smelly, and I realized I had retched and defecated and urinated. A mixture of mucus, tears, blood, vomit, feces, urine, and sweat were in my mouth and on my hair, face, head, and the rest of my body. I held on to the side of that cage with my left hand and used the other to wipe my eyes and push my hair aside. I spat.

I looked at my feet; they appeared to have been replaced by rubber. My stomach contracted, and I turned my face to heave. I was cold and lightheaded, and I shook, my palms bleeding. When they finally stopped assaulting me, they untied me, turned the cage back on its side, and pulled me out by the ankles. They had to help me stand.

Sharp darts of pain spread from my toes up my legs and hips and lower back. I spewed. I lifted a hand to wipe my mouth and stopped when I noticed a long strip of skin hanging from my finger. The old one, holding the bloodied stick close to my face, yelled and ordered me to walk, and I whispered I could not.

"Move. Now!"

I became angry again and screamed at them.

"Why don't you just kill me? Go ahead, I don't care. Kill me."

I lowered my head. The old woman put her face in front of me and used one end of the stick to raise my chin. She told me to look at her. I obeyed.

"*I* will not kill you, but if you do not walk, I'll put you right back in that cage and beat you again."

I put my right foot forward. I stopped because it hurt, but the old woman pointed the stick in the direction of the cage, and I put the left in front of the right, and so I moved, even though it seemed to be on a path of burning coals. I felt hot liquid leaking from my wounds, but I had stopped crying, gratified that they were not going to assault me again today.

They led me back to the same building where I was before the beating, but to another room this time, also with no windows and a pallet on the floor. There were four torches in the room. The old woman told me to sit. It was better to be off my feet, even though the pain was still severe and throbbing. They stared at me for several moments before they all left.

With no one else in the room, I had time to think and became afraid of what was going to happen next. The old woman had said she would never murder me, so I looked about the room for something I could use to hurt myself. The only idea I had was to set myself on fire using one of the torches, but that seemed too painful and slow, and my feet were already burning.

A short while later, two different priestesses, also dressed in black and who had smooth skin and clear eyes, came into the room. These two were clean, with no dried blood or black paint on them, and had their hair tied back. One held a large cup and a bowl and said I should use it to rinse my mouth. It was difficult to hold the items. I saw there were mint leaves floating on the water, and I obeyed. One of them poured water from a pitcher on a side table into a clean cup and gave it to me. I had not realized I was thirsty and drank three cups in a row.

"My name is Priestess Yoltzin, and this is Priestess Toci. Now, dear, what are you called?"

I did not say my full name because it was part of life with my family, and it was so special that not even they used it to address me, but I did not want to lie and risk getting another beating. My mother had told me that when I was born the soothsayer said the day was unlucky and consulted the calendar for a better time to acknowledge my arrival in the world. That turned out to be six days later, with an uncommon name, Treasured Flower of My Heart, that, for the rest of my life, would counteract the misfortune of having had an ill-starred birth date.

Priestess Yoltzin repeated her question.

"Um, my family calls me 'Flower.'"

She said they would allow me to continue to use the name "Flower," as a special sign they forgave me for my disobedience. She added they were not only priestesses but healers, too, and were going to care for me until I was better. Their gentleness only made me sadder.

"We understand you miss your family, and we did, too, when we first came here. But from now on, you'll see, as long as you continue to obey, everyone is going to treat you well, and we will never again hurt you. All right, dear?"

I wanted to cry.

"We're going to undress you and then carry you into the bathroom next door so you won't have to walk. Then we'll bathe you. Is that all right, dear?"

I hesitated about being naked again, but then I nodded, because I smelled awful and was uncomfortable. They removed my soiled clothes. I curled my body. I felt afraid and lonely and small.

Together they lifted me, and we went into an adjacent room, also brightly lit, and they sat me on a stool where one of them told me to open my mouth wide. She looked inside it and then ran her fingers along my gums. It was an odd sensation as she poked and rubbed. She pronounced my teeth healthy; then she taught me how they wanted me to clean my teeth and tongue and handed me a small, rough cloth with a paste on it made, she said, from ground geranium root, salt, and chili pepper. She produced a small, sharp wooden stick from her pocket and picked food from between my teeth and said I was to do that every night, using a mirror, after cleaning my mouth with the cloth. She added that it was important to care for my teeth so they would not rot and fall out.

They washed my hair, face, and body with a soft cloth and soap and rinsed me; then they put me in a filled bathtub containing herbs I could not identify. I gasped when I first touched the water because it was cold, but then it was soothing on my feet and hands. They took turns cleaning my body and face again with another cloth and washing and rinsing my hair. One of the priestesses handed me a soft cloth and told me to wash myself between my legs. They rinsed me; then they lifted me again and put me in another tub, this one filled with clean water. After that, they dried and wrapped me in a cloth. Together they carried me out of the bathroom and down a hallway to another room, also with no windows and lit torches, but this one had large vases on the floor filled with pretty flowers and a pallet covered by a colorful sheet.

While I was on the bed, they helped me put on a white tunic and applied sap from the maguey plant to my hands and feet, the same Mama used at home to treat our wounds. They rubbed on an ointment one of them said was to prevent infection; they wrapped my hands and feet with strips of fabric. When they had completed those tasks, one of them left for a short while, returned with a pitcher, and poured a cup of water she set on a small, low table next to me. She went out again while the other stayed and helped me sit and drink. I tasted a flavoring I could not identify that reminded me of an herbal tea Mama gave us when we could not fall asleep; it was not unpleasant.

A priestess returned with a plate of warm flat maize cakes and roasted turkey, and, with their assistance, I ate until I was full. Then I put my head on the pillow and closed my eyes. Someone covered me, and I went into a state where my mind showed me no story.

Chapter Two

THE SPANIARDS

The Spanish monarchs, Isabella and Fernando, appointed the first inquisitors for the Archdiocese of Seville on 27 September 1480. Tomás de Torquemada, Isabella's confessor, who would amass a vast fortune from his duties as an inquisitor, reorganized the Inquisition and named it The Tribunal of the Holy Office of the Inquisition. The Inquisition held substantially more prosecutions against women than men.

In 1480, when Marina González was thirteen and her family lived in Seville, a Christian mob of men tried to burn down her father Juan's store. Juan, then named Abrahán Ben-David, went to the constable to report the attack, but the official said there was nothing he could do, as they had not witnessed the crime and Juan had not produced a Christian to corroborate his complaint.

Juan left the precinct and returned to his shop, where he continued working with his assistants, but that night, as he was walking home, a group bloodied his lip and kicked his back until they cracked a rib. Someone yelled, and men ran out of the neighborhood's synagogue, where Juan's father-in-law was the chief rabbi, to help, and they steadied him and took him inside, where a physician treated him.

Juan recovered from his wounds, but Christians on the street continued to torment him by yelling epithets. Juan did his best to ignore them and would have continued to do so, but four months later, his Christian customers stopped going to his store, even though all owed him substantial amounts for what they had taken on credit.

Many other Jews in Seville who were undergoing similar experiences were converting to Christianity, but what finally made Juan decide to take the same action was what occurred one night as he was approaching the door to his home. Men called him anti-Semitic names and said they were there for his beautiful daughter.

"Let us come in with you so we can all have her, and we'll leave you alone after that. Or we can wait until you go to sleep and break in through the window. We know where she sleeps—we've seen her looking outside."

Juan walked faster and, at his house, unlocked the door and went inside, locking it behind him. Isabel, his wife, and Marina were crying, as they had heard everything the men had said. The boys were doing their homework in the study. Juan went to the storage room for a hammer and nails and secured all the windows and installed another lock on the front and rear doors. Then he sat downstairs all night, periodically checking that everyone was safe.

In the morning, before dawn, Juan washed and dressed, prayed, had breakfast, and told his wife no one else could leave and that she should be careful about letting anyone inside. His sister, to whom Marina was apprenticed as a seamstress, usually arrived for her in the late morning to take her to her shop, but Juan said Marina could not go out that day. He departed and asked neighbors, two kindly families on his street, Jewish and Christian, to watch over his family.

Juan went to the synagogue, which was connected to the rabbi's home, where he related to his father-in-law what had happened, including the threat to Marina. He asked permission for himself, Isabel, and their children to convert to Christianity, as it was the only way he knew to get the authorities to protect them.

"I'll think about it, but any consent must be conditioned on your agreement that the conversion would be only for how you conduct your lives in public—you would still have to practice Judaism at home," the rabbi said.

"And, you can visit us at home and continue to attend services unobserved as often as possible. In the meantime, I know *conversos*, people who converted from Judaism to Christianity, who work at the palace, and I'll speak with them about procedures for converting."

Juan told his wife and daughter what he and his father-in-law had discussed, causing Isabel and Marina to cry. When two weeks had passed, Juan's father-in-law told him he consented to the family's conversion, but they had to continue practicing the most important Hebrew tenets in private. He gave Juan names of two *converso* courtiers who were expecting him to discuss the procedures of how to convert.

Juan went to the palace and met with the men, who advised him that the family's conversion had to be convincing and that they had to follow all Christian religious instruction. They could no longer observe Jewish holidays or go to temple. The children were required to go to a Christian school or be tutored at home by a clergyman. They had to go to church at least once a week, on Sundays, and attend Bible study classes. The family had to take Christian names and, if they had any more boys, they could not be circumcised.

The courtiers that day introduced him to a friar at their church, and Juan spoke with the priest to make arrangements. In less than a month, the church witnessed the baptism of Juan and his family. Isabel and the children cried most of the time; Juan never again saw his wife smile. They were nervous at church and found it difficult to remember exactly how to cross themselves, pray, or perform any of the rites or customs that came easily to Christians.

The family's life stabilized gradually during the first two years of their conversion, and when they became known in their community as Christians, all harassment ended. The Christian shoppers returned, and most even paid debts they had previously incurred. Marina returned to work with her aunt and became highly skilled as a dressmaker and, with the money she earned, contributed to the family's savings for her dowry.

By the end of 1482, however, the Inquisition investigated *conversos* in Juan's neighborhood and deduced that Isabel was practicing Judaism. The inquisitorial judges ordered the constable of their district to arrest Isabel and seize her jewelry and fine clothes. When they arrived at her house and searched, they found and took a jewelry box and gowns and dragged her to a wagon. Isabel was alone, as the boys were at school, Juan at the shop, and Marina working with her aunt.

She saw several people she knew on the sidewalk and pleaded with them to go to her husband and tell him what had happened. The constable and his deputy tied her hands with rope, pushed her into the back of the wagon, and delivered her to the courthouse. When a neighbor went to Juan's store and informed him of Isabel's arrest, he sent an assistant to his father-in-law to relay the news, and then he went to the courthouse.

An officer took him to his wife and allowed him to stay with her while the inquisitor read her the denunciation. He said she could return home and had thirty days to appear before them to defend herself against the charge of having Judaized, or practiced Judaism.

After he took Isabel home, Juan went to his father-in-law and asked him to send someone to their home to perform a divorce under Jewish law. That night, a rabbi dissolved their marriage. Isabel, with the help of their families, escaped to Lisbon, where they had relatives.

The following day, the Inquisition posted the denunciation against Isabel on the doors of Juan's home, on St. Peter's Church, and at public buildings throughout the city, and had it read aloud at the church and at the main plaza. Thirty days later, when Isabel did not appear at the tribunal, the Inquisition held a trial in absentia, declared her a heretic, and sentenced her to excommunication and death by burning at the stake. No one ever found Isabel.

Juan stayed in Seville for a year after Isabel fled before he moved his family to Toledo. He was unable to get a good price for the sale of his shop in Seville and thus could not open his own business in Toledo, where his only means of earning income was working for someone else, selling fabric. Once the family was settled, Juan asked his relatives to introduce him to possible suitors for Marina but explained that, with children to support, he had to use most of Marina's dowry for their living expenses. The only man with interest was a *converso* named Francisco de Toledo, who at least had his own store. They arranged the marriage that took place the following year.

Marina's first child, Catalina, was born in January 1487, and twin boys, Tomás and Miguel, followed in 1489. All the children were baptized, but at home, Marina did not do much to practice Christianity, and it was her husband who ensured they celebrated Christian holidays and went to Mass most Sundays.

Marina and her family were entering church for midnight Mass on Christmas Eve in 1490 when she noticed the Inquisition had posted an Edict of Grace on the main entrance. Marina did not read it, but she trembled because she assumed it had been posted to target her and, believing the Inquisition would stop investigating her if she confessed, after Mass she approached a priest and asked to speak with him privately.

She said she wanted to confess regarding the Edict of Grace. He told her to return to church January 5 to formally admit her sins, but, in the meantime, she should celebrate Christmas and the holidays. Marina and her family went home, and that week, they went to Mass twice, and she attended Bible study.

On January 5, however, Marina awoke with a fever, and Francisco went to the church to inform the priest, who accompanied him to his house to hear her confession that she had Judaized until Christmas 1490. The priest forgave her sins and granted her reconciliation with the church.

Francisco's spice business was not successful, and Marina, from the beginning of their marriage, had to supplement their income by buying fabrics from her father at a reduced cost and sewing dresses to sell and by renting rooms in their home to relatives. Marina, by the time they had moved to Toledo, made wedding gowns for wealthy *conversas* and Jewish women in the city.

Two years after Marina had confessed pursuant to the Edict of Grace, the Inquisition began a prosecution against her. The tribunal's chief constable, his deputy, and the notary of the sequestration, all armed, accompanied by four laborers, went to her house one morning after Francisco had left. Marina was feeding the children when she heard pounding, followed by a demand to allow entrance to the officers of the Inquisition. She told the children to be quiet, went to the door, and opened it to see the men, one of whom announced he had a warrant for her arrest and seizure of her personal belongings.

"What? What do you mean? What is this all about?"

"You have been charged as a heretic by the tribunal. I have orders to take you to the courthouse right now."

"This has to be a mistake. In any case, I can't leave my children alone. I'll go to the court later and explain they made a mistake. I haven't done anything wrong. If people have been making things up about me, they're just liars. I'm a good Christian. Please leave me alone."

Marina tried to close the door, but the constable stuck out his foot, then pushed it, almost knocking her down, and the men went inside.

"What are you doing? Get out of my house! Get out—now!"

The constable and his deputy grabbed her and, as one stood behind and pulled back her arms, the other locked a chain around her wrists. Marina cried. When the children heard her, they screamed and went to their mother. Marina fell. She struggled to remove the chain, but it was secure.

"Where's the servant who helps you with the children?"

"I don't have anyone right now. Please, please sir. Untie me—just untie me. Have a heart! Don't you see how upset my babies are?"

"Where is your husband—at his shop?"

"Yes, yes. Please go get him. He'll tell you this is all a big mistake. You have the wrong person. Please, sir, at least untie me so I can take care of the children. They won't stop crying until you do."

The children now were clutching Marina. The constable directed his deputy to leave and return with Francisco and the others to locate Marina's valuable possessions, including all the wedding dresses she was making.

"What is this all about? Are you claiming I'm a criminal just because you want to steal my things?"

"You're lucky I don't slap you for accusing me of theft. I'm here by decree of the Inquisition. It says so right here on the warrant that I have to arrest you and seize your belongings."

"Please, sir, take this thing off my wrists. I just want to care for my babies. You see they're afraid and won't stop crying."

"I'll do it, but you'd better not cause trouble. If you do, you see I have a weapon, and I won't hesitate to use it."

He unlocked the chain, and Marina hugged her children close and kissed them. A while later, the deputy returned with Francisco, who was sweating, and his face was flushed. When they entered the parlor, the children ran to him.

"My children, my wife—what have you done to them? The deputy said you're arresting my wife? For what? She hasn't done anything! She's a good woman. You have the wrong person."

"That's not for any of us to decide. I'm just following the court's orders. You can make it easier if you tell us where you keep all the jewelry and cash. Where's your lockbox?"

"We are not rich people. I sell spices, and my wife is a seamstress."

"You're lying. We'll go on looking."

The men found women's clothing, including a wedding dress trimmed in gold thread, but not a box containing Marina's diamond jewelry and other items her mother had given her. She had never worn them, saving them for Catalina. The constable chained Marina's wrists. She and the children screamed, and Francisco pled with the official to release her, which he ignored.

He told Francisco to hold the children or they would be hurt if he had to separate them from Marina. Francisco obeyed; the agents took Marina outside, where neighbors had gathered, some to yell epithets at her, as the men pushed her into a cart and departed. Francisco took the children to Marina's father's home and then went to the courthouse.

At the tribunal, the chief prosecutor read aloud the allegations. Marina had been baptized but now was a heretic because she had continued to follow the Law of Moses and its rites, even though after her confession she had been reconciled with the Catholic Church. After that, "like a dog going back to its vomit," she rested on Saturdays by doing no household work, ritually purged meat of fat, did not eat pork, had no picture or figure of any saint in her house, no sign of being a Christian, and no cross. Marina asked for time to answer the charges, and the chief prosecutor granted three days.

She turned to leave, but the chief prosecutor yelled at her. "Where do you think you are going? You are remanded to jail to await trial. Warden, take custody of this prisoner. And bind her hands in case she tries to run."

The warden complied and secured her wrists.

Marina cried, "No, no, please. Please don't! I can't! I can't go to jail! I have my babies to take care of, and I just can't, I can't go to jail. Please, sir! I'm afraid—let me go home, please. I beg you."

No one replied.

"Please, sirs, would you at least let me speak with my husband?"

He nodded, and Marina approached her husband. She whispered in his ear. "Sell some of the jewelry in the lockbox and hire that lawyer, Diego Tellez, for me. And take care of the children and my brothers, and don't bring them here. Tell them I'm sick in the hospital."

Francisco tried to embrace Marina, but the jailer and his deputy pulled her away from him and told him to leave. She dropped to the floor. The men pushed Francisco away, and a deputy escorted him out as the warden and a guard led Marina to the entrance to the cells, located in the basement. When they reached two floors underground and went through an opening, Marina saw a cage containing about twenty women prisoners. She screamed and tried to free herself, but they would not release her.

The captives laughed and jeered. "Come here, sweet thing! What, you're too good to be with us?"

Marina kicked the warden's leg, and he slapped her, drawing blood on her lips.

"You dirty bitch! I was going to be nice and put you in with the whores, but now we have a special place for you—where you'll stay until you learn to behave."

Marina was faint. They removed the chain from her wrists and guided her one more flight down, to the lowest level of the basement, the area for solitary confinement. A lone dim candle provided the only light. They pushed her inside a cell through an opening. She fell to the dirt floor, and they closed and locked the grate before leaving.

Marina screamed. She heard laughter upstairs and cried until she went to sleep. Sometime later, she stretched her legs, kicking over a bucket and its contents, a mixture of feces, urine, and blood, that soaked her dress and undergarments. She vomited. She was thirsty and noticed a pail with the hook of a ladle sticking out and considered investigating whether it contained water, but because it was dark she knew she would not be able to tell if it was clean. She almost called for someone to bring her something to drink but changed her mind, assuming it would be futile. She needed to relieve herself but held it in until it became painful; then she pulled down her underclothes and squatted on the ground, although with difficulty, because her joints were stiff.

The lining of her mouth seemed to be breaking. She crawled and smelled the water in the pail; it seemed clean, and she drank. Marina sat, leaning against the wall, thought about her family, and silently prayed in Hebrew. She heard a squeak. She yelled as she crawled to the front of the cell. The vermin ran. Marina spent several hours sitting on the ground in one position, reciting her favorite prayers and rocking herself, with her arms tight around her knees, afraid to close her eyes.

After a while, she heard someone coming down the stairs. A burly jailer arrived, carrying a bucket and a tin bowl and spoon.

"Take the bowl and hold it so I can give you porridge."

Marina did not move.

"If you don't get it now, you're not getting nothing else to eat for a long time. You want it, or what?"

Marina was silent, and he left. No one else came until hours later, when the same jailer arrived with another bucket, this time with stew. She ignored him, and he left, and for the next two days, three times a day, the only person she saw was the man with his pail.

The warden and his deputy arrived the following day and took her upstairs, past the women's section. No one said anything and, as her eyes adjusted to more light, she stumbled on the stairs. A woman guard met her on the main floor and led her to a room where there was a pile of clean clothes and toiletries Francisco and her father had delivered. She told her she would leave so Marina could wash herself, comb her hair, and put on the clean clothes.

The guard returned and directed her to a room where Francisco and Juan were waiting. They embraced. Marina at first could not speak because she was crying. Her husband said he had hired a Christian woman to care for the children when he was at the shop and to cook and clean. The children cried constantly and asked when she would be home, but they were well. Francisco had brought her food and a jar of juice. She ate and drank.

Marina, Francisco, and her father met with the lawyer, Diego Tellez, and they discussed the denunciation and what Tellez would tell the inquisitors. He reviewed with them a document he had drafted, the answer to the complaint, which Marina signed. Escorted by the warden and his deputy, they went to the courtroom to stand before the tribunal, where Tellez entered on Marina's behalf a plea of not guilty and filed her reply, denying each allegation. Marina demanded her property be returned. The inquisitor ordered her back to jail to await trial. She screamed and tried to flee, but the deputies seized her. She kicked them and scratched the face of one, but they subdued her, chained her wrists, and dragged her back to solitary confinement.

As before, she saw only the same guard, three times a day, with his bucket of slop. She ate a few spoons of food at each meal. One day, a warden and a deputy arrived to chastise her for being disobedient. She ignored them; they entered the cell and kicked her several times. She was silent but wept after they had departed. When the jailer went to feed her, she ate a bowl of pork stew but vomited most of it after he had left. Her body and clothes were soiled, her hair was falling out in patches, and she had itchy skin, boils, and sores. The following day, she menstruated, and the blood soaked through her undergarments and dress.

The next day, she heard footsteps, footsteps that stopped near her cell, and her heart beat fast. Marina stared but saw no one. She lost consciousness and awoke hours later. She thought about her family as she rolled up her left sleeve and pinched her arm with her right thumb and index finger, digging her now long and soiled fingernails into her flesh. Blood flowed. She smiled and chose another spot and repeated the procedure six times, until she went to sleep.

The jailer woke her by banging on the cell door with his ladle. He did not say anything; he just held up the bucket with swill. He dropped the pail and placed it on the floor outside the cell and left. Later, the warden and the deputy arrived and unlocked and entered the cell.

"Uuugh, what a nasty bitch. It smells like shit and piss and blood in here."

They raised her, and she was limp as they took her upstairs to a medical examining room, where they laid her on a table. It was daytime, and the shutters were open. The light hurt her eyes.

A physician and his assistant, a prison matron, entered. "What do we have here? Help me take off her dress."

Marina opened her eyes. She tried to hit them but was too weak. They removed her dress. She was embarrassed to be in her undergarments but stopped resisting. The physician examined her arms and hands. She had large infected wound sites on her left arm covered in dried blood and soil, and her fingernails on her right hand were covered in the same mixture. Her jutting cheekbones stretched the skin on her face. The physician shook his head. Marina screamed as they applied an astringent liquid to her injuries with a cloth, digging inside to remove soil and clotted blood. She fainted and regained consciousness when they put smelling salts under her nose. They had wrapped her left arm in bandages and washed and cut her fingernails. Marina cried.

"Mrs. González, we are going to need you to compose yourself and get up from the table so you can wash yourself and put on clean clothes that your husband brought you. Then, you will be transferred to a different area, in the section with the other women, but in your own cell, where you will sleep on a clean cot and eat specially prepared food and good drinking water."

Marina said nothing.

"Please answer me. Do you understand what I am saying? Answer me, Mrs. González."

Marina nodded. The woman closed the shutters to the window.

"Good. You can use the basin with water and the soap and extra pitchers of water next to it and the paste that is there for your teeth. That package over there has your clothes and shoes and other personal items. We will go out. When you have finished, open the door; we will be outside."

They left. She took off her garments, washed her body and hair, dried herself with towels, cleaned and rinsed her mouth, combed the strands of what was left of her hair, and dressed. She walked to the door and opened it to find the physician, the warden, and his deputy waiting for her.

"Very good, Mrs. González. Well done. Someone will deliver the rest of your things to you there," the physician said.

They escorted her to the women's area she had seen her first day at the jail. She barely noticed this time when the prisoners jeered.

"Hey, they said you was a Jew. You too good to be in here with us?"

"Be quiet, or I'll put each one of you bitches in the hole, too, if you say anything else," the warden said.

They stopped speaking. He and the deputy helped Marina inside a cell that was separated from the women, on the far side of the same floor. Marina later learned that Francisco had paid special fees so that she could have her own section and additional services. It not only had a cot with a mattress and clean sheets, a pillow, and a blanket, but there was a bowl with soap and a towel. The floor was wood instead of dirt. There even was a chair at a small table. The warden told her to sit down and that someone would bring her food. Francisco had also paid for someone to remove her waste bucket twice a day, but she could smell the stench coming from the group of other women. Marina sat, as instructed. The men went out and locked the gate behind them.

Ten minutes later, two workers arrived, and one of the women yelled at them.

"When're you going to take out the buckets full of shit and piss?"

"I told you, when they spill over, you stupid slut."

"Fuck you, you animal."

"Want me to call the warden to come down and break your ugly face again, you dumb whore?"

"Who're you to be calling somebody 'dumb' and 'ugly'?"

"At least I'm not a whore. And I don't have to put up with this when I go home and I'm away from you nasty bitches."

Some of the women yelled at him to stay. "Don't punish us for what she said. And when're you bringing me a present, like before? Come on—you know I'll suck you off again if you bring me some real food."

Smiling, he distributed the food. In the meantime, another jailer, as some of the women in the cell watched, set up Marina's dinner: roasted pork, bread, clean water, red wine, and cake. The men left. For the next three days, Marina ate some food at all her meals and slept for long periods of time. Each day, the wounds in her arm hurt less. On the fourth, they took her upstairs to see the physician; he examined her, removed the bandages, cleaned the wounds with an ointment, and replaced the cloths on her arm. They returned her to her cell.

On 8 January 1493, the Inquisition presented its case with neither Tellez nor Marina present during any part. The first witness, Pedro de Teva, said Marina refused to eat pork, she only pretended to do chores on Saturdays, and she had made unleavened bread. Fernand Falcon, Marina's cousin, spoke next and said he was in Francisco's house the day they arrested her and seized her goods and that he saw no sign she was a Christian.

Juana de la Cadena, who was married to Diego Falcon, Fernand's brother, called Marina a "Jewess," said Marina did laundry on Fridays, went out all day on Saturdays, and did housework on Sundays. Juana also testified that Marina worked by sewing on Sundays to earn money for her daughter's dowry. Juana added she often saw her and other *conversas* walk about on Saturdays, to show off their evil lineage. Gracia de Espina said Marina cooked and cleaned on Fridays and Sundays and observed the Sabbath on Saturdays.

The Inquisition informed Tellez when the prosecutor had completed its case and granted him permission to submit a list of questions he wanted the inquisitors to ask Marina's witnesses at the trial, pertaining to whether she had committed any of the acts alleged in the complaint. Marina's six witnesses testified she was a Christian, went to church, and worked in the household on Saturdays.

The proceedings continued; with Marina present in the courtroom, the tribunal announced its verdict on 18 April 1493. The

Inquisition declared Marina a relapsed heretic and ordered her to be tortured by water and that if she did not thereafter confess, she had to prove her innocence with the testimony of eight Christian witnesses. They commanded the warden and his deputy to chain her and take her to be interrogated. Marina went limp and fainted.

Marina had her eyes closed as they took her out of the courtroom to another area. She did not resist when the jailers, now including a specialist in interrogation techniques and a matron, who removed Marina's dress, placed her on a rack four feet wide by seven feet long, and secured her with chains by the wrists, waist, and ankles. The specialist told Marina to open her mouth wide. When she obeyed, he pushed in a metal clamp to keep her jaws open; then two men raised the rack at an angle twenty degrees to the horizontal so Marina's head was down and her feet up.

The specialist, from a height of twenty inches, poured water from a jar for forty seconds, filling her mouth, throat, sinuses, and trachea. Marina coughed, and water spurted out her nose. The specialist poured more water, and Marina twisted her head to the side, so he cupped his hand around her mouth to prevent the liquid from spilling.

Marina cried. A combination of mucus and blood, from the clamp breaking the lining of her mouth, dribbled down, covering her eyes and soaking the hairline on her forehead. The specialist and the warden then tilted the rack so Marina's head was up and her feet down, and the matron removed the clamp. The specialist asked her if she admitted she was guilty of the charges. She was silent.

The matron replaced the clamp, and they lowered her head once again. She held her breath as the specialist poured a pint of water into her mouth. He waited until she could no longer hold her breath and poured in more water. She choked, and bile poured out of her mouth; she thrashed, causing the irons binding her to cut into her skin.

They raised the rack and took out the clamp. The specialist asked her if she denied the allegations. Marina made a vague statement that she hoped would be acceptable as an admission, because she did not want to hurt anyone she knew by turning them in. She said a neighbor, whose name she could not remember, fasted for Jewish holidays and observed Saturdays as Sabbath and that that had happened more than a year ago. They untied her and helped her stand. The matron assisted with her dress, and they led her back to her cell.

The tribunal ordered her brought before them, on 20 May 1493, without her attorney or family present, and told her to confess. She was silent. They asked her if she was a good Christian. She said she was not and did not believe in any of the evil teachings of the Catholic Church. She said she hated Christians and that it was true that she had not converted to Christianity. The inquisitors stared at her and offered more time for her to obtain witnesses to prove she had not Judaized. She replied she would not inform on anyone, was not interested in continuing the proceedings, and asked to be executed.

The chief inquisitor said their patience was depleted and set the date for her execution. They said she could pay an additional fee so the executioner would choke her to death with a rope before burning her body at the stake. A deputy delivered the written judgment to Francisco's shop and provided instructions for paying the extra charge for the executioner's special service.

Francisco went to see Marina's father. They agreed to tell the children Marina had died from an illness at the hospital. Francisco handled the procedures, and he and her father visited

Marina a final time in a room located on the main floor of the courthouse. She weighed less than a hundred pounds, almost all her hair had fallen out, and she had sores on her face and body. Juan and Francisco stared at the floor as she said she wanted no one from the family present at her death. She asked Francisco and Juan to take care of her children and brothers and Francisco to use all the money from her savings that remained for Catalina's dowry and to give Catalina, when she married, all the jewelry in her lockbox.

2 June 1493 was a cloudy and windy day, but, as there was no rain yet, the tribunal went forward with Marina's execution at one of the squares in the city. A substantial crowd gathered in a large circle around a pyre and stake the warden's staff had constructed, surrounded by dried faggots and straw. They had passed a cord through a hole bored in the wood at the top of the stake.

Ten officials, including members of the clergy, escorted Marina, bound in irons at the wrists and ankles and dressed in clean clothes and new shoes Francisco had delivered, from the jail to the square. She walked slowly, her head down. She did not cry or resist when they tied her to that stake, arms next to her body, at the head, waist, and ankles, and, to strangle her, they secured the cord around her neck.

A friar led the congregation in prayer and pled for Marina's soul, commending her to God. A captain in the royal military waved to the executioners standing on either side of Marina. One lit the fire, but as the other was pulling the rope to choke her to death in accordance with Francisco's wishes, so she would not suffer the pain of being burned, a breeze blew the flames and scorched the executioner, and he retracted his hands and stopped choking her.

Marina panted as heat from the incineration caused the lining of her trachea to swell and the skin on her feet to crack open and release fluids and make a hissing sound. She fainted. It took two hours for her heart to stop beating and her organs to fully cook and burst.

Chapter Three

THE MEXICA:
MOCTEZOMA

As chief priest, my duties were to ensure that the gods continued to make the sun rise, the rains fall, and the Earth produce human life and food, by presiding over the rites that nourished our deities and paid them our debts. Most divinities prefer warriors in offerings, but according to our calendars there is substantial need at all times for subjects, forcing us to use slaves, regionally bought men, women, and children—those I demanded as tribute from the territories—and local criminals whom I had sentenced for violating certain laws.

I selected future deity impersonators for two important reenactments at the compounds where we housed and educated young men to play the part of the Lord of the Smoking Mirror and girls to impersonate a goddess. The ceremony involving Coyolxauhqui, the Moon Goddess, is a reenactment of the events that took place when Huitzilopochtli annihilated Coyolxauhqui and her brothers, the Four Hundred Southern Gods, to prevent them from murdering the Mother of the Earth.

Once the girls arrived at the compound, they were not permitted to leave until they had been selected to impersonate a deity in a rite. The girls' fathers were not told where they would be taken, only that they now belonged to me. Sometimes, family members regretted having sold their daughters when their financial circumstances improved, and they made inquiries of local officials, who dispatched a military officer to warn them they would be imprisoned or suffer the death penalty if they did not stop asking questions.

One day last year, at the female compound, the senior priestess said she had twenty girls who were the proper ages, and of those I had seen ten the prior month. The senior priest who accompanied me relayed my responses to her, because I do not speak directly to women outside my family. I said I was not interested in seeing the ones from the last inspection, as I had determined them to be flawed. She said she had no more candidates who were fifteen years or older.

The senior priest ordered the senior priestess to leave the room so he and I could speak, and she bowed and departed, walking backward. I was angry she had only ten candidates of the required age other than the ones I had rejected earlier, some of whom had dog faces, others moved like animals, had crooked or yellow teeth, hooked or flat noses, or uneven eyes—several had scars from pustules.

I did not raise my voice, however, because I always speak in a soft tone, as it is undignified for the emperor to yell or otherwise call attention to himself. He called the senior priestess back in, and she explained the number of impersonators of suitable age was running low because of the frequency of ceremonies. She departed.

Another priestess entered with ten young women, ones I had not seen the prior month. Each one's hair hung loose to her waist; they stood before me in a row with their heads lowered, but not so much as to obscure their faces. They were unshod and dressed identically in simple garments, skirts made of black maguey cloth, short to the knee. Then, the priestess led a handsome girl standing to my far left to stand before me.

Her hair was thick, black, and shiny. Her visible skin had no scars or pustules, her lips were full, arms and legs firm but not muscular, her ears were the same size, and she had a nose that was small and not flat or hooked. She was thin but with a womanly bosom. I always perform the same inspection for each candidate, with the priest telling her what to do. He ordered her to smile, and her teeth were white and even.

"You may look up at His Highness, but only until he nods, and then you must lower your head again."

She looked at me boldly, which I liked. Her eyes were evenly spaced, of the same size, and long, topped by neat eyebrows, and the whites truly were white and clear. I nodded, and she lowered her head; I indicated with my hand that she should move back to the row. I was disappointed by the rest and realized why the priestess had placed the perfect one at the beginning of the line.

The others each had at least one defect; two of them were just ugly. The senior priestess left with the nine rejected girls, the one whom I had selected remaining. Another priestess led her to the center of the room, where she tied a small bell around each of the young woman's calves.

The girl danced, and, as she moved, her skirt rose, and I saw her thighs, which, like her arms and calves, were firm. She performed with full confidence. When she had finished, the priestess left the room with her, both walking backward, heads bowed.

The senior priestess returned with the second group of girls. I turned down the first five, but the sixth in the row was lovely, and I chose her as the second candidate. As I was about to dismiss the rest, my eyes followed a shaft of sunlight shining on a third girl I was interested in, last in the row, tall for fourteen. My heart beat fast.

Even though I could not see her entire face because her head was bowed, I knew this girl was extraordinary. She was not comely; no, she was spectacular and—she became *my* sovereign. This girl would not impersonate Coyolxauhqui—this girl *was* Coyolxauhqui. I saw myself kissing and touching her smooth skin, as I silently deliberated whether to use her in the rite or keep her as a concubine.

She trembled. Her hair was the deepest black with a burnished cast of blue, and it contrasted with her reddish-brown skin, her skin, her skin, her skin absorbed illumination from the window and converted her face into a palette of copper. I did not want to stop staring at her, but she forced me to turn and look outside.

She had changed the firmament; the heavens now were orange and crimson, as if the sun wanted to set, even though it was mid-day. I made myself focus on the task and whispered to the priest to keep this girl in the room.

"His Majesty orders you to remove all the other girls, except the last one in the row. What is her name?"

"Yes, sir. Sir, we call her 'Flower.'"

"Where is she from?"

"Xochimilco, sir."

When the other candidates had left, the senior priestess brought her to me; the girl had her hands tightly clasped in front of her body. The priest nodded, and the woman told her to look up at me. I held my breath.

She was a commoner, but there was something dignified about her mien. Her eyes were full of tears, and several escaped onto her cheeks; I wanted to wipe them away with the tips of my fingers. I did not rush my inspection. Never had I seen such a personification of Coyolxauhqui.

I nodded, and the priestess told her to lower her head; another escorted her out. Flower was not ready to participate in the rite at that time. I ordered the senior priestess to educate her for another year and specified there could be no mistakes with Flower. She had to be delivered to me pure. The priest told the priestess to confirm Flower was a virgin.

"Yes, holy sir, I examined her myself, when the official first brought her here, the way I do with all the candidates, and her maidenhead is intact."

I commanded Flower to be trained as a warrior, in addition to her other studies, and the priestess to order the finest cotton clothing and bed linens for her. Flower was to sleep alone in her own room but with a priestess to guard her at night. She replied that there were no female warriors at the compound, and I instructed her to send a messenger to the military headquarters and ask for a female warrior to go there and teach Flower.

After I asked how she was doing in her academic classes, the priestess said very well in all of them, even outstanding in her reading and writing, so much so that she had her own tutor in those subjects. I ordered the priestess to contact the Royal Academy in Tenochtitlan to obtain a priest to teach Flower four days a week in reading and writing.

The matters having been concluded, and upon returning to the city center, I resumed my normal schedule, presiding over judicial hearings, meeting with governmental officials and spies on different issues, and granting audiences to noble subjects and tributaries from throughout my empire. There were always so many people who sought an audience with me that every morning they formed a line that stretched outside my palace.

I have thought of Flower since I first saw her last year and remain mesmerized by her, sometimes needing to stop myself from having her brought to me from the compound. If I took her as mine, I constantly chastise myself, I would anger Huitzilopochtli, who would punish me for my misdeed. By allowing her to be educated another year, I gave myself time to make a decision about what to do with her.

After returning from the compound, I received reports about the bearded foreigners from five spies who had just returned from the outlying territories, and this provided a distraction.

The month after I first saw Flower, I ordered the senior priestess at the compound to send me the candidate in the first group I had selected and held the initial step in the Coyolxauhqui rite. When she arrived at my residence, attendants led the impersonator to a chamber and into the care of two concubines, whose role in this part of the ceremony was to render the young woman compliant so she did not balk and refuse to perform in the sacrament the following day at the Main Temple.

All three had drunk *iztac octli* before I went to the room, as was the practice, and I heard them laughing as I approached the door; that was a good sign, because sometimes the impersonators could not stop crying when they were removed from the compound and its now-familiar surroundings.

Sacred herbs burned in censers, pine torches brightened the space, and, earlier that evening, four thousand flowers had been placed in vases around the room. I was pleased when I saw the young woman; light from the fires showed the priestesses had done an excellent job, as usual, of dressing her like Coyolxauhqui. She wore a battle uniform made of fine cotton and had little warrior's bells attached to each of her calves. Jewelry of two-headed serpents made from copper circled this Coyolxauhqui's arms, legs, abdomen, and head. Her hair was wrapped with a striated cloth, and they had painted bells on her face and Earth-monsters on her knees, elbows, and ankles.

She smiled and then covered her face with her hands after looking in my direction. The concubines knew what to do. I sat on a bench, across the foot of a bed that was covered with a white cotton sheet to soak up Coyolxauhqui's blood after I penetrated her, and I watched as she drank more from a silver cup, until she fell onto the mattress, on her back. She and the concubines laughed.

The concubines undressed themselves, removed her uniform and the jewelry from around her abdomen, arms, legs, and head, and took off the cloth covering her hair. She did not protest her nakedness. She had full breasts and small black nipples and almost no hair on her pubic area. One of the concubines kissed the impersonator's mouth and bit her lower lip, and I became stiff as the women caressed her skin and breasts and rubbed between her thighs. She closed her eyes.

I parted the front of my robe, under which I was not wearing a loincloth, and gestured to one of my concubines to continue to play with her and the other to kneel before me. She took me in her mouth and sucked until just before I was ready to release my seed, at which point I patted her head.

The concubine on the bed bent down in front of the impersonator and put her face between her legs. The impersonator moaned. I was so hard I could sit no more, and the other concubine and I walked to the bed. As she helped me remove my robe, I was thinking only of Flower.

The Coyolxauhqui impersonator smiled when she saw me. The concubines spread her open, which made the little bells chime and released a scent of sacred herbs, the forest, and the sea. Pretending she was my Flower, I knelt between her legs, and, as I entered her and broke her hymen, she screamed, punching my shoulders with balled fists, but I did not stop until I had released my seed.

I pulled out. The concubines stood. I rose from the mattress. One was holding my robe for me. I put it on and left the chamber; my attendants were waiting for me outside to escort me to a steam bath. The concubines folded the bed linen with the impersonator's virginal blood and gave it to a priest, who sent it to the base of Huitzilopochtli's statue, where it remained throughout the next day's ceremony.

We followed identical procedures in every Coyolxauhqui rite. In the morning, after the first stage, when I lay with the impersonator, I rose early, before dawn, and prayed in my chambers. Then priests accompanied me to the House of Fasting, where local nobles and visiting dignitaries were waiting to pray together and engage in penance by bleeding our earlobes, using small bifacial knives, before the Coyolxauhqui impersonator arrived at the Main Temple.

After we completed our duties at the House of Fasting, priests and attendants went with me to a room under Huitzilopochtli's statue, where they helped me dress. I put on a new uniform that was similar to what I wore in battle, and they made blue diagonal stripes on my face and covered my arms and legs in blue paint. I wore a headdress decorated with precious stones and feathers, and while I was preparing, forty priests were outside, at the altar.

To release robust fragrances, we burned torches made from pine wood, incense, and sacred herbs on standing braziers; we offered Huitzilopochtli food, including roasted maize cobs, and gardeners from Xochimilco delivered forty thousand flowers to the altar. The scents from all these offerings were intoxicating and created an ethereal scene for all participants near the altar.

The concubines who had joined me the night before remained with the Coyolxauhqui impersonator at the palace until she left the next morning for the Main Temple, because she could not be left alone. They knew to pamper her and allow her to sleep late, and they gave her food and beverages, including *iztac octli*, as much as she wanted. After the meal, the concubines took her to a steam room, where they bathed and perfumed her and reassured her they would be waiting for her when she returned to the palace after the ceremony at the Main Temple.

Priestesses were waiting in another room to dress her in a battle uniform and again adorn her with double-headed serpent jewelry, wrap her head in a striated cloth, paint fresh bells on her face and Earth-monsters on her knees, elbows, and ankles, and tie the little warrior bells around her calves. She stepped into gold-toned sandals, and someone gave her a golden bow and a gold-tipped arrow and, when fully dressed, she was transformed into the living image of Coyolxauhqui.

The concubines and priestesses bowed and kissed her hands before they delivered her to the attendants, who took her through the palace gate, where crowds had gathered to see her. As trumpets played, the people shouted to praise the new Coyolxauhqui, and, when she was in her litter, they followed her until she arrived at the steps leading to Huitzilopochtli's altar. Thousands had come to watch. Most were commoners, but there also were rulers and noblemen, including some of my enemies, in certain sections.

Attendants took the impersonator to the bottom step, and Eagle Warriors who represented the Four Hundred Southern Gods stood directly behind her in orderly rows. Musicians played, and I emerged from the enclosed area at the top, beneath Huitzilopochtli's statue. Surrounded by priests, I walked until I faced Huitzilopochtli.

I could not see Coyolxauhqui, but a priest confirmed she was with the Four Hundred Southern Gods, two of them helping her climb. A priest announced when they had reached the altar, in front of a large round stone; then just four stood with her, as the rest had moved away, 198 on each side.

I turned to look at her; she was not holding her bow and arrow and swayed and struggled to keep her eyes open—thanks to the *iztac octli*—as the four Eagle Warriors prevented her from falling. I raised my right hand and, as the priests and I chanted, the Eagle Warriors gently placed her on the stone, face down, and pressed on her shoulders, wrists, lower back, and thighs. So far, she had been following all the parts of the ceremony she had rehearsed at the compound.

Two priests dressed in black, their faces and hands painted the same, approached her. While the Eagle Warriors secured her, a priest inserted a small flint knife, about the length of my open hand, that was thin and finely pointed at both ends, into the base of her skull, to sever the spinal cord. The Eagle Warriors turned her around. She could not move, not even to close her staring eyes, but tears fell down her face.

The priests used flint knives, each curved at one end with a handle on the other side, to cut into her chest. Precious red liquid, almost black, shot out, spraying the priests' and Eagle Warriors' faces. Her own face twitched because she tried to scream as she died. One priest carved out her heart. He handed it to me, and I put it in a pocket, where the blood soaked the fabric.

The other priest had removed her liver, which he kept. Her blood flowed along a groove on top of the stone, through an opening, and into a bowl on the ground, and, when the ceremony had been completed, four priests and I poured it on our heads to coat our hair and faces.

The Eagle Warriors helped the priests turn Coyolxauhqui's body back around, onto her abdomen, and, in the process, the cloth covering her head fell off. They worked together to raise her head above the stone and tautly hold it.

A priest knew where to slice—between the base of her skull and the top bone of her upper spine. When the head had been severed, they handed it to me and I walked to the top step. I bent down and kicked it hard. It flew, her long, long black hair soaked in blood, until it landed on the ground in front of the bottom step. The people cheered.

The priests chopped off Coyolxauhqui's arms and legs and separated her torso from her abdomen. As they dismembered the rest of the body, I faced Huitzilopochtli, removed Coyolxauhqui's heart from my pocket, and squeezed out all the precious liquid onto my chest; then the priest next to me did the same with her liver. We lay the shriveled parts on the ground in front of the Supreme God.

When the priests had finished, they placed all the remaining pieces of her body on the top step and, one by one, I threw them down the stairs. Coyolxauhqui's dismembered body and head remained there until night, when the priests gathered and rearranged them, as if they formed a whole, and placed them before Huitzilopochtli, where they stayed until vultures and fire ants had eaten the flesh and her bones were taken to be used to make sacramental objects.

A priest removed and discarded her brain and later placed her head on a skull rack inside the Main Temple that faced east and the folded cotton sheet with her virginal blood in a room for storing sacred items. As was customary, after the sacrifice, I returned to my residence, where I bathed and changed into new garments, presided over a celebratory meal, and then granted audiences to official visitors and heard reports from them and others about events in my territories.

Several weeks after this year's Coyolxauhqui ceremony, I went to the deity compound to select a subject for the next year's rite of the Lord of the Smoking Mirror and to observe Flower's military training. As ordered, the priestess had obtained a female Eagle Warrior from the military headquarters to train Flower. When we arrived inside the women's section, the litter carried me to the inner courtyard, where they teach the few impersonators who learn how to fight.

I pushed aside the litter's covering so I could see Flower as she practiced archery. She was dressed in a uniform, and her hair was tied in a warrior's knot, but the garments had the unintended effect of making her appear smaller.

Flower and the Eagle Warrior stood facing a deerskin target that was tacked onto a wall, and a priestess was sitting on a chair, watching them. Flower could not even place the arrow properly in the bow by herself, and the soldier behind her kept doing it for her and holding her hands as they released the arrow together; that was unacceptable. A priest who had accompanied me left his litter to stand next to mine; I instructed him to dismiss the Eagle Warrior and have a priestess take Flower back to her quarters and order the senior priestess to meet us in the hall.

I told him what he needed to say to the priestess, and when she joined us, he asked why Flower was crying when we first saw her, and she replied that the girl was afraid to be in my presence. He asked what she knew about the Coyolxauhqui rite.

"Just as we taught her, sir. She knows the impersonator has the honor of going to His Majesty's palace to be with him the night before the ceremony at the Main Temple, sir."

"Does she know what it means to 'be with' the Supreme Ruler?"

"Yes, all the girls are taught when they turn fourteen about having relations with the ruler or with a nobleman, sir."

I said I was dissatisfied with the present arrangement of having her trained by a female warrior and ordered her to speak with the senior priest of the men's compound to find a male Eagle Warrior to teach her how to fight and to order new battle uniforms and gear made for her, ones that fit properly.

"Now, His Highness instructed you to be present when Flower practices military skills, and, because you disobeyed him, His Highness orders you to engage in penance by letting out your blood, under the senior priest's supervision, for two days. And should you fail to be present at any of Flower's future military instruction, he will order the death penalty against you. His Highness will return in one month to see what progress she has made."

Her hands shook, and her head fell lower as she confirmed her understanding.

Back at my palace, I heard accounts from spies about the progress the foreign warriors were making on their march from the coast. As I had instructed him, Teudile, one of my stewards on the coast, was visiting the leader of the foreign men, now on the mainland with the Totonacs at Potonchán, to learn what he could about them, embed my spies among two thousand slaves I offered the leader to build three hundred huts, and deliver gifts from me.

"Supreme Ruler Moctezoma, this is what happened when Teudile arrived at the foreigners' camp. Teudile introduced himself to the leader as your servant," a spy said.

"'I am here on behalf of the Supreme Ruler and Speaker, Chief Priest, and Master Judge Moctezoma to welcome you and present these gifts of precious stones and fine feathers,' Teudile said."

"'Please thank your ruler, and tell him I look forward to meeting him soon,' the leader replied. 'And please tell him I am here as an ambassador of my Majesty, ruler of most of the world, who sent me to see these lands, now part of his empire, and to speak with the people. He expects me to write him what I learn. Please give your ruler these presents from my motherland. Please tell me, how old is your ruler, and how does he look?'"

"'He is a mature man. Because he is a warrior and commander of our military, he is strong and lean. Do you mind showing us your war animals? They are quite fascinating,' Teudile replied."

"'Certainly. It is my pleasure, and do not fear—we will fire some of our weapons, but away from everyone, just so you see what they are like.'"

"Supreme Ruler," the spy now said to me, "the foreigners pretended to fight each other, using swords like the one you have at the War College. And their weapons that shoot fire—they were so loud we covered our ears and fell to the ground! And their warriors tied bells on the armor of their large war animals that look like deer and rode them on the beach. It was amazing how they controlled the animals!"

I returned to the compounds a month after I had ordered the priestess to have Flower trained by an Eagle Warrior from the men's compound. I arrived at the area where archery instruction takes place at the women's section as Flower was releasing an arrow; it hit the target at the outer ring. Her new instructor, who had his own bow and quiver full of arrows, was standing by her side. He, too, judging by his flawless appearance, was a would-be deity impersonator who lived at the male compound next to the women's. Both he and Flower were dressed in thick quilted cotton uniforms and shod in the sturdy deerskin shoes we wear at war.

Flower now was a little heavier and, with clothing that fit her, she no longer looked frail.

There were four other arrows in the target close to the one I had seen land. While they were far from the target's center, she had markedly improved from the first time I saw her practicing with the woman. As I watched, Flower reached back into her quiver, nocked her arrow to the bow, looked at the target, and released the arrow; it landed by the others on the same outer ring. She retrieved another arrow. I told the priest who had accompanied me that I was ready to go to the men's compound.

"I am interested in the warrior who is training the young girl called Flower as a Lord of the Smoking Mirror. Tell me about him," I said to the senior priest.

"Yes, Your Highness. He is an Eagle Warrior named Teputzitoloc who was captured in battle two years ago, and he is now seventeen, Your Highness."

"I will leave him to continue to train Flower, then, for the time being, because his skills are remarkable, but I'm thinking of substituting him for next year's candidate in the rite. Bring the impersonators in."

I selected another candidate for the Lord of the Smoking Mirror ritual. It was mandatory for impersonators of this god to appear perfect because he had no visible defect, such as a scar or misshapen feature. I returned to my palace.

Chapter Four

THE XOCHIMILCA: FLOWER

When I woke in the morning, I felt sharp, rapid darts of pain in my feet and up my legs and hips and lower back, and I remembered the day before and what those people had done to me. I thought about my family and of killing myself and cried, softly, because I was afraid someone would hear and tell the old priestess.

I could not understand what I had done to deserve any part of the horror I experienced from when I first heard those men screaming at Papa. My head hurt, and I became angry.

"Why am I here? Why, why am I here—why am I here?" I yelled. "I want to go home. I want to go home—now!"

One of the kindly priestesses appeared.

"Now, now, dear. You said you were not going to misbehave again. Sh-sh-sh. You don't want the senior priestess to hear you, do you? And dear, know this: the senior priestess has a duty to inform the Supreme Ruler's officials about any girl who continues to misbehave, and they could punish your family, by imprisonment or worse. Do you understand what I just said, dear?"

I stopped weeping.

"Is that clear? I must hear your response."

I accepted that I had no route out of this place.

"Yes."

"That's a good girl. Do you need to relieve yourself?"

I said I did; she left and returned with a chamber pot, and I took care of my needs without having to walk. She brought me a cloth, soap, and a bowl of warm water and helped me wash my face and the parts of my hands not covered by bandages. She went out, came back with a tray of hot cornmeal with honey on top, sliced fruit, and lemongrass tea with honey, and put it on the table next to me. She helped me sit with my back resting on the wall; then she put the tray on my lap and sat on a chair by the door to watch me. As I was hungry, I ate and drank everything.

Afterward, the two priestesses took me to the bathroom, where I sat on a chair as they removed the bandages; my feet and hands were still swollen, but not like the previous day. I had a cool bath, and they dried me, took me back to the room, and settled me in the bed, where they applied fresh dressings to my injuries. They put a small bell on the table next to the pallet and told me to ring if I needed anything before going out. I became angry again but said nothing.

I thought about my family and that we had normal lives, just like everyone else in our village, and I could not think of any reason why I had been singled out to be taken from my home. I rang the bell, and one of my minders appeared. I asked what was going to happen to me after my hands and feet were healed, and she said I would be moved to the main section, where I would live with the girls who were nine to eleven years old, and there I would begin my education. In the coming days, I continued to try to obtain information from them and asked why I had been forced to go there.

"Please don't disobey us. It's time to stop asking questions, dear. You don't want us to report this discussion to the senior priestess, do you, dear?"

My heart beat fast.

"No, no. But I can't sleep, and, and, there's nothing to do. Can you take me outside?"

She said they could not do so until I had fully healed, but she would ask the senior priestess if I could have paper and paints to practice drawing characters.

"Can you draw any characters, dear?"

"Yes, just ones that have to do with farming and the market. You think she'll let me do that?"

"Yes, dear, I do. We've already told her how you have been behaving so nicely."

Later the priestesses brought a basket with paper, brushes, and paint. I had seen such fine writing tools only at the markets. They helped me sit up and put a wooden tablet on my lap. They arranged the paper so it was flat and placed three brushes and three small cups with paint in red, blue, and yellow colors by the paper. They told me to draw all the characters I knew.

I painted those having to do with farming and the markets, numbers, lakes, boats, and canals. It took me some time to finish each character, because I wanted to do a good job, and I still had bandages on my hands. I put down the brush after some time and looked up. They reviewed the completed papers.

"Dear girl, you're quite advanced. We'll show them to the senior priestess, and I think she'll want to place you in a class with older girls, maybe with the twelve-to-fourteen-year-olds."

"But, but I'm only ten."

"Yes, dear, we know that. You'll be with the older girls only for your reading and writing classes. For everything else, you'll be with the younger girls. Do you want to paint more?"

They put the completed papers on the floor to begin drying. They gathered all the filled sheets, but not the blank paper or the basket with the rest of the paints and brushes, and left. When they were gone, it was my turn to be surprised. I was sorrowful and missed my family. I wanted to go home more than I had ever wanted anything, but I did enjoy painting characters, which distracted me from my pain. Papa never could afford any of those writing tools, and I could not believe the people who had caused me such pain were the same ones who had given me an opportunity for an experience that, I was sure, only the ruler, noblemen, and priests and priestesses had.

For the next six weeks, I did not see any of the priestesses who had beaten me or anyone else—just the two who had taken care of me from the beginning. I sometimes heard sounds—music and chanting—but the walls were thick, and everything was muted. Every day was the same routine: They woke me at dawn, removed the poultices from my feet and hands, and helped me bathe and wash my hair. Then they dried me and took me back to the pallet, where they dressed me in a clean tunic and replaced the bandages. I then had breakfast, and afterward, they helped me clean my teeth.

Every day I sat on my pallet and drew and had my meals. All that time, I could not see outside. I knew when it was daytime only because they told me so when they arrived in the morning. My hands and feet were healing, but they did not let me walk around the room or to and from the bathroom until the seventh week, when I felt almost no pain and all the swelling had gone down. It felt good not to be carried, and they let me walk in a hallway next to my room.

I constantly thought about my family, including all of my grandparents, who lived in a mountain village named Ixhuatepec and whom we visited every other year after harvest. We walked to see them, of course, and went with my uncles, aunts, and cousins on journeys that took about eight days each way.

We cooked and slept in the open, and those travels were among my favorite times of the year. When the little ones were tired, my parents and the older girls carried them. Papa and the other men knew how to hunt, and they would go into the woods and bring back deer or turkeys to roast over fires. We also ate well because Papa and the other men took along nonperishable goods to trade for fresh food. We usually spent three weeks with our grandparents, who always begged my parents to leave us girls with them, but Papa and Mama declined to do so, saying they needed us at home. It was our people in the mountains who would give us sanctuary in the days of hardship to come.

One night, eight weeks to the day after I had been abducted, a priestess told me I would go outside in the morning to attend a religious ceremony featuring one of the older girls, and then I would move to a dormitory. I was happy when I heard I would be leaving my cramped quarters, and I asked what was going to happen the next day. She said they would wake me before the sun rose to bathe and dress. They instructed me to watch them and do the same at the temple.

"When the ceremony ends, we'll present you to the priestesses who are responsible for the nine-to-eleven-year-old girls, and then you and the other new girls, five in your age group, will be led to your assigned dormitory."

I had many questions and was agitated about going outside, but I knew they would not say anything else, so I obeyed when they told me to bathe and clean my teeth. It seemed as if I had just fallen asleep when they shook me awake and accompanied me to the bathroom, where they had prepared the tub. When I had finished drying, they reentered with black garments—a long skirt and a long-sleeved tunic; they helped me dress and comb my hair and gave me sandals similar to ones I wore to work in our field.

When I was ready, they escorted me to the hallway, and we walked outside. It was cold; I breathed deeply, and the air smelled of pine. I was glad to feel it on my skin. In the distance, I saw orderly rows of girls, standing by women holding illuminating torches. I shivered.

A priestess handed me a lit torch, and when it seemed as if everyone was present (because no one else was joining us), a priestess chanted, and we marched. My memories of that chilly dawn are unclouded. The sky was black and the stars bold. I saw the temple; it was made of dark stone and had an altar at the top. The crowd slowed as we arrived at the staircase, where we faced steps leading up to the altar. The priestesses and girls in front of me climbed until everyone either was at the top, on the steps, or on the ground, where my priestesses and I were standing, in two columns, with an aisle in the middle.

I was close to fires in braziers emitting a pungent aroma, a combination of flowers, pine, and some type of incense or herb I could not identify. Once I had breathed in the scent a number of times, I could not control my thoughts. Pictures appeared, some outside my head, but each quickly vanished. Other scenes formed, only to travel in my brain before they were gone. Then, without meaning to, I leaned to my right, and a priestess put her hand on my shoulder.

Now I am happy and with my family and everyone is smiling and we just worked in our field and swam in cool water under a hot sun and fished and roasted what we'd caught and ate as we sat cross-legged on the grass, and now my hair is almost dry, but the dampness on my neck feels good and we peel newly ripened mangoes, and I tear into mine and I wipe nectar off my lips with the back of my hand and I hate the strings in the fruit and how they get between my teeth, but oh, oh, oh, it is worth it to taste the juice as it rolls down my tongue.

A priestess covered my mouth, and I suddenly remembered where I was. My other guard signaled with a finger over closed lips, and when she seemed satisfied I was not going to laugh or say anything, the first one removed her hand from my face. There were about forty priestesses above us at the head of the stairs singing and chanting, some playing instruments, and I heard bells but could not see who was making the sounds. After a while, the music ended and the chanting stopped. Two priestesses who were at the top held torches, throwing light on that old woman who had tormented me on my first day in that prison. My heart beat fast, and it was difficult to breathe.

I felt lightheaded, and could not think about anything other than how she led the others and ordered someone to strike me, as my head was upside down in that wooden cage. I closed my eyes but still saw her.

She is standing before me, waving that stick in my face and I am back in that room, surrounded by smelly people, and I am naked and on the floor and they spread my legs and she shoves her finger in me and I cry, but quietly, because I know if I make a sound they will assault me harder and harder or put that piece of wood in me. I hate her, I hate them, and I want to go home so my mama will hold me and tell me everything is good and we are together and no one ever again will take me from my family.

I wiped tears off my face and steadied my sight on the ground. I heard singing, and moments later, one of my minders lifted my chin, and I saw a young woman, wearing remarkable garments and jewelry, ascending the stairs. I had never seen anyone dressed that way.

She held a bow and arrow, and the jewelry on her arms appeared to be of snakes. She had on a short skirt, a blouse showing her midriff, and a patterned cloth wrapped around her head. At first, I could not see her feet, but when she reached the top, I saw she was wearing gold-toned sandals and had small bells tied around her calves. She and four priestesses walked together until they stood before a god, where they bowed their heads; then all five marched to a large round stone.

The young woman allowed the priestesses to help her lie on it on her belly, and they put their hands on her shoulders, waist, and thighs as they prayed. The musicians resumed playing, and the priestesses released her. She stood, and all five walked up to and entered an opening in a wall to the left of the altar, followed by the others there, and the rest of us returned to the buildings.

I worried about what was going to occur next, but the rhythmic sounds our sandals made on the dewy grass had an unexpectedly calming effect. Groups of women and girls broke away from the larger congregation and went in different directions, but I was in a section that walked toward a large two-story white house. We entered a hall that had rows of tables and benches. My guardians led me to stand by a wall, and when it seemed as if no one else was coming in, I heard the chime of bells coming from a side door. The old priestess who had tortured me arrived.

My minder squeezed my shoulder and tilted my head up, raising her eyebrow, and I knew not to cry. She released me, and I looked in the direction of the vile woman, who was with three other women. They went to the front of the room. I looked at the floor.

"I greet you in the name of the Supreme Ruler and Speaker, Chief Priest, and Master Judge, the Honorable Moctezoma. You will live here and learn how to become deity impersonators until you are called upon to serve at one of our most important religious rites. You were chosen for your intelligence, so you will study religion, how to read and write, history, music, dance, and other courses. The reason you will receive a fine education is that it will make it easier for you to be able to impersonate a goddess.

"Now, listen carefully: Understand that I will get daily reports from the priestesses about how you are conducting yourselves, and I will not hesitate to administer punishment to any girl who is not obedient. If her behavior does not improve, the severity of the punishment will get worse and worse, until she completely submits."

She turned and went out through the same door she had entered from, but her companions remained. My heart calmed. My minders led me to the three priestesses at the front and presented me to them, as the other priestesses standing with their girls did the same. Priestess Yoltzin and Priestess Toci smiled, and each put her hand on my shoulders before walking away; I wanted to cry and beg them to stay, but I knew this would have been considered misconduct.

After we had been introduced, one of the new priestesses, who seemed to be the most important of the three, instructed all the girls to sit at the tables, and we obeyed. A priestess gave us further orders, but I was focused on the other girls, wondering who they were, where they were from, how they had arrived there, and if they also had been assaulted.

"My name is Priestess Citlalmina, and my assistants are Priestess Eztli and Priestess Ahuiliztli. Welcome. This is where you will live until you are called to serve the gods as a deity impersonator at the Main Temple at Tenochtitlan or a temple somewhere in the empire of the Supreme Ruler and Speaker, Chief Priest, and Master Judge, the Honorable Moctezoma. I will explain to you soon, after you have had a meal, more about your lives here and what is expected of you."

The three priestesses watched us as women came in through a side door and gave us venison meat pies, flat, round corn cakes, vegetables, fruit, and tea. When we had finished eating, the servants removed everything and left.

Priestess Citlalmina addressed us and said the ruler's representatives had chosen us because we were special, as the gods had given each at least one extraordinary skill.

"In most cases, we do not yet know what that talent is, and we will have to wait until it develops during your education. Whatever your unique trait is, at the end of your time here, you will have the necessary skills to play the role of a goddess."

She explained that, to be able to impersonate a deity, we had to be as close to perfect as possible, and everything we would learn here was meant to turn us into godlike human beings. She said we would never have to work, as servants would do everything for us.

"Now, we understand that you miss your families, and I am sure you are wondering when you will see them again. Most girls are called upon to serve as deity impersonators when they are fifteen or sixteen years old. But once a girl participates in a ceremony, she can choose to return to her village or enter a temple and train to become a priestess."

I wanted to smile. The priestess continued to speak—who knew about what?—as all I thought about was how to survive and then perform a ceremony impersonating a goddess at a temple. Then, I remembered that, because Papa had said to those men who abducted me that I was ten, I would have to spend at least five years in that place rather than three before I could go home. I wondered if I should tell them I was really twelve, but, no, Papa had to have had a good reason for saying I was younger, and I did not want the ruler's officials to harm him if they found out he had lied to them.

I made myself listen to the priestess and vowed I would excel at everything they taught me so they would choose me to perform in a ceremony five years from now.

She said the most important study was religion and would include how to interpret the moon and stars and our calendars, the 260-day ritual calendar, and the 365.25-day solar calendar that consisted of eighteen months of twenty days plus five and one-quarter unlucky days. That afternoon, the priestess spoke about how the sun, Earth, moon, and stars were made by our gods, beginning with our Supreme Creator, Ometeotl, who had four sons, three of whom made other gods, the world, and humans.

When she ended the introduction to religion, Priestess Citlalmina said it was time to go to our new home, and she and the others led us through a hallway to an attached two-story house. We went upstairs—my first time on a second floor—into a sunny dormitory that had windows and thick pallets covered in colorful linens and blankets. There were flowers in vases and unlit torches throughout the room and shelves where, Priestess Citlalmina said, each of us had piles of clothes and rows of sandals and other personal items.

She said the daily schedule was to rise at dawn the first four days of the week to pray next to our pallets, go down for breakfast, go back upstairs to bathe and clean our teeth, get dressed, and return to the first floor to study. As I was in a writing class with twelve-to-fourteen-year-olds, I went to a different building for that course. On the fifth day of each week, we would have a ceremony at the temple or, if it was raining, at the main assembly hall.

The first night in the dormitory, everyone was quiet, and I wanted to speak to the other girls but did not want to break the rules and risk being punished. I was thinking about my family and started crying softly. I noticed a girl in the bed to my right signaling to me. She was looking at me as she tapped a finger on her closed mouth, to let me know I should be quiet. A priestess yelled at us.

"Flower and Yaretzi, why are you girls not asleep? If you do not go to sleep right now, I will report you to the senior priestess in the morning!"

Yaretzi's kindness in trying to keep me out of trouble brought more tears to my eyes, but eventually I fell asleep.

The next morning, they rang a bell to wake us.

"Everyone, rise and wash before breakfast."

I got out of bed slowly because I was unsure about what to do next. When Yaretzi spoke to me, I was relieved.

"Come, Flower. I'll show you where everything is and what to do."

"That is good of you, Yaretzi, to help Flower," a priestess said.

Leading the way to the bathroom, Yaretzi pointed out the shelves where they had stacked supplies and garments. We washed and dried ourselves and put on clean clothes, and then the priestess took us downstairs. A priestess consented when Yaretzi asked if she could sit next to me.

I began the reading-and-writing class with the twelve-to-fourteen-year-old group. I was disappointed that Yaretzi was not in that class with me. The teacher, Priestess Eztli, made each student say her own name. It was evident who was new, because we spoke softly and kept our eyes focused on the floor until Priestess Eztli told us that, from then on, we always had to look into a person's eyes when addressing someone to show we were confident. She added that, because we were training to be deity impersonators, we had dispensation from the ruler to look into anyone's eyes but his without permission.

After introductions, Priestess Eztli told the students who were not new to go into a room next door to practice their writing and told the rest of us to remain. After they had left, she showed us manuscripts written on long strips of paper, painted in bright colors on both sides, that had been folded into large pleats, similar to ones I had seen at the marketplaces.

She let us touch them and said the paper was made from the bark of the wild fig tree, and, because I was curious, later that year, Priestess Eztli gave me private lessons on how to make it, which we then used in writing class.

Priestess Eztli told us the ruler, priests, priestesses, and nobles knew how to write, and she emphasized what an extraordinary privilege it was that, although we were commoners, we would become literate. The new girls like me already knew how to do one form of writing, the most basic—how to paint or draw pictures of words we needed to know for our family's trade.

That was the most useful for our empire, she said, because drawings of words could be understood by anyone, but to an educated person, writing was more than pictures of objects, persons, and places.

She explained that, in the days to come, our teachings would include two other substantially more complex forms, one of which had to do with characters or signs that stood for sounds, ideas, and concepts. When those characters were combined, we would use them to form complete thoughts on paper.

The other method of writing, she said, the most complicated one, was when one drew characters or signs that represented certain sounds. This was used when a word was impossible to conceptualize. Instead of trying to write the difficult word, one replaced it with a word that sounded the same but was easier to paint.

That first day, we practiced writing words we knew. At midday, a bell rang outside the room, and Priestess Eztli told us to put down our brushes. She took me back to my house to eat. Yaretzi and I arrived at the same time and sat together again after she asked a priestess for permission.

"Girls, it is all right if you sit together at meals, as long as you continue to behave."

Later that week, after school, Priestess Citlalmina escorted a group of us, including Yaretzi, to a stone hut and into a room, where a priestess handed each of us a short black skirt and a matching long piece of fabric that she instructed us to tie around our chests. All the girls needed help tying the fabric. When we had changed, she led us into a steam room.

We recited a prayer thanking the gods for our blessings, and then each girl sat on a wooden stool. At first, I felt uncomfortable because it was hot, and I was perspiring heavily, worse than in the middle of summer when I worked at the field, but eventually the heat made my shoulders drop and the weight of my bones and muscles lost their tension. Priestess Citlalmina told us to close our eyes and breathe deeply, and steam traveled the cavities of my nose and down to my chest.

A priestess behind me said, "Flower, dear, I'm going to rub oil on your shoulders and neck. Is that all right?"

Using the pads of her fingers, and at times the palms of her hands, she worked an oil with a pleasant scent deep into the flesh of my neck and shoulders and along the bones of my upper back, concentrating on the area between the base of my skull and the top of my spine, until she removed the knots that, from my first day in that place, had made the upper part of my body clench. For the rest of my time there, I would undergo this steam-room ritual once a month. Once during a meal, Yaretzi and I tried to discuss that experience, but a priestess told us to be quiet.

Over time, the rough skin I had from being a farmer disappeared from my knees, elbows, hands, and feet. The priestess who four times a year cut my hair often told me it was the loveliest she had seen. I often thought about my family but found sustenance in the goal of seeing them again after I had played the role of a deity in a ceremony at a temple outside the compound. I was no longer as sad as when I had arrived.

My daily life, however, took another pivotal turn when I turned sixteen, or, as my captors believed, fourteen.

Chapter Five

THE SPANIARDS: CORTÉS

In the name of the Most Holy Trinity, which is the Father, the Son, and the Holy Spirit, and the magnificent Virgin Blessed Mother, my Advocate, Amen. Know ye who may read this revised report of the conquest and pacification of New Spain, which is in the Indies across the Ocean Sea, for the Emperor Carlos, fifth of this name, King of Spain, my sovereign Prince and Lord, that I, Don Hernándo Cortés, Marques del Valle de Oaxaca, Captain General and Soldier of the Faith, wrote the following chronicle to set my conscience free so I may receive eternal life, and I pray my Savior, Jesus Christ, the Holy Redeemer, will have mercy on me and admit my soul to Glory, there to praise and magnify Him.

I did not intend the letters I wrote the monarchs to convey a complete account of events that transpired when I conquered the mainland, as they were designed to obtain permission to pacify the inhabitants of New Spain and form a government on the Crown's behalf. Those summaries, unfortunately, gave my enemies opportunities to skew the record and destroy my reputation with lies.

Here, however, I will set down the truth and show, despite allegations to the contrary, that my chief goals, from when I was in Cuba and had resolved to attain them or perish in the endeavor, not only were wealth and renown, but also to win Christian souls for the Lord and an empire for my Majesties. In the end, no one acknowledged I was the only one with the valor to subdue a realm mightier than any my rulers had ever fought, including the Saracens of Granada.

Diego Velázquez de Cuéllar, governor of Cuba, chose me as commander general of the third fleet from Cuba to the Yucatán, after the failed voyages of Francisco Hernández de Córdoba and Juan de Grijalva. He summoned me to his house in San Cristóbal de La Habana and ordered me not to reveal to anyone what he was going to say because many others, intoxicated by Grijalva's reports of treasures in the Yucatán, coveted the appointment.

"You and I are going to enter into a confidential verbal agreement. But the written contract, which will control how you conduct yourself as commander of the expedition, will be public, and those are the terms the Council of the Indies will know about. So, again, keep our conversation just between the two of us. Do you agree to that?"

"Yes, Governor—of course. Absolutely," I said.

"You say the words easily, but I know you too well. This time, you had better keep your promises, or I guarantee I will replace you as commander, at *any* stage of the expedition."

"Our conflicts are all in the past, Governor. I greatly appreciate this opportunity, and I will not disappoint you."

I could not stop thinking that being appointed to lead this venture was going to prove to be the most important event in my life.

My heart was beating fast, and my throat was dry, so I paused to drink. He stared at me with furrowed brow. I feared he was about to change his mind.

"Governor, you have not misplaced your trust in me. My earlier misadventures were the foolish actions of an immature man. Think about what you have accomplished with me at your side. We have pacified and built Cuba from an island of thatched-roof huts to a prosperous colony. Yes, I promise to obey *all* your orders—those written and those you tell me today."

"You always could make a pretty speech. I think you know that I picked you because you are intelligent, you proved yourself in previous pacifications, and you're not a milksop like the other two I sent to the Yucatán. But always bear in mind that you are hotheaded—and try to control yourself at all times.

"Let's proceed. You may use your judgment during the expedition in unexpected circumstances. Now, if you reach a stage that you believe is appropriate, you may establish a colony.

"Now, this, of course, is not in the written contract: the principal basis of the expedition is for you to locate sources of significant quantities of gold, pearls, and precious stones to prove the land is wealthy, so the king will grant *me* the titles I requested so *I* will conquer the Yucatán. Is that understood?"

"Yes, Governor. I understand."

"Good. Here's the contract. I'll call in the notary to witness our signatures."

I left Velázquez's home and went directly to speak with naval suppliers to place my orders for goods. Three weeks later, when Velázquez noted the scale of my venture and that I had not requested his assistance, he sent Amador de Lares, his accountant and advisor, to my house.

"Listen, I'm only the messenger here, so don't be angry with me. Velázquez orders you to stop all your preparations for the expedition. He—he is going to replace you. But he said he will reimburse you for what you have already paid."

"Is he demented? He must be, if he thinks I'm not going forward with this venture!"

What Velázquez did not know was that, when I had learned he was looking for someone to lead the third voyage, I befriended Lares and induced him to persuade Velázquez to choose me as commander.

"Well, those are his orders, and you know he has authority to remove you at any time. There are plenty who are willing to take your place."

"Well, he and everyone else on this damned island can go to hell. I'm staying on as commander of this expedition."

"Be careful. He's thrown you in jail before, and he'd do it again."

I put my hands on his shoulders.

"Listen to me, Lares: You don't want to be stuck here under his thumb all your life keeping his books, do you? If you help me, I promise to send you gold and precious stones from the Yucatán. What do you think about that? I can make you a rich man."

"Only if you promise me, with your bond as a gentleman, to send enough gold and jewels to make me rich, will I do as you ask."

We shook hands.

"Wonderful, my friend. For now, please keep me informed about what he plans to do to me at each step so I can continue to prepare and then sail."

I not only proceeded despite Velázquez's orders but also considerably increased the number of vessels and men.

Velázquez, who supplied the majority of food and dried goods to merchants in Cuba, thereafter tried to prevent me from buying more provisions, but most ignored him, because no one was willing to turn down money. He persevered and officially canceled my commission and selected Luis de Medina to lead the undertaking. Lares promptly notified me of that decision and said Velázquez was sending a messenger on foot with documents to Medina in the morning.

This act, as I interpreted it, was a breach of our agreement because I had given consideration by disbursing almost everything I owned for the enterprise, so I conferred with my brother-in-law, Juan Suárez.

"Velázquez is sending a courier with Medina's certificate of appointment. Intercept him on the main road, and do what you have to do to get those papers. Do you understand? And he'll be armed, so make sure you are, too."

Juan told me the man refused to release the documents, and so they fought; Juan had to use his blade, resulting in the postman's death. He gave me the document; I read it and threw it in the fire.

I accelerated performance of all tasks, including sending armed men to the slaughterhouse for all available meats—from hogs, cows, and sheep—for the ships so the cooks could begin salting them. Several hours later, the butcher, an obese man, arrived at my home. He had difficulty breathing, and his face was sweaty. His chins quivered as he spoke.

"Sir, your men took all my meats, on your order, they said, and gave me just a small amount of money. If you don't compensate me, I will have to report you to the governor!"

"I have permission from the governor to obtain supplies for an important expedition that will benefit all of us. You can see him about obtaining additional payment, if you would like. But, in the meantime, I ask that you not trouble the governor with your complaint and accept the only valuable item I have left."

I gave him a thick gold necklace with a cross I was wearing. Late that night, the slaughterman reported what I had done to Velázquez, and, at dawn, the governor went to the quay, where I was directing men from shore. He stood close and pointed at me.

"I cannot believe you have betrayed me, my friend. Why? Why are you doing this to me, after all I have done for you?"

"Forgive me, but all the plans have been made, according to your orders and the contract we signed," I said.

"When you made plans without speaking with me first, you violated the terms of our verbal agreement, so I had to appoint someone else, someone who will follow the rules I set. If you insist on going forward with this betrayal, you can be sure this is not the end. I will see to it that you will not be the one to assert control of the new lands."

He shook his head, turned his back on me, and departed. I continued with my duties.

We left Santiago de Cuba on 18 November 1518 with six vessels and left one to be careened. As we needed more food and wine, we stopped at Macaca, where a messenger delivered letters from Velázquez for two of my captains, Diego de Ordaz, Velázquez's cousin, and Francisco de Orozco, telling them to delay my departure.

I encouraged them to disobey by promising them riches. I induced Velázquez's courier to join my voyage and coaxed Ordaz to go with us to Trinidad to seek assistance from Velázquez's ally, Francisco de Verdugo, who gave me provisions, four horses, and fodder.

To obtain more food, I sent Ordaz on a brigantine to seize a ship on its way to Darien and to confiscate its bread, bacon, and salted chicken; because I impressed the owner of the pirated craft with my audacity, he also joined my expedition.

At Trinidad, I persuaded a number of men to enlist with me, some of whom had been on Grijalva's expedition, whom I valued because of their experience in the Yucatán. I also sent word to Sancti Spíritus to solicit additional captains, soldiers, and crew.

From Trinidad, we went to San Cristóbal de la Habana, where most officials refused to assist me, but I hired the crier to announce my venture and spoke with the tithe and tax collectors, who made monetary donations for the journey in the name of God and the Crown and sold me provisions at reduced prices.

While we were in San Cristóbal de La Habana, a courier from Velázquez delivered a document, this time ordering Ordaz to arrest and take me prisoner to Santiago de Cuba. I spoke with Ordaz.

"I need help with your cousin. I have to find a way to make him stop trying to keep me from launching this voyage. Please, write him a fabrication that you tried to capture me by tricking me into boarding the messenger's boat, but that I had realized it was a ruse and feigned illness."

Ordaz complied. We reembarked and departed, and I held muster at Cabo Corrientes. There were ten vessels present, including mine, *Santa María de la Concepción*, a *nao* with a capacity of one hundred tons. I had a total of 610 people, not including three hundred Cuban Indian and African slaves, men and women, who were servants and porters.

I took thirty-two crossbowmen, thirteen harquebusiers, and fifty sailors from Spain, Portugal, Genoa, Napoli, France, and Greece, and I hired experienced pilots who had been on Córdoba's and Grijalva's expeditions.

To placate Ordaz, whom I wanted on the voyage because of his experience and financial resources, I took his two sisters, who were expert horsewomen and, with their black maids, would fight alongside the men in the conquest of Tenochtitlan.

I also took Melchor and Francisco, Yucatán Indians whom Córdoba and Grijalva had captured and taken to Cuba, as interpreters.

The voyage was expensive because we needed materials to engage in pacification: swords, lances, crossbows, harquebuses, sixteen horses—which neither Córdoba nor Grijalva had taken on their expeditions—for the captains and horsemen, modern artillery from Seville, ten bronze culverins and four falconets with extra ammunition for each piece, a launch loaded just with supplies, and one hundred mastiffs.

On the advice of men who had sailed with Grijalva, I paid Indian women who lived near San Cristóbal de La Habana to make thick, quilted cotton uniforms similar to ones the men said the Indians wore in the Yucatán, that arrows could not penetrate, although all of us horsemen and captains also had full suits of armor made of iron plate and steel helmets and other protective gear, and the horses had iron plate barding. We took hourglasses for ourselves and a significant number of glass beads, bells, needles, and pins, and iron and steel tools, such as hammers and axes, for trading and gifts.

We departed Cabo Corrientes on 18 February 1519, after I had ordered my captains to keep my flagship in sight at all times and, if separated, to meet at Cozumel, but no one should land before me. We fought wild storms the first night, causing one of the pilots to lose his rudder, which he recovered in the morning by jumping into the water.

We continued sailing. As we approached Cozumel, I noted it was almost identical to the other islands we had colonized, but here, the sea was more green than blue and the sand white.

When my craft arrived near the beach, I saw that Pedro de Alvarado, one of my most important captains, and his crew had disembarked. He later explained he had explored and found most inhabitants had abandoned the island, but he had captured some he found hiding in a temple and took turkeys and other objects from the homes.

I instructed everyone to get off the ships, and as we approached the beach by boat, three Indians jumped into a canoe, trying to flee, but we caught them and put them in chains. They trembled as I questioned them, using the Yucatán Indians, Melchor and Francisco, as interpreters.

"Our chieftains, when they saw your vessels in the distance, emptied the towns and ordered our people to hide in the forests."

I offered to free the men if they delivered a message to their rulers.

"We did not come here to harm anyone but to inform you about our religion, the Holy Catholic Faith, and also about our Majesties, the Catholic queen and king, so that you and other Indians in these parts may accept them as your sovereigns."

The natives appeared to lose their fear when they heard these words, and after we removed their irons they said they would return in five days and departed. I released the people Alvarado had seized and chastised him and jailed his pilot, in a hut we built for that purpose, for not having been at muster.

Two days later, when all our ships but one were present at Cozumel, I inspected the island and encountered a woman, her children, and servants who had remained behind. All the people we saw had their shameful parts covered. The women here, even the servants, wore tunics as well as skirts.

"Here are toys for the children," I said to the woman. I gave the little ones wooden carved animals and the adults scissors and mirrors, in which they looked and laughed. I smiled.

"Please, do me the favor of telling your chieftain that we are here in peace. Really, we mean none of you any harm. I would just like to speak with him, and if he comes back with his people, we promise to treat them well."

I showed her a bell and then rang it.

"Here, take him this bell and these beads. And tell him I have more gifts he may be interested in."

The woman left with her children. The chieftain returned with his subjects the next day. I restored to him the items Alvarado had taken and gave him glass beads, scissors, and mirrors, and at my request he gathered a number of villagers in the square.

I preached about the evils of human sacrifice, evidence of which I had observed at the structure where they bowed to their false gods. They consented to become good Christians, and the chieftain permitted us to place an image of the Virgin Mary and a cross inside. Then I ordered a friar to hold Mass.

The three Indians I had sent as envoys returned eight days later, but almost all the towns in the vicinity were still largely empty. To prevent other natives from trying to escape, I ordered two captains, each with two hundred men, to patrol the coast and speak with anyone of high rank whom they encountered and say I wanted to meet with them, but I directed the Castilians not to hurt anyone or their property.

After four days, my captains returned with twelve Indians, whom I advised we had come in peace but would not leave until we had spoken with all the chieftains. I released one to take them a dispatch and, in two days, he came back with a well-dressed man who claimed to be the ruler of the island. He asked me what we wanted.

"We have not come to harm you or your people," I said, "but to teach you about our Holy Catholic Faith and tell you we are subjects of the most powerful king on Earth. All we ask of you on our Majesties' behalf is that you are willing to freely become vassals of our monarchs, as we are. If you do so, we promise to leave you in peace."

"If that is all you desire, I will call for all the leaders," he replied.

I granted him permission to send men to bring them but made him stay with us. The next morning, seven chiefs arrived, and all pledged to become subjects of the Catholic king, as long as we caused them or their people no injury, and they obeyed when I ordered them to make everyone return to their homes.

That afternoon, I learned, from questioning one of the lords, the fate of certain Castilians who years prior had been shipwrecked in the region and whom the Indians had taken captive. He said they were across the sea, to the west, in Yucatán, so pursuant to his advice, I sent four native Indians in a canoe with a substantial number of glass beads and a note stating I had sent a ransom to their jailer and would wait for them at Cozumel.

They returned six days later without the Castilians, stating that they had delivered the payment and paper to someone who said he would give the items to his chief, so I ordered eight Castilians to go search for them, but a storm prevented them from leaving.

The following day, however, we saw a canoe coming in our direction and, when it was close to shore, we were glad to hear a man yell, "I'm Father Geronimo de Aguilar. It's me—it's me. I have your letter. I'm one of . . . one of the ones you're looking for."

A group rowed out to meet him and helped him onto a boat. He barely looked Spanish, as he was dark brown, like the Indians, had long, unkempt hair, and wore a loincloth under a frayed cloak. We were excited, because he was one of us and now was out of danger, but I especially so, as I assumed he had learned to speak well the language of the Indians who had kept him captive, and I needed an interpreter who was fluent in both Castilian and the native tongue.

After we had fed Aguilar and given him clean clothes and san-dals and let him sleep inside a hut, my captains and I spoke with him, and he explained what had happened to him and the others.

"We were on a ship, in March or April 1511, on our way to Santo Domingo, but we were shipwrecked near Jamaica when our ship hit shoals, and everybody got on different boats. I went in one with nineteen others, including two women. We didn't have food or water.

"Then, we lost sight of the others in the other boats, and ten of the men in my boat—they died, they died, and we, we threw them overboard. Then, a strong current came and pushed us west, all the way to the Yucatán, and we landed on the beach.

"Straightaway, some Indians on the beach took us, and they killed five of us and took the other five of us captive, including the two women, and put us in cages, but they gave us plenty of food and water. Gonzalo Guerrero and I feared they were fattening us to sacrifice us and eat our flesh.

"One day we, Gonzalo and I, heard screaming, as the other three begged the Indians not to kill them. But about three weeks later, he and I broke out and ran, but we didn't get far because a chief from a different tribe captured us and made us his slaves.

"About a month later, we heard that the other three Castilians had died, and then the chief sold Gonzalo to another village. From time to time, travelers who stopped where I was gave my chief reports about Gonzalo, and because I was obedient and worked hard in the cornfields and cutting wood and drawing water, the chief sometimes, when I asked, told me what was happening with Gonzalo.

"So, then an Indian came to the village where I was to give my chief the ransom and letter you sent. The chief was happy with the payment and freed me. He gave me food and water to take and said I could go to the village where Gonzalo was and even sent one of his warriors as a guide.

"But Gonzalo, he did not want to leave because he had accepted his chief's offer to become his military advisor so he would not be a slave, and Gonzalo even took an Indian wife, and they have three children. He barely looks like a Spaniard now, because of the way he dresses, and he has his nose and ears pierced and his face and body permanently painted."

Aguilar asked us if we had been in those parts a year prior; I replied some of us had, under a different commander, Grijalva. When I inquired why he wanted to know, he said Gonzalo had counseled his lord to attack that expedition.

We let Aguilar recover from his ordeals for five days, as we gathered food and water, and then my captains agreed with me that it was time to resume our voyage.

Chapter Six

THE MEXICA: MOCTEZOMA

I was a child of ten when I became a man; that year, Father retained an Eagle Warrior to teach me advanced archery skills at the Imperial Complex, in the courtyard of our palace. About six months after I began archery training, the new instructor told me that, because I was doing well, practice was also going to take place at night for the next five months and, after that, when I turned eleven, I would begin hunting lessons in the woods with Father and his senior Eagle Warriors.

The next day, my teacher and I began practicing at sunset and ended about six hours later. There were more armed Eagle Warriors in the courtyard than during the day. He took me back inside when we were finished, and my mother was there without her ladies but with a male attendant, who escorted me to my chambers, while she returned to hers.

My skills continued to improve, and I hit the target's center every time, even when the moon was not bright. Late one night, I turned around and looked up at the terrace and was surprised to see my mother there, alone, observing us. My instructor stopped our lesson because he was disappointed that I was distracted.

"In battle or even hunting, if you focus on anything other than the task at hand, that could mean your death. From now on, every time, before you nock your arrow to the bow, you must repeat these words to yourself. It doesn't matter who your target is. It doesn't matter if eighty thousand other warriors are on the field. It doesn't matter if it's raining or the sun is so hot you feel like you're going to faint. Nothing. Repeat after me: Only four things matter: me, my bow, my arrow, and a point on the target."

"Only four things matter: me, my bow, my arrow, and a point on the target."

We resumed, and I never lost concentration, but when I thought we had ended, he said Father had given him permission to punish me and teach me a lesson. I had to spend the rest of the night until daybreak in the courtyard kneeling on the ground. He said I could relieve myself first, but I could not drink anything, and he would go with me to watch me. I was afraid. We went inside, and when we returned to the range, he ordered me to kneel, hands crossed on my head, and then he departed.

My arms hurt in moments and sagged; a guard told me to raise them or he would send for my instructor. My knees pressed into small stones that felt like daggers. I became dizzy and thought I had been there for days. I was thirsty and, even though I had relieved myself before my ordeal had begun, my bladder was full, and I needed to urinate.

As I fell asleep, the two guards by my side caught me, and one told me to put my hands back on my head. I pushed away one who shook me.

"Sir, you don't want the Supreme Ruler and Speaker to hear that you couldn't take your punishment."

I opened my eyes and put my hands on my head. *Father would be proud*, I told myself, *when he learned I had withstood my penance like a true warrior.* My mouth was dry as when I had been playing with my sisters on the beach on the eastern coast, where we went on holiday during winter.

I wanted to cry, but my resolve to be brave for Father's sake prevented tears from falling. For the remainder of the night, until just before dawn broke, I picked a point to stare at, on a gate at a distance, and many times silently repeated: *Only four things matter: me, my bow, my arrow, and a point on the target.*

My instructor arrived just as there was an arc of light in the sky. He told me to rise and lower my hands and escorted me inside so I could relieve myself and then go with a priest who was waiting to take me to my religion class. I was numb, unlike before my punishment, and felt no pain, hunger, or thirst as I sat through my morning classes.

When it was midday, a priest led me to my chambers, where servants fed and gave me beverages, and, after I had eaten, someone took me to my bed, where I slept until dusk, when attendants woke me and accompanied me to the steam room. I bathed, cleaned my mouth, washed my hair, dressed in a new uniform, dined again, and returned to the courtyard for archery lessons.

A few weeks later, my instructor complimented me on my progress because I never lost focus and hit the precise center of the target every time. That night, after practice, when I was back inside the palace, I realized I had not seen my sisters in days, and, after I bathed and dressed, I went to my mother's chambers. A guard, head bowed, was standing outside her door; I asked if she was awake, and he answered in a whisper.

"Yes. Yes, Your Highness. She is."

I heard something.

"Step aside," I ordered.

He obeyed, and I went into my mother's sitting room near the dining area, where she and her ladies spent time during the day, and I walked through a long hallway that led to her bedroom and other private quarters. I stopped when I heard sounds coming from the end of the corridor.

My instructor was grunting and repeating my mother's given name. "Song. Song. Song. Song." She moaned. As I moved, my sandals squeaked on the bare floor, and the noises ended. I slowed down, and as I approached the end of the hall, my mother turned the corner and came to me. She was wearing a robe, and her long hair was tousled.

"What're you doing here, idiot? Get out! Go back to your rooms!"

I went to my quarters and was sitting on my bed, thinking about what to do, whether to tell Father, when she arrived, fully clothed and now wearing a head covering. I thought she would be contrite and plead with me not to tell Father.

"You didn't see a thing, so if you're thinking about telling your father some lie about something you think happened, you'd better not."

That made me angry, and I raised my voice.

"I'm telling him what I heard—that my archery instructor was in your bedroom and that he sounded like, like an . . . animal and . . . and . . . he used your name; he, he called you 'Song, Song, Song, Song.' I know what you were doing, you dirty whore."

She lifted her hand to slap me but stopped midway and folded her arms across her chest. I cried and wiped my face with a corner of my tunic.

"You'd better stop speaking to me like that. I'm your mother, and I was born a princess. And I was royalty even before I married your father. And you, you're just a child."

"I'll call you what I want. And just because I'm a boy doesn't mean anything because, because you're, you're just a woman. And—Father is the Supreme Ruler and Speaker and . . . and I'm a prince."

She was quiet for a moment.

"Yes, you're a prince, but you're a fool, too. Just because you heard someone say my name doesn't mean anything, you simpleton."

I stood and pointed at her. Everyone said I was tall for my age, and we were about the same height. "You—you'd better stop; stop calling me bad names, or I'll tell Father."

"You're not telling your father anything about what I called you or what you think you heard. You want to know how I know you're not going to tell him a thing? Well . . . do you?"

She smiled. I was silent and stared at her. I did not want to tell Father what she had done because in law classes I studied the code my great-grandfather Ilhuicamina had enacted. The penalty for adultery, one of the most important crimes, the tutor had explained, when a married woman lay with a man who was not her husband, was death for both parties.

I had also learned that all laws, even ones involving a capital sentence, applied equally to everyone, including the ruler's own family. I knew, however, that I could not betray Father and had a duty to tell him what had happened that night.

"Here's how I know you'll stay quiet about this: If you tell your father what you think you heard, I'll take your precious sisters with me back to my hometown, and you'll never see them again."

I lowered my head. She laughed.

"Good. I knew you would see things my way, you dolt."

I whispered, "Where are they now?"

"They're in your father's wing. I wanted them out of my way."

She left. I slept poorly that night. The following morning, when I went to breakfast in Father's wing, my sisters were there, and they ran to me, their long hair bouncing.

"Oh, why can't you stay with us? We miss you! Let's play!"

"Run, and I'll try to catch you, but I don't think I can."

I slowly chased them around the hall.

"You Eagle Warriors are too fast for me," I said.

They giggled.

"I have to stop now, because I have to eat before I go to school, and, the truth is, well, I'm really embarrassed to admit it," I whispered. "You're too fast for me, and I'm tired."

They sat on either side of me and told me their adventures since I last had seen them.

When my archery lessons resumed, my instructor and I acted as if nothing had transpired, but he seemed distracted and did not know what to do with his hands for most of the exercises. He was even more unctuous than usual, constantly addressing me as "Your Highness." A week later, my father and I were at breakfast when he dismissed everyone but me.

"I have noticed you are sad. But I commend you for continuing to do well in your studies and military training.

"Son, I know everything that happens in every part of this palace, and I am dealing with the situation, and soon you will participate in resolving the matter. I need you to continue your lessons and studies as if nothing has happened and to keep this between us. I have one question for you. What did your mother say to keep you from telling me what you found out?"

"Father, I'm so sorry, Father. I . . . I . . . wanted to tell you; I did, but . . . but, she, she said, Father, she said she would take Jewel and Emerald with her to her home, and I would never see them again. Father, can she do that?"

"No, little Moctezoma, no. She does not even have the power to leave through the gates of this palace without my consent. Your sisters are safe, and they are being watched, as is your mother. But I still need you to keep quiet about this to give me time to arrange their punishment and for evidence of their crime to develop."

My archery training with my instructor continued until about three months later, when Father's chamberlain entered my chambers after I was finished with my academic and religious studies for the day. He said Father wanted to see me and accompanied me to his private rooms, where he was waiting.

"Sit down, son. I have to tell you something that you will find distressing, but I am certain you are old enough to know the truth. Son, your mother and instructor are being arrested for the crime of adultery."

Father, of course, knew I had studied the law against adultery.

"Son, I cannot be lenient on behalf of your mother because she is a member of my family, and so she will suffer the same penalty as the instructor. I have sentenced both to death by shooting. Your mother, because she was royalty, will be escorted to the military headquarters by litter and the instructor by foot to be imprisoned there.

"You will execute the man, and then you and an experienced Eagle Warrior will execute your mother. I have chosen you for two reasons.

"First, I want to improve your chance of being selected by the Council of Elders as the ruler when it is your time. This will be an opportunity to prove to them not only your skills and that you understand our laws must be equally applied to all, including the ruler's own family, but also that you are courageous enough to execute any criminal, even your own mother.

"Secondly, you must punish your mother for speaking to you in a disrespectful manner and forcing you to withhold information from me. What do you think, son—are you prepared to carry out their sentence?"

I was shocked and sad and thought about what he had said for some moments before I replied with what I assumed he wanted to hear.

"Yes. Yes, Father. I am, and I promise I won't disappoint you."

Father asked me to spend time with my sisters that afternoon and said they would now live with his first wife, whom they adored, but I would continue to live in my own wing. I did not want to show him how I felt about having to kill my mother, but I could not suppress my emotions and cried.

"Son, you will learn to never display your emotions in front of anyone. Ever. It is a sign of fear. And you should not be sad about my or anyone's death, son, because we all die. Now, always remember: No man who fears death can be a warrior. A true warrior, in fact, welcomes death, because a warrior's home is not here in the Middleworld, but in the Overworld. And if a man cannot be a warrior, he cannot be a ruler—and you, Moctezoma, were born to be a ruler."

My shoulders slumped, and I wanted him to embrace me and call for two cups of hot *chocolatl* flavored with spices.

"Is there something else you want to say?"

I wanted to leap into his arms and sit on his lap, as he used to let me do before I turned six, and even though I was being brave about what I would have to do to my mother, I wanted to tell him I was sad about her, too, and not at all sure I wanted to kill her, even though she had betrayed us.

"Father? I have another question. What . . . what will you tell Jewel and Emerald about . . . Mother?"

"They'll think she went to her hometown. In time, I will tell them that your mother passed away. It is best if you do not tell them the truth."

My sisters jumped up and down when they saw me again and asked me to review their lessons. They were progressing well with their characters, and both had good hands for drawing and painting. Father arrived and told me I could go to the archery range if I wanted to practice. So I left them and shot for several hours with my stone- and eagle-talon-tipped arrows, and, after dinner, I played games with my sisters until it was time to go to bed.

I awoke on my own, well before dawn, bathed, and, as Father had instructed me, dressed in a warrior's uniform to join him for prayers at the chapel. I ate and drank little at breakfast. I prepared two quivers, one with stone-tipped and another with eagle-talon-tipped arrows, and we departed the palace in Father's litter.

When we arrived at the military headquarters, he led everyone who was going to be present at the executions, including my maternal grandfather, other rulers, my brothers, noblemen, and the senior members of Father's government, to the area where archery training took place.

As at the palace courtyard, there were targets on high walls; that day, however, two human marks, my mother and my instructor, were secured to poles next to each other, each one bound by the waist and ankles, wrists tied behind them. Both had their heads bowed.

My instructor wore a loincloth made of maguey fiber. My mother was wearing a short robe made of cotton, but it was untied, and her swollen breasts and belly were exposed, but at least she was wearing a garment to cover her lower parts. *Princess Song. She was royalty before she married Father.*

A general ordered me to take my place in the firing line of my instructor. I gave my quiver with eagle-talon-tipped arrows to an attendant and assumed my shooting stance. The general lifted his hand, and I nocked an arrow to my bow. Absurdly, I found myself wondering whether my instructor would be impressed with my focus and my aim.

I picked a point on my target and released a stone-tipped arrow. It landed on my teacher's right thigh, and his body jerked, but he clenched his teeth and did not make a sound. Blood appeared. The second arrow landed on his left thigh. There was more blood, but no cry from him. The third arrow pierced his upper-right chest. He screamed. Blood dripped. The fourth arrow hit his upper-left chest. He wailed and looked at me.

"Stop. Stop. Please, stop. No more—I'm begging you."

The fifth arrow landed in his abdomen, right above his groin. He yelled. I was still as I watched tears roll down his face and mucus cover his mouth.

"Please, please—just finish it. Finish it. I'm begging you. Do it fast."

I slowly reached into the quiver for my next arrow. He whimpered.

"Please hurry. Please, finish it, fast. I beg you—just . . . just kill me! Kill me, quick!"

I paused. He continued to cry, softly now. I nocked another arrow.

"Please, I'm begging you! Hurry, hur . . . ry. Hurr . . ."

Only. Four. Things. Matter. Me. My. Bow. My. Arrow. And. A. Point. On. The. Target.

The sixth arrow landed near his heart. By then he evidently was in too much pain to howl and was quietly weeping and murmuring.

"Wa-wa . . . ter. Please . . . wa-ter, so thirs, thirs, so thirs . . . ty."

The next four arrows flew in rapid succession, and each hit his chest, which now was gore. I gave the attendant my quiver and gestured for the one with eagle-talon-tipped arrows. I took a few steps to my right so I was in the firing line of my mother. An Eagle Warrior stood to my left. I had decided that morning that, because she had given my sisters and me life, I would use only one arrow to kill her, but I soon realized Father knew me at least as well as I knew myself. The Eagle Warrior and I nocked arrows to our bows and pointed.

Princess Song was royalty before she married Father. My mother raised her head and stared at me, her round eyes full of tears, but she did not beg. Even though she had never showed me physical affection, she had always made sure the servants prepared my meals exactly as I liked them and would scold them if my soup was not the right temperature or my venison was cold. Although Father refused to spoil me by letting me drink *chocolatl* anytime I wanted it, my mother let me have it whenever I was in my chambers.

The general signaled, and the Eagle Warrior and I released our arrows; we shot her heart at the same time. I lowered my bow. As her body convulsed, the Eagle Warrior, whose presence I then fully understood, shot her belly, three times. The general walked over and escorted me to a room where Father and the others were present.

Father approached me and put his hand on my shoulder.

"Well done, my son. Well done."

We sat, and as attendants served us beverages, Father explained what was going to happen next. Everyone was staring at me, no doubt to see my reaction, but I resolved to not display emotion.

"The male's body will remain tied to the post until he has finished bleeding to death. The female's has, by now, been taken down. Her body will be flayed, and a priest will wear her skin at a ceremony this afternoon. Then, because she was royalty, her body will be cremated."

I risked my voice cracking, but there was something I had to know. "What about . . . the baby?"

"In accordance with law, and the sentence I issued, they will place it with the male on the banks of the lake, to be eaten by buzzards."

We returned to the palace, and attendants walked me to my chambers. I rested and bathed before putting on religious vestments. When I was dressed, Father, his retinue, and I went to the Main Temple and walked up the steps to Huitzilopochtli's altar, where we prayed.

We turned around as musicians started playing, and at a distance I saw a priest covered in a cape, dancing as he neared the temple, and others chanting funereal songs as drummers walked on either side of them. A large crowd of commoners was marching behind the clerics, and the one who was wearing what I now realized was my mother's skin reached the bottom step leading to Huitzilopochtli's statue, stopped, and bowed to the god.

The grim cloak had no face but long hair, and many loose strips of skin hung from the area where my sibling used to be. He performed an elaborate routine as he held on to the cape so it would not fall off, and at the end of the dance, he did not climb the stairs but walked back in the direction he had come.

Father led everyone who was at the top to a room underneath Huitzilopochtli's statue, where we prayed before returning to the palace for a feast. I had no appetite but forced myself to swallow something, hoping Father would not notice I was sad, regretful I had killed my mother. He said I looked tired and should go to bed early.

I cried most of the night but promised myself it would be the last time I wept. It was my tenth year, and I had become a man.

Chapter Seven

THE XOCHIMILCA: FLOWER

The priestesses did not say there was a men's compound for deity impersonators next to us, and I did not find out that it existed until my fourth year. They also kept us ignorant about each other by forbidding us to speak about our lives at home, and a priestess, even at night in the dormitory, was present to hear what we said.

If girls ventured into an unauthorized topic, such as how they treated us, a priestess would tell us to be quiet. I often cried in bed, but quietly, when I thought about my family. I was glad Yaretzi had become my friend. She helped to ease my loneliness even though we could not speak freely.

I performed my first practice ceremony at the temple in the compound the year I turned my falsified age of fourteen. Priestess Ahuiliztli told us we would begin learning how to perform the ritual to pretend we were deities in the event we were chosen to be featured at an outside temple when we turned fifteen.

One day, she unexpectedly took ten of us who were fourteen years old out of a history class to a different place, where the senior priestess and others were waiting for us. When I saw the old woman, my heart beat fast, my face became hot, and I felt sharp pain in my toes. I tried not to let my mind wander back to my arrival at the compound, but I saw images of the women beating my feet and the old one putting her finger in me.

"Greetings in the name of the Supreme Ruler and Speaker, Chief Priest, and Master Judge, the Honorable Moctezoma. Now that all of you have turned fourteen years old, you will pass into the next important phase of your training and education by practicing how to perform in one of our empire's major religious ceremonies. First, let us close our eyes and pray."

As everyone else chanted, I suppressed a smile and forgot about the disturbing memories by thinking about going home to my family after I had impersonated a deity. I still hoped it would be next year, and I believed I had done everything possible by studying hard and being exceptionally good at most subjects to make them select me.

The senior priestess left after the prayers, and Priestess Citlalmina told us to go to a table that had clothing, sandals, jewelry, and other objects. One by one, she showed them to us; then she rang a bell, and servants entered to assist the priestesses with dressing us. After we had put on the garments, someone tied a striped cloth on my head, helped me with pieces of jewelry for different parts of my body; two-headed serpents circled my arms, thighs, abdomen, and head, and I tied little bells painted in blue around my ankles.

We stepped into gold-toned sandals, after they painted designs on us—bells on our faces and Earth-monsters on our knees, elbows, and ankles. I thought we were ready, but the priestesses handed us each a bow and arrow, smaller, but otherwise similar to those I had seen warriors and guards carrying. The clothing, sandals, jewelry, belt, and other objects fit each girl perfectly. Even the bows were different sizes to match her height—mine was the largest—but the priestess said we would not actually use them because they were just to be held.

They took us to the temple at the compound, where we rehearsed walking up the stairs and how to conduct ourselves once we reached the altar. We practiced there the entire morning, marching in two columns up and down, with the priestesses correcting us to make sure we moved at the same pace.

One day, Priestess Citlalmina told our group that one of us would rehearse the ceremony at the temple in the compound before everyone, but we would not know who was to be chosen until the next morning, before dawn. I slept well, despite being excited about the possibility of being the one to practice the ritual.

The next morning, Priestess Citlalmina shook me gently, and, when I awoke, she said I would play the role of a deity at the sacrament. Torches had been lit; I looked around and saw that other priestesses were waking the rest of the girls. I jumped out of bed, but Priestess Citlalmina had a grave expression—almost sad—about my enthusiasm.

She instructed me to bathe and then go to the changing room, where she and Priestess Eztli had set everything I needed on a table. They helped me dress, tied a striped cloth around my head, put on the serpent jewelry, and repainted the designs on me; I then stepped into the gold-toned sandals. Priestess Eztli handed me a bow and arrow, and they escorted me downstairs through the main door and, when we were outside, I saw two columns of girls accompanied by priestesses.

Priestess Citlalmina told me to walk up the aisle, and, once I was just in front of the steps, four priestesses stood beside me, two on each side, and we waited as musicians played at the top. Everyone, except for the senior priestess and her assistants, was marching. We heard bells ringing at the altar, our signal to ascend the stairs.

It felt peculiar to be the center of attention of so many people, but I was pleased I was going to be seeing my family again, maybe as soon as the following year, and I focused on climbing at a steady pace, as we had rehearsed. It seemed the closer I was to the gods, the more potent was the scent of burning incense and herbs, a smell I knew well by then. But my thoughts still wandered as I breathed in the scent, and I was somewhat anxious about being near the old woman when I reached the top. When I did, I looked at the ground.

I knew from prior rehearsals to hand the bow and arrow to a priestess standing in front of me and then to walk to a large, round stone, where the four priestesses who had walked with me helped me lie down on my belly while they pressed down on my wrists, shoulders, thighs, and lower back. I stayed in that position for several moments, with the rough stone on my cheek, until they released me.

When I rose, I followed in a line led by the senior priestess, and we went through an exit, where Priestess Citlalmina was waiting to accompany me to my dormitory.

"My dear, you did a lovely job today—lovely, indeed."

They introduced fasting for a day, once a month, and Priestess Citlalmina told us that learning to go without food was essential to participate in certain rituals involving the consumption of sacred plants. It was not challenging to deprive my body of nourishment by not having breakfast, the midday meal, or dinner because we drank large amounts of water and tea, and it was another way I could show I was seriously preparing to be a deity impersonator.

My life continued without incident until two months and one day after I had rehearsed for the first time at the temple before everyone. That evening, as we were about to eat, Priestess Citlalmina told the fourteen-year-olds we would begin our fast after dinner to prepare us for a ritual in which we would consume a sacred medicine called *peyotl.*

The following afternoon, the priestesses led us to a round hut, where they directed us to an inner room that held plants with pink, red, and yellow flowers, lit torches on braziers, and mats placed on the floor in a circular pattern. We sat. When everyone was settled, they signaled us to participate in a chant, and when we had repeated it a number of times, a servant entered with a tray of what looked like small, green buttons and handed it to Priestess Citlalmina, who took a piece, placed it in her mouth, chewed, and swallowed. She passed the tray to Priestess Eztli on her right, who followed the same procedure and then gave it to the girl next to her.

When it was my turn, I imitated the others and put a piece in my mouth and passed the tray to Yaretzi, who was to my right. It was so bitter I was about to spit it out, but Priestess Citlalmina ordered me to chew and swallow it. I obeyed, but the taste remained on my tongue, and I felt nauseated. I looked at Yaretzi as she chewed; she was grimacing. I remained still and silent as the tray made its way around the circle to Priestess Ahuiliztli, who ingested the last piece. We sat for some time.

The colors on the flowers are so bright and sharp, I was blind before this moment. I hear rocks fall down the mountain where my grandparents live and a jaguar cry in the ruler's park. The torch is huge and almost in my face, but I am not afraid it will burn me. It runs away, back to the corner, and now is tiny. The pinks, reds, and yellows on the plants jump off, fly around the room and return to their original setting. I looked at Yaretzi, and we laughed. *My chest, face, and neck are one piece, and I am unable to move them for a while.*

We could not stop laughing, and two other girls joined us; we held our bellies and fell. We pointed at each other and commented on the creatures and animals in the air. The priestesses had their eyes closed and were smiling, too. I felt happy and glad I did not spit out the plant. My eyelids were heavy, and I tried to keep them open to say something to Yaretzi.

I heard my name, opened my eyes, and saw that the priestesses were in the process of awakening all the girls and telling us we were leaving the hut and returning to our dormitory, and those of us who wanted dinner could eat, and the others were to go to bed. I chose sleep, but Yaretzi stayed downstairs. I did not rest much that night because I felt the lingering, euphoric effects of the medicine, although I did not see bizarre images, as before, and instead thought about my family and how I was going to see them soon.

I believed I was going to repeat the ceremony with that plant in the coming days, but while other girls went to the circular hut, three others, including Yaretzi, and I were not allowed. I later overheard an older girl telling someone that those who had laughed during that ritual were never again to be included. While I liked the joy I felt after eating it, it was acrid-tasting, and I was glad to no longer have to be part of that experience.

Three and a half months later, one evening while the fourteen-year-olds were having dinner without the younger ones, Priestess Citlalmina announced that we were going to try the beverage called *iztac octli*, which was unlawful to drink except under the supervision of priests and priestesses. I became angry, remembering that I had been abducted from my family to punish Papa for consuming *iztac octli*, and I thought of refusing it, but I was resolved to being obedient at all times. I drank; my heart beat fast, and my mind became muddled, but I had a sense that my body was releasing tension. I put down the cup, and, immediately, a priestess told me to drink more.

The second sip unsettled my stomach and made me more light-headed, yet I realized that the deep misery I had since I arrived at that place was gone. I finished the cup, and they refilled it several times. Afterward, they escorted us upstairs and helped us prepare for bed. I washed myself slowly and several times swayed. A priestess put me on the pallet and covered me; I fell asleep.

In the morning, I was nauseated until midday and would have the same symptoms almost every time I drank *iztac octli*, but they never had to force me to do it, because I liked not caring about the circumstances of my life for those brief periods.

One afternoon, Priestess Citlalmina spoke to the fourteen-year-olds about the procedures for being selected by the ruler or a nobleman to impersonate a deity outside the compound.

"The senior priestess will know ahead of time when the ruler or a nobleman will be at the compound to select an initiate. We priestesses will prepare you to be examined. Now, when the ruler or nobleman is in the hall used for making selections, the senior priestess will lead you in, and you will stand in line, each of you facing forward.

"You must keep your heads down until told to look at the ruler or nobleman and, if the ruler or nobleman is interested in looking at you more closely, the senior priestess will tell you to step forward and follow other instructions, such as to dance as you have rehearsed in class.

"Now, when the ruler's representative tells you to look up, you can look at the ruler's face but, after that, when you are ordered to lower your head, look at the floor immediately. Failure to obey would lead to severe punishment if you look at the ruler's face without permission."

I trembled when she said that, once we were selected, we would go to the ruler's or nobleman's palace the evening before the ceremony at the temple outside the compound.

"You will be taken to a room in the palace where you and the ruler or the nobleman will have sexual congress, just as if you were married and this was your wedding night. The purpose of this union is that, as a deity impersonator, the woman transfers her divine essences to him and in so doing increases his vitality."

I was confused about what my sister had told me about being intimate with her husband and that it hurt at first, but then she enjoyed it. The difference was that even though our parents and his had arranged the marriage, she loved him and found him attractive. The thought of having sex with a complete stranger, let alone one old enough to be my father or grandfather, was repugnant, and I became afraid.

I had thought it was going to be easy to impersonate a deity when it seemed all I had to do was put on odd clothing and jewelry and walk up the stairs of a temple, but this was a distressing new piece of information. My eyes filled with tears, and Priestess Citlalmina stopped speaking and walked over to me and asked why I was crying. I did not answer her, and she ordered me to stop or she would tell the senior priestess. Tears continued to fall, but I wiped them with my hands and forced myself to be quiet.

"There is no need to be upset. This is a tradition that has been going on for a long, long time, and it is not going to end now. And remember, once you have done everything that is required of you, you can choose to return to your family. Tell me you understand and will continue to be obedient."

"Yes."

"That's a good girl. And I forgot to say earlier that, if the initiate wishes, before she lies with the ruler or a nobleman, she can drink *iztac octli* or consume *peyotl*."

I was glad I could be drunk during my ordeal with the ruler or nobleman, but I became sad and worried again when I realized that, once I no longer was a virgin, and returned home, perhaps my family would be ashamed to take me back.

The next critical event in my daily life took place later that year. One afternoon, I was in writing class with my tutor, and Priestess Citlalmina interrupted us, saying the senior priestess had ordered me to the reception hall. I was about to ask why I had to go there to see that woman. No one had told me the night before about any special occasion, but I thought better of it, put down my brush, and went with her.

We walked to the rear entrance of a building at the inner court-yard where they had beaten me. Now I was afraid, but Priestess Citlalmina did not seem angry at me or indicate in any way that I had done something wrong, and it did not seem I was about to be punished. I was glad to see Yaretzi and other fourteen-year-olds in a group led by a priestess going toward the same door and was relieved I was not the only one to have been summoned to stand before the senior priestess. We went inside a room to find her and other priestesses standing in front of a table that held stacks of black clothing. The old woman addressed us.

"Candidates, I have called you here because the Supreme Ruler and Speaker, Chief Priest, and Master Judge Moctezoma has ordered me to select ten of you to appear before him, right now, and be examined as candidates to perform as deity impersonators at the Main Temple in Tenochtitlan. Each girl will have two priestesses to help her change her garments and comb her hair. Now, move!"

I did not even have a chance to look at Yaretzi to see her reaction to all of this. A priestess already had a short tunic and skirt in her hands and told me to begin undressing and take off my sandals. As soon as I had my clothes off, I put on the other ones, and she started combing my hair. When all the girls were ready, we were told to form a line and directed where to stand, with the senior priestess at the front and Priestess Citlalmina at the end, behind me.

"Remember to keep your heads bowed and your eyes looking down at all times, unless you are told to look up."

We marched out to a hallway. Bells rang, and a priest opened a door. The senior priestess led us inside a large, sunny hall. Then all the girls stood in a row facing forward. I stared at the floor.

"The Supreme Ruler and Speaker, Chief Priest, and Master Judge Moctezoma commands you to dismiss all the other girls, except the last one on the line. What is her name?"

"Flower, sir."

"Where is she from?"

"Xochimilco, sir."

The other girls walked out. It was quiet. The light in the room changed; it seemed the sun was about to set, even though it was early in the afternoon. My heart beat fast, and I could hear it, and it seemed all the blood in my body rushed to my face. I could not believe some man had asked my name.

My eyes became teary, but I forced myself not to make a sound because I was afraid of being beaten; I clasped my hands in front of me to prevent them from shaking. The idea of moving made me even more apprehensive, and I did not know how I was going to manage if ordered to do so. Someone walked and stood near me, and I smelled the senior priestess's putrid odor; she put a hand on my lower back and pushed me forward. I trembled.

Even though I was still looking down, I realized I was in front of Moctezoma, because he was seated on a chair placed upon a platform, and I could see his sandals, decorated with gold and emeralds, and that he was wearing a garment trimmed in fur, feathers, and gold thread that reached down to his ankles. His feet were dark brown like Papa's, but Moctezoma's were clean and smooth.

My legs felt weak, as if they could not support the rest of my body, but I knew that, if I fell, I would receive a thrashing worse than the first. I locked my knees, straightened my back, and breathed slowly but could not hold back tears.

"Look up at His Highness, the Supreme Ruler and Speaker, Chief Priest, and Master Judge, the Honorable Moctezoma," the senior priestess said.

I memorized his face: It was oval, and he appeared older than Papa, with black circles around his eyes and deep furrows in his brow. His nose was long, with narrow nostrils, and he had a full mouth. He had on a crown adorned with gold and jewels and pink, white, orange, and red feathers, and he wore a golden necklace and earrings, a greenstone nose pendant, a greenstone earspool, and a small, round greenstone lip plug set in gold that dangled from his lower lip. His hair appeared to be tied in a warrior's knot.

We stared at each other, but then, as I kept my head raised, I inspected the rest of him. The skin on his face and throat was darker brown than on his bare arms, and he wore gold cuffs embellished with red stones arranged in the shapes of flowers. He was holding a decorative cane and had on a colorful cape tied in a bow on his right shoulder made of thick and brightly colored cotton trimmed with fur.

There was something about the way he was studying me I could not understand; he was almost sad but also as if he were inspecting me the way merchants looked at slaves they were planning to buy at the market. That made me angry at this man, who had ordered his representatives to take me from my family, and I wished I could relay without words that I did not want to have intercourse with him and that he should release all the girls at the compound and return them to their homes.

The senior priestess told me to lower my eyes and head. She stood next to me, and we walked backward and out of the hall. We retraced our steps to the first room, where Priestess Citlalmina was waiting for me, and she helped me change into my other clothing and escorted me back to class. Neither of us said anything on the way there, even though I had many questions, including what was going to happen to me next and whether the ruler had chosen me for a ceremony.

When we arrived, the teacher said I should resume my work and acted as if nothing had just occurred, but she seemed melancholy, not cheerful as usual.

The rest of that day proceeded and ended normally, but my daily life soon was to change in extraordinary ways.

The next morning, Priestess Citlalmina woke me when all the other girls were still asleep and told me to bathe. As I was drying myself, she returned with a pile of clothing and sandals.

"These are new. From now on, you will dress only in cotton clothing and sandals like these. Put them on, and comb your hair; then go downstairs to the hall."

The tunic and long skirt, both in black, were of the softest cotton, of the same quality Mama and the girls used to make warriors' uniforms to sell at the market or to pay taxes, and the sandals seemed to be of deerskin, not like the ones made of thick maguey fiber we wore at home and the ones I had been wearing in the compound.

When I was dressed, I learned the reason why, by law, cotton was reserved for the ruler and nobility: it felt wonderful on my skin and not itchy like clothing made from maguey fiber. I concluded that the ruler had chosen me to impersonate a deity at the Main Temple in Tenochtitlan.

After having seen him, I still thought engaging in sexual intimacy with him was going to be repugnant, but I wanted to leave the compound and return to my family more than anything else, so I was delirious that he had selected me.

I went downstairs and followed Priestess Citlalmina down a hallway and into a large, pretty room that had two windows facing the forest, flowers in vases, and four torches on braziers. There was a bed covered in bright linen, a table with writing materials on it, and a stool. She spoke to me in a monotone voice, and her face was without expression as she said that, from then on, this was where I would sleep, alone, but that when I was here, someone would be outside my room, in the hallway.

Chapter Eight

THE MEXICA:
MOCTEZOMA

I, Moctezoma, as Chief Priest, like the rulers before me, am responsible for delivering the blessed word to everyone in my kingdom. We are not the first world; there were four suns before us, each eradicated by a different catastrophe; we now live in the fifth, and, one day, the omens say that, soon, it similarly will be obliterated.

Our time in the Middleworld is divided into epochs: 4-Jaguar, wrecked by unbroken animals; 4-Wind, razed by tempests; 4-Rain, decimated by firestorms; and 4-Water, demolished by torrents.

After the fourth sun had vanished, there was darkness for fifty-two years, and, at the end of that period, the divinities convened at our first homeland, Teotihuacan, to discuss who among them would create the next existence and bring forth a new aeon. To meditate on the question, they engaged in penance, performed rituals for four days, and gathered around their eternal hearth.

Two deities, Nanauatzin and Tecuciztecatl, volunteered to make a new sun by jumping into the sacred fire and putting on garments

suitable for this grave action. Tecuciztecatl approached the con-
flagration, but, while he did not even touch it, a flame seared the
skin on his forearm, and he became afraid and walked away. He
returned for a second attempt, and again failed. Tecuciztecatl tried
a third time to penetrate that blaze, but finally acknowledged he
did not have the courage to do so.

The other gods ordered Nanauatzin to endeavor to complete the
task and encouraged him by saying he was brave, so Nanauatzin
closed his eyes as he approached the fire and did not stop, even
though it seared his flesh.

He became strong; he felt no dread, moved forward, and, all
at once, without thinking about what was going to occur, hurled
himself headfirst into the inferno. Tecuciztecatl resolved to be as
intrepid as Nanauatzin and also threw himself in. An eagle flew
down from the sky and joined the burning gods.

A jaguar saw what the eagle had done, and it also jumped
in; since then, our warriors, depending on how they perform
in battle, are called Eagles, as I am, or Jaguars, the lesser title,
and our fighters have no aversion to death because the deities,
to reward us for our service, reserve a separate heaven for us in
the Overworld.

When the sacred fire had cremated the celestial beings, the rest
of the creators sat in vigil to see where Nanauatzin would appear
at dawn and shine as the next sun. After they had waited a long
time, they noticed the sky reddening everywhere in the world, but
still the orb did not ascend.

In four days, the gods understood that the light star could not
find his fixed place in the sky because, as he climbed, he was not
steady and swayed, and he was not yellow, but red. The remaining deities, about a thousand, concluded they had to find a way to

assist him and decided to be brave and sacrifice themselves, like Nanauatzin and Tecuciztecatl, by ordering the God of Wind to slay them. But even though he blew violently, again and again, he could not murder them all until he disguised himself as Quetzalcoatl.

He then executed each one, causing the sun finally to soar in the east, bringing forth 4-Motion, the fifth and current era, that also will be extinguished, this time by massive tremors, after which it will be ruled by Earth-monsters. To avert that day, it is my duty, as Chief Priest, to nourish the creators with human blood.

Huitzilopochtli, God of the Sun and God of War, was born the first time to the Supreme Creator Ometeotl and the second, to the Mother of the Earth. Mother Earth was engaging in penance by ritually cleaning the Hallowed Mountain when she saw a ball of fine feathers floating down, and she caught it in her palms and placed it inside her robe; when she had finished sweeping, she reached to remove the ball, but it had disappeared.

That evening, she felt movement within her womb and discovered the feathers had impregnated her. It was not long before her offspring, the Four Hundred Southern Gods and their only sister, Coyolxauhqui, the Moon Goddess, concluded that their mother, who existed only in female form and did not have a mate, had brought shame upon them.

Coyolxauhqui became wrathful and told her brothers, who agreed, that they must punish Mother Earth for her wickedness and kill her because she had dishonored them, as no one knew who had fathered what she carried. Mother Earth cried when she found out her children were planning to slay her; she touched her abdomen and, for the first time, heard her son speak.

"Honorable Mother, do not be afraid: I know how I came to be, and it was through no wrongdoing on your part, and sweet, compassionate mother, I already know what to do. I will care for you and not allow my sister and brothers to cause us any harm."

She was now at peace. The next day, Coyolxauhqui continued to incite her siblings, and they came together to plan war against Mother Earth but knew they had to prepare well because she was mighty. Each god was like a general of a separate army; everyone sharpened their blade, made a new bow and arrows with barbed points, and twisted their long hair in a tight warrior's knot.

Coyolxauhqui, who wore the gold-toned sandals of a goddess, directed them and gave each one clothing designed for battle and the little bells every soldier ties around his calves when he wants to intimidate the enemy.

Nothing she did to her appearance marred her exquisite heavenliness: two-headed serpents encircled Coyolxauhqui's arms, legs, abdomen, and head, which was wrapped with striated fabric. She painted bells on her face and Earth-monsters on her knees, elbows, and ankles.

When the Four Hundred Southern Gods and their sister were ready, they marched in orderly squadrons to the holy mountain, and Coyolxauhqui led them as they climbed to the summit, where Mother Earth delivered Huitzilopochtli. The Four Hundred Southern Gods and Coyolxauhqui stepped back when they saw Huitzilopochtli born to the Mother of the Earth as a fully mature god.

Girded and splendid, he held a shield made of bronze and eagle feathers in one hand and his mother's blue fire-serpent weapon in the other, covered himself in diagonal stripes in child's paint color on his face and blue pigment on his arms and legs, and secured his warrior's knot in place with long feathers from the blue plumage of the macaw.

He started with his sister, whom he reached in one instant, and she screamed when he thrust the double blades of the fire serpent into her chest to withdraw her heart. She fell. He tucked her heart in a pocket of his uniform and reached down and severed her head; then he kicked it, and it rolled, eyes open, until it rested on the ground at the base of the sacred summit.

Huitzilopochtli lifted her decapitated body and threw it off the peak and, as it dropped, it crashed into the side of the mountain and broke into pieces, with her arms, legs, feet, hands, and torso scattered at the base of the blessed alp.

Huitzilopochtli turned next to his brothers, who now cowered after having seen what he had done to their leader. He removed his sister's still-beating heart from his pocket and squeezed onto his chest all its blood, emeralds, and rubies and disposed of the empty and shriveled organ off the mountain.

The Four Hundred Southern Gods quivered as they begged Huitzilopochtli not to kill them, but he granted them no mercy and chased the weaklings off the venerated apex and, to toy with them, slowly tracked them four times around the base of the mountain.

Several times they attempted to take the offensive, rattling their bells and clashing their shields, but they could not defend themselves against Huitzilopochtli's choler. His fury would not be quenched, and it deafened him to their appeals to allow them to surrender.

When he elected, he closed the gap between them and deracinated almost all, and as the bodies of the Four Hundred Southern Gods lay on the battlefield, he stripped them of their gear and ornaments, which he made part of his own insignia.

To this day, we reenact the confrontation between the siblings Huitzilopochtli and Coyolxauhqui because it is a parable of the conflict between the sun and moon and an allegory of the positions held by men and women.

Because female blood contains a capability of regeneration, males, because of their innate intellectual and physical superiority, have a duty to dominate and control them to regulate this extraordinary and mysterious force.

Chapter Nine

THE XOCHIMILCA: FLOWER

The first night in my own bedroom, I missed Yaretzi and how we would whisper at night and giggle about nonsense until a priestess ordered us to sleep. And I regretted that we could not speak about this change in my life. She continued to live in the dormitory upstairs with the other girls and go to the same classes, so I assumed she had not yet been chosen to perform as a deity impersonator outside the compound. In the morning, I ate with Priestess Citlalmina, and afterward, we went outside.

"Flower, the only class you are going to attend for now is dance."

I was shocked.

"But why?"

"That is the only order I have right now from the senior priestess. And stop asking questions."

We went to a hall where the only other person present was a dance instructor. Priestess Citlalmina sat on a chair against the back wall.

"Flower, you are going to have a private class with me every morning the first three days of the week."

"Why? I don't like dancing! When am I going to my reading-and-writing classes?"

"I don't know, and it's not my place to make those decisions. The senior priestess ordered me to give you individualized attention in dance because you're not doing well in that course."

I raised my voice. "I'm not dancing, and I want to go to my reading-and-writing class instead!"

I heard Priestess Citlalmina's footsteps. She stood in front of me.

"From this moment on, you will obey everything you are told to do, without asking questions, and, if I have to report you to the senior priestess, you will be punished exactly as you were the day you arrived."

I shook. She returned to her seat. My legs were not steady, but I followed every command and danced as well as I could for the rest of the class.

Three weeks later, a priestess arrived and escorted me to another room, where Priestess Citlalmina and a woman about my height and wearing a warrior's uniform were waiting for me. I had seen a few women fighters at the market and sometimes around the city center when we went to pay our taxes.

"Flower, this is Eagle Warrior Atl, and she is here to teach you how to handle and shoot a bow and arrow. You will obey everything she tells you to do. Is that clear?"

"Yes."

"Good. First, here's a uniform; we will help you put it on."

My uniform had a tunic with long sleeves and matching pants made of quilted, natural-colored cotton, with no adornments. Priestess Citlalmina told me to take everything off; I was uncomfortable doing so in front of a stranger but had no choice. They seemed unconcerned that the clothes were too large for me.

"I'll accompany you and Eagle Warrior Atl to the courtyard, where you'll have archery lessons," Priestess Citlalmina said.

I wanted to cry because that was where they had beaten me, but I was grateful that they had not killed me. I lowered my head to look at the ground.

"Let's go—follow me," was all the Eagle Warrior said.

We went outside, entered a building, crossed a hallway, and passed into another room, which opened into a courtyard. No one was in the courtyard, but I recognized it as the area where they had put me in the cage. My heart beat fast as images of that day appeared in my mind. I walked behind Atl until we stopped next to a table where someone had placed a bow and a bag full of arrows.

"This is where you'll practice shooting, two times a week, the first and third days. Be ready, with your uniform on, after your noon meal for me to bring you here."

She picked up the items on the table.

"Now, we keep our arrows in this bag we call a 'quiver.' Our goal every time is to shoot an arrow into the middle of that target there on the wall. Now, I'll move into position and shoot, and you'll watch. Then you'll go to the target and pull out all the arrows, bring them back to me, and put them in the quiver. Then you'll put on the quiver, and I'll stand behind you and show you how to do everything, where and how to stand—that is, what we call the proper stance."

She stood in a lane that led to the target. She emptied her quiver in moments, and every arrow hit the center. I retrieved them all and put them in my quiver.

She told me to stand with my feet wider and make the toes face forward, helped me put on the quiver, and handed me a bow, larger than the one I had used to rehearse at the ceremony at the temple. She instructed me to remove an arrow and nock it on the bow, but because my hands were shaking and wet from perspiration, I could not get the arrow to attach to the bowstring. I tried to nock the arrow several times until she stood behind me and put her hands over mine to help me shoot. We practiced that way many times.

One morning, Priestess Citlalmina took me to a room in a building facing the courtyard, where a priest was waiting, standing by a table and two chairs across from each other. He was young and clean, with no blood on him, and his hair was tied in back.

"Flower, this is Priest Matlal, your new tutor in reading and writing and poetry recital. You will study with him the first four mornings of every week, after breakfast until your midday meal."

I smiled, and he bowed his head. Priestess Citlalmina went to the back of the room, where she remained for the entire lesson. Priest Matlal told me to sit at the table; I obeyed. He opened a manuscript and asked me to read. This was difficult, because I did not know numerous characters.

"There is no need to worry, Flower. I am here to teach you advanced reading and writing. I am a teacher at the Imperial Academy, the same one the Supreme Ruler and Speaker, Chief Priest, and Master Judge Moctezoma attended, in Tenochtitlan. I just wanted to know how much you already knew. Let's begin."

I spent the morning learning new characters, and I would continue to study with him for the next year. Each day my vocabulary increased because I practiced drawing or painting words, including a few of the difficult ones I knew from before, and I also spent part of the time reading from manuscripts.

One day there was another key development, one that would have the greatest impact on my life and on events to come. Priestess

Citlalmina, maybe because she pitied me and knew how I reacted to being in the presence of the senior priestess, broke her recent curt manner of speaking to me.

"You're getting a new archery instructor tomorrow, Flower, a male Eagle Warrior. So, I'll take you to the practice area after your midday meal, but the senior priestess will be with you from now on during those lessons."

That next afternoon, I changed into my uniform, met Priestess Citlalmina in the hallway, and we left. I was amused that I had not seen men in four years, and now I was going to have two of them teaching me. When we arrived at the range, the person I focused on was not the old woman, who was sitting on a stool located behind the place I stood to shoot; no, my eyes focused on the young warrior.

I walked faster, barely hearing Priestess Citlalmina, who said she would return for me after the lesson, and did not think about what I would say when I reached him. He spoke first, and I was annoyed that the senior priestess was going to hear what he had to say, because I did not want to share any part of him, not even his words, with anyone else.

"I'm Teputzitoloc. Let's begin. Show me what you know so far. Go ahead and pick up the quiver, put it on, nock the arrow, center it, and shoot."

I was disappointed that he wanted to practice immediately and did not say anything else about himself, as I had many questions for him, from when and where he was born to where he lived. Instead of doing as he said, I admired his beautiful face, whose features were harmonious, each one the right size and shape.

He spoke again, startling me. "Now! Go ahead—pick up the bow and quiver, and show me what you can do."

Despite commanding me about something important, his voice was lovely, and I wanted to kiss his mouth. Surprisingly, with steady hands I confidently put the quiver on my shoulder, picked up the bow, and went into my stance in line with the target. I nocked my arrow to the bow, but when I shot, the arrow landed on the ground in front of the wall. My face was hot. He told me to pick up the arrow, put it back in the quiver, and hand him all the items. Then he put them back on the table.

"I'll explain to you the rules of archery, one step at a time, and you'll practice each step for as many days as it takes, until you have mastered each skill, and only then will we move to the next step. First, though, by this evening, you'll have new uniforms that will fit you properly and protective gear and shoes like mine. When you arrive here tomorrow afternoon, you'll be wearing them, and you'll bring the other items with you."

I wanted him to smile so I could see his teeth; I suppressed a giggle. He told me to walk with him to the target so he could explain something. At the wall, he pointed at the center of the target as he whispered that he was here to teach me on the order of the Supreme Ruler and Speaker.

"That means that anything we say or do, he'll hear about, anything that's not directly related to archery. So, you have to stop acting silly and not paying attention to what I say or do. And just . . . just do what I say!"

He turned around and walked away, and I felt foolish and hurt but grateful he had more sense than I because I could have, or maybe even already had, put us both at risk.

Chapter Ten

THE SPANIARDS: CORTÉS

We left Cozumel, after giving the chieftains more presents and leaving them in a peaceful state. We sailed until we reached the mouth of a river, now named the Grijalva, that was too shallow to navigate by ship, so I took two hundred men to explore by boat. Indians confronted us as soon as we arrived at a town called Potonchán. Aguilar interpreted for me.

"We come on behalf of the Catholic king," I said, "and ask for food and water and your permission to land, because we have nowhere to sleep, other than the close quarters of our boats, and it is too late to return to our ships at sea."

A well-dressed man wearing an elaborate headdress replied. "Meet us at the square in our town tomorrow morning, but do not land here today."

Their archers took their positions and nocked their arrows, and I shouted to my men that we should depart and directed them to a beach away from the town, where we slept without incident, although we took turns staying awake to patrol.

We used the darkness to land more soldiers, including cross-bowmen and harquebusiers from the ships, but no horses, and, at dawn, we went to the square in Potonchán, where several Indians arrived with a meager amount of food, cooked turkey, and maize cakes.

"Take the food, and leave," one said.

"No! We will not depart until we have explored these lands that belong to our Majesties, whose vassals you are, and because of this, you have a duty to let us into the interior. Our monarch demands gold. If you bring us a large container of gold and enough food and allow us to see your land, we will leave, but not before then."

"We do not care what kind of stupid arguments you make—we are not letting you in," one holding a large axe answered.

They left. We waited four more days at the beach, but they brought us only a few turkeys and maize cakes. On the fifth day, I ordered a captain to take two hundred men on a road we had discovered the night before, leading to Potonchán. Indians soon arrived, armed with bows and arrows, lances, and bucklers, scream-ing at us to go.

"If war is what you are looking for, you have found it, because we will do what is necessary to defend our people and our land," one said.

The Indians shot at us, so I commanded my harquebusiers to fire cannon from a boat. When our counterattack had killed about three hundred of the enemies, the remainder, about one hundred, fled, although our own weapons, unfortunately, had wounded a few Castilians. We obtained control of the town by slaying the men, women, and children who had not escaped.

The next day, I interrogated captured prisoners and told them to go with a message for their lord that the battle had been their fault for failing to submit to the Catholic Majesties and that I wanted him to come see me.

I sent Spaniards to follow them and bring me back more captives. The following morning, twenty chieftains came to my camp, with a few cheap trinkets and promises they would be peaceful and bring us food in the morning.

"These are from our ruler," one who seemed to be of rank said. "He said to tell you this is all the gold we have, and it is a gift so that you should leave."

"Tell him we prefer to do him and this town no further harm," I replied, "provided we are not attacked, but that I have taken legal possession of this land on behalf of the most powerful monarchs in the world, whose vassals he and all his people are. And, if he willingly agrees to obey our Majesties, they will grant all of you favors and protect you from your enemies."

"Our lord said that, if you agree to leave, we agree to serve your king and be his subjects."

"That is fair enough. And we will leave, on his word, because we have other lands to see and people to whom we will deliver the word of God. And I am glad he has agreed we can be friends. Now, we have no food, so bring us some, but we need a lot more than the stingy amount you brought us before. And tell your ruler he'd better be here in person when you return."

"He will be here tomorrow."

Two days passed, no one had returned, and we were hungry. We could have sent a boat to our ships to bring us provisions, but I assumed the Indians were watching us from hidden positions to see what we would do, and had we capitulated, I reasoned, the next town would have been even more difficult to possess. I ordered four captains to take two hundred and fifty armed soldiers inland for food.

They later reported that, as they neared the cornfields in a village named Centla, a significant number of natives assaulted them with arrows and stones, wounding twenty Castilians, and if two of my soldiers had not informed me of the battle, so the rest of us could assist them, the Indians would have killed my men. We fought most of the day until the rest of the natives fled, our interpreter Melchor with them, and then took our wounded back to camp for treatment.

That night, I sent boats to the ships to bring back food and water, weapons and ammunition, and, for the first time, horses, ten of them. On land, the animals did not want to move at first and were unsteady, so I ordered the most experienced captains to ride them on the beach until they were comfortable.

Combat resumed the following day. I commanded six captains to lead a vanguard of three hundred men to the site of the previous day's action outside town and two captains with one hundred men as the rear guard. I went on foot with twenty soldiers, along with ten knights, who had attached small bells to their horses' breastplates.

The frontline came upon a large group of warriors, and they fought. The rear guard, the cavalry, and I arrived two hours later, and we battled hard until we had killed more than eight hundred, a good number of whom the horsemen speared, making it easier for the foot soldiers to prevail against the remainder, about two hundred.

My military, as I had ordered, afterward gathered at a large edifice we had located earlier by a farm, where we administered medical care to sixty injured men, including three horsemen, buried our two dead, and sealed the wounds of three horses using the fat of an obese Indian we had dismembered for that purpose. Then we returned to our headquarters.

Once there, I interrogated the captives we had seized and then freed two who were captains, on the condition they return to their ruler with my message that he should come to me. Later that day, two leaders arrived with good presents, well-made cloaks and plenty of food, and one said they wished to do whatever was necessary to avoid further injury to their people and asked for leave to bury their deceased.

"I have said repeatedly that we came in peace and never wanted to fight with you," I told him sternly, "that we wanted to be friends. But you used us poorly and only pretended you had agreed to be vassals of our royal Majesties. You ridiculed what I told you, but now you know that there is only one true God, that he is all-powerful, and he is on the side of our monarchs, not of your stone idols."

"Yes, we see that now."

"I need to speak with your ruler; tell him to come here to ask for permission to bury your dead."

They departed. Within an hour their ruler, a rotund man who required twelve slaves to carry him in a litter and whom we called when he was not present "fat chief," arrived, with more food and a good number of valuable gold and turquoise items. He also brought us twenty women, whom I divided among my captains. In response to my request, he formally became a vassal to our Majesties and pledged peace.

"Do you truly believe that, or are you simply saying it so we will leave?"

"Yes, now we believe everything you told us."

"Good, but first, tell me: Were all the warriors who fought with you from this vicinity?"

"No, eight neighboring provinces joined in war against you."

We stayed five days as guests of the Indians, during which time they gave us small quantities of gold they said they had obtained through trade, as, they claimed, their land had no sources for that metal. Their region, however, was rich in agriculture and plentiful with fruits of the sea.

The ruler obeyed my order to repopulate the town before we left, and I preached a sermon advising that it was evil to worship false idols and instructed the chaplains to install a wooden cross atop the Main Temple and the Indians to kneel before it and pray according to our Holy Catholic Faith.

I asked the chieftain why they had assailed us, even though we had asked three times that they submit.

"My brother, the ruler at a town called Champotón, had accused me of cowardice by not defeating a prior expedition of your people. He also said that Melchor, your former interpreter, when he escaped from you, had gone to Champotón, where he reported that you could be defeated if we fought you day *and* night, because you foreigners are few in number."

"You turn that traitor Melchor over to me right now!"

"I can't," the chief said with a smirk. "He fled from Champotón when he learned about your victory." My final query was the source of their gold, and he said it was "from the empire in the direction of the sunset" and words I then did not understand: "Culua, Culua, Mexico, Mexico."

It was the ruler of Potonchán who provided one of the most useful tools at my disposal in the conquest of New Spain. Among the twenty women he gave me was one I named Marina. The chieftain said she spoke not only the languages of the Indians of Potonchán and of those who lived along the coast but also, significantly, the same tongue as that of Mexico, the wealthy inland empire. Aguilar and Marina, working together, would be the key to my ability to communicate with the Mexicans, as I would always have them by my side whenever I needed an interpreter. The method I used was to speak to Aguilar in Castilian and he interpreted to Marina in Mayan. Marina, in turn, interpreted from Mayan to the language of the Mexicans.

In the months to come, Marina told me her story—that her father was a lord at a village called Painala, and her mother his concubine, and he had sold Marina to merchants, who had traded her to buyers from Potonchán. I gave Marina to Alonso Hernández de Portocarrero, a captain, and instructed him to teach her Spanish and use her only as a domestic servant, not as a concubine.

We healed and collected food and water at Potonchán; then we resumed our voyage to the port which the Grijalva expedition had named San Juan de Ulúa, where many natives gathered on shore to observe us, and, as it was evening, I directed my men to stay on board.

The following morning, I disembarked with three hundred men and horses. Native men on the beach directed us inland to a location where we made camp. The next day, a well-dressed Indian accompanied by warriors came to our base and asked if we were peaceful, and when I assured him we were, he said his name was Teudile, a representative of the Mexican Empire, and was there to deliver gifts from his sovereign. A short distance behind them stood about two thousand natives who, judging by their meager dress, appeared to be slaves.

"I am delighted to know this, and such friendship will be greatly rewarded. I want to give you a token of our future favors. Would you do me the honor of putting on these clothes I brought from my land?"

Two of my men helped him dress in a linen shirt, a velvet coat, and a belt with a gold buckle, after which he said he had made arrangements to obtain gold ornaments that were in transit for our Majesties.

"Please tell me about your king," I asked. "What is he like?"

"The most important thing you should know about him is that many, many princes and nobles serve the Supreme Ruler and Speaker, Chief Priest, and Master Judge Montezuma," Teudile replied.

"I would like to meet this man you say is great," I said.

"I'm interested in your large war animals," he replied.

"I understand you don't have these animals anywhere on your lands," I said.

"No, we do not. And I would like to know how you control them, as big as they are."

"It's my pleasure to show you. Watch my horsemen closely; see how they hold the reins and touch the animals, and listen to sounds the riders make."

I ordered the riders to parade the horses and play at battle. All the time, Teudile had painters drawing on easels.

"Thank you; that was enjoyable. I have to go now, but I will leave enough slaves to build you and your men huts, because the rainy season is about to start. But I'll come back tomorrow with more gifts."

The next evening, he returned with a large chest containing valuable gold pieces, fine cotton clothing, ornate featherwork, and food, and I thanked him and gave him goods for his emperor— pearls, an elaborately decorated armchair, and a velvet cap with a medal of St. George. He left.

That night, in a meeting of my captains, we concluded that, because there was so much wealth in these lands, we should continue the expedition to serve God and the Crown and found a permanent base we would call Villa Rica de la Vera Cruz.

"You do understand," I explained to the noblemen, "that by the decisions we just made, we have legally invalidated Velázquez's orders, and we now have to obtain authority directly from the Crown to proceed with the pacification and colonization of the Yucatán."

Everyone agreed I should write our Majesty a petition, but, in the meantime, we needed administrators, so they voted me mayor and chief justice of Villa Rica and, in the name of the king, appointed me commander of the Royal Armies, until such time as the king wrote back with official grants.

Teudile returned the following afternoon with Mexican lords and additional gifts: two magnificent gold and silver discs, engraved with delicate and diverse figures, both as large as cartwheels and so heavy six men were needed to lift and carry each, one representing the sun and the other the moon; gold and silver jewelry, numerous pieces made of gold in designs of animals and other objects; ten bolts of cotton cloth; featherwork; and more food.

"Please tell your ruler that I am deeply appreciative of these wonderful gifts for my Majesty. Did he send word about when I may visit him?"

"Unfortunately, you cannot go to the capital because the Supreme Ruler is in the midst of presiding over religious festivals. Also because the rains are about to begin, the route there is dangerous."

I gave Teudile and the Mexican lords gifts of Spanish clothing and an ornate glass cup for Montezuma.

"Please tell your ruler that I will see him because my Majesty has commanded me to do so." The men departed.

In the morning, men who said they were Totonacs, inhabitants of this territory, arrived from a town called Cempoallan located about seven leagues away.

"We know Montezuma is plying you with presents, and we came to warn you about his duplicity."

"Why do you say he is duplicitous?"

"Where do we begin? The Mexicans are extraordinarily wealthy and powerful because they know how to fight in war. But when they first approach you, they pretend they want to be peaceful. Once you do not give in to their demands, that is when they threaten you with force."

"Thank you for this information. Is there anything else you can tell me about them?"

"Do you know that they have spies everywhere? But you'll hear from us again soon, and we will tell you more." The Totonacs left.

Around this time, a group of Castilians said they were ready to end the expedition and complained that I had not given them any gold.

"The amount of gold the Indians have given us is but an infinitesimal amount compared to the wealth that awaits us in Mexico, and when we have completed the pacification and conquest of these lands, we will *all* be rich. Please, be patient and continue to work hard. And let us do this: we will take an inventory of all the valuable items we have so far, set aside the royal fifth to send to Spain, and then divide the rest among ourselves." That seemed to mollify them.

Teudile came back one morning with cotton goods, jade, featherwork, and a message from Montezuma.

"The Supreme Ruler orders you to leave and return to your lands."

"No! We will not leave until I go to your capital and meet with your Supreme Ruler."

"Well, then, we have no more gifts for you, and we are taking back our slaves." They departed.

I sent one hundred men north to locate land that would be suitable for establishing a settlement, and the rest of us went back to San Juan de Ulúa. While they were gone, Teudile came to see me with more gifts, of gold and cotton, and again with Montezuma's statement that we should not go to Tenochtitlan. I insisted that we were going to visit him.

After ten days, my men found nothing, so they turned back. But on the return, they found an area that, as I had specified, had a good harbor to keep our vessels safe from strong gales. The entire expedition departed, now with the men who had come back from exploring. That night we rested at a river bank, where one hundred Totonacs arrived, provided us turkey and flat corn cakes, and invited us to Cempoallan; we left after eating.

At their city, the ruler's chamberlain welcomed us and offered us a palace as lodging and presented gold, cloaks, and featherwork. We toured the area, and, one day, accompanied by fifty soldiers, I paid a formal visit to the ruler, who responded to my queries about Montezuma.

"He is the ruler of nations, territories, cities, and countless vassals. But he has numerous enemies, for the same reasons we despise him. The tributes he exacts from us are oppressive, and he regularly enslaves our people, particularly warriors and beautiful young women and girls, to be sacrificed in his capital, Tenochtitlan."

"Why don't you go to war against him?"

"You clearly do not know how great is his power and wealth. He would squash us like insects if we tried to fight him."

"If you did want to attack him, how is his capital fortified?"

"Security of the Mexican capital is impossible to breach, because it is built in the middle of a major body of water, Lake Tezcoco, and Montezuma has three causeways linking Tenochtitlan to the mainland, all of which he can disable at any time."

"So, is it your opinion that Mexico cannot be conquered?"

"No, it is not impossible, but . . . almost so."

"If you were to take Mexico by force, how would you do it?"

"Well, the truth is, I would never think about it. The Mexicans have been the most powerful empire for hundreds of years, and, because of that, they have the best weapons and warriors, and they would crush a small kingdom like mine."

"So you allow your people to just continue to suffer?"

"That is how it has been and will be, until the gods make the Mexicans fall."

"Are there other kingdoms that are in the same situation as yours?"

"Of course—that is why Montezuma is so wealthy. He has plenty of tributaries."

I pressed the chieftain no further that day. We would stay in the area two weeks, during which time we walked around the city, including the ceremonial center, where I freed ten slaves awaiting sacrifice, displeasing the ruler, who claimed his idols were going to punish him, so, for that reason and because I agreed with my friars that it was not yet time to end ancient traditions, I returned the captives.

As we prepared to leave, I asked the ruler whether he could spare any slaves to serve us as porters. He gave me four hundred, and he sent messengers to the chieftain of a small, fortified Totonac town named Quiahuiztlan on high cliffs by the sea, near Villa Rica, to say we were going to visit him.

We departed Cempoallan and marched in formation with the artillerymen in the vanguard. Halfway through Quiahuiztlan, we saw no one and later learned it was because most inhabitants had fled. When we arrived at the top of a hill, fifteen Indians wearing tall headdresses, designed with colorful feathers and embellished with gold and jewels, and ornately decorated cloaks and sandals, were waiting.

"Do you come in peace?"

"Yes, we do. The lords of Cempoallan suggested we visit your ruler. Would you please escort us to him?"

They led us to his palace. The ruler complained that the tribute Montezuma exacted was burdensome and that his officials captured their women and children as slaves or to be sacrificed. As we were speaking, an official interrupted us to say a group of five Mexican tax collectors had arrived to perform their duties, and the ruler excused himself, saying he had to prepare a reception for them. I asked him not to go, as I had a proposal for him.

"Why don't you send Montezuma a message that you have had enough of this treatment? Seize the bureaucrats and jail them, and post your warriors to guard them, and if Montezuma later confronts you, you can say it was all my doing. What do you think?"

Chapter Eleven

THE XOCHIMILCA: FLOWER

The day I met Teputzitoloc, we practiced all afternoon until Priestess Citlalmina arrived to take me back, and the rest of the day and that night I could not stop thinking about him, not even when I dreamed. The next morning, no one had to wake me, and I rushed to writing class and ate fast at midday so I would have time to comb my hair and dress in one of the new uniforms Priestess Citlalmina had placed in my room. The warrior's costume was more comfortable, without all the extra fabric the old one had.

I also took the gear Priestess Citlalmina had left, and she escorted me to the training area, where I was surprised to see Atl with Teputzitoloc. She was there to help me put on a finger tab, a chestguard and ear protectors, and a bracer, a sheath that prevented the bowstring from scraping my arm or catching onto my sleeve, after which she departed.

For the next three months, Teputzitoloc taught me new skills, and I practiced each until I was fairly competent, but, at first, he had to repeat how to grip the bow and place the arrow on the string. He moved on to the setup, the point just before I released the arrow, and he instructed me to keep most of my weight on the balls of my feet, hips opened slightly, and my buttocks flexed to keep my middle section tight to support my shot.

The next task I had to learn was how to draw the string back to just below my chin and inhale deeply and then to move my head and use it as a reference point to focus my aim, release the arrow, and begin reaching into the quiver in a smooth, calculated motion to retrieve the next arrow.

Early on, he taught me the most difficult skill—to have the proper mindset before I shot by eliminating all other thoughts and distractions—that all warriors must learn without thinking. It was one proficiency that, during war, could mean the difference between life and death.

"You memorize these words I'm going to tell you, and say them to yourself just before the setup. Only four things matter: me, my bow, my arrow, and a point on the target. Repeat them before each time you get to the setup, until you feel comfortable saying them to yourself without thinking."

I silently repeated the phrase and worked hard to remember to say it to myself after that, because I was determined to learn to shoot an arrow so well that the man I loved would be proud of me. After the first four months of training me, Teputzitoloc told me that because I always hit the center ring of the target, we would begin practicing at night, which he had already cleared with his superiors.

"Who are your superiors?"

He looked behind him at the senior priestess, and I followed his gaze. She stared at him.

"I'm not allowed to discuss anything with you that does not directly relate to archery."

I was disappointed, of course, but I knew the venomous woman would report any insubordination on his part to his overseer, so I did not pursue the topic. We continued practicing and stopped only for brief rests. Although we spoke only about archery, we sometimes stared into each other's eyes, and he allowed himself to smile.

We did not pause for dinner, and I was hungry and thirsty, and my arms and shoulders hurt, so I slumped, and my arrows were landing outside the innermost ring. Teputzitoloc said my stance was incorrect.

"You have to push your buttocks out more as you squat to improve your balance."

I felt hot whenever he said anything about my body.

"Stand properly, and shoot the rest of the arrows in the quiver, and as soon as I see days of consistent improvement, I will move you to the next step, hunting in the woods. Go ahead, now!"

He gave me no time to react to the news that I would be able to go outside the compound. I adjusted my feet and tucked my tailbone. *Only four things matter: me, my bow, my arrow, and a point on the target.* I released the arrow, which hit inside the innermost ring.

I emptied the rest of the quiver, retrieved the arrows, and began again until I had practiced hundreds of times. He said we could rest, and I put my weapon down on the table. I turned to see Priestess Citlalmina standing ready to take me to my room.

I rested in there a short while, and then Priestess Citlalmina said it was time to go back; by the time we had arrived at the range, it was dark, and Teputzitoloc and the senior priestess were there.

I picked up the quiver and bow and went into my proper stance. The moon was not bright, so I could not see the rings on the target that were visible by daylight. I squinted. *Only four things matter: me, my bow, my arrow, and a point on the target.* I released the arrow, but it did not appear to have hit the innermost ring. Teputzitoloc said we should go to the wall to get a better look. I followed him, and when we were there, he whispered.

"From now on, when I have something important to tell you that I don't want the senior priestess to hear, walk with me to the wall after I say I have to show you something on the target. But we'll always have to speak quickly and briefly because the priestess and the guards watch us closely.

"Before I can tell you something, you have to confirm never to repeat it, not to anyone at all."

"No, of course not. I won't repeat anything to anyone else. I promise."

"Just listen. Don't ask questions. I will begin telling you everything tonight, but I can tell you only a bit at a time so we won't make anyone suspicious. There . . . there is a compound across the road for male deity impersonators, where I live."

"So you're also going to—"

"Flower—I'm serious. Follow my instructions. No questions! Let's go back."

As we walked back to the firing line, he said the rings on the target were intentionally dark-colored to make it difficult to see them, because training included being able to shoot well under all conditions.

Twenty-seven nights later, my arrows all landed in the innermost ring, even though it was pitch-dark. One afternoon, Teputzitoloc gave me news. He looked not at me but at the guards' station. His voice was unchanging in pitch as he told me something exciting that was about to happen to me.

"Because you have made excellent progress, I have permission to take you hunting in the forest tomorrow. Make sure tonight you go to sleep early, and eat a lot in the morning and at midday. And Flower, we will be accompanied by soldiers from Moctezoma's military headquarters in Tenochtitlan. They will be there to watch both of us."

I smiled and wanted to yell: *"I'm going outside the compound!"*

That evening, at dinner, they gave me only water to drink, and I rested well, even though I was excited about going outside the compound and spending time with Teputzitoloc. I followed his instructions at meals the next day and in the afternoon dressed in my uniform, put on my protectors, and left for the practice range with Priestess Citlalmina.

At the courtyard, Teputzitoloc was standing in front of a large group of people, mostly male warriors and slaves. Four of the bondsmen were in groups of two, bearing two small, narrow litters that were open, with fabric only on top and bottom, with mats to sit on. As I approached, I counted nine male warriors, including Teputzitoloc, as well as Atl and the senior priestess. It was evident Teputzitoloc was the only male deity impersonator present, because he was perfect in every way. While the other men had scarred skin, long noses, and thin lips, my beloved had no prominent features, and his dark skin was clear and smooth.

When Priestess Citlalmina and I reached them, Teputzitoloc told me to join him at the table where we normally kept the weapons. I obeyed.

"This is your new quiver. It is painted in bright colors because it has two sections, for two types of arrows—red ones, in the red section, like the ones you have been practicing with, made of stone tips, and white ones in the larger section, with tips made of bone talon.

"Now, you are used to pulling out one kind of arrow, but at war a soldier must be ready to withdraw the proper arrow quickly, according to the goal of the shot, so we will practice that in hunting. How can you tell which arrow is which, quickly, but without looking at it?

"Close your eyes. I'm handing you two arrows. Hold one in your right hand and the other in your left. Now, feel the fletchings. The one in your right hand, the bone-tipped arrow, has larger fletchings than the one on your left, the stone-tipped arrow."

I practiced shooting at the target according to his commands to shoot to kill, with a bone-tipped arrow, or just to shoot, with a stone-tipped one. I emptied my quiver as Teputzitoloc ordered, and then I retrieved the arrows from the target and repeated the practice. Each time I was a little faster finding the correct arrow than the last but was much slower than when I had only one type of arrow to choose. It was late afternoon when we stopped practicing at the range.

"It's time to move your training to the woods. Flower, you will carry your own quiver and bow, but first, Atl will show you how to put on a pouch filled with dried food and an empty pouch for water to fill in the woods and a knife in its holder," Teputzitoloc said.

Atl directed me to stand behind Teputzitoloc, who was at the head of the line, while she was in back of me, the priestesses in the litters following her, and the rest of the warriors bringing up the rear.

We proceeded to the exit, where guards in uniform opened the gate for us. I was excited about being outside the compound, even though I knew I was going into the forest only to practice archery and would return, but the brief respite from captivity and the fact that I would be with Teputzitoloc so thrilled me that I almost bumped into him and had to slow my pace. We reached twenty guards, facing us, in a row.

One spoke to the senior priestess. "Where are you going, and by whose permission?"

"The senior priest of this academy has an order from the Supreme Ruler and Speaker, Chief Priest, and Master Judge Moctezoma to take an initiate for military training in the forest."

The line of sentries parted, and Teputzitoloc resumed walking as the rest of us followed. He later told me that every time we went hunting, unseen spies accompanied us. As we marched, I now observed what I had not been able to from the litter they had brought me inside that first day, including tall trees which flanked the entrance to the compound.

Everyone was silent, and, after some time, we arrived at and crossed an intersection, entering thick woods. It was cool, with a light breeze. Once we had stayed on a narrow path for a while, we could not continue in a straight line, so we moved by navigating around pines, oaks, and bushes.

There was little light or sound. As we continued and my legs became tired, I stumbled and put a hand on the trunk of a tree to break my fall, but Teputzitoloc and everyone else kept walking. I wanted to sit, or at least lean against something, but no one showed any signs they wanted to rest, and I did not want Teputzitoloc to think I was weak.

He spoke without turning around. "Flower, walk faster. This is part of your training; warriors have to go long distances, and we do not travel in litters. Now. Pick up your pace."

"Can we at least get some water?"

"When I say so, not before. And you are out of place for speaking to me."

We proceeded until Teputzitoloc ordered us to follow him to the stream, where we filled our water pouches, drank, and rested on the ground until he told us to move again, but we had not gotten far when, a short distance away, I saw two deer eating from bushes.

Teputzitoloc whispered, "Get into your stance and shoot to kill the one closest to you."

I looked around me for a good spot, walked there, and got into my stance, but with my hands shaking, I pulled out a bone-tipped arrow, aimed, and released. The arrow did not fly anywhere near the animals. Both deer fled before the arrow landed on the ground next to the bush. I wiped my sweaty palms on my uniform. Teputzitoloc directed everyone to resume walking. We had not gone far when we saw another deer ahead of us. He stepped out of my way.

"Shoot."

My arrow seemed to graze the animal, but it ran and disappeared. Teputzitoloc signaled that we should continue, and soon we came upon other deer eating, but my shot similarly failed. We saw perhaps eight more deer, each escaping my attempt to wound or kill it, but eventually, I became determined enough and took one down with a bone-tipped arrow. It was not dead when Teputzitoloc and I reached it; the animal was panting and had its eyes closed. Its chest was rising and falling quickly, so I could see its heart was beating fast. Teputzitoloc told me to stab it in the chest.

I hesitated.

"Now!"

I took the blade out of its holder. The deer's long eyelashes fluttered, so I looked away from its face and, using both hands, plunged the knife in, and, a few moments later, it had stopped moving. It did not please me that I had ended its life, but I was glad I had finally learned to hunt. Teputzitoloc said we were going to stay in the forest until I had used all the arrows in my quiver.

When Teputzitoloc announced it was time to return to the compound, we took along five deer I had killed. At dinner, I ate venison, and Priestess Citlalmina said the senior priestess had ordered all the animals to be cooked for our compound.

As the days and weeks progressed, Teputzitoloc continued to teach me, and when my skills had improved enough, he pointed out small wildcats in the forest that I also learned to dispatch. In just eleven and a half months, I automatically repeated the phrase he had taught me—*Only four things matter: me, my bow, my arrow, and a point on the target*—and always hit the innermost ring of the target or took down an animal.

Shooting proved instrumental in how I would handle the devastating information I learned from Teputzitoloc about our lives, why we had been abducted and forced into captivity, that joined us and dictated how he and I comported ourselves in the cataclysmic days to come.

Chapter Twelve

THE MEXICA: MOCTEZOMA

Our first ruler, 128 years ago, was my ancestor, Acamapichtli, of royal Toltec blood, who began constructing Tenochtitlan. To provide sweet water for the residents of Tenochtitlan, Acamapichtli designed the aqueduct that begins at the spring at Chapultepec.

Ilhuicamina, my great-grandfather, was perhaps the most successful ruler in history. His notable accomplishments included beginning the construction of the Main Temple in Tenochtitlan and a decree of new laws, ordinances, and statutes. Twenty-eight years after his installation, Ilhuicamina died, and the Council of Elders in Tenochtitlan and the rulers of Tezcoco and Tlacolpan elected my father.

Three consequential wars took place during my beloved father's rule—victories over Toluca and Tlatelolco, but his defeat at the hands of the Purépecha stands to the present day, as no one has been able to conquer them. When Father conquered Tlatelolco, he installed a governor, my uncle Ahuitzotl, in place of its formerly independent ruler.

Father went to war against the Purépecha when I was twelve.

"Please, Father! Take me with you to fight!"

Father smiled and put a hand on my shoulder. "No, Moctezoma. While you are a brave and superior warrior already at your age, you are not ready for combat."

"Yes, I am, Father! Yes, I am!"

"But you see, the fact that you don't simply accept my decision and that you continue to debate the matter is a sign you are not ready. It shows you would not obey your commander's orders. At war, such disobedience would surely lead to your death, my son. And what kind of father would I be if I let you go to war unprepared?"

I bowed to Father.

"I understand, Father, and I'll stop asking."

"I know you mean well, son, and I appreciate your enthusiasm. But you will have time when you are older to prove yourself on the battlefield."

The Purépecha soundly defeated us. They killed or took as prisoners twenty thousand of our warriors and wounded many, including Father.

Father spoke about the Purépecha loss with my uncle Ahuitzotl and me when they returned to Tenochtitlan. He ordered everyone but us out of the room where the physicians were treating the injuries he had sustained when the enemy's copper arrows penetrated his shoulder close to his neck and his right side near his chest. Father was gaunt and could not even lift his head from the pillow. Fresh bandages the healers had wrapped around his waist were showing blood. He spoke softly about what he had learned from the Purépecha War, and we had to lean close to hear him.

"Moctezoma, most of what I am going to say is for your benefit. And . . . it all stays between the three of us . . . because I am going to make admissions of my failures, what I did not do properly, so that you will learn from my mistakes.

"My chief mistake was not to obtain authentic evidence before we went to war, so my decision to fight was based on lies the enemy fed me. That happened because I did not use my entire web of spies and counted on information from only a select few, ones who had been reliable in the past.

"And I was stunned when we went to war and learned the Purépecha had converted our spies and paid them to give us false statements. The misinformation the agents gave me was that the Purépecha had only about fifteen thousand soldiers.

"When the war began, two subdivisions, each of twenty thousand Purépecha warriors, surrounded our army of twenty-four thousand.

"But you know if the numbers had been almost equal, we could have beaten them," Father told me, "except . . . except, there was another significant deception by those . . . spies. Well, it was not really a lie—it was a consequential omission.

"The omission was that we recently had begun experimenting with copper to use in our weapons, and the generals and I used some of them against the Purépecha, but because we had not finished learning how to make them, none of our lower-ranked warriors had them.

"The Purépecha, however, because they have numerous copper mines and have perfected the use of that metal to make weapons, had not only copper arrows but also copper spears, swords, shields, and even breastplates.

"Every single Purépecha warrior, that is, forty thousand warriors, had copper weapons, shields, and breastplates. Is it surprising they slaughtered us and only four thousand of us survived?"

I forced myself to appear stoic.

Father continued, "I did not know the Purépecha meant to fight to kill, rather than capture warriors to offer to the gods in sacrifice, and that was a development we have to monitor and adjust to, if necessary, in terms of how we decide whether to go to war and prepare for and engage in battle."

That was the last time I saw him alive. As is customary when a Supreme Ruler and Speaker, Chief Priest, and Master Judge dies, we held Father's funeral the next morning, at the Main Temple, where a crematory fire released the soul that lived in his heart.

The clerics had dressed him in a cloak trimmed in fur and feathers, a headdress adorned with feathers and jewels in butterfly designs, a greenstone nose pendant, religious vestments, and a quilted cotton uniform, all to signify he was an emperor and Eagle Warrior.

Priests sacrificed four of Father's attendants in offering to Huitzilopochtli and cremated them after extracting their hearts and placing these on Father's pyre. The blaze that burned Father's body and everything else on his pyre, including food and drinks, not only released his and his servants' souls but also protected and led them to the highest level of the Overworld, the ninth, where they would arrive after a twenty-year journey.

After Father's death, the Council of Elders elected Tizoc, another of Father's brothers. And when Tizoc died, the Council of Elders chose my dear uncle, Ahuitzotl, who treated me like a favored son, under whose reign the Main Temple was finally completed.

Together we rebuilt and significantly expanded our intelligence network, especially far north, along the coast of the eastern seas, and south, even beyond the lowlands. We perfected the use of copper and bronze for making shields and arrows and other tools, and we obtained new spies, paid them more than any other power in the world paid theirs, and granted them the best titles of nobility. To the present, I have agents embedded even in territories where the principalities, such as the Maya, are neither my tributaries nor my enemies.

Eighteen years ago, when I was the age of thirty-four and a commander in the military, the Council of Elders elected me to succeed my uncle Ahuitzotl after his death. No one can inherit the title Supreme Ruler and Speaker, Chief Priest, and Master Judge, not even those of us who are legitimate sons of an emperor, and, since the founding of Tenochtitlan, even those of royal lineage must prove themselves worthy of this, the most important position in the world.

My coronation was consistent with installations of our prior emperors and served to reinforce the fact that I am not only above all humans but that I am no longer even one of them. The ceremony began with a lesson in being lowered and humbled in a room at the Main Temple beneath Huitzilopochtli's statue, where I removed my fine clothing and put on a loincloth made of maguey fiber, and the rulers of Tezcoco and Tlacolpan, high priests, noblemen, and my attendants escorted me to the base of the altar. There, one priest painted my face and body black and gave me a green garment to wear, and another handed me a tobacco gourd and a green cotton pouch decorated with small pieces of human bones.

Next, they perfumed me with incense, signaling the musicians to play large conch-shell trumpets. When the sacred harmonies ended, four noblemen dressed like me led me down the temple steps to the House of Fasting, which also functions as a military headquarters, where we engaged in four days of penance and purification by fasting and ritual bathing, and each morning walked up the stairs to stand before Huitzilopochtli, where we bled ourselves, pricking the skin on our arms, using needles we made from the maguey plant.

On the fifth day, after the high priests pronounced me representative of the gods, everyone went to a celebration at my residence, where the ruler of Tezcoco crowned me.

A week after my coronation, I conducted the traditional inaugural war against our enemies the Tlaxcalans, whom we had never been able to conquer, the purpose of which was to seize a significant number of sacrificial subjects, and I offered the hundred warriors we captured to Huitzilopochtli within a day of my return to show Him my gratitude for elevating me.

To consolidate my authority and silence most of Ahuitzotl's senior officials, I killed them.

Chapter Thirteen

THE SPANIARDS: CORTÉS

The ruler smiled when I suggested he send Montezuma a message that he was tired of his mistreatment by seizing Montezuma's tax collectors and jailing them. But he said he feared Montezuma's retaliation, so I patiently persuaded him by repeating his grievances, adding that our weapons were far superior to Montezuma's.

"I pledge my army to defend you and your people if Montezuma tries to punish you. You have my word."

He finally consented, and his warriors arrested the tax gatherers, binding them with collars and beating the ones who resisted and imprisoning them in a building, after which I met with the ruler and his chieftains; they took an oath to the Spanish Majesty and became our allies.

"Now that you are vassals of the Crown, I relieve your principality from having to pay tribute to Montezuma, and I instruct you to send messengers throughout all the Totonac villages informing them that they are now free from their Mexican tax burdens."

The ruler obeyed and dispatched the envoys.

"What do I do about the tax collectors? Should I have them killed?"

"No, you should not," I said. "I will deal with them. For now, my men will guard them."

Late that evening, when it appeared everyone was asleep, I met with the Castilians to explain my scheme, and we initiated it that night. The interpreters spoke with the Mexicans first, without my presence.

"They screamed at us and called us dirty dogs. And they know we had them jailed. They taunted us by saying that if the Totonacs rebel against Montezuma because of us, he will destroy all of us," Aguilar said.

After Marina and Aguilar reported back to me, they went to the captives, accompanied by two captains, and, as I had commanded, one of my men chose two of the prisoners and took them to me, but quietly, so the local Indians could not find out. I addressed the tax officials.

"Because of my friendship with Montezuma, I will help you. But only on the condition that the two of you go to him and tell him I was offended by how the Totonacs abused you and that I helped you escape and prevented your harm.

"And tell Montezuma I will persuade the local ruler to allow me to take the other three men to one of my ships on the coast, where Montezuma can send someone to retrieve them. As for the two of you going to the capital, six of my men will take you by boat and leave you in Montezuma's territory.

"And, this is important: I want you to tell Montezuma I was disappointed he will not grant me an audience, as all I want is to obey my monarchs' orders to see him and his empire."

In the morning, the ruler of Quiahuiztlan was incensed.

"You let two of the prisoners escape! Because of that, I'm going to kill the rest."

"No, please. That is not necessary and might start a conflict. Montezuma might attack us if you do so. As we are not now in a position to go to war with him, I propose we hold them on one of my ships at the harbor. What do you think?"

He consented. I thanked him for his hospitality and promised to speak with him again when I had fully developed my strategy to proceed against Montezuma.

We departed to our base, Villa Rica de la Vera Cruz, that we officially founded on 28 June 1519. With my carpenters, I drew the initial plans for the town, which included houses and a main square with stocks in the center, enclosed by a church, the municipal hall, military barracks, a marketplace, arsenals, the slaughterhouse, and a jail. Everyone participated in the construction, and even captains, knights, and I carried dirt and stones and dug foundations.

As we were building, emissaries of Montezuma arrived, one named Motelchiuh, a military official in Tenochtitlan, two of Montezuma's nephews, and four old men of high rank, all accompanied by numerous servants, stating they were here on behalf of the emperor and his nephew, Cacama, king of Tezcoco.

They presented me with more gold objects, cotton cloaks, and featherwork; then they delivered Montezuma's latest denial of my request to go to Tenochtitlan, for the reason that he was too ill to receive me at the time, but he thanked me for freeing the tax collectors.

"The Supreme Ruler and Speaker, Chief Priest, and Master Judge Moctezoma asks you to cease encouraging the Totonacs to rebel against him and to order them to resume paying their tribute," Motelchiuh said.

"If Montezuma had not refused us an invitation to his capital, we would not have approached the Totonacs, who have treated us well. And I took appropriate action by telling the Totonacs to stop paying Montezuma tribute because they have formally pledged their allegiance to my Majesty, and they cannot now serve two masters."

We stared at each other in silence for several moments. When they did not reply to my statement, I gave the visitors glass beads for Montezuma and themselves and, as entertainment, asked a captain to parade and show the horses galloping on a grass field.

That evening, we provided the guests with huts, and, as they were settling into their quarters, I sent one of my captains with four soldiers to tell the ruler of Quiahuiztlan that Montezuma's ambassadors were at my town and that I was releasing to them the remaining tax collectors. The Mexicans departed the following day.

The chief of Cempoallan, less than a week later, sent word asking me for military assistance, as Montezuma had started war against the Totonacs from his garrison in a hill town called Tizapancingo and was destroying their farms and assaulting their people because they had declared themselves no longer subject to Mexico.

"Tell your lord that, as I have promised on behalf of the Crown to protect him and his people against all enemies, I agree with his request, but I need his assistance. Tell him to coordinate with the ruler of Quiahuiztlan to send me as many warriors as possible and one hundred slaves to serve as porters. And I want everyone to meet at my base so we may leave together and deal with the Mexicans as one force."

The next day, two thousand Totonac fighters arrived at Villa Rica, by which time I had assembled most of my military, four hundred soldiers, all sixteen horsemen, crossbowmen, harquebusiers, and porters to carry the cannon. I was excited about my first challenge against Montezuma.

When we reached the outskirts of Tizapancingo, the Mexicans confronted us. They had painted their faces and bodies and wore elaborate featherwork. As soon as they saw us, they turned and ran into the town, and we pursued them, but the horses slipped, and we were unable to climb the hill made of stone.

All the horsemen dismounted and, with the foot soldiers, we chased them until we were at the main gate. We had to break it open to enter, and after we subdued and seized the enemy, I sent them to the chieftain of Cempoallan with the order that no one should be executed.

We marched toward Villa Rica and stopped at Cempoallan, where the ruler gave us huts to sleep in. In the morning, he formally became our ally and, to seal the pact, gave us eight girls, all daughters of men of rank, and then we left for Villa Rica.

In the early evening, a ship commanded by Francisco de Saucedo, which I had left in Cuba to be careened, landed at our town, bringing news that the Crown had granted Velázquez the right to trade and establish settlements in Yucatán.

Saucedo gave me a copy of a document that had proper seals and other marks of authenticity. I was astounded to discover the sizeable grants the king had conferred on Velázquez.

He and his heirs were entitled to the yield from my expedition, and the Crown would take only one-tenth of all gold from him, rather than one-fifth. That night, I met with my captains.

"After careful consideration about how best to accomplish the goals we have set for ourselves in this land, I have decided that we are going to send not only the royal fifth to Spain but also the entire first spoils of the gold, silver, and jewels, so the Crown will grant us permission to conquer Montezuma's empire."

No one said anything to me in response, but they whispered to each other, many shaking their heads.

"If you have anything to say about my announcement, be bold enough to say it so we all hear you."

Still no one did, but I knew they were dissatisfied. I should have done more that night to find out who was vehemently opposed to my plan, because I could have taken action against those men before they had time to form a plot against me.

That week, I found out Velázquez's allies were preparing to overthrow me and return to Cuba, on the way intercepting the ship with the king's treasure. Their scheme was to seize the brigantine and kill the captain, but one member of that group informed me, so I ordered captains to arrest and interrogate the conspirators. When those actions had been completed, I carried out their sentences.

I hanged Juan Escudero and Diego Cermeño, cut off a foot of the pilot Gonzalo de Umbría, jailed two others for five days, and subjected the rest, except Juan Díaz, because he was a priest, to two hundred lashes each. Then, I commanded the captains to beach nine of the twelve ships but first remove all that could be reused, such as guns, rigging, anchors, sails, compasses, rudders, and cables.

I entrusted the treasure to representatives of Villa Rica, Portocarrero, and Francisco de Montejo, with a directive not to stop in Cuba or anywhere else in the Indies, and I sent Emperor Carlos, who was in Flanders at the time, a copy of the list and a separate description of the land and its people.

I later learned that the ship with the treasure sailed to San Cristóbal de La Habana, not directly to Spain. Portocarrero and Montejo, contrary to instructions that I did not want Velázquez to know anything pertaining to what I had sent the king, disembarked at Cuba, and Montejo sent someone to Santiago de Cuba to inform Velázquez that he had three hundred *castellanos de oro* in treasure on the ship.

Further, a sailor on Portocarrero's ship who was partial to Velázquez had concocted a plot with another in Villa Rica to inform Velázquez about the voyage, but, fortunately, by the time Velázquez heard about the scheme and tried to stop the vessel in the Bahama Channel, it was gone.

Velázquez thereafter wrote the vice-regal court in Santo Domingo and the Council of the Indies in Seville to lodge complaints against me, but the court in La Española ruled in my favor, and so did the king, as I had taken measures to ensure that he had his own copies of my letters.

After Portocarrero and Montejo had left for Spain, I appointed Juan de Escalante commander of Villa Rica, with 150 soldiers, two harquebusiers, and two horses, to protect the town from Velázquez's further attempts to interfere with me. We went to Cempoallan, where I summoned all the Totonac chiefs who were our allies.

"We are about to launch our conquest of Mexico. On behalf of my Majesty, I thank you for being our friends and for your kind assistance. Now, we still need your cooperation. Would you please provide us with two hundred slaves to carry our artillery and one hundred of your best warriors?"

The chieftains complied.

About a week later, while we still were at Cempoallan preparing, a messenger brought me a shocking letter from Villa Rica stating that Francisco de Garay, governor of Jamaica, had arrived nearby and landed but had reembarked after my soldiers told him I was commander of that territory.

He and his men continued sailing along the shore, so I immediately departed with ten foot soldiers and returned to our base. As we were near our town, we encountered five men who identified themselves as being with Garay. One Spaniard asked me my name and, when I provided it, said he was serving me notice of process and held out a document I refused to touch, so he dropped it on the ground by my foot.

"I am presenting you with documentation," he said, "proving the Honorable Francisco de Garay has discovered these lands and is here to establish colonies. He orders you and your men to immediately vacate these territories and return to Cuba, or, if you prefer, he is willing to grant you an audience to resolve division of the lands."

"You tell your master to meet me in Villa Rica, and he and I will discuss this matter when I have a moment. Step out of our way," I said.

"Sir, ah, the governor said to tell you he does not want to meet in person, and we're the only ones from the ships to land, and that's why he sent us. . . ."

I grabbed him by the throat and told my men to seize the others.

"You tell Garay that I will speak only with him, not his underlings, and if he refuses to meet me in my town, then I have better things to do and am continuing my voyage. And, if he has the courage to see me, tell him he can find me on the way to, or at, Cempoallan."

I ordered three of my soldiers and three of Garay's envoys to remove their outer clothing, after which I instructed my men to put on the garments of Garay's men, and we bound and gagged them. When that was done, dragging our charges, we walked back in the direction of Cempoallan for about one hour, in the event Garay had others in the vicinity observing us, and then we stepped off the road and turned around.

That night, crawling behind bushes and trees with our captives, we moved along the shore until we were at the beach directly across from Garay's fleet, where we hid until noon the next day, watching the Castilians, hoping some would land. No one did, so my three soldiers, dressed as Garay's envoys, as I had instructed them, walked close to the water and waved white cloths and yelled at the people on the ships.

Not long thereafter, a group of men boarded boats and sailed to us until they were close, but only six disembarked, two crossbowmen and four harquebusiers, and my soldiers fired; one of the enemies would have killed someone, but his fuse failed to ignite.

The men on the boat fled, abandoning their allies, and Garay and the rest of his fleet already had hoisted their sails and departed. Those of his men I had captured, except for three soldiers who joined my expedition, I sent as prisoners to Villa Rica. We returned to Cempoallan.

Chapter Fourteen

THE XOCHIMILCA: FLOWER

They guarded me always, even when I was in bed, and sometimes I awoke to find a priestess standing over me, claiming she had heard me making sounds in my sleep. When we were at the range, warriors watched us from their station inside the front gate, as the old woman sat on a chair behind Teputzitoloc and me. Not long after we had begun night lessons, she snored, making it easier to speak, although we whispered, and did not spend much time at the target because guards still watched us.

One day, after I had been hunting in the woods for three months, Teputzitoloc started telling me the reason why Moctezoma's people had abducted and imprisoned me. He frowned as he spoke.

"I have to remind you that you cannot repeat what I'm going to tell you."

"I promise. I won't say anything to anyone."

"The main difference between the female and male compounds is that all the men were captured at war and are being taught how to impersonate a god called the Lord of the Smoking Mirror."

"Who is he? I've never heard of him."

"I'll have to tell you about him another time, because the sentries are staring at us. But this is important: Do you know about the goddess Coyolxauhqui?"

"No, but why is she important?"

He straightened his arm and almost touched my shoulder with his fingers, but then abruptly pulled back his hand.

"I'll tell you more the next time you practice. Now get the arrows from the target, put them in the quiver, and shoot—and repeat the exercise three times in a row!"

Even as I obeyed, I kept thinking about what Teputzitoloc was going to say.

The next day, he announced I was going to learn how to use a slingshot and handed me one. I said my father had made ones for my sisters and me to play with.

"But I'm going to teach you how to use a slingshot as a tool for war, a weapon, not a toy, because you can take down or even kill a man with a slingshot. Find as many small stones as you can. Try to find sharp ones, about one hundred, and put them in the pockets of your uniform."

I followed his commands and walked a distance from the range to collect stones, and Teputzitoloc joined me and demonstrated by bringing down a bird that crashed into the ground, twitching. I cried; Teputzitoloc became angry and screamed at me.

"What's wrong with you? At war, you'd have to murder human beings! Stop crying, right now. I said, 'Stop crying!' In this exercise, you have to kill a bird."

Even as I spoke, I knew I sounded like a spoiled child. "I don't want to kill anything. And it doesn't matter because I'm not going to be a real warrior, anyway. Just a pretend one in a silly ceremony."

His tone was gentle as he stared into my eyes, and we were the only people on Earth.

"You have to trust me. You need to learn those skills. And your reaction today showed me you're not ready to hear about Coyolxauhqui or why you're here."

I stamped my foot. "I *am* ready! Just tell me what you have to say!"

He lowered his voice, and it was deep, almost a growl. He pointed at me.

"I said, 'No!' I will tell you when *I* think you're ready, and not a moment before!"

I shrugged my shoulders. The next two times at practice, I did not speak to him, except to greet him and say goodbye, and simply followed his instructions. But in a few days, I asked him what he had wanted to tell me. He ignored me and turned away.

It was not until a month after he had broached the topic, when we heard the senior priestess grunting in her sleep, that we spoke at the target.

"Just answer my questions. Describe the ceremony you practiced at the temple in the compound."

"The priestesses dressed me in strange clothing and jewelry of serpents, they painted designs on me, and then we marched up the steps to the altar; they helped me on top of a large round, stone face down. They pressed on my back, thighs, and wrists for several moments, and then they told me to rise to conclude the rehearsal before escorting me back to the house."

"Did they say if the ceremony here is like the one outside?"

"Yes, they said exactly like the one outside."

"What did they say is going to happen after the ceremony outside the compound?"

"I can go back to my family or become a priestess."

He was silent; tears formed in his eyes. He turned away from me and wiped his face with the sleeve of his uniform.

"What? What's wrong? What did I say to upset you?"

"We have to go back to practice!"

I walked in front of him and wanted to turn around and kiss him, as I yearned to do every time we were together. I tried to think of something I could say to make him smile. How Teputzitoloc told me my fate showed he loved me and that I was not alone in my cursed existence.

The following night, we spoke again at the target.

"Do you know what is going to happen to you the night before the actual ceremony outside the compound?"

I was relieved to be able to tell someone it was going to be difficult for me to lie with that man.

"Well, what I'm going to tell you is going to make you more than upset." He furrowed his brow. "What I'm going to tell you is more horrible than you can imagine. So please prepare yourself. The reason I'm telling you the truth is that perhaps there is a way we can do something to prevent what's going to happen the morning after you sleep with Moctezoma and they take you to the—"

Since the sentinels were staring at us, Teputzitoloc said he would have to continue another time.

"No, please. I can't wait. Please—tell me now!"

His voice cracked as he spoke. "I'm sorry, but the guards are watching and—and I'm not sure you're strong enough to bear what I have to tell you now. So think about how you're going to react when I do tell you the truth. You'll have to promise me you will not cry or scream when I tell you what Moctezoma plans to do to you.

"And, Flower, know this: if anyone else finds out when you know the truth, we will be killed, immediately."

I wondered what he could say that was so horrific that they would murder us. At that moment, I understood those of us born on an ill-starred day could not escape our predestined doom. I agreed to his terms not to betray how I felt, and we resumed practicing, but one night a week later at the target, I learned my fate.

"Because of how well you're being treated and no one in the men's compound has ever heard of a male warrior teaching in the women's side, I know Moctezoma is particularly interested in you and that he has chosen you to play the part of Coyolxauhqui, the Moon Goddess, who was the sister of Huitzilopochtli, God of the Sun and God of War.

"What happened to her was that, because she told her brothers, the Four Hundred Southern Gods, to murder their mother, Huitzilopochtli killed and dismembered Coyolxauhqui. You will impersonate Coyolxauhqui at the actual ceremony at the Main Temple. And that ceremony, that ceremony, Flower—that ceremony re-creates when Huitzilopochtli killed and dismembered Coyolxauhqui."

He could not control his trembling hands, even after he had placed them firmly against his sides.

"Flower, that's what . . . what Huitzilopochtli did to Coyolxauhqui, and that's . . . that's what they're going to do—to you."

I did not initially understand what he had said and heard only that a god had murdered his own sister, but eventually my mind acknowledged the second part. My palms perspired, and my heart raced. I had a sensation I was spinning and almost lost my balance.

That's what they are going to do to you.

Darts of pain traveled from the soles of my feet and up my legs to my lower back, and I clenched my jaw. I was going to die. I was going to die—at the age of sixteen. *I was going to die.*

"Please, don't scream, and, again, you can't tell anyone that you know this, or they'll immediately kill us both. Just continue to act like before when you go back to your house, in every way, all the time. Promise me."

I could not move, until he yelled at me.

"I don't care if you're tired—move!"

We practiced until Priestess Citlalmina arrived to take me back. She asked if something was wrong and why I was walking slowly, but I did not reply. When she repeated her question, I wanted to scream at her.

I hate all of you! What kind of people are you? How can you be part of a scheme in which you devote yourselves to preparing others to be murdered? No human being should know when he is going to die, and I deserve to live—just as much as anyone else.

She stopped walking.

"You answer me, right now. What's wrong with you?"

I crouched and vomited.

"Oh, poor dear," she said as she handed me a cloth to wipe my face.

She accompanied me to my room, where she sent a priestess for a bowl, water, soap, and towels, and I heard her tell someone else to bring tea with mint leaves. I removed my uniform, and, when the woman brought the items and left, Priestess Citlalmina helped me clean myself, put on sleeping clothes, and get in bed. A servant brought the beverage and placed it on a table near me.

All that time, my mind could focus on nothing else: I was going to die. I recalled the day those men abducted me from my family, and now it all made sense—even why Papa said I was younger; my father had wanted me to have two more years of life. Teputzitoloc was wrong, though, to have revealed my fate, as there was nothing I could do.

"Flower, dear, I think your tea is cool enough to drink. You seem to be in a world of your own. Did anything happen today at the range that made you upset?"

I was about to say I knew they were going to execute and dismember me and did not care if they assassinated me tonight but reconsidered because of what Moctezoma would do to my family if he had to murder me before I had sexual intercourse with him. I said my stomach was sick, and she said a good night's rest would make me feel better. I drank the tea as she stood next to me. It tasted odd. She went out.

My heart was beating fast, and I saw pictures, perhaps hundreds of times, in rapid succession, sometimes outside my head upon the wall, of me face down on the stone, dressed and jeweled as when I practiced the ceremony at the temple, but the images always ended just before someone chopped my neck. I cried, sometimes loudly, and my nighttime guard entered the room, carrying a torch.

"Flower, should I call Priestess Citlalmina? What can I do for you?"

I asked her for the chamber pot, which she brought. I retched. She lit two braziers before she left and returned with Priestess Citlalmina, who was frowning. She bent down and, with the inside of a wrist, touched my forehead and throat and said that, if I did not feel better, I would not be able to go to classes. I had not thought about the next day and was glad I would not have to face anyone, including Teputzitoloc, and eventually slept.

When I awoke, it was late morning. I stayed in bed and did not rise to paint or read. My mind continued to revolve around the day they were going to kill me. No one ever had discussed in religion class anything that had to do with death or what happened to us in the afterlife, and now I knew why: it was because they did not want to even inadvertently hint that they were going to kill us.

Soon I would cease to exist. I no longer would breathe, see, hear, speak, eat, drink, walk, paint, read, write, or bathe, and I would never again see my family.

Oh, and Yaretzi! They were also going to kill that sweet girl who had made my life in this place a little better.

I remembered the first day, after they had beaten me, how I had wanted to die, and it made me realize now, when death was certain, I wanted to survive, and this took me back to Teputzitoloc. I wept, but this time quietly, as I wanted no one to come into the room. With a blow to my head, I had just realized why he was in the men's compound. I had been unfair by being angry at the man who so cherished me that he had risked his life to tell me how I could try to save mine. I decided to compose myself and return to classes and archery practice the next day.

In the morning, I rose, bathed, had breakfast, and went to reading and writing class, where I painted characters, and Priest Matlal said he was glad I was better. After my midday meal, I went to the range with Priestess Citlalmina, and Teputzitoloc began the slingshot lesson that we continued until night, with brief rest periods. We spoke when the senior priestess went to sleep.

"They said you were sick and canceled training, and I was so worried about you. Flower, I'm so sorry I didn't tell you before, but if I don't get a chance to later on, I love you."

I said nothing for a few moments, just to savor those words.

"I love you, too, and have from the first day. You don't have anything to be sorry about. I'm the one who has to apologize. I . . . I'm sure you understand how I felt after you told me everything, and I didn't let on to anyone what I knew, and I really did get sick.

But, Teputzitoloc, I was very selfish. I didn't even think about you; you're in the compound because they're going to . . . to do the same thing to you?"

"Yes, but, no, no. Don't cry. Don't. It's different for me because warriors learn not to be afraid of death, and it is considered a sign of cowardice if they resist a death that is honorable, such as after impersonating a god. And all deity impersonators are killed fast and can eat *peyotl* or sacred mushrooms and drink *iztac octli* beforehand and on the final day."

He added that all warriors go to a special heaven in the afterlife, but nothing he said gave me comfort.

The next time we could speak safely, he told me how I could try to save myself.

"Flower, you can try to persuade Moctezoma to let you live with him as his concubine."

"No, no, I couldn't. And since you have confirmed they are going to kill you, too, there is no point in my living. All I ever wanted before I met you was to go back home to my family. If the ruler kept me alive as a prisoner in his palace and killed you, I would have nothing."

"Flower, please believe me when I say I'm truly prepared to die, but I'm determined to find a way that you can live."

Chapter Fifteen

THE SPANIARDS: CORTÉS

The march to Mexico resumed the morning of 16 August 1519 with a Castilian army of fifteen horsemen, three hundred foot soldiers, including crossbowmen and harquebusiers, fighting mastiffs, and 250 Indian and African slaves from Cuba as porters.

A native commander named Mamexi led eight hundred Totonac warriors and slaves, who carried our artillery and built us huts at every camp. My spies informed me Montezuma had at least fifty agents embedded with the Totonacs who continuously relayed intelligence to him.

We went south for two days to avoid the steepest point of a mountain thirteen thousand feet high that the natives called Nauhcampatépetl but that I named Cofre de Perote, until we reached a fortress town, part of Montezuma's empire, where they treated us well.

From there we climbed and crossed a misty col I named Nombre de Dios to a post also in the Mexican Empire, where the people provided us food and lodging, and we stayed for two days.

We continued and descended to an uninhabited flat route through desert country with no water sources, where ten Cuban Indians who had no warm clothing died during hailstorms, and, because the ground was frozen, we could not bury them.

We went north to stay away from a barren zone that the Totonacs warned us about and went through poor towns, where a chief gave us a gold necklace, cloth, and two girls. We proceeded through villages and climbed to a mountainous area, and south on a ridge that fell to a lovely valley we crossed to enter a pine forest.

We left the woods to arrive at the next important location, a wealthy town called Zautla, where Montezuma had a military base and the chieftain, Olintecle, gave us food and comfortable lodging. The next morning, I questioned him.

"Are you Montezuma's vassal, or do you owe him some other allegiance?"

"Who is not a vassal of Montezuma? Montezuma is the ruler of most of the world!"

"Well, actually, it is *my* king who is the most powerful monarch on Earth. In fact, Montezuma soon will be one of *his* subjects."

He stared at me. I asked for gold samples to send to my Majesty.

"We cannot give you gold, or anything else of value, unless the Supreme Ruler and Speaker, His Royal Highness Montezuma gives us permission to do so," Olintecle said.

"Is that so? Well, very soon I will order Montezuma to make you give me gold or anything else my Majesty desires."

I pressed him no further, but he presented me ten pieces of cheap jewelry, maize, and four women. We stayed there four days, during which time two lords from towns several leagues away visited and gave me a small quantity of gold and eight girls.

"What is the best route to Mexico?"

"You should go through a wealthy territory called Cholula," Olintecle answered.

I repeated to Mamexi what he said.

"No, Montezuma controls Cholula, and that's probably why Montezuma told Olintecle to tell you to go through there. Tlaxcala is the better route, because it's not only closer to here, but I think the Tlaxcalans would consider becoming your ally against Montezuma."

I told Olintecle I had decided to follow Mamexi's advice.

"No, you should reconsider that," Olintecle said. "That is a bad plan. Do not travel to Tlaxcala, because the Tlaxcalans are a major Mexican enemy, and we can't protect you against them. Please—do not go that way!"

We traveled to another territory that was a border between Mexico and Tlaxcala, where we stopped to await return of Cempoallan messengers I had sent to Tlaxcala to inform the chieftains there I was going to visit them. When they did not return after eight days, we left for that region.

We walked through the valley and came upon the frontier of Tlaxcala, a nine-foot-high stone wall with only one entrance that had a thick battlement on top and extended the distance connecting two mountain ranges.

I took horsemen and fifty scouts to explore, and, after about four leagues, as we came upon a hill, two knights ahead of me were the first to notice about thirty Indians dressed for battle, armed with swords and bucklers, who fled when the horses approached them. I sped forward and waved at them in a beckoning manner.

They screamed and threw sharp spears at us, killing two horses and wounding two knights and three other Castilians, one of whom died several days later. Battle was joined. I sent a horseman to bring back reinforcements, and soon more than a thousand of the enemy entered the field around the same time our soldiers arrived.

We suffered harm but killed about sixty of them, capturing twenty prisoners. We went to our camp, where we rested and treated our injuries with fat from an obese native we cut open, as we had no oil or medicine, and for dinner, we ate small dogs, because the local Indians apparently had fled and taken their provisions with them.

Several hours later, envoys who said they were from Tlaxcala arrived, bringing with them three of my Cempoallan messengers.

"We come to tell you the warriors who attacked you were not Tlaxcalans and to invite you to visit our chieftains. Also, our chieftains will pay for your dead animals."

"Tell your masters I will see them soon."

The Tlaxcalans departed. That night, we took turns patrolling the camp. At dawn, we left post and several hours later arrived at a small hamlet, where we came upon two of my missing Cempoallan messengers.

"A Tlaxcalan chieftain almost had us killed!" one of the envoys said. "But we broke out of the cage they had put us in, and we ran."

Several thousand Indians appeared, not too far away, and I sent three Tlaxcalan prisoners to them to say we wanted peace. They responded by shooting at us with javelins, arrows, spears, and stones.

We fought for several hours, until we forced them to retreat; then we followed them near the forest, at the edge of which we realized they had posted warriors to ambush us. They surrounded us and slashed off the head of a mare and would have killed the horseman if ten of us had not rescued him. Combat continued. We beat them, and, afterward, I seized a small temple on top of a hill.

The next morning, we left base, and at the first village we came upon burned homes and murdered about one hundred inhabitants and captured more than five hundred; then we returned to camp with our prisoners.

The following day, however, a significant number of Indians, armed and painted for war, went to the outskirts of our headquarters, and we went out and fought them hard. To hasten victory, I commanded the swordsmen to thrust at the bowels of the enemies and the horsemen to plunge lances in their eyes, but the Tlaxcalans continued to do battle until late at night, when they finally withdrew. We dispatched a substantial number of them and they, only one of us, but they wounded all the horses.

At dawn, we did not wait for the adversary to come to us and traveled a new route to the Tlaxcalan provinces, where we set fire to the first fifteen villages, one of which had more than four thousand houses. We killed more than twenty-five thousand people, but as we carried the banner of the cross, God spared us harm.

At noon, we returned to our headquarters, and before resting I sent Tlaxcalan prisoners to their lords with the message that they should make peace and grant us safe passage on our journey to Mexico. They departed.

No one returned until two days later, when sixty Tlaxcalan lords arrived with others, carrying food. The noblemen refused to state the true purpose for their visit, claiming they were just delivering provisions. I ordered one of them taken to a hut, where I interrogated him by repeatedly plunging his face into a bucket of water, each time until just before he drowned. He confessed after several rounds.

"Xicotencatl the Younger, a Tlaxcalan captain general, is going to attack you tonight and sent us to spy on you and inspect your camp. We're supposed to search for exits and count how many huts you have so we can burn them."

To confirm his story, I took another spy and similarly interrogated him. He gave the same account.

In the center of our base, surrounded by my military, after my soldiers bound them in irons around the upper arms and ankles and held them in place, with a broadsword I cut off the hands of fifty of Xicotencatl the Younger's men and told them to relay a message.

"You can come by day, or you can come by night . . . as you please, but . . . either way, you will see who we are."

I doubt most of them, or any, heard what I said, as the injured ones howled and pressed their stumps on their bodies or the ground as they tried to prevent blood from gushing out. A few fainted; I ordered my men to deposit them outside and push the rest through an exit; then I commanded everyone to fortify the camp by placing cannon and soldiers at strategic points.

That night, I sent out scouts, but most of us in camp stayed awake, except for the horsemen, whom I instructed to rest until we needed them. Sometime around one in the morning, my men returned to report the enemy was advancing down two hills, so I left, and, by moonlight, two of my captains and I observed them watching us from a distance.

We did not leave post for three days, except once to briefly skirmish with Indians who had gathered just outside to shout at us. On the third night, I left with one hundred foot soldiers, seven hundred allies, and all the horsemen, but one league away, five of the horses fell and would go no further, so I sent them back with their riders.

At dawn, we attacked two towns, pulling out people from their homes and killing them, having ordered everyone not to burn dwellings and the Castilians not to use guns to avoid warning neighbors in adjacent villages we were near.

We proceeded to a large city my scouts had previously identified that had more than twenty thousand houses; there, we burned structures and used ammunition to murder residents, as now we wanted other inhabitants in the streets. Men, women, and children ran outside, attempting to flee, but we were swift, and those we did not shoot we brought down with other weapons.

It had not taken long to dispose of about five hundred when high-ranking Tlaxcalans found me as I was on my horse, chopping off people's heads. I stopped when my interpreters called out to say the chieftains wanted to speak with me. I approached them, holding my bloodied sword, but did not dismount. One addressed me.

"Please, please sir. We beg you. Order your men to stop . . . to stop . . . stop killing our people. We are now your Majesty's vassals, and, and we are ready to serve him and serve you, in any way we can."

I looked around, and, as far as I could see, my soldiers and allies continued to attack. I paused before I replied. "Do you truly and genuinely submit as vassals of my Majesty, the Catholic king? Or are you pretending?"

"It's true! It's true! Please, sir—order them to stop—now. Please. We beg you! Stop—yes, we honestly obey! We submit. We submit!"

I sent soldiers to all the fighters, Spanish and Indian alike, to order them to stop the assaults and go from street to street to relay that I had commanded cease-fire. The chieftains thanked me. I addressed them.

"Now I need to hear from you that, this time, you are serious about obeying my Majesty's orders and that you have become our allies."

"Yes, sir. Yes, sir. We agree to obey. We are your king's vassals. Thank you, sir, and, sir, we invite you and all who are with you to join us for a meal after you have had time to rest. We will have food prepared at a place by a spring just outside of town. Would you do us the honor?"

I accepted their invitation. They departed, and I waited for the Spanish Army to join me at the edge of town, where we slept for several hours. Then, wearing our bloodied clothing, we went to the appointed location for an elaborate feast, and, after we had eaten, I spoke with the chieftains. They repeated their pledges, and when I was satisfied they had been pacified, we returned to camp.

The next day, Xicotencatl the Elder arrived at our base with fifty noblemen.

"We apologize for our prior conduct and came to explain why we opposed you. We did not know who you were. We are an independent people who have maintained our way of life by going to war against anyone who threatens us, including the Mexicans, who have never been able to subjugate us, although they have conquered everyone around us and boxed us in.

"That has affected us in important ways, especially since Montezuma does not permit his tributaries to trade with us. For example, we do not have salt, because we have no access to a salted body of water. And we don't have cotton, which we cannot grow because it is cold in our territories."

"I appreciate your apology and now understand why you fought us," I replied. "We came here in peace, hoping you would join us against Montezuma. Now that you are vassals of my Majesty, you are part of a military that is much more powerful than Montezuma's. And I understand your warriors have experience fighting Montezuma, so together we could defeat them quickly. And there are important benefits that would accrue to you if you pledge warriors to us, you know."

"Yes, we do have excellent warriors, and we are enemies of the Mexica. So, yes, we want to join you against Montezuma," Xicotencatl the Elder said.

"That is good news, and you soon will see, after we beat Montezuma, that your people will gain numerous advantages, including military protection, salt, and cotton through our partnership," I said.

We recuperated in Tlaxcala for twenty days, and I knew all the time Montezuma's spies were with us because the Cempoallans had explained, when we were at the coast, that he would embed agents posing as porters and servants and to build huts, and even women pretending to be concubines. They also had said Montezuma's agents employed the messenger-relay method, so anything important I said or did could be sent to him in a matter of hours. I used that knowledge to create my succeeding plan.

Much would be said about the pacification of our next destination, Cholula, a wealthy and populous territory near Montezuma's capital. In a letter to my monarch, I lied when I said the Tlaxcalans had told me not to go to Cholula because there was a plot on the part of Montezuma to assassinate us.

The truth was that the Tlaxcalans had never said anything like that, and Montezuma's alleged scheme to murder us was an important component of my overall strategy. Cholula would be one of the key campaigns in the conquest of New Spain. To succeed there, I had to spread a false rumor for the benefit of my soldiers and our allies to make them enthusiastic about participating in the most challenging military operation I had devised to that date.

At Tlaxcala, to make plausible the fabricated threat that the Cholulans were plotting to kill us, I swore my captains to secrecy regarding our plans and told them to spread hearsay to the rest of the Castilians and our confederates that Montezuma had sent the Cholulans an army of 100,000 men to attack us. Then, because the ruler of Cholula had not been to visit me at Tlaxcala, I sent an envoy asking him and his chieftains to do so, and they sent me three men of no rank.

"This is what I want you to say to your overlords, and listen carefully. 'I am a representative from the highest Majesty in the world and should not be addressed by the likes of you, or even your masters, who themselves are barely worthy of such an honor. Tell them to appear before me in three days to proclaim their obedience to my king. Should they fail to be here in the specified time, I will destroy them.'"

The next day, a contingent of leaders from Cholula arrived.

"Sir, we have not been to see you because well, well, honestly, we are afraid of our enemies, the Tlaxcalans. But now that we know you come in peace and you mean us no harm, we invite you to our province, where you and your people will be warmly welcomed."

"I now understand why you have not visited me. But before I can go to your province, I need to know that you are sincere. Will you willingly proclaim yourselves vassals of my Majesty?"

They took the oath and departed.

A critical part in the conquest of the Mexican empire was about to start at Cholula.

Chapter Sixteen

THE MEXICA:
MOCTEZOMA

Seventeen years ago, my spies brought me accounts of bearded, white- and black-skinned men sailing the southeastern seas who had stopped at a group of small islands not far from our coast. I ordered warriors to a large populated island, called Coba, located about eight days in an easterly direction from Ah-Cuzamil-Peten, to learn if those people knew anything about these strangers, but my envoys had to return to land because of a fierce storm that almost destroyed their ships.

I heard nothing else about those men until about twelve years ago, when my sources reported another sighting of them, in the same area as before, but closer to the shoreline; then, four years later, my spies brought me, from one of my trading posts, a large wooden chest they found on the beach containing worthless jewelry, odd clothing, and a sword made from an unknown type of metal.

The day after I received the items, I took the weapon to the military headquarters, where I tested it by fighting an Eagle Warrior; he used a sword made of copper and I, the foreigners' one, and, just as the blades clashed, theirs sliced ours into two bent pieces. There was silence on the grounds.

I ordered the soldier to use an obsidian sword, and, as soon as the foreigners' sword hit his, the obsidian shattered into bits, but the new metal had not changed. I commanded him to use a heavier copper sword, and that one twisted from the new metal's impact. Finally, I struck a large rock with the foreign blade, and the blade dented at the edge but did not crook.

I stored the unbreakable sword in a locked chamber close by at the War College in the Imperial Complex and sometimes took it out to practice against Eagle Warriors. My weapon makers agreed that wherever the metal was from, it was a land well beyond any with which we had had contact.

Perhaps a month after my agents gave me the box with the blade and other objects, a messenger who had just returned to Tenochtitlan delivered a folded manuscript from a professional merchant who was trading by the eastern sea that depicted ships, larger than any of ours, on the water, but they appeared to have houses on them. I called a meeting with my senior advisors and showed them the picture and asked what we should do.

"Supreme Lord, I don't see there's any cause for worry. Whoever these men are who have arrived on our shores, they found a way to build houses on their ships. They must be men from the islands in the eastern seas," one of the advisors said.

The rest of the counselors concurred, but I disagreed; even before I knew anything about them, I was uneasy, and even afraid, I must admit, about these strangers. My advisors' sanguine responses irked me, and I turned to my senior priests, who also vexed me because they were equally indifferent, and I ordered them to return to the Main Temple to engage in penance.

Six years ago, there was another landing, this one apparently intentional and closer to my trading posts on the northeastern coast, but those foreigners did not stay long, and I learned little about them.

There were few accounts after that about any bearded men, but what I did hear was significant: about four years ago, a group of them constructed a settlement on the mainland, well to the south of my empire and the lowlands.

About two years ago, however, I was astonished to learn from my spies that another group of more than one hundred foreigners had arrived near the coast of the Maya of the Ekab Kingdom, where I have local paid informants. The ruler, when he heard these people were in his territory, sent advisors in ships to welcome them.

The strangers invited some of the Maya on board one of their ships, where they gave them beads, clothes, fabric, and food. The following day, the Maya returned and asked them to land, and they did, but the Maya ruler had ordered his warriors to arrange a ruse in the forest, where a unit of Maya warriors attacked them. The Maya gravely wounded about twenty of them.

The momentousness of that event, however, has little to do with what the Ekab did to those men, since I know them to be fearless, but rather with what I learned about the foreigners, who killed about fifteen Maya. All the bearded men not only had superior metal blades like the one I received eight years ago, but they also had weapons that released fire and could kill the target on impact. Every informant described the sound the fire-shooting weapons made as deafening thunder and the smell the burning projectile created like rotten turkey eggs.

The foreigners reembarked after the battle and sailed, but they did not return from where they had come, instead continuing until they reached another Maya village. The ruler there, however, did not make war against them and even invited them to stay as guests and fed them well, but when they did not leave after a reasonable time, he ordered them to go.

The strangers resumed traveling and stopped at a town where the Maya invited them to land. They took them inside a temple where they were preparing a sacrificial rite. The priests, making signs with their hands, indicated the strangers should leave before the beginning of the ceremonies. The bearded men prudently departed.

The foreigners, however, continued sailing until they arrived at another Maya town, where they went inland and took control of a well to fill barrels, after which they went back to their ships and slept close to shore.

The ruler of that town, I understand, having heard what the strangers had done in other places and about the weapons they had, planned an assault and, to intimidate them, ordered his warriors to beat their drums at night.

At dawn, the foreigners awoke, and before they had realized that they were surrounded by Maya warriors on all sides, the Maya attacked, using arrows, obsidian swords, spears, slingshots, and stone- and copper-headed axes, murdering about twenty-five invaders and wounding the rest, including their leader, forcing them to flee and return to sea.

For more than a year after that, my intelligence web was silent about these bearded men, but I knew they were not gone from our lands for good because they had shown they were hungry for gold and had vastly superior weapons they were willing to use to get it, so I continued to send spies, diplomats, and professional merchants along the eastern coast, far north and south, to seek any knowledge about them.

About a year and a half ago, yet another force of bearded men landed at Ah-Cuzamil-Peten, but these men were different: They had a fierce determination to impose their will and their customs. In an unprecedented action no stranger has ever performed on anyone else's land before winning a war, to my knowledge, these men raised the flag of their home in a Maya temple and ordered one of their priests to hold their own religious ceremony there. My informants, not understanding the foreigners' language and religion, could not explain their rites in any detail.

The foreigners next went to Champotón, where at first officials greeted them politely and permitted them to enter their town. The foreigners asked for gold; their hosts replied by telling them to go, but they did not comply and instead stayed the night and requested food and water, which the Maya supplied.

The strangers again demanded gold, and a functionary gave them a mask of gilded wood and two gold plates but repeated they should leave. They refused, and when the ruler threatened them, the invaders charged. They introduced yet another fantastic weapon, described to me as a large metal cabinet that shot a missile of fire that frightened and confused the Maya, three of whom the strangers murdered. The Maya, however, were not without success, as they wounded about forty of their enemies and killed one.

The foreigners continued their voyage along the coast; the next important report I obtained was that the Totonacs, one of my most productive tributaries, enthusiastically welcomed them ashore. The bearded men stayed there for ten days and enjoyed themselves, and not even their constant requests for gold irritated the Totonacs, who gave them a few bars and small golden items before they left.

The Totonacs, according to reports I received, already knew about the strangers' powerful weapons and their contacts with the Maya before they welcomed them. I have concluded that the Totonacs approached them with the sole purpose of pointing them in the direction of Tenochtitlan.

The foreign men sailed northerly afterward, but Huaxtecs attacked them on the water, causing the bearded men to use their large weapon that looks like a cabinet to shoot fire at the Huaxtecs, killing four of them and sinking one of their boats. The battle coincided with the beginning of the rainy season, which made sailing difficult, and the foreigners returned to sea and departed.

Chapter Seventeen

THE XOCHIMILCA: FLOWER

I had resigned myself to my fate until one night, once the senior priestess was snoring, when Teputzitoloc whispered information after ordering me not to interrupt him.

"I am Tepanec, and my father, a merchant, met my maternal grandfather, who was from Tlatelolco, at a market, and they arranged for my parents to marry. This is relevant to us because the Tepanecs and the Tlatelolca have joined forces with other principalities to overthrow Moctezoma. Many nations despise the Mexica because they kidnap our people and sacrifice them. But they are the most powerful and wealthy rulers, and no one has been able to destroy them. Recently, though, there has been an opening.

"Foreigners from across the sea in the eastern coast from an island called Coba have invaded our lands and are murdering many people as they march to Tenochtitlan. But Moctezoma refuses to fight them, while other rulers think he should go to war with them to expel them.

"Now, the leader of the opposition to Moctezoma in Tlatelolco is named Cuauhtémoc, Moctezoma's cousin, who is searching for more warriors, the best ones. My family on my mother's side, because they are wealthy, powerful, and connected to Cuauhtémoc's people, have been able to send me messages that they and the resistance in Tlatelolco are trying to help me and others in the compound flee to become soldiers in Cuauhtémoc's armies.

"And, here's why this is important to you. One of Moctezoma's officials, who transfers deity impersonators to and from the compounds, told someone in the men's section that your father has been working for your release with a group that has ties to Cuauhtémoc's people by bribing agents with valuable goods."

I did not understand what he had just said. I held my breath for a few moments. My heart beat fast.

"Did you just say Papa has been trying to rescue me?"

"Yes, he has!"

I did my best not to scream. Then I smiled when I found out my family had not abandoned me. Although I realized it was not at all likely I would escape my destiny, I was reassured that I had kept them out of danger by not revealing to Priestess Citlalmina that I had learned the truth.

The days continued their normal pattern, and I experienced joy when I was with Teputzitoloc, but, alone in my room, I slept or stared out the window. At the range one time, after the old woman had fallen asleep, I dropped the bow and arrow and quiver and wept. Teputzitoloc told me to follow him to the wall and said I had to stop crying.

"But how? How do I stop? I love you, and it hurts so much that we're never going to be together after they take me from here."

"I want to cry, too. But I don't want it all to end now, and I wish you wanted to fight to live as much as I want you to."

I took deep breaths and made myself think about the present, that just being with him made me happy, despite everything, and I forced myself to smile. We returned to the firing line, where I lost myself in hitting the center of the target.

The day arrived. Priestess Citlalmina said Moctezoma had called me to Tenochtitlan to impersonate a deity at the Main Temple. I barely listened to her. I had never kissed Teputzitoloc or touched his skin. A knot formed in my throat; now I wanted time to pass fast, so I could die.

"Dear, aren't you excited about your big day and that you'll be going to the ruler's palace?"

I stared into her eyes and reached for a ceramic pitcher to smash her face. She blinked. I pulled back my hand.

"Well, well, that's all right, dear. I understand you're apprehensive, but . . . but, well, it will turn out well, you'll see. I'll . . . I'll leave you alone."

She scurried out of the room. I did everything they ordered, and every morning I bathed and ate breakfast, went to dance class, and, in the late afternoon, before dinner, they took me to the steam room. They washed my hair with soap made from the avocado seed and rinsed it with a mixture of water and lime juice, and they rubbed my shoulders and neck with floral scented oil, and, afterward, back at the house, I drank *iztac octli* with my evening meal.

Once, in the hut next to the steam room, they made me eat sacred mushrooms, most of which I vomited, but the small amounts my stomach did not reject made me see pictures of corpses cut up in pieces, and I screamed and tried to run outside. The priestesses caught me and held me down until I was calm.

All the time, I thought about my family and Teputzitoloc and concentrated on what everyone looked like, but my parents' and sisters' faces were blurry.

One afternoon, Priestess Citlalmina led me to a room in one of the buildings around the inner courtyard where seamstresses were waiting so I could try on costumes to wear at the palace and the Main Temple.

When we had completed that task, Priestess Citlalmina said she was going to take me to the range, where the woman Eagle Warrior named Atl, who had taught me before Teputzitoloc, was going to show me how to carry a bow and arrow like the one I would have at the actual ceremony.

I must have shown my disappointment that I was not going to see Teputzitoloc, because she spoke to me curtly and ordered me to move fast. I almost dropped to the ground when I realized I was never again going to see him. Priestess Citlalmina left me. Atl greeted me and began her lesson with no preliminary discussion, and she showed me an arrow, painted in gold and with a gold tip, and a bow, also painted in gold.

"Now, you're not going to actually shoot the arrow at any time during the ceremonies, but we want you to get used to it now, since it and the bow are much heavier than the ones you've been practicing with. So, go ahead. I've heard you're excellent at shooting now."

I loaded and shot, but the arrow landed on an outside ring. She told me to go with her to the target. There, she spoke quickly, as she pointed at the innermost ring.

"I have something very important to tell you. Just listen, and don't ask any questions. I will make everything clear to you. Teputzitoloc has a plan so I can help him, three other warriors from the men's compound, and you to escape, but it has to happen soon, before

Moctezoma's officials take you to the palace. I can't tell you everything at once, so make sure you miss the target and sometimes aim for the ground during training, so we can return to the wall to speak."

We went back to the wall every time I shot off the target, until I had heard what I had to do. Now I was exhilarated. I learned that this was a propitious time to flee because Moctezoma was consumed with the interlopers and not focused on other matters.

Atl was a high-ranking Eagle Warrior and instructor at Moctezoma's military headquarters in Tenochtitlan and also a spy. She had access to information about the impending arrival of the foreigners in Tenochtitlan that Moctezoma, contrary to advice from his brother Cuitláhuac and his nephew Cacama, ruler of Tezcoco, not only had decided not to go to war against the invaders but was going to surrender his empire to them.

Atl and many other warriors in Moctezoma's armies agreed with a number of factions that wanted to fight the foreigners, including Cuauhtémoc's, and had joined forces with them. The Tlatelolca had approached and enlisted her to help Teputzitoloc and three other Eagle Warriors in his compound to escape and become soldiers in Cuauhtémoc's military.

"The Tlatelolca paid large sums to bribe officials and others, inside and outside the compound, to help the warriors escape and look the other way, and your father also contributed money so that you can try to escape with them. Your father, in fact," Atl said, "has been working with the Tlatelolca since before Moctezoma's people took you by spending time with women who posed as prostitutes but were spies for the Tlatelolca resistance, because he wanted their help to prevent your abduction."

"I know I'm not supposed to ask you questions, but I have to try. Is it possible for my friend—her name is Yaretzi—to escape, too?"

"No, I'm sorry. It's risky enough getting you and the men out. Now, you have to learn to follow orders, so no more questions!"

It made me sad that Yaretzi had to stay.

During one of the conversations at the target, Atl handed me a long, thin flint knife with a handle in a sheath that I put in my pocket, and, when training was over, I returned with Priestess Citlalmina to the house. I went to my room before my bath for clean clothes and hid the weapon in the fold of a manuscript.

I obeyed all orders that evening and the next, but the following night, at dinner, I refused *iztac octli*, saying my stomach was unsettled. Before going to bed, I opened the shutters and stayed awake. I thought about my family and Yaretzi, who had become like a sister to me. I saw her at practice ceremonies, and the priestesses allowed us to greet each other. I was unhappy to be leaving her behind.

When it was late and crickets made high-pitched rapid sounds, I went to the window. As Atl had instructed, I watched until slaves put out most torches on the grounds, and I changed into a long-sleeved, quilted, black daytime tunic and a short black skirt with an undergarment and put on deerskin shoes.

I took the knife and removed it from its case. The priestess guarding me in the hallway snored, and I parted the fabric covering the door. Light from a fire burning on a stand showed her sitting on a bench, head tilted, drooling saliva, her long hair greasy, her face a map of gnarled creases.

I walked to her and sealed her toothless mouth with a hand and thought about what the other old woman did to me that first day—*she forces her blood-caked finger in me and orders the others to beat me with that stick*—and she opened her eyes.

Her rupturing ribs made snapping sounds when I plunged the blade deep into her emaciated chest, as far as it would go, to the handle. She jerked, causing more bones to break, but her breathing ceased, and I held her as she fell to the side.

I left the dagger inside her and gently laid her on the floor. I wiped her saliva off my hand on my clothes and walked through the hall to the main exit. When I stepped out into bracing air, the woman warrior who was posted there and whom the resistance had paid to help me flee, waved to signal it was safe to keep going. I saw no one else and went to a cluster of greenery to the right of the building.

I searched for and found under the shrubbery my regular bow and a quiver full of eagle-talon arrows. I took the items and went in the opposite direction from the inner courtyard where I practiced archery.

Dragging the bow and quiver, I crawled, even though a blade of grass cut the skin on my leg and drew blood and breaking twigs crackled, to reach an area by the smaller entrance to the compound located on the western side.

I stayed flat on my belly to observe four watchmen inside the gate, not the two I had expected to be there, and waited as I looked at the top of the right section of the wall behind them. The full moon turned the skin on my hands metallic gray. A bird glided above me and screeched, and the guards looked up.

My heart was thumping, and my mouth was dry, and I fought not to cough. I trembled, because I was not certain I could shoot all the sentries quickly, as Atl had instructed me, and worried the signs would not come, so silently I repeated, about fifty times: *Only four things matter: me, my bow, my arrow, and a point on the target.*

I was cold and cupped my hands to breathe warmth into them. Then I heard whistling and other noises outside the compound and saw a piece of white cloth on top of the wall to the right of the gate.

The guards turned to investigate; and I stood and put on my quiver, nocked an arrow, and I ran. They had their backs to me, and I stopped, went into my stance, and began shooting. They yelled as they dropped. I reached them. They were on their sides, twitching, and I aimed, this time at their throats.

When I was sure they were dead, I opened the gate and smiled when I saw Teputzitoloc, Atl, and three male warriors, all dressed in black uniforms. Eight guards lay motionless outside on the ground. We went into the dark woods. The others moved ahead of Teputzitoloc and me.

"Keep walking fast. Flower, I'm so happy the plan worked, at least so far. I'm so relieved that Moctezoma—"

"Shhh, let's not speak about that now. I'm so happy to see you, and I wish we had time to be alone together. I love you so much!"

"I love you, too! But Flower, from this point on, everything is going to happen quickly, and we have to keep our wits. We can't for a moment become distracted, or we'll become careless and captured again.

"Flower, we won't be able to see each other again until the war is over because you're going to be in the women's army, and Cuauhtémoc wants me to serve directly with him. And as an Eagle Warrior, I will not have any contact with you other than through messages, if that. But Flower, think about where you want to go after the war is over, and I will meet you there. Atl told me your father went to your ancestral village. It's Ixhuatepec, correct?"

I confirmed the information. We walked mostly in silence. I wanted to hold his hand but had to be content with being next to him.

"There is something I need to ask you. Is there any way to try to rescue a friend I made in the compound?"

"No, Flower, I'm sorry. If I could, I would release everyone in both compounds. But we're in danger. Moctezoma is going to do everything he can to catch us. But Cuauhtémoc has promised to end human sacrifice and close the compounds when we win."

We slowly navigated around dense trees and pushed aside bushes, as there was no path, taking brief rests, until the sun rose. Teputzitoloc told the others to go ahead.

He put his arms around me and pulled me so close I felt his heart beating.

"Flower, I love you so much, and I wish we could escape somewhere to be together."

"I love you, too, and as much as I want to fight the foreigners *and* beat Moctezoma, I'd rather run away and spend the rest of my life with you somewhere far from here!"

"I would, too, but we're going to fight for all our people, not just for ourselves. Oh, but let's forget about everyone else for now."

He caressed my arms and hair as I held on to him, and I rested the side of my face on his chest. Then we kissed. I was in rapture. He put his hands on my lower back. I wanted him inside me. He gently pushed us apart.

"We have to go and . . ." He kissed me again, and we held each other.

"Flower: Always remember today and what we have to look forward to after the war. Let's go."

He held my hand as we ran to join the others. We reached a deserted path by the water. We were about to board one of six empty boats tied to poles, when someone shouted to halt.

We saw four warriors at a distance and obeyed. They walked toward us and, when they were near, Teputzitoloc and Atl shot and killed them.

We embarked, and Atl, two other warriors, and I picked up poles, stuck them in the soil, and pushed; Teputzitoloc and the other warrior used oars to make us go faster. We moved in a northerly direction as Teputzitoloc ordered us to watch for warriors who might cause us trouble.

We sailed, at a good speed, until we were near Tlatelolco. Teputzitoloc instructed us to slow so we would not miss a farmer who was meeting us. Not long after, we saw a number of boats loaded with goods and searched for a large blue one with pictures of mountains painted on the sides.

Atl identified the man and waved at him; as it had been arranged, he motioned us to approach, and, when we were next to him, he threw Teputzitoloc a filled sack. We continued until we had to kill ten sentries on shore who told us to stop; then we landed and ran into the woods.

There, we changed into clothes the man from the blue boat had given us, similar to his, removed our shoes, took our hair out of warrior's knots, and returned to the water, where he was waiting for us. We boarded and helped him steer north to a canal leading to the market at Tlatelolco, and when we arrived and had secured the boats, we each took two sacks, one containing our bows and quivers wrapped in thick cloths and the other filled with vegetables. I was now a fugitive but prepared to begin the next stage of my life as a warrior.

Book Two

A COMET IN THE SKY

Chapter Eighteen

THE XOCHIMILCA: FLOWER

The market was still beautiful and lively and crowded. I searched for the street where our stand had been located, even though I knew Papa was not there. Atl had told me that after he had given the Tlatelolca resistance bribes to help me escape, my parents, sisters and their husbands, and the little ones had fled to the mountains, along with many others, because the foreigners were slaughtering massive numbers of people on their march to Tenochtitlan from the eastern sea.

No one paid any attention to us as we reached the booth of the farmer who had helped us and put down his sacks containing the goods that he was going to sell at the market. Three members of the Tlatelolco resistance, also dressed as laborers, led us away from the market. Teputzitoloc and I said our farewells as we walked.

"I'm so very sad that we can't be together. I don't know if only married people are allowed to say this, but I love you, and . . . and I wish we could sleep together," I said. He smiled.

"I think you know I feel the same way. Flower, I love you, too. And I'm also unhappy we can't be together, but I'm confident that we will win this war and be together afterward."

We continued to repeat how we felt about each other, and I enjoyed hearing him say he loved me. We reached an area that had two-story houses. Tears came to my eyes. Teputzitoloc and I looked at each other before a woman led Atl and me to one of the homes. We stayed there that night with other women warriors.

At the house, a woman introduced herself as a general in Cuauhtémoc's armies and said we were going to be trained to fight against foreigners who had invaded our lands. In the morning, after our meal, dressed as farmers, we left in small groups at staggered intervals and walked to the waterside, where we boarded boats and sailed to a secluded area on the mainland at the base of a mountain.

We climbed to reach a military camp of a thousand women warriors, where everyone but me, I found out, had been a soldier or spy in Moctezoma's military. I would remain there until Cuauhtémoc ordered me to Tenochtitlan.

At the base, General Ameyalli, a female Eagle Warrior, assigned me to a battalion of one hundred led by Captain Cipactli. Training was radically more arduous than what I had experienced at the compound with Teputzitoloc, where my main task had been to learn how to shoot with a bow and arrow or a slingshot.

I was blissful, of course, to be away from that prison, but I did not know anyone at the base, and I so missed Yaretzi. I hoped she was well and that Moctezoma had not chosen her to be sacrificed.

At the camp, I learned advanced archery and how to shoot stones with a slingshot, using targets significantly farther away than those at the compound, and training included using other weapons—axes and spears tipped with sharp flint heads. I practiced how to protect myself with shields as other soldiers shot at me, and I spent hours each day making fifty arrows with tips of stone, wood, obsidian, flint, and bone.

Captain Cipactli, a stocky woman, often forced us to practice two days at a time, with no sleep, and she kicked us hard when we closed our eyes or fell on the ground. It was cold at night in the mountains, sometimes freezing, but Captain Cipactli did not permit us to build fires to warm ourselves if we were in the woods.

General Ameyalli spoke to us about the foreigners and said they had large animals that looked like deer, and the soldiers *rode* them and directed them, and it was possible to kill the animals and the men atop them with eagle-talon, flint, obsidian, and bone arrows from a distance.

At a small lake by the camp, on a military ship that seated sixty warriors and had room for weapons and supplies, we practiced how to shoot while standing. We learned to balance ourselves and not fall by crouching slightly so we could maintain a proper stance on water. That way, we could shoot by day or night, no matter the weather. We also learned to hide in reeds to ambush and kill enemy crews.

Every few days, General Ameyalli made the same speech.

"You are here to learn to fight not only the foreigners and their Tlaxcalan and other dog allies, who are killing, enslaving, and raping our people, but also Moctezoma, who has surrendered to the invaders. You will learn to fight to take back our lands!"

One day, though, she gave us new information.

"Now, listen carefully. The Mexican nobles of Tenochtitlan, who oppose Moctezoma's policy of appeasement, have joined Cuitláhuac, Moctezoma's brother and Cuauhtémoc's cousin, to fight. And Moctezoma is not as well guarded as before, so Cuitláhuac and Cuauhtémoc have assigned spies to watch him for when he is vulnerable to attack."

Late one night, General Ameyalli and Captain Cipactli went to my quarters and ordered me to follow them. They were silent as we walked along a path. I trembled from fear and cold. They led me to a hut where only the three of us were present. General Ameyalli addressed me.

"Repeat after me: I swear, under the penalty of death, that I will not reveal to anyone what I am about to hear."

I obeyed.

"Teputzitoloc sent me a message that he has recommended you to participate in an action with agents Cuauhtémoc has embedded in Moctezoma's military to execute Moctezoma," General Ameyalli said.

I was shocked.

"This is the plan: Cuauhtémoc's spies told him the invaders have ordered Moctezoma to make a speech tomorrow to a gathering of Mexican leaders, from a terrace of the palace where the foreigners have imprisoned him, because the Mexican noblemen have been attacking the invaders. And this is the most important part: Cuitláhuac, Cuauhtémoc, and the nobility want to rattle the invaders by killing Moctezoma."

I was surprised that Cuitláhuac and Cuauhtémoc believed they could murder the most powerful man in the world.

"Now, one of Cuauhtémoc's generals ordered us to prepare you for tomorrow, when you will be on that balcony, and you will participate in the murder of Moctezoma."

I shook.

"Captain Cipactli will take you to Tlatelolco while it is still dark. There, you and she will sleep in a women's barracks and, when it is light, you will dress in the uniform of a warrior in Moctezoma's army."

We sailed, and, at the barracks in Tlatelolco, they assigned me a pallet, in the officers' section, next to Captain Cipactli. She went to sleep, but I stayed awake for some time because I was worried about my mission and whether I would do well. I was glad that I was not going to be the only one to shoot at Moctezoma. Eventually, I went to sleep.

Captain Cipactli woke me.

"Flower, here's some tea. Quick—drink it, and eat these nuts. That's all you have time for before you wash yourself and put on this uniform."

When we were ready, a litter took us to the main gate at Tenochtitlan, and then we walked to a large two-story house on a street across from the palace where the foreigners had imprisoned Moctezoma. Captain Cipactli stayed downstairs, and I joined nine of Cuauhtémoc's men purportedly to protect noblemen standing in rows behind us on the second-floor balcony. I was in the front row.

What no one had told me was that Cuauhtémoc was going to be present on that balcony, also in the first row. Cuauhtémoc and his bodyguards arrived after us. He was not in warrior's uniform; he was handsome, wearing a tall feathered and jeweled headdress and a cloak ornately embroidered with fur and gold thread. He was surrounded by Eagle Warriors behind him, one to my right, and Teputzitoloc on his other side.

As previously instructed, I reviewed the buildings and people in front and to the left and right of us for anyone who might attack those on our balcony. Teputzitoloc stared straight ahead, so we did not have an opportunity to exchange glances.

The plan was that I would distract Moctezoma by doing something to make him notice me, and then Eagle Warriors on my balcony would shoot him, and, if I had the opportunity, I also could aim at him. General Ameyalli and Captain Cipactli had warned me, however, that Moctezoma's warriors on the terrace would try to kill me if I did so.

It was quiet, even though we were outdoors, as we waited for Moctezoma to appear. I marveled at the view of the beautiful palaces on the broad thoroughfare.

Moctezoma, surrounded by warriors and attendants, came out of a door to an abutment on the tower of the palace and walked until he was facing Cuauhtémoc. I thought about what he had done to me and how, if I had not escaped, he would have raped me and then murdered and dismembered me.

General Ameyalli had directed me to initiate the plan of drawing Moctezoma's attention as soon as a nobleman on my balcony began speaking.

"Moctezoma is a vile and cowardly man for bowing to the dog invaders and their allies," Cuauhtémoc said.

My heart was beating fast. I did not hear everything Cuauhtémoc said. I wiped my sweating palms on my uniform; then, slowly and in an exaggerated manner, I adjusted the bow on my shoulder and retrieved an eagle-talon-tipped arrow from the quiver. Moctezoma stared at me.

"Moctezoma no longer has authority as the ruler, so our people do not have to obey him or even listen to the lies he tells us on behalf of his puppet masters," Cuauhtémoc was saying.

Eagle Warriors and I shot at Moctezoma, but his men covered him with shields. I put down my quiver and bow, retrieved a slingshot and stones from my pocket, and pelted him through gaps between the shields. Several landed on his chest, forehead, and temple.

He fell, and his men lifted and moved him indoors. The soldiers on my row, except for Teputzitoloc and the other bodyguard, who escorted Cuauhtémoc off the balcony, continued to shoot at him.

No one from the palace retaliated after we had shot Moctezoma, and, when he was gone from the terrace, Cuauhtémoc's men led me to the entrance to the stairs and down and outside the building to a nearby safe house. They left me with a family who made war uniforms. Hours later, General Ameyalli sent four women warriors for me and all of us, disguised as laborers, went to one of Cuauhtémoc's bases in Tlatelolco.

Chapter Nineteen

THE MEXICA: MOCTEZOMA

Although the invasion by these foreign men is a constant worry that forces me to commune with Huitzilopochtli in sacred-mushroom rituals at least once a day, I cannot control whether to think about Flower, because she mesmerized me the day I met her. I still do not know what I will do after I bring her here and finally know her intimately. Some days I believe I will have the fortitude to go forward with the sacrificial offering, but other times I want to take her to my hunting lodge and never return to the capital.

It is my duty, however, to protect my people from all harm, including the current one, so I am confident that, if I pray and engage in penance, Huitzilopochtli will grant me the power to master my emotions and offer him Flower.

When the bearded man, whom I shall call the leader, arrived at Potonchán, the most significant intelligence was that he had among his men a white man who spoke not only their language but also Mayan, and was one of two men the Maya had enslaved eight years ago.

At Potonchán, the Maya attacked the invaders with arrows, spears, and stones fired from slingshots, but the leader countered by ordering his men to go ashore with their fantastic weapons, and, once on land, the foreigners killed or captured more than four hundred Maya, although the Maya wounded twenty white men.

Two days later, a battle took place when more than two hundred bearded men located fields of maize guarded by armed Maya; this time, the foreigners had to retreat but returned the next day.

It seems the Maya could have won the second battle because it was difficult for the bearded men to fight on farmland containing numerous irrigation ditches. The reason the Maya lost was because of a monumental fact: the foreigners removed from their ships, for the first time, a most sensational animal—one that does not exist on our lands.

My sources have difficulty describing it to me, but they all agree it looks like a large deer. It is incomprehensible to me that they mount this animal, which is exceptionally swift, my spies said, and control it with ease as it goes wherever the rider directs.

The Maya, according to my agents, were frightened by the beasts and the loud noise they made. It was the combination of weapons that shot fire, metal swords, and animals that look like monstrous deer that defeated the Maya.

The invaders that day killed more than five hundred Maya, but not one of the bearded men died, although the Maya wounded about fifty of them. As part of their surrender, the Maya gave the foreigners small amounts of gold and turquoise, all they had, and twenty women and girls, whom the leader divided among certain of his men.

He then asked the Maya the location of sources for gold, but the Maya explained they had none, and, in yet another key development, they said I controlled all sites for gold and silver. The leader and his men spent about three weeks at Potonchán, holding religious ceremonies and destroying the Maya gods' statues and installing those of their own god and the goddess who is his mother.

There was another significant event at Potonchán, in addition to the bearded men's possession and use in battle of animals that look like immense deer. The Maya ruler gave the leader a woman whose noble father had sold her to these Maya and who was fluent in both Mayan and our language, and he and his interpreter began teaching her their tongue.

The foreigners sailed along the coast until they arrived close to shore at a Totonac town. The next morning, two hundred or more foreigners landed ashore with weapons, their large war animals, and fighting dogs, and the Totonacs greeted them with food and copper and silver plates.

The following day, my representative, Teudile, accompanied by six hundred slaves, visited the leader and gave him twenty large valuable jewels and thirty cloaks. Teudile's hidden objective for being there was to plant a number of my spies in the foreigners' camp by saying the slaves were there to build the leader and his men huts.

My senior advisors and I agreed to send the leader more items to let him know he need not go to Tenochtitlan to receive substantial quantities of valuable objects, so I delivered four large chests containing gold jewelry and bows, arrows, breastplates, and staffs made of gold.

When my spies delivered their reports, I called a meeting of the Supreme Council of Elders. We failed to reach a consensus whether we should try to prevent the foreigners from coming to Tenochtitlan. I asked Cuitláhuac, who had been quiet during the meeting, to speak.

"My position is unequivocal: we must prevent the foreigners from entering Tenochtitlan, at all costs, or they will conquer us."

Cacama at that time took an opposing stand.

"Why are we treating these foreign men any differently than we do other official visitors? After all, their leader claims to be an ambassador of an emperor from across the eastern seas. Don't we risk potentially alienating his ruler, one who has weapons superior to our own, not to mention fearsome animals they have trained to fight at war?"

I subsequently learned yet another consequential piece of information: twenty-two Totonacs had visited and told the leader that their ruler had proclaimed independence from me and was amenable to serving the foreign emperor because they wanted to end their status as my tributary.

Teudile returned to the leader after the Totonac visit.

"The Supreme Ruler Moctezoma orders you not to go to Tenochtitlan!"

The leader approached Teudile. "You tell your master that I have a higher command than his from *my* Majesty. I will not leave these lands until I have visited Tenochtitlan!"

Teudile left, taking away my slaves. I kept spies in the area, however, mainly embedded among Totonacs. The leader sent warriors to explore the coast, and, when they had returned, all the foreigners and their servants went to a village called Quiahuiztlan, where he engaged in hostilities against me by colluding with the local lords in a ruse involving imprisonment of five of my tribute collectors.

The bearded men departed after that to Quiahuiztlan to build a post at a nearby location by the water. Cuitláhuac, Cacama, senior advisors, and I concluded I had to send someone other than Teudile, who had been ineffective, as my ambassador to speak to the leader. Two of my nephews and four senior advisors went to the foreigners' base with gifts and assured the leader that, at a future date, I would receive them.

The next important development was a battle against the foreigners that I instigated, not because I wanted to try to defeat them but as a way to learn more about them, in particular their military skills, war animals, and weapons. I sent one of my generals to my post nearby to make displays showing we were preparing to use force to suppress and reconquer the Totonacs.

Two days after my army had begun military preparations, the leader, many of his men, about sixteen riding their large war animals, and a troop of Totonacs arrived. Our fighters confronted them outside that town, which is gated and built on a steep hill, and the white men on their large animals attacked.

My warriors fled, but the foreigners followed them, although their animals were unable to climb the hill, giving my soldiers time to close the gates behind them. The strangers, all on foot, broke into the town, disarmed whatever of my men they could find, and handed them to a Totonac chief.

Before returning to his base, the leader ordered destruction of statues of gods and altars at Totonac temples and forced priests they encountered to cut their blood-caked hair, complaining it was foul. In at least one temple, the foreigners rebuilt an altar, on which they placed a painting of a goddess and two long wooden sticks affixed together at the top. Then they ordered Totonac priests to maintain the newly installed altar to their god and his mother.

About three months later, the bearded men began their march to Tenochtitlan. The leader left his newly constructed post and took three hundred of his men, their large animals, eighty fighting dogs, about a thousand Totonacs to carry equipment, food, and ammunition, and roughly 160 brown- and black-skinned men whom they had brought from their lands as slaves.

The foreigners and their allies spent several days in Zautla, and the leader met several times with Olintecle, the ruler there, who tried to discourage him from proceeding through Tlaxcala. From Zautla, the leader went to Tlaxcala.

They traveled for some time until they came upon about fifteen Otomi mercenary advance guards the Tlaxcalan leaders had retained to attack the foreigners, but who instead fled.

The leader and his men pursued the Otomi, and the Otomi responded by using swords to kill two foreigners and wound several of the large animals.

The Tlaxcalan army arrived, ready for battle, with substantially more warriors than the foreigners, but the invaders killed about thirty Tlaxcalans. The foreigners retreated and continued on their course, but the Tlaxcalans again assailed them, this time with more Otomi mercenaries, and they fought until the strangers forced back the Otomi.

The following morning, the invaders' campaign against the Tlaxcalans and Otomi was different. Now the leader did not attack only warriors, but he and his army also murdered inhabitants in multiple villages or cut off their noses, ears, limbs, feet, and the testicles of the men.

The next day, Tlaxcalan messengers arrived at the foreigners' camp with substantial amounts of food, including turkeys and flat maize cakes, but afterward, that very afternoon, the entire Tlaxcalan army and Otomi warriors assembled to face the leader, who escalated his massacres and burned ten towns, resulting in Tlaxcala's decisive defeat.

I then sent representatives to the leader's camp on a hilltop near the Tlaxcalan border, with gifts, including gold, to inform him of my decision to become his emperor's subject, and to ask about the required amount of tribute and taxes, a sum I agreed to pay on an annual basis.

I offered gold, silver, cotton, and precious stones, and my emissaries reiterated that he and his men did not have to go to Tenochtitlan for our arrangement to be carried out, as I would deliver the goods to him at a designated place and time.

The leader, however, refused to enter into that bounteous agreement, and his peremptory reply was that he would continue the journey to Tenochtitlan, after stopping at Tlaxcala. He continued his war against that state by attacking more people on the outskirts, until Tlaxcala fully capitulated and its rulers sent food and slaves to the foreigners' camp.

To counter the Tlaxcalan gifts, I sent more presents of my own, along with word to the leader that he should not trust Tlaxcala. The foreigners did not leave their camp for days in order to recuperate from wounds sustained in battle. The Tlaxcalan rulers again went to him and gave him jewels and persuaded him to agree to visit them.

When the leader and other injured members of his expedition were better, they and the Totonacs departed to Tlaxcala, where the Tlaxcalan lords welcomed the bearded men and let them rest and heal for twenty days.

The time they spent with my enemies was yet another important event, as it was then the foreigners and Tlaxcalans formalized their alliance against me and joined forces to advance toward Tenochtitlan. To seal their contract, the Tlaxcalans gave the leader about three hundred girls and two noblewomen, and the leader reciprocated by ordering gifts, including significant quantities of salt, for his new confederates.

Chapter Twenty

THE SPANIARDS: CORTÉS

We left Tlaxcala, and Cholulan chieftains met us in the outskirts, accompanied by musicians and chanting priests, to escort us to their city, where they put the Castilians in comfortable lodging, and the captains and me in a large house with an inner courtyard.

Several hours later, Montezuma's agent arrived.

"The Supreme Ruler wants to know how much you want to be paid as annual tribute to your Majesty and whether in items such as gold, silver, precious stones, cotton, or slaves. The only condition is that you do not go to Tenochtitlan. As a token of future payments, he sent you a substantial quantity of gold and cotton."

"You thank Montezuma for his gifts, but tell him I am going to visit him!"

We spent our first two days scouting the city and the countryside, but, on the third, because Aguilar and Marina said chieftains were evacuating people from the city, I directed two captains to seize an Indian from the street who appeared to be a nobleman and bring him inside to me.

"What are your leaders planning?"

"I don't know anything."

I interrogated him various times by submerging his head in a tub of water to the point he almost drowned, until he confessed.

"The lords have ordered the women and children to be sent to the forests for their safety."

I pushed his head in the water once more and took it out, and then I slammed his face on the floor. I pressed the sole of my boot on his neck. He coughed.

"I swear! I swear! I told you everything I know—I swear!" I released him and allowed him to flee.

It was time to implement my plan, but first I sent two captains with the interpreters to bring me noblemen, as many as were willing to come without force, and to say I wanted to speak with them before departing the city. They returned with twenty.

"I will release two of you, accompanied by my captains and soldiers, to leave and gather five thousand slaves and deposit them in the gated courtyard at the Main Temple. Go, now!"

When they had completed that task, the Castilians and noblemen came back, as I had ordered, to confirm my soldiers were guarding the five thousand bondsmen at the temple.

"Good. Now, you four, go bind all the chieftains at our lodging in irons and lock them in a room."

Outside, I fired a harquebus to signal the Castilians and our allies, who now were camped near us, to burn houses and other buildings in Cholula and outskirts.

They drove the inhabitants out, and we assaulted every man, woman, and child in the streets with swords, harquebuses, crossbows, knives, axes, arrows, and mastiffs, gore dripping from their snouts and pieces of flesh stuck to their canines. In about twelve hours, we had killed about twenty thousand, including the five thousand slaves trapped in the courtyard at the temple.

Blood soaked the ground, making it slippery, and we stumbled on viscera, an arm, leg, or other body parts strewn about, and the effluvia from feces and urine made me nauseated. When we had murdered all in our path, I returned to our lodging and released two chieftains to tell the noblemen I had not imprisoned to bring back the residents who had fled and remove all debris, including the dead.

In about a week, many of the people had returned. We remained in Cholula twenty days to rest and prepare for the advance on Tenochtitlan, during which time Montezuma sent diplomats to ask whether I had a response to his prior query. I told them what to say.

"You sent me your word when I was in Tlaxcala that you were my friend and ally, but once I arrived in the vicinity of Cholula, I saw evidence you were planning to lure and kill us to prevent us from going to Tenochtitlan.

"So now I will enter your capital ready for war and prepared to use whatever force is necessary against you and your people. It is your decision whether you will submit to me in peace. The fate of your empire rests in your hands."

"Sir, our Supreme Ruler Montezuma knows nothing about these events. Please, please give us time to investigate and speak with our Supreme Ruler."

I consented, and they returned the following day with gifts—gold plates, fifteen hundred articles of cotton, a substantial amount of food and beverages—and a reply from Montezuma that he was not involved in any of the hostilities that had taken place in Cholula. He again urged me not to go to Tenochtitlan.

"Tell your master," I said, "exactly as follows: 'My Majesty requires me to go to your city and see it for myself to send him an account.' Now then, here is something else you must tell him, and should I learn you did not do so, I will find you and slit your throats. Tell your emperor he is not to leave Tenochtitlan, or he and his people will suffer great harm."

It was only after this last warning that Montezuma finally conceded and said I was welcome at the capital. He sent guides to accompany me there on a route north of the volcano Iztaccihuatl that followed the Atoyac River, but the Tlaxcalans suggested Montezuma had chosen it as a place to ambush us. To search for alternate directions, I sent a team of Castilians and Tlaxcalans to the volcanoes Popocatepetl and Iztaccihuatl, the lower peak.

They went near Iztaccihuatl but could not go farther because it was spewing hot rocks and the area was windy, with significant amounts of snow and ash. They did, however, find a road to a col they walked on and from there saw, in the distance, the towers of Tenochtitlan.

When they returned to Cholula and reported what they had observed, I spoke with Montezuma's guides and said we had found a better way to go than what they had advised, but I did not reveal it to them at the time.

We renewed the march and departed Cholula on 1 November 1519, accompanied by the Mexicans and two thousand Tlaxcalans, but unfortunately not the Totonacs, who had chosen to go home with many valuable gifts from me thanking them for their service.

We ascended to forests of mixed pine trees, full of deer, bobcats, and alpine rabbits; then, we climbed up, into the snow and barren lands, to reach the col. I ordered everyone to halt so we could savor the superb view of Tenochtitlan, surrounded by the blue waters of

Lake Texcoco, and my heart beat fast, knowing I was close to the seat of Montezuma's empire.

We crossed the pass, enduring severe cold, and about twenty Spanish soldiers and others lost fingers and toes that had frozen. Then we descended onto a forked road, the entrance to which was blocked by tree branches, which the Tlaxcalans cleared before we proceeded.

We came upon a large, well-built, vacant edifice outside a town the Mexicans maintained for military purposes, where the Castilians and Montezuma's ambassadors stayed; it was comfortable, with a fireplace in each room, and we had plenty to eat.

We departed in the morning and marched to a Mexican tributary called Chalca. That night, about ten curious Indians arrived at our camp to observe us, so we killed them. At sunrise we walked again, past woods, until we descended at lake level two leagues away in a large town, still in Chalca, where the chieftains quartered us in good houses.

We stayed there two days, during which time Mexicans visited and said Montezuma had asked them to provide whatever we required. The local ruler gave us gold, provisions, and fifty girls.

Our next stop was Chalco, the capital of Chalca, the first town we saw on the lakeshore, where Montezuma sent me gold, jade, cotton, and a message protesting our arrival. Montezuma warned I should not go to Tenochtitlan, as the roads were dangerous and there was not enough food for everyone. He added that, if we returned to our home, he would send us regular tribute payments of gold every year. I repeated we would depart after we had met him and had seen Tenochtitlan.

Chapter Twenty-one

THE MEXICA: MOCTEZOMA

When my agents reported the foreigners' massacre at Cholula, I stopped prevaricating about what I was going to do and concluded that I would pretend to submit to the leader, while formulating a strategy to expel them. I decided to order Flower brought to me so I could offer her in sacrifice to Huitzilopochtli in exchange for his protection from the invaders.

Since I had seen her the first time, images of Flower were firmly lodged in my mind, but more so now, probably because the closer the invaders were to Tenochtitlan, the sooner I had to offer her in sacrifice to Huitzilopochtli. Thoughts of lying with her did not ease my distress about having to kill her.

I was meeting with a diplomat when my chamberlain and senior military advisors interrupted us; I assumed they had additional information regarding Cholula. They bowed, and I asked the diplomat to excuse us and leave the room. The chamberlain's hands shook, and the advisors were silent, their hands clasped in front.

"Most Revered Honorable Lord," the chamberlain said, "uh, Most Revered Honorable Lord—"

"Speak!"

"Most Revered Honorable Lord, there has been an incident at the female compound for impersonators and—and—and—"

"And what?"

"The impersonator, Flower, has, she, she escaped, she escaped with others."

I did not understand him. No one had ever fled a compound for deity impersonators. Since before my time as ruler, we have had the most secure systems in place to prevent such an occurrence, including the use of guards who were Eagle Warriors. I asked an advisor to explain what the chamberlain had said.

"Most Revered Honorable Lord, we just spoke with two captains who were posted at the compounds and came here to report the situation, and they said Flower, the candidate you asked to be delivered, disappeared late last night with four male impersonators with the help of a woman Eagle Warrior named Atl. They apparently killed a priestess and guards."

I could not think clearly. I stood and paced. I sent for the captains who had come from the compound to report the news and individually questioned them. Their hands shook as they stared at the floor.

"Su-Su-Su-Supreme, Supreme Ruler and Speaker Moctezoma, the deity impersonator you ordered, she, she, she—"

"Speak now, or I will cut out your tongue!"

"Sir, uh, uh, she escaped. The girl, Flower, she escaped with the help of a female warrior and others, others at the male and female compounds."

I addressed the chamberlain and advisors.

"Why did no one from the compound come earlier?"

"Most Revered Honorable Lord, the senior priest and the general responsible for security at the compounds ordered them to the palace to tell you only in the late morning."

"Those imbeciles! Now it will be more difficult to catch them! Keep the captains at the palace, and send for four of my defense ministers from the military headquarters," I ordered the chamberlain and advisors.

"Also, send Eagle Warriors to bring the senior priest and priestess and every priestess who taught or cared for Flower from the compounds, and detain them at the cells in the Main Temple. And have the priests at the Main Temple prepare for the sacrifices of the senior priest and the priestesses to Huitzilopochtli tonight. I will preside. As for the general at the compound, bring and place him under arrest at the military headquarters until I issue further orders. Now, go!"

The defense ministers arrived.

"I want to know how your subordinates allowed impersonators to flee the compounds. You two: Go to the compounds now to conduct an investigation. Find out exactly how the impersonators escaped. The rest of you wait for the general at the military headquarters.

"When the general arrives, question him about what he has done so far to capture those who escaped. Then prepare another plan to search for them. And keep him under arrest. And if you find the deity impersonators, including the girl Flower, and Atl, take all alive. Do not harm any of them, in any way. Just seize them, and take them to the Main Temple until I issue further orders."

When I was alone, I sat and put my head in my hands. My love had left me. I would never hold her or kiss the smooth skin on her extraordinary face.

I ordered my chamberlain to have senior priests prepare for the sacred-mushroom ritual in the chapel at the palace so I could commune with Huitzilopochtli. My selfish and sentimental action in not sacrificing Flower when I had the chance had placed my empire in jeopardy. In my prayers, I begged His forgiveness for not having sacrificed Flower and for my thoughtlessness in wanting her for myself. I promised Him I would now do everything in my power to find her and give her to Him.

That night, I went to the Main Temple and offered Huitzilopochtli the senior priest and ten priestesses, including the old woman. I killed each one myself and assisted the priests with dismembering them, and we left their parts on the ground in front of Huitzilopochtli's statue.

The following day, I sent for another impersonator from the compound, but I knew she would be no substitute for my Flower. While this girl was handsome, with all the proper features in the right places, my Flower had an empyrean quality. This girl would pretend to be a goddess. But my Flower, oh, my love was divine.

I had no interest in having sexual intercourse with the impersonator or anyone else, so I told them to deliver her to a cell at the Main Temple. We sacrificed her the same afternoon she arrived.

Every day, I met with the advisor responsible for coordinating the search for Flower and reviewed what had been done and provided my thoughts on other strategies. I believed Teputzitoloc, the impersonator who was Flower's archery instructor, had hidden her somewhere in a distant location, but I could not devote substantial resources to look for her when I had to continue to rule, hear and decide legal matters, and, most importantly, deal with the invaders.

As for the foreigners, I instructed my diplomats to advise the leader the best route from Cholula to Tenochtitlan was north of Iztaccihuatl, along the Atoyac River. I heard they had gone a different way because they thought I would ambush them. But I had no intention of doing so. To the contrary, I told all my people to treat them well on their journey because I did not want to give them an excuse to attack anyone.

Chapter Twenty-two

THE SPANIARDS: CORTÉS

S tarting at dawn, we traveled four leagues and set up camp by the lake at a small town, half of which was built on water, but we did not rest because we had a skirmish with the local Indians, enemies of Tlaxcala, and killed forty.

In the morning, as we were about to depart, one of the advance scouts I had sent out rushed back to camp.

"There are rich-looking Mexicans marching toward us!"

"Follow these six captains and me," I ordered the armies.

We went out. Four Indians stood at the entrance to our base, one of whom spoke.

"We announce the approach of Cacamatzin, Supreme Ruler and Speaker of Tezcoco."

Not long after, a litter leading a caravan arrived. The head litter was decorated with green feathers, gold, silver, and precious stones set in designs of trees, borne not by slaves, but by well-dressed noblemen. Twelve lords descended from other litters to clear stones and debris off the ground in front of the first litter and then opened its covering to assist Cacamatzin, Montezuma's nephew, to exit.

Cacamatzin was spectacular. He held a scepter and wore a tall crown of precious stones, orange, red, yellow and blue feathers, and, from his ears and around his neck, arms, and wrists, jewels encrusted with precious stones. His cloak, trimmed in fur, was orange and fell to his feet, and he was shod in sandals embellished in gold. We bowed to each other.

"I come on behalf of Montezuma, Supreme Ruler and Speaker, Chief Priest, and Master Judge of the Mexican Empire," he said, "who asked me to welcome you and provide you with anything you may need. But he also pleads with you not to go to his capital, as he cannot attend to you there as you wish."

"Thank you for your welcome and greetings, but I am annoyed with these interminable requests that I not go see the Emperor Montezuma. How many times do I have to tell you? I am going to Tenochtitlan!"

Cacamatzin did not reply. I gave him gifts from Spain, including three pearls I maintained for special occasions, after which he said they would lead us to Tenochtitlan, and he boarded his litter. The caravan turned and set forth, and we followed.

We went on a road along the shoreline and passed Mixquic, an exquisite city built on water with towers and well-designed houses. Then we traveled for one league on a narrow causeway, in width about the length of a lance, that led to a Mexican principality, but I decided not to rest there.

I heeded the advice of our Mexican guides to enter a different causeway, onto a peninsula, to stay one league from Tenochtitlan in Iztapalapa, a prosperous city ruled by Cuitláhuac, Montezuma's brother, where Cuitláhuac and other lords welcomed us near the Hill of the Star, an extinct volcano.

We stayed only one day but enjoyed the lovely province, with its large two-story houses made of stone and flat cedarwood roofs, enclosed gardens, ponds, courtyards draped with cotton awnings, fruit orchards, and canals that led directly from the lake to the noblemen's homes. As presents, Cuitláhuac gave me gold and thirty girls. We departed Iztapalapa for Tenochtitlan the following morning, 8 November 1519.

We entered the Mexicaltzingo Causeway and marched west for one-half league, to the entrance to the Iztapalapa Causeway. We followed it to where it and the Coyoacán Causeway merged to form the main North-South Causeway to Tenochtitlan. We continued, and when we were about a league from the splendid city of Tenochtitlan, everyone stopped, permitting us to enjoy its magnificence.

I had to relay orders to the allies to compose themselves because they shouted war chants and whistled and cheered, causing the horses to elevate their heads, curl their upper lips, and flag their tails. The mastiffs jumped, barked, wagged their buttocks, spun, and even nipped their handlers in the leg.

Montezuma had granted permission for our allies to make camp on the outskirts of the city, so we left them there before continuing to Tenochtitlan.

At the end of the northern limit of the Iztapalapa Causeway, Cacamatzin led us onto a wide and lovely street, flanked by palaces and other buildings, to a fortress that had two towers, surrounded by a wall with merloned battlements.

A group of men of high rank met us at a gate and directed us to an area where Montezuma, who had come to welcome us, had stationed his litter, borne by noblemen and covered with a canopy decorated with gold, silver, jade, and flowers. As we approached, lords swept the ground before him, and the litter bearers knelt, as others helped the emperor to descend.

Montezuma wore a tunic made of fur and trimmed in feathers, a headband made of gold and feathers, golden earrings, a jade nose pendant, and a jade earspool. A labret of a blue hummingbird set in gold pierced his lower lip. He held a decorative cane. He had on ornately designed sandals, while all the well-attired chieftains were unshod, except for Montezuma's brother, Cuitláhuac, and his nephew, Cacamatzin, who stood on either side of him.

I separated from the group around me and moved forward to join the four horsemen in front, dismounted, and walked until I was before the emperor, but when I stepped to embrace him, Cuitláhuac and Cacamatzin put their hands on me so I would not touch him.

Montezuma gestured to his brother to stay with me and hold me by the arm; then he went ahead with Cacamatzin to join the noblemen, who bowed to them and formed two columns. Montezuma asked me to stand before him.

I instructed Aguilar and Marina, who, on her own accord, had taken off her sandals and was barefoot, and never looked at Montezuma, to interpret that I was going to remove a necklace of pearls and glass beads. I placed it around Montezuma's neck. Montezuma ignored her as she, head lowered, spoke to him; henceforth he would treat her in that manner.

He said he and I should walk together, as the lords accompanied us by his side on a broad thoroughfare, where well-attired boisterous men, women, and children pointed at us from balconies and the flat rooftops of sumptuous buildings.

After some time, we paused when a servant arrived with a box, which he opened in front of the emperor, who removed two long necklaces, each designed with eight shrimp pendants made of gold and red snail's shells, that he put around my neck.

We moved again until we arrived at a street on which was located an enormous and handsome palace off the main square that Montezuma explained had been his father Axayacatl's and had been prepared for us. The Spanish foot soldiers went to smaller houses on the nearby grounds, and the captains, knights, and interpreters stayed with me.

They led us to the palace, where Montezuma had been raised and lived until he became the emperor, at which time, as was the custom among Mexican emperors, he had his own residence built. He said he was leaving us to settle ourselves but would return after we had a meal.

After we had eaten, Montezuma's courtiers called for me and led us to a large room facing an interior courtyard and gardens, where they asked me to sit on an ornate chair. Montezuma arrived about twenty minutes later to sit on a throne that had been placed there, as servants arranged gifts on a table—gold, silver, featherwork, and embroidered cotton garments.

We asked about each other's health, and I commented that Tenochtitlan was grander than I had imagined, and we exchanged other pleasantries. He presented me with the items, and I thanked him for his gracious welcome and generosity; afterward, he bid me a good evening and left.

The palace had cavernous halls, and our bedrooms were furnished with thick mattresses, cotton bedding, and pillows stuffed with down, and each of us had a number of servants. Since we had been in Iztapalapa, I had ordered the Castilians and allies to be on alert at all times, and, that night in Tenochtitlan, I posted Spanish sentries outside my rooms, in the event Montezuma attacked us. Even though it was the first time since leaving Cuba I had a comfortable bed, I did not sleep well.

Chapter Twenty-three

THE MEXICA: MOCTEZOMA

When I first saw the invaders, I focused on their amazing war animals; although my artists' renditions of the beasts had been accurate, they were astounding to the eye. They were as tall as commoners' houses. The men astride them rubbed the creatures' flanks, I later learned, to keep them calm.

Then I looked at the men. They were not really white skinned; their skin either was pink or slightly brown. Some were black. All the foreigners had beards. A few of the pink ones had yellow hair and, I would notice when I was near them, several, like the leader, had blue eyes almost the color of the eyes of some fish, which I had never seen on a person. They all emitted a horrible body odor, and I had to refrain from covering my nose when I was close to them.

Then I focused on who I assumed was the leader, standing by my litter. He wore foreign clothing and what appeared to be armor and a helmet made of metal. He had a sword, like the one at my headquarters, and other weapons attached around his waist. A foreign man and the native woman, the interpreters, stood next to him.

Four men, armed and wearing metal armor from their heads to their feet, were on the war animals, also partially covered in metal armor. Soldiers holding drawn metal swords were behind, and others, some astride their war animals, wore quilted cotton armor similar to ours.

The leader moved forward and held out his arms as if to embrace me. I was grateful Cacama and Cuitláhuac blocked him to prevent him from touching me. I motioned to Cuitláhuac to stay with the leader and directed them to proceed to where Cacama and the noblemen were now standing. I addressed the leader.

"Welcome to my capital."

"Thank you, Emperor, for granting my request to visit you."

"We will speak freely when we are indoors, after you have rested and dined."

"I look forward to conversing with you and learning more about this lovely land. Before we go, I would like to present you with a gift."

He removed the dirty necklace he was wearing and placed it around my neck. He smelled of stale sweat. I sent an attendant to bring two necklaces with gold pendants in a box to me. I gestured, and the leader and I walked together on the street, with everyone else behind us.

He was about my height and trim like a warrior. Even though I did not understand what he was saying, the man's voice was not loud or abrasive to my ear. He did not use his hands as he spoke, and he made no sudden or exaggerated movements. It was easy to converse with him, even by the use of interpreters.

The residents, nobility of the area, were gathered on their balconies to observe, and there was a feeling of a festival. The necklaces arrived, and I placed them around the leader's neck.

We resumed our walk, and I led them to my father's palace, the one I used for visiting heads of state and diplomats, and left them in the care of my staff. I returned later, after they had dined, and I presented the leader with numerous other gifts.

The first five days, the leader and his men walked around the city, accompanied by my people and spies. On the sixth day, the leader asked for a meeting with me at my palace. His face was red and mottled. He evidently still had not bathed, and his clothing was dirty. He raised his voice.

"You conspired with your governor Qualpopoca to kill six of my men."

"That is not true! Absolutely not! Qualpopoca was simply doing his job of collecting tribute from the Totonacs, who told him you had ordered them not to pay, as they were now vassals of your emperor, so Qualpopoca gave the Totonacs notice that he would use his military to make them pay.

"And it was your representative at your base on the coast who started hostilities, and your men who initiated the fighting. Qualpopoca and his military had only defended themselves. But I do admit that it is true that Qualpopoca's army defeated them and killed six of your soldiers and a number of Totonacs."

"I don't believe you. And because I have to explain to my king what happened, I demand that you send for Qualpopoca and his son and several others so I can conduct an investigation on behalf of my monarch."

"I will agree to do that, but only because any investigation you conduct will prove my and Qualpopoca's innocence."

He then shocked me by asking me, in a calm tone, to stay with him at the Palace of Axayacatl. I stared at him for several moments, unsure if he was serious. "I will not do so, and I cannot understand why you would suggest such a thing."

"Well, I want us to spend time together to learn more about each other," he said.

"But you are welcome to visit me here at any time."

"But don't you think it would send a signal to your people that you and I are friends if we stay in the same residence?"

We continued in this manner for two days. He offered an enticement, that he would have his carpenter build four ships and then take me and other lords sailing on the lake. I had seen their ships in drawings; even their smallest were larger than our largest, and I was curious about them. We both knew he could force me to do his bidding at any time, but, as he had not threatened violence, I negotiated important concessions.

"You must agree that I will govern as before and be free to leave the palace whenever I want to."

"Yes, absolutely, but I ask only that you are always accompanied by my captains or me."

I ordered apartments prepared for myself and my chief wives and younger children. I was satisfied that my capitulation had prevented a violent seizure of power, massacre of my people, and destruction of Tenochtitlan.

Now, confined to my father's palace, but in my own quarters, I continued to meet with my spies, administrators, advisors, diplomats, the nobility, and merchants and to hear and resolve legal matters.

"My Majesty, who is also head of our church, lives across the ocean, farther, much farther beyond the seas than where the island called Coba is located. In the country of my birth, where my family lives, we have numerous great cities, and the countryside is bountiful with many farms," he said.

He used terms and names I did not understand relating to his religion.

"Our ruler lives in cities in different nations as head of the church. He never stays in one country long because he has to travel to deal with the spiritual needs of many, many people.

"Unlike your people, we know there is only one God who has a son he sent to Earth to save us by dying for our sins. The son of God has a mother, who is our advocate with God."

He asked me questions about my empire, chiefly about sources for our gold and precious stones, which I evaded, but he had no interest in hearing details about our religion.

"Really, I have preached to other rulers in these lands about your vile practice of sacrificing humans, yet it does not appear that any of you listen to me. You must end human sacrifice!"

"Let me explain why we engage in the sacred ritual."

"No! It is a practice only for savages, and I am surprised an empire as advanced as yours still engages in such depravity. I want you to end it immediately, and I want you to let me put our holy paintings and statues in the Main Temple."

"Absolutely not! Our gods would become angry."

He dropped the matter, but, then, as he would do almost every day, he returned to asking about gold and requested I produce ledgers for gold-producing regions. I did show him books, but they were all for silver, as I knew the woman interpreter would not be able to read them, because even her verbal language was rudimentary.

My men delivered Qualpopoca, his son, and fifteen others to Tenochtitlan. The leader and his men tortured them into saying I was guilty of conspiring with Qualpopoca. I repeated my innocence. The leader ordered me to watch as the foreigners and the Tlaxcalans burned the seventeen men to death in the square by the Main Temple.

Chapter Twenty-four

THE SPANIARDS: CORTÉS

M ontezuma provided me guides, and I explored the city with my captains and visited the massive Main Temple, with its forty tall towers and internal chapels, surrounded by a high wall in a precinct as large as a town of five hundred inhabitants.

In response to my queries about their ubiquitous canals and system for obtaining sweet water, the Mexicans explained they had an aqueduct that began at a location called Chapultepec, made of two mortar pipes, one they cleaned while the other was in use.

After I was satisfied we had seen enough of the capital, I conferred with my captains, and we decided it was the appropriate time to assert control over Montezuma to initiate the next step in the pacification of the Mexican Empire.

Although I knew it to be false, I accused him of colluding with Qualpopoca, Montezuma's governor in a town called Nauhtla, to have six Castilians murdered.

The truth was that Qualpopoca had demanded tribute payments from certain Totonacs, who refused to pay, saying I had relieved them of that duty. Qualpopoca threatened them with military action, and when Escalante, whom I had left in command of Villa Rica, heard this, he went to Nauhtla to demand gold.

Upon Qualpopoca's refusal, Escalante declared war. The Mexicans outnumbered the Castilians, and some of my men deserted Escalante, whom the enemy killed, along with five others and a substantial number of Totonacs. Qualpopoca captured, sacrificed, and beheaded a Spaniard.

I asked Montezuma to send for Qualpopoca, his son, and certain others. He sent messengers to Nauhtla.

"Would you do me the favor of staying with me until your men return with Qualpopoca? It will also give us an opportunity to know each other better," I said.

Montezuma frowned.

"Please, do not be offended; you will remain free to govern your empire. It is important to me that everything continue to run smoothly, you know. And choose whatever rooms you would like, and order your servants to make you as comfortable there as possible."

Montezuma was silent as he stared at the floor for several minutes with his hands limp on his lap before he replied that, as Supreme Ruler and Speaker, Chief Priest, and Master Judge, he could not leave his palace to stay in one where he had lived before he was elevated.

It was not easy to persuade him to yield. I spent two days negotiating with him. I cajoled him by reiterating that he would continue to govern as before, which was true, chiefly because I did not want the production of wealth to cease or slow.

"You will receive all favors due to you, and I will not harm you or any of your people, noble or common, if you agree to stay at my house. Please, I need you to agree to do this willingly and peacefully, and to show it publicly, so no one will think of rebelling, or that I am taking you by force," I said.

He finally relented and ordered the apartments he wanted prepared at the palace where I was staying. He called for sixty of his lords to escort him, and those of us present followed them outside and watched as the chieftains helped him into a litter and walked alongside it in a procession.

Every day thereafter, most of the time, unless I was out with my captains, I spoke with Montezuma or, if he asked me, visited his animal park or House of Birds. In December that year, I designed four brigantines that my carpenter built, and I used them for pleasure and scouting, taking Montezuma and his lords on the lake, and several times we went hunting at his lodges on the mainland. Most days, Montezuma spent time with scribes writing and painting a book.

On other occasions, I wove in questions about locations of gold-producing areas and asked whether he had any ledgers I could inspect. He had someone bring books I asked Marina to review, but unfortunately she recognized only a few sites—which, I later found out, were only for silver.

Two weeks after, Montezuma's vassals produced Qualpopoca, his son, and fifteen others, also of high rank. I ordered them put in chains at a governmental building nearby, where I interrogated them by repeatedly pushing their heads into buckets of water until they almost drowned. They all confessed to killing the Castilians and said Montezuma had ordered the murders, so I sentenced them to death by public burning.

At the square, I watched as Tlaxcalan and Castilian captains shot Qualpopoca with arrows before his execution. When I later spoke with Montezuma and told him what Qualpopoca and his men had said, he denied assassinating the Spaniards.

Shortly after I had arrived in Tenochtitlan, I sent spies with Cacamatzin when he returned to Tezcoco. My spy told me, "Commander, we found out that the incident with Qualpopoca has led to plans against you by Cacamatzin and other lords, and they have devised a plot to kill all of us and our Tlaxcalan allies and depose Montezuma."

I called for two captains, and we made an arrangement with Ixtlilxochitl and Coanocohtzin, Cacamatzin's brothers, who wanted his throne, to trick Cacamatzin and other lords by concocting a scheme to deliver them to me in Tenochtitlan. I told Ixtlilxochitl what to do.

"Tell Cacamatzin and the other rebels with him to meet you at a canal near your city, where you purportedly will join them in a blockade of the capital and an attack against Montezuma and us."

Cacamatzin and the noblemen agreed and boarded Ixtlilxochitl's canoe, but when they arrived near our lodging, my soldiers took them into custody.

Cacamatzin petitioned me to release him and promised me gold in exchange, and, at his direction, I sent a team of Spaniards to his major-domo in Tezcoco. Even though they returned with fifteen thousand *pesos de oro*, I told Cacamatzin I wanted more and ordered Alvarado to go to Tezcoco with him.

When they did not return after a day, I sent someone to investigate, and he learned Alvarado had tied Cacamatzin to a stake and burned him with brands because he had produced only another nine thousand *pesos de oro*. They brought Cacamatzin back to the capital, where I imprisoned him.

The events surrounding Cacamatzin and the other insurgents caused me to realize that they could not have been the only Indians conspiring against me, so I summoned Montezuma and the other lords to stand before me.

Addressing the lords, I said, "Although His Highness is living here, let me assure you he is being treated well. He is with me temporarily so we may get to know each other and so I may report to my Majesty what I have learned about these lands and all the people who are now his vassals. It is the will of my king that Montezuma should remain in power of this empire and continue to govern, and they expect everyone will continue to obey him, as they did before I arrived."

I dismissed the noblemen.

"It is important that you watch them for any sign of dissent," I warned Montezuma.

After much coaxing, Montezuma and his lords agreed to become vassals of my emperor and, to seal the pact, he gave me gold, jewelry, and three of his daughters. One of them was Tecuichpo, later christened Dona Isabel, his eldest legitimate daughter, who had been married at the age of eleven to Cuauhtémoc, Montezuma's cousin, Prince of Tlatelolco.

In two weeks, Montezuma had shown, by obeying whatever I asked of him, that he had accepted being a vassal to King Carlos.

I told Montezuma, "We need to see the areas where you obtain gold so I may prepare a thorough account of the land."

He obliged by providing Indians to accompany Castilians to certain provinces, where they inspected sites at rivers and brought me back samples of gold of good quality.

After I had sent expeditions into the interior to search for gold and territories that would be suitable for expansion and

colonization, I turned to the next step in the process of pacification. One day, after ensuring that Montezuma and the lords I had
detained were secured, I took ten Castilian soldiers, carrying tools,
and two Spanish priests to the Main Temple, where I instructed
Andrés de Tapia to lead us as we ascended the steps that led to
the altars of two idols.

We found at the top, in some places about two inches thick,
blood on the walls and gore on the ground and, in multiple rooms,
filled racks of dried skulls, including one solely of small ones, of
decapitated babies and children.

When I had seen enough, I sent two men to our lodgings to
bring back forty Castilians, and, as we waited for them, we wrecked,
without regard to what they were, statues and other objects and
smashed them by throwing them down steps or with iron bars.

The native priests howled and begged us to allow them to save
certain gods, and I permitted them to hide them somewhere away
from the Main Temple. We resumed the demolition, including of
a particularly ugly idol they called Huitzilopochtli.

When the other Castilians arrived, they joined us, and together
we completed the task of destroying the objects of false worship.
Afterward, I ordered the Indian priests to remove all blood from
innumerable sacrifices on the altars with lime and instructed our
friars to install images there of the Virgin Mary and St. Christopher.

As the cleaning was taking place, our clerics consecrated
the church and celebrated a mass. We showed the Indians how
to care for it, to burn incense and candles that we would teach
them to make, and always to decorate the area with fresh flowers
and branches. I assigned one of my older soldiers to remain and
supervise them after we departed. All killings ended at the Main
Temple in Tenochtitlan.

Chapter Twenty-five

THE SPANIARDS: CORTÉS

One afternoon in April 1520, Montezuma's messengers arrived from the coast to say many ships had arrived there, and the following day two of my Cuban Indians delivered a letter from Villa Rica about vessels that had docked at the harbor we called San Juan. I assumed they were from Velázquez with orders to remove me and force me back to Cuba.

I sent two Castilians to enquire. After five days, four other Castilians arrived in Tenochtitlan from Villa Rica, and one of them gave me a report.

"The fleet in our port belongs to Velázquez under the command of Pánfilo de Narváez, who has ninety horsemen and eight hundred foot soldiers. Narváez's men say Velázquez obtained royal decrees empowering him to name Narváez captain general and lieutenant governor of Yucatán and to take you back to Cuba in chains to face criminal charges.

"And Narváez did not permit the messengers you sent to return here—and he turned everything into chaos. He sent letters to our men at Villa Rica and our Indian allies, telling them to rise against you and join him. Now the lands you left pacified are in revolt or soon will be!

"And Narváez is telling everybody that, despite Velázquez's orders to arrest you and take you to Cuba, he intends to kill you and any member of your expedition who does not abandon you!"

The following afternoon, two more Spaniards from Villa Rica came to the capital with more shocking news.

"The natives have rebelled and joined Narváez. And we found out that Narváez and Montezuma have been communicating and that Montezuma sent him gifts of gold and other valuables. And Narváez has even built a base by Cempoallan, and many of the Spaniards of Villa Rica fled from him into the mountains to stay with a friendly Indian chief."

I wrote to two of my captains, Juan Velázquez de León and Rodrigo Rangel, whom I had sent to explore the interior, to meet me with their soldiers in Cholula.

I met with Montezuma but did not mention that I knew he had sent a delegation to Narváez and had sent him presents.

"Now that you are the Catholic king's vassal, you will receive many favors from him for your services and gifts. But I need you to continue to assist us. I have to go to my base on the coast, but I will leave the rest of my men and our gold and jewels in your care. I am leaving only because I must, to deal with newly arrived enemies from my own land."

I departed on 2 May 1520 with ninety Castilians, leaving Alvarado in command of Tenochtitlan and the surrounding cities with 120 Castilians, including all harquebusiers, the cannon, and the Tlaxcalan allies. We encountered a friar I had sent to the coast, who gave me a letter from Narváez claiming that he had royal decrees and that I should go to him at Cempoallan.

"I heard Narváez and Montezuma are corresponding, that Montezuma sent him gifts, including a gold medallion, and that Narváez persuaded a chief who was a vassal of Montezuma to side with him," the priest said.

We resumed our journey but soon happened upon a small group of Narváez's men, who claimed they had orders for me, so I directed my captains to chain and have them follow us, and we continued marching. Fifteen leagues from Cempoallan, a priest arrived from Villa Rica, along with Andrés de Duero, a resident of Cuba and one of Narváez's representatives.

"Captain General Narváez orders you to Cempoallan to officially acknowledge that he is now in command of these lands," Duero said, "and he has all the Castilians and Indians of the region as allies, and, if you fail to do so, he will use force against you, but if you submit and obey him, you may leave peacefully with all the ships and provisions you need."

"You tell Narváez he will have to show me these alleged decrees and that, according to the laws of Spain, these matters will have to be resolved by the court in our town, of which I am chief justice."

We debated and reached an agreement.

"Narváez, with ten of his men, and I, with the same number, will meet with a surety on each side so he can show me the documents he claims he has."

We drafted mutual letters of safe conduct, and Narváez's men departed. Duero later returned with the pass signed by Narváez.

"I will pay you ten *pesos de oro* to tell me Narváez's true plans," I said.

"Pay me first, and give me your gentleman's word that you will let me leave unharmed after I tell you."

I agreed and paid him.

"Narváez is going to have two of his men kill you while the other eight fight yours."

I wrote Narváez that I had found out his plan to murder me and would not meet with him, and if he had a valid decree from the Crown, he should send it to me. If not, I said, he should stop calling himself captain general, under the penalty of criminal punishment that I would personally administer. An adjutant handed an envoy and me hourglasses, and we coordinated the time. I then sent that envoy with another to command all of Narváez's followers and allies to appear before me at ten the next morning, or I would arrest and sentence all as traitors to the Crown.

On the way to the coast, we met Gonzalo de Sandoval, one of my captains, leading a force of my Castilians on the road, who said the natives at Villa Rica continued to rebel and refused to work for us. I assigned him and eighty men to lead us. We followed, and that day all of us arrived at Cempoallan, just outside Narváez's base.

"When Narváez heard we were in the vicinity, he left his camp with eighty horsemen and five hundred soldiers and approached, but he only surveyed the area before returning inside his camp. Then he went to sleep inside a thatched-roof hut atop a temple, with captains guarding him below on platforms," my scouts reported.

It was time to attack, even though there was a tempest and the night of 28–29 May 1520 was black. I sent out Sandoval with Tapia and sixty soldiers, and the rest of us followed until we came upon two of Narváez's scouts outside their camp; I captured one, but the other fled to warn Narváez of our arrival.

I interrogated the prisoner by choking him until he nodded he would speak in response to my queries. He told us how Narváez and his men were situated in their encampment.

We resumed our march. When we arrived at Narváez's base, we killed the sentries at the entrance without making much sound, and I bribed the master gunner with gold to permit us to stuff each cannon located in front of the barracks with beeswax.

We came upon shacks of the cavalry, where we cut off the cinch straps of all their sleeping horses tied to posts next to their lodging.

No one in the camp knew about our presence until we were in the center, where many of the soldiers were located. Narváez, as our spies had said, was with other armed men on the tower, and we climbed fast to reach him, with Sandoval ahead. A gun fired by accident, injuring no one but rousing the enemy.

Sandoval approached Narváez's hut. Narváez was outside. When he saw my men, he and his guards fled back into his hut, and Sandoval set it on fire, partially burning Narváez and the other occupants.

Narváez would not concede defeat, so one of my soldiers took out his right eyeball with a spike. Narváez then surrendered, begging for a physician, as he whimpered and covered the empty socket with the sleeve of his coat. Ignoring his plea, Sandoval removed all the papers Narváez had in his possession, jailed him and four of his captains in irons in another building, and posted two of our men as sentries. After a period of time, he called for a physician.

The documents Sandoval delivered to me were Velázquez's orders for Narváez to take me back to Cuba in chains to face criminal charges. I burned these orders after reading and instructed Sandoval to watch Narváez, after which I returned to my army.

My men seized the enemy's artillery and fired on them, including those running down the steps attempting to escape. Narváez's horsemen fell when they mounted their animals because of the cut cinch straps, and Narvaez's soldiers could not fire most of their weapons, as the rain had wet their gunpowder and we had filled their cannon with wax.

Narváez's captains submitted once they learned we had captured him. Satisfied we had beaten his army, I visited Narváez, who was lying on a cot. The physician had covered his eye socket with a bandage and treated his burns, but drying blood covered his face and chest. I dismissed the physician.

"The doctor, the doctor you sent me, he took good care of me. Thank you." Narváez fell silent for several minutes. "I bet you are overjoyed that you beat me," he said.

I inspected my fingernails before replying. "No, I regret you came here and forced me to fight you. And, really, this has been one of my easiest chores. My men have instructions to ensure you are comfortable. And you should not hesitate to send for me if you need anything else."

I left the jail and began the next stage of my operation by sending a captain and ten soldiers to Port San Juan to escort Narváez's ships to Villa Rica. They sailed to our town, where I met them and commanded everyone to unload all equipment, including sails and rudders, provisions, and any booty of war, including gold, and deliver it to the storehouse to be maintained in reserve. Once that had been done, I ordered Narváez's ships run aground, except for two I sent to Jamaica to purchase other necessities, including mares and livestock.

We lost only two men in the engagement, and Narváez, fifteen, although we captured everyone we wanted to and took their weapons. The village at Cempoallan, founded by Narváez, however, was in ruin, and all its residents had abandoned it, as Narváez and his men had looted everything of value.

I ordered two of my captains, each with four hundred of Narváez's men, to seize as many slaves as they needed and to start construction of new towns at the port of Coatzacoalcos and the Pánuco River.

Another captain, with a force of Castilians, escorted Narváez and the other prisoners to the Pánuco River, and I commanded Juan Velázquez de León and Rodrigo Rangel back to the interior to continue their work, each with four hundred men.

I set free the prisoners of war, except Narváez and his top captain, and offered to return their guns and horses if they joined my army, which they accepted. I persuaded Narváez's physicians and notaries to go with us. I sent six of Narváez's captains on foot to Tenochtitlan, with forty others, including my men, but, on the way, Mexicans killed them all.

Chapter Twenty-six

THE MEXICA:
MOCTEZOMA

Five months after the invaders had reached Tenochtitlan, messengers brought me word from the coast that more foreigners' ships had arrived. Before I revealed this information to the leader, however, I sent word back to my spies in the region with instructions to investigate who these men were, identify their leader, and subtly determine whether he was an ally or foe of the foreigners in Tenochtitlan.

Three days later, my spies identified the new commander, who said he had orders from his governor to expel the foreign leader in Tenochtitlan. I instructed my agents to deliver gold as gifts for the man and to propose we join against the foreigner who was in my capital.

The leader confronted me.

"What do you know about the men who arrived on the coast?"

"That's all I know—that men from your home are here."

"Yes, they are enemies from my land, and they are here to try to usurp me. I have to go there to deal with them, but I need to know I can rely on you to watch over my men and our gold and jewels," he said.

I promised to do as he requested, and he departed one morning, leaving behind one of his captains and forty soldiers. Before he left, the leader placed one of their large weapons that looked like a cabinet at the front entrance to the palace.

The leader went to battle at the new arrivals' camp, defeated them, and took their commander captive. Now I could no longer communicate with the leader's enemy.

A disaster took place in Tenochtitlan while the leader was away. The foreigners and the Tlaxcalans massacred more than three thousand, mainly lords and priests, as they celebrated at the Feast of Toxcatl at the Main Temple. The captain the leader left behind, I later found out, had claimed we were planning to attack them. That was not true.

The leader's captain had ordered us to stay inside the palace, guarded by foreigners. While the massacre was taking place, the men at the palace executed my nephew Cacama, other lords, and most of my attendants; then they chained me and others.

The Feast of Toxcatl had gone ahead without incident the first two days, with noblemen, many of whom were related to me, and priests engaged in rituals, including praying and dancing. On the third morning, however, the invaders and several hundred Tlaxcalans went to the Main Temple and posted sentries at the three exits to the square where activities were taking place.

The captain shouted a signal, "Let them die!"

I questioned agents of a few survivors, some of whom had escaped by climbing over a wall, and they said that our people who had perished, all unarmed, had tried to defend themselves, but the foreigners and Tlaxcalans cut off their hands, sliced open their abdomens to pull out their intestines, and beheaded and dis-membered them. Many tripped on their own entrails that dragged on the ground behind them.

The attackers took the jewelry off the corpses. Some who lived had pretended to be dead and covered themselves with blood, viscera, and body parts. When they had murdered the lords in the courtyard, the enemy turned to the audience, who had run out of the square into the streets, and similarly killed them and others.

Some of my warriors had chased the invaders and tried to break gates to the palace, but the foreigners murdered them and prevented the breach. Our people did not stop trying to enter. They almost managed to go inside when the foreigners' large weapon at the front door did not discharge, but, as they were about to go in, the captain put a knife to my throat and ordered me to go on the rooftop to command my people to stop their attacks.

Embarrassed that I was in chains, I addressed them. "My people, we cannot win. They have superior weapons, but I am still your Supreme Speaker and Ruler, Chief Priest, and Master Judge. Obey me, and leave. This is for your own good."

My people listened and departed, and their assaults ceased for a time. Over the next several days, however, their attacks resumed, and the invaders remained under siege.

After the massacre at the Main Temple, I used my spies to communicate with Cuitláhuac and our cousin Cuauhtémoc, who was in Tlatelolco, and instructed them to organize against the for-eigners. I appointed Cuitláhuac commander of the military, and he coordinated with Cuauhtémoc.

They placed battalions of warriors throughout Tenochtitlan, and, when my spies sent messages that the leader and his force were on their way back to Tenochtitlan from the coast, Cuitláhuac and

Cuauhtémoc finalized their strategies, closed the main marketplaces in Tenochtitlan and Tlatelolco, and ordered residents to stay indoors.

I was unable to do much regarding military action from the palace, for fear confidential orders to my commanders might be intercepted, but I managed to speak privately to Cuitláhuac.

"Tonight, go and burn all four of the invaders' ships to deny them an easy escape once our armies attack and set fire to the fortress the invaders built in Tenochtitlan."

The leader returned one morning, about a month after he had left for the coast, but this time, he had an army of more than twelve hundred foreigners and twenty-five hundred Tlaxcalans. I sent him a message welcoming him back and asking to see him. He did not respond, and several more times that day, I requested a meeting with him, all of which he ignored.

As I had arranged with Cuitláhuac and Cuauhtémoc, as soon as the foreigners were back in the palace, our armies disabled all the causeways, making transit throughout Tenochtitlan burdensome.

When the leader learned this, he sent out a large force to fight our warriors, but they were ready for them and killed more than ninety of the enemy and injured the rest, whom they chased until the invaders were back inside the palace.

The next morning, the interpreters arrived in my wing to deliver an order from the leader to reopen the market at Tlatelolco.

"Tell him that the people will not listen to me, as I am not allowed to speak with them directly and have lost all authority," I answered.

They left and returned with the leader's reply that he was not going to permit me to go out.

"Say to him I offer to send my brother Cuitláhuac, who still has the respect of our people, to negotiate with the merchants."

The leader agreed, and I sent a representative, after speaking with him privately, to Cuitláhuac with the command to hold an emergency session of the Council of Elders to formally depose me and elect Cuitláhuac as the new Supreme Ruler and Speaker, Chief Priest, and Master Judge.

Our warriors did not halt their assaults on the foreigners; some wrecked a wall in the palace, hurled lit torches inside, and almost entered, but the leader's men repelled them. Our fighters were relentless; in one day, they murdered more than eighty more of the bearded men and injured others.

Battles around the city took place over the next three days, and I could hear shouting and shooting of the invaders' weapons, even late at night. The leader, when he realized we had outnumbered his forces and they could not prevail, finally came to see me, with his interpreters. His face was red as he yelled at me, standing face to face.

"You colluded with my enemy on the coast, and it's your fault your people rebelled. But I have another army coming."

From my spies, I knew this was not true.

"If your subjects do not stop fighting me, I will obliterate everyone in Tenochtitlan and Tlatelolco," he went on.

I tried to speak, but he would not permit me, and he continued to scream, pointing at me, spittle shooting from his mouth, calling me a "traitorous dog." His breath was sour, and his body had a rank odor.

"You pledged to become a loyal vassal of my emperor, but you were not sincere. Unless you speak to your subjects and make them stop attacking us, this will be the end of your empire!"

He continued this way for a while until he wore himself out; then he gave me an order.

He said, "Be ready in the morning to address Cuitláhuac or his representative and your noblemen, who will be on the balcony of a house across from the palace, and command them to stop attacking us."

Chapter Twenty-seven

THE SPANIARDS: CORTÉS

One morning, while I was still at Villa Rica, messengers from Tenochtitlan arrived with calamitous news that the Indians of Tenochtitlan had revolted.

"They burned our four brigantines and the fortress we built, and they tried to mine it, almost murdering the men stationed there! Everyone begs you to go back."

After learning what had taken place in Tenochtitlan, I wrote to my captains Juan Velázquez de León and Rodrigo Rangel, informing them of the events in the capital and commanding them and their forces to meet me at Tlaxcala along with eight hundred men who had joined us from Narváez's expedition. I departed for that city, where I held a parade of our men and counted seventy horsemen, 1,130 Spanish foot soldiers, and twenty-five hundred Tlaxcalans.

We arrived in Tenochtitlan on 24 June 1520, St. John the Baptist's Day, shooting cannon and guns. The city was deserted and silent, and I later learned that the marketplaces in both Tenochtitlan and Tlatelolco had been closed.

We went to our palace, where we found everyone worn and hungry, and because they were short on drinking water, they had dug a well in the courtyard that produced only dirty water.

As to my dealings with Montezuma back in Tenochtitlan, I at first refused to see him, despite his repeated requests, because his and Narváez's incipient plans to join forces against me caused me to leave Tenochtitlan to dispatch Narváez, fomenting the rebellions against us.

The most pressing issue was to formulate a strategy to suppress the Mexican insurrection; the other important matter was that we were low on food because the insurgents had closed the marketplaces.

The following morning, 25 June, I sent the interpreters to instruct Montezuma to order his subjects to reopen the market at Tlatelolco, but he said he could do nothing from inside the palace. I replied I was not letting him out, and he proposed I allow him to send another lord who had authority, his brother Cuitláhuac.

I permitted Montezuma to outwit me by consenting to his scheme, because as soon as I had freed him, Cuitláhuac called an emergency session of the Council of Elders, who deposed Montezuma and elected Cuitláhuac as the new emperor, and Cuitláhuac went to Tlatelolco to make an allegiance with Cuauhtémoc. Cuitláhuac became commander-in-chief of the opposition, and Cuauhtémoc his second-in-command.

I dispatched two soldiers to Villa Rica to say we were alive and had secured Tenochtitlan, although the rebels had murdered ten of our men, but in less than one hour, my envoys returned, bawling, because Indians had beaten them. The Spaniards said the natives had disabled all the causeways and most bridges over the canals in the capital.

I ordered Diego de Ordaz and three hundred soldiers to commence hostilities against the rebels, but the force had been marching only about twenty minutes when Mexicans on rooftops pelted them with arrows and stones, killing ninety Castilians and injuring the remainder, chasing them back to our palace.

A sizeable contingent of howling Mexicans, perhaps thirty minutes after, succeeded in breaking through a wall with axes and launching lit torches to set parts of our building on fire, and they would have entered but for our crossbowmen.

I commanded the breached wall to be repaired, and the rest of us went out to fight. The enemy murdered ten and wounded more than eighty of us, and one of their arrows severed off the tips of three fingers of my left hand.

Battling continued over three days, but we did not advance because they replaced their fallen as soon as they were down and assaulted us at all hours, even using tactics designed to cause fear, by displaying outside our windows the heads of Spaniards tacked on poles, or decapitated bodies representing a figure they called Night Axe.

We murdered a few, but with insufficient gunpowder, no warning of their attacks, and because they were numerous and highly skilled with their weapons, including the women warriors who fought alongside them, and pelted us with stones from the rooftops, we were at a disadvantage.

Our inability to defeat the natives was taking a toll on us, and it appeared they would beat us, so, after discussing the matter with my captains, I ordered Montezuma to speak with representatives of the rebels and tell them to stop fighting.

I told two captains to negotiate with Cuitláhuac to be present with other lords to listen to Montezuma's speech on a balcony at a house across from our palace.

At the appointed time the following day, 26 June, we escorted Montezuma to the roof of our palace to address Cuauhtémoc, whom Cuitláhuac had sent in his place, and Mexican captains and warriors gathered on the balcony of a house across the street.

I watched from a position of safety, and only Montezuma's Indian attendants were with him as he walked to a breastwork that jutted out from a tower.

He was about to speak when he focused on something on the edifice facing us, and I moved forward and turned my head to see the object of his interest—a young woman, exceptional in beauty, dressed as a warrior. Cuauhtémoc, who was standing in the front row not far from the lovely soldier, spoke and called Montezuma a coward and other pejorative terms.

Montezuma had not uttered a word when the insurgents shot him with arrows. His men protected him with shields, and the exceptionally handsome young woman put down her bow, picked up a slingshot, and retrieved stones from her pocket.

He was still as they hit him with missiles on the forehead and chest so hard he fell. His bodyguards lifted him and carried him away, back inside, where Montezuma's physicians treated his wounds. He would develop a fever and remain ill in bed for days.

We went out to fight after the rebels wounded Montezuma, but we made no progress and negotiated a truce with them that night.

War resumed at dawn, 27 June, when they returned with reinforcements who were fiercer than the ones from the first day, and as we dispatched or wounded any, others promptly replaced them.

We moved outside the fortress, leaving sentries there, to take three bridges, burn houses, and kill a significant number of civilians. We skirmished, but the adversary always had reserves, and that day they murdered seventy Castilians and wounded more than eighty.

We were thirsty because the water from the palace well was salty and fetid; and the stones, the stones that the men, women, and children threw at us from the flat rooftops were constant. Cannon did not help; when we fired into a crowd, more people substituted for them.

At nine o'clock the night of 27 June, I sent a captain with the interpreters and soldiers out to negotiate another suspension of hostilities, until the following midday, and we went back to the fortress to give ourselves time to build three wooden engines. Each machine was rectangular and designed with enough space to carry twenty-five soldiers, including harquebusiers and crossbowmen, to shoot through small windows.

At the appointed time to resume the war on 28 June, we sent out the siege machines, borne on the shoulders by Tlaxcalans, but the Mexicans would not bend; with stones, arrows, and spears, they pelted the engines and damaged them.

That day we saw, in separate areas, Indians directing their troops, one of whom was Cuitláhuac, and the other his cousin, Cuauhtémoc.

In the evening, under another cease-fire, six Indian captains approached me.

"Cuitláhuac demands you leave our land."

"We are going nowhere! And I order him to submit."

"The war will end only when all of you have departed."

The following morning, 29 June, after we had repaired the engines, we took them out again to attempt control. The enemy had replenished their forces, which now included even more women, many who were not even warriors, as evidenced by their attire.

We battled until midday, and they continued to hit us with stones, killing ten Castilians, wounding most of us, and destroying the war machines. We returned to the fortress.

That afternoon, the opposition recaptured the Main Temple when hundreds climbed the stairs to the top, leaving guards below armed with long lances. I commanded men to breach the tower, and they tried numerous times but to no avail, as the rebels forced them back down, causing the Indians on the streets to cheer.

I joined the attack to lead a force of five hundred Spaniards and Tlaxcalans, even though my left hand hurt from the wounds I had sustained on three fingers. The swollen stubs were infected, and my hand had changed from red to purplish blue. The skin on that hand was cold and crackly and released a putrid-smelling discharge.

The rebels assaulted us, but we made progress in burning the Main Temple, and that demoralized the Indians, causing them to enter into discussions.

"Do you not see you cannot beat us?," I asked. "We will not end this war until either the city is razed to the ground or none of you remains alive. It is your choice; your fate is in your hands."

"We do not care how many of us die," a captain replied, "and you are correct in one respect. We have two choices, but they are: we either will perish from the Middleworld or kill all of you and your dog allies. And you are close to losing, because we have dismantled the causeways, and we control the aqueduct and food."

We continued this way for an hour, until it was obvious neither side would capitulate. That night, with the Tlaxcalans, we incinerated more than three hundred houses on one street; then we moved on to another and set fire to yet more buildings, especially those that the enemy, from their rooftops, used as vantage points to attack us, until I lost count.

We returned to a thoroughfare where they had defeated us the previous day, because it was the only access to the Tlacolpan Causeway to the mainland, and secured it, and, by the time we had retired, we were in charge of four bridges and had filled canals under them with adobe, clay, and stones. We stationed guards there so they would not be retaken.

The next morning, 30 June, we fought and won more bridges. The rebels asked for a meeting, so I spoke with a mediator, one of their priests.

"The terms are that you will stop fighting us, you will rebuild the bridges, repair the roads, and serve my Majesty as before," I said.

"And what will you do for us in exchange?"

"Well, of course, we will stop fighting you. But that's a good way to begin working out the other details, don't you think?"

"Yes, I agree to that. Both sides will cease fighting."

I returned to our garrison to rest and have a meal, but, as I was eating, a Spaniard interrupted me.

"The insurrectionists have recaptured the bridges and killed five Castilians!"

We put on our steel armor and helmets and ran to the stable, mounted our horses, and went out. As we pursued fleeing Indians, we were stupefied to see the Tlacolpan Causeway filled with tens of thousands of Indians and thousands more on canoes on both sides.

We reached the last bridge before the causeway, but the Indians, who shot us with arrows from their boats, killed a significant number of horsemen, and almost all the horses fell into the water.

Horses on the road ran loose, in circles. My head hurt, even though I was wearing a helmet, because they had hit me with numerous stones. My horse had arrows stuck in its flesh.

I resolved we should abandon the city that night and ordered everyone back to the fortress, and, on the way, we made sure we had four well-guarded bridges.

When I reached our garrison, where we had hidden the gold and jewels, I informed the Castilians that we were departing and told captains to relay my decision to the Tlaxcalans.

The rest of us packed the valuable goods, including much of the gold, on mules in the stable, and I distributed the rest to my captains. I directed men to prepare the Mexicans I had imprisoned in the fortress for departure, including Montezuma's son and daughters.

I returned to the palace to deal with Montezuma, who was recuperating from his injuries. I went to his chambers, where a torch burned in each corner. He was asleep, snoring lightly. I heard yelling in the streets.

I ordered his physicians and servants out and to close the door behind them and, when they had obeyed, removed the bed linen on him as I covered his mouth with my hand.

He opened his eyes and tried to push me away, but his grip was weak. I unsheathed my blade, and five times plunged it deep in his chest, as his body jerked.

When he had stopped breathing, I took my hand off his face, replaced the blanket, put my knife back in its case, and walked out.

"The emperor has died from his wounds. Bury him in Tenochtitlan," I said to his attendants.

I never learned what they actually did with his remains. My captains and I dispatched the other lords at the palace, one fighting so hard we had to stab him forty-seven times to kill him.

We departed and reconvened outside with the rest of our force. Sixty men carried a portable wooden bridge the carpenters had made to use on gaps in the causeway to flee Tenochtitlan that night, 30 June–1 July 1520.

Sandoval led the vanguard; behind them were the Castilian women and Montezuma's son and daughters, including Tecuichpo and Doña Ana, who was carrying my child.

The Tlaxcalans followed, with Velázquez de León and Alvarado commanding the rest of us in the rear guard with sixty horsemen. Those in charge of the gold, most of which we had melted into bars, and other treasure marched near me.

The cavalry, infantry, our prisoners, and the allies, about seven thousand of us, had crossed four bridges and were about to go on the Tlacolpan Causeway to the mainland, when natives screamed.

"The enemies are fleeing! The invaders are running!"

Chapter Twenty-eight

THE SPANIARDS: CORTÉS

I commanded the soldiers to remove our portable wooden bridge so the rebels could not follow us onto the causeway, but it had become fixed, so we abandoned it. They murdered most of the Spanish vanguard at the next crossing.

War cries and drums sounded. A countless number of Indians on the water and those who crossed our disabled bridge assaulted us, and we fired at them with the little gunpowder we had left, but they jumped in the water to escape injury. Other obstacles we faced were the vast numbers of people on the causeway, preventing us from moving quickly, and the noise and assaults by the enemy, frightening the horses and causing them not to obey their riders.

Five horsemen and one hundred foot soldiers helped the women and Montezuma's children to cross as other Spaniards and I swam to the mainland with our horses, before leaving the animals and returning to rescue those still on the causeway.

Many dead Castilians and others had fallen into a breach the enemy had made on the causeway. We collected the injured and helped them escape.

I looked back at Tenochtitlan and saw bright fires consuming the spectacular buildings of the city. Cuitláhuac and Cuauhtémoc had defeated us.

The enemy chased us out of the city until we reached Tlacolpan, where my people had gathered in a square to wait for us. They were confused, all injured, and no one knew what to do.

"The captains and I have assessed the situation. I know everyone has questions about what happened to the rest of our people. I pledge to figure out how to reach a place of safety.

"Unfortunately, the Mexicans killed more than six hundred Castilians and most of our horses, leaving us with only thirty animals, and three thousand Tlaxcalans and the mules loaded with gold and jewels have disappeared."

Soon, the adversary approached, and I ordered everyone to hurry, until we arrived at the countryside, where I made another tally and learned the Mexicans had killed Montezuma's daughters Doña Ines and Doña Ana, who was carrying my child.

We advanced. Our force reached a village where we skirmished, but not for long, as I commanded a retreat to Citlaltépec because of injuries to my head from stones hurled by them. The adversaries continued to pursue and assault us, killing four horsemen and their horses and injuring many of us. At camp, we were so hungry we ate grass.

We departed Citlaltépec and walked for about two days, still with no food but what we pulled from the ground. Then we climbed a pass on the mountains to descend on a road leading to a town called Otumba.

It was there my scouts informed me that Cuitláhuac had been pursuing us with an army since we had fled Tenochtitlan, but had since returned to the capital, although he left a force to fight us. At Otumba, the Mexicans assailed us, leaving more of us injured.

In the morning, even though I was weak from hunger and my stomach growled, we marched and on a hill saw a group of Mexican captains, whom the Tlaxcalans identified because they wore spectacular uniforms with feather insignia in black and white. I took five horsemen, and we attacked, killing each one with lances.

With the loss of their leaders, especially the one carrying their pennant, the Mexican troops became disoriented, causing them to retreat. We suffered injuries, including another gash to my left hand, but no deaths.

The leaders of Tlaxcala visited me and advised us to travel to the city of Tlaxcala to recuperate. We followed their counsel and stayed three weeks. It was there, with my captains, that I completed my plans for the conquest of Mexico and investigated the cause of the uprising in Tenochtitlan.

"After you left to deal with Narváez," Alvarado said, "the Tlaxcalan captains told me the Tenochtitlan lords were going to assault us during the Feast of Toxcatl. The few of us left here were afraid, so I had to do something to prevent the ambush.

"But before the feast began, some Mexican lords and priests asked me for permission to reinstall their statue of Huitzilopochtli at the shrine in the Main Temple. I said 'No.'

"Then I looked for proof of the Mexicans' plans to kill us. I interrogated several of Montezuma's relatives until they confessed there was a Mexican plot afoot to murder us."

At Tlaxcala, some Castilians died from their wounds; others were crippled. The three fingers of my left hand wounded at Tenochtitlan had to be amputated to prevent gangrene. A number of Spaniards had lost confidence in our ability to prevail and wanted to return to Cuba, but I implored them to remain steadfast.

We went to Tepeaca, where we and the Tlaxcalans attacked, climbing onto roofs to push off those who had sought safety there and using our mastiffs to tear apart people. We murdered four hundred and captured the rest for enslavement, after which the Tepeacan ruler conceded and became a vassal of my Majesty. I sold the women and children to my men, each for ten pesos.

I sent Olid with a force to a village called Quechula. When they arrived, they came upon all its inhabitants, the men armed, standing together in a field. Olid told them that, if they submitted peacefully and followed the Castilians, he would not harm them. They put down their weapons, and Olid escorted more than two thousand men and more than four thousand women and children to Tepeaca. At our camp, I told my soldiers what to do with them.

"Separate the men from the women and children, and shoot and kill all the men. Brand all the women and children."

In the entire province of Tepeaca, we murdered about twenty thousand. When we had completed pacification of the territory, we founded a new post on 4 September 1520, a town I named Segura de la Frontera.

The Crown still had not responded to the petition I had sent on 10 July 1519 with Montejo and Portocarrero, but I concentrated on the next task of building of ships. I ordered Martín Lopez, my chief carpenter, to Tlaxcala.

"Take all the tools, experienced craftsmen, assistants, armed soldiers, and slaves, as many as you need of everything, to cut down oak and pine trees, sufficient to make thirteen brigantines."

Around that time, fortunate events significantly altered the strength of my military. A ship arrived near Villa Rica from Velázquez intended for Narváez with thirteen soldiers, a large supply of provisions, and a mare. One of my men asked the captain, who had a letter ordering Narváez to take me prisoner and send me to Cuba in irons, to see me at Segura de la Frontera, where I persuaded him to join me in the conquest.

A second ship thereafter also landed by Villa Rica, and its captain, with eight soldiers, six crossbowmen, a mare, and a substantial amount of supplies, went to Segura de la Frontera and enlisted with us. An expedition subsequently arrived at Villa Rica, part of a fleet belonging to Garay.

The party had disembarked when local Indians attacked them, so the Spaniards fled and swam to their vessels, but as they were escaping, one ship sank. Some drowned, and others swam to another ship that had landed at Villa Rica with sixty men and went to Segura de la Frontera to become part of our endeavor.

Garay, further, had sent Miguel Díez de Aux to Pánuco, but, having found no one there, he went to Villa Rica; they sent him to me with fifty soldiers and seven horsemen. Still another ship, also belonging to Garay, landed, and forty soldiers and ten horsemen who had weapons ended up at Segura de la Frontera. Then, a vessel my father and our associates in Castile had sent arrived at the coast with supplies, provisions, muskets, gunpowder, crossbows, and four horses.

The ships added two hundred men to my expedition, and I used two of the vessels to obtain additional personnel and goods—one to Hispaniola for horses, crossbows, guns, and powder, and the other to Jamaica to recruit men and purchase mares for breeding.

On 27 December 1520, we departed Tlaxcala for Tezcoco, our base for launching the conquest of Tenochtitlan. We advanced until we ascended a mountain range and reached a saddle more than twelve thousand feet high by the headwaters of the Atoyac River. We rode to a place from where we could see Tenochtitlan. Almost all the towers were gone.

We stayed in Tezcoco with no aggression from the residents as we continued to prepare our assault against the Mexicans. My next task was to investigate and pacify the southern perimeter of Lake Tezcoco. I left Sandoval with a force at Tezcoco and took two hundred Spaniards with me. We marched along the shore of Iztapalapa.

Mexicans appeared when we were about a league outside that city, on canoes and by land, and battle was joined. They disabled a causeway that also functioned as a dike, and we and our allies commandeered the canoes of civilians trying to escape, murdering more than six thousand men, women, and children by the end of that day.

At night, I ordered houses on the shore plundered and burned. The water from the raised dike now was ferocious, and that night we still were trying to reach safety. Unfortunately, we lost most of our spoils, and some of the native allies drowned. At dawn, the lakes were level again, but enemy warriors on canoes covered the waters, so we went in another direction back to Tezcoco.

In January 1521, the Mexicans formally installed Cuauhtémoc as emperor, and he escalated military preparations. Cuauhtémoc did manage to defeat two villages around the lake that had become our allies and made them join him, so I took two hundred soldiers there to burn many of their homes and eject the Mexicans. The chieftains apologized and again pledged as vassals.

By early May 1521, when we had made significant progress on the new ships, I issued commands designed to worsen the conditions of the Mexicans and test the enemy's readiness for battle. I instructed Alvarado and Olid to supervise the leveling of the Iztapalapa Causeway leading to Tenochtitlan, but Mexicans in canoes attacked them with stones, wounding thirty Castilians. On 23 May, Alvarado and Olid took a force and destroyed the pipes of the aqueduct at the spring at Chapultepec, the Mexicans' main source for sweet water.

Chapter Twenty-nine

THE XOCHIMILCA: FLOWER

At one of Cuauhtémoc's bases in Tlatelolco, I contin-ued training to fight and making arrows under the command of a woman, Captain Tlachinolli. All the time I thought about my family, Teputzitoloc, and Yaretzi, but I was not worried about my family's well-being because I assumed they were safe in our mountain village.

Captain Tlachinolli relayed Cuauhtémoc's new orders three days later.

"Cuauhtémoc called our battalion to Tenochtitlan because the invaders just burned more than three hundred houses in one night. He and Cuitláhuac now want to overwhelm them with significant numbers of our warriors stationed throughout that city. We will deploy to a district near the Main Temple, where we will kill the invaders and their dog allies with every weapon we have."

The campaign to eject the invaders escalated that day, and Cuitláhuac and Cuauhtémoc still had plenty of Eagle and Jaguar

Warriors in their armies, even though the enemies' weapons that shot fire killed many.

Captain Tlachinolli spoke to our battalion at the end of that day.

"Our Supreme Ruler Cuauhtémoc is proud of how well you have fought. We have made great progress and are close to making the invaders run from our cities! You should also know that Cuauhtémoc appreciates the contribution of women in this war, and he has pledged that we will not be forgotten when we rebuild our nations.

"But the war is not even close to being over. He commands us to continue to fight hard, no matter what difficulties lie ahead.

"Who here will continue to fight the dog invaders who are murdering, raping, and enslaving our people and stealing our lands? Who here is willing to fight them to the end?"

Everyone stood and cheered. Someone started a chant, and I joined in.

"I will fight the dog invaders! I will fight them to the end! I will fight them to the end! I will fight them to the end!"

Captain Tlachinolli quieted us down.

"Moctezoma is dead. He was murdered by the invaders."

I was surprised they had to kill him, as many times as we had hit him.

"Now, Cuitláhuac and Cuauhtémoc have ordered our warriors to intensify our attacks against the invaders. They have assigned companies of warriors in a strategy to force the invaders and their allies to flee Tenochtitlan on the Tlacolpan Causeway, the only one we intentionally have not completely disabled. The strategy is that warriors will assault the enemies' flanks from the lake, on both sides of the causeway."

My battalion and a hundred others sailed and arrived at the Tlacolpan Causeway, from which we could see fires burning in

Tenochtitlan. We waited until we heard the signal—screams that the invaders were trying to escape, followed by people running onto the causeway.

On our ship, Captain Tlachinolli ordered us, "Stand at attention, and prepare to shoot."

She pointed at the foreigners, some of whom were on their large war animals.

"Shoot them and their animals first and then everybody else on the causeway, their allies, and any Mexicans who have joined them."

The foreigners, our scouts said, were low on a powder they needed to make their weapons shoot fire. Although some of them defended themselves with these weapons and killed warriors on our ship, the rest of us brought many of them and their animals down and made them fall into gaps our warriors had created on the causeway.

We trounced them because we had significantly more warriors, all armed with bows and arrows, on the lake attacking them from both sides as they tried to escape, and because there were so many people on the causeway, they were unable to discharge their weapons that shot fire. Another factor in our success was that they were focused on fleeing, but we, on fighting.

That night, Cuitláhuac's and Cuauhtémoc's armies murdered at least six hundred foreigners and more than three thousand of their allies. We wounded and drove out the rest, and Cuitláhuac and one of his armies chased them for a distance on the mainland.

Cuitláhuac's and Cuauhtémoc's cataclysmic blunder, however, was to allow the invaders to escape, rather than exterminate them when they were weak.

After we drove the foreigners out, Cuitláhuac and Cuauhtémoc reopened the markets and began to rebuild Tenochtitlan. Cuitláhuac and Cuauhtémoc had agents embedded with the Tlaxcalans, so they knew almost everything the invaders did after we had ejected them.

They were preparing new strategies to return to fight us, this time adding a maritime component, ships they were building at Tlaxcala that warriors of Cuitláhuac and Cuauhtémoc three times tried to destroy.

Cuitláhuac governed for only a short period because he died, reportedly from a disease the invaders had brought to our land. The Council of Elders elected Cuauhtémoc to formally succeed Cuitláhuac, but Cuauhtémoc had already been functioning in that capacity.

Cuauhtémoc ordered us to deepen canals under bridges, build bulwarks and other entrenchments, and make and stockpile weapons. He designed longer lances and attached the invaders' blades the armies had seized from them, and, for the first time in history, General Ameyalli said, a ruler substantially increased the number of women warriors in the Mexican and Tlatelolcan armies.

I remained in Tlatelolco for a time after we had driven out the invaders, but then Captain Tlachinolli sent me back to my base in the mountains to continue training. I would not be deployed again until two weeks before the invaders returned, in Tlatelolco.

Book Three

AUGURIES OF INIQUITY

My Heart has no flaw. She is virtuous,
supernal, and her eyes are long and bright.
And she is made of luminous red clay.

Earth-monster signs line this hetaera's face.
Bicephelous snakes circle her arms, yet:
My Heart has no flaw. She is virtuous.

My Song, my wail, warrior's bells must toll.
I aim—a body, but two brains; chimes ring.
And she is made of luminous red clay.

Midday: The moon and three stars shine as a
captured bluebird bears a golden diadem.
And she is made of luminous red clay.

Chapter Thirty

THE XOCHIMILCA: FLOWER

At camp, we continued to make arrows and practice shooting. My captain forced me to focus on training to fight, but every night on my pallet at the barracks, I thought about Teputzitoloc.

He puts his arms around me and pulls me so close I feel his heart beat. His body is hard. I embrace him.

"Flower, I love you so much, and I wish we could escape somewhere together."

"I love you, too, and I want to spend the rest of my life with you!"

He caresses my hair. I hold on to him as I rest the side of my face on his chest. We kiss. I want him inside me.

"Flower: Always remember what we have to look forward to after the war."

I summoned the courage one day to ask my captain whether she had heard anything about him.

"No, I am not privy to his whereabouts and, even if I were, I would not have authority to reveal such information to you."

"Captain, I'm sorry if I overstepped my bounds. I just, I just want to know if he is well."

"As far as I know, he's still alive. That's all I can tell you. Now, get back to work."

About eleven months after we had ejected them, the foreigners and their native allies left Tezcoco, their base, to attack Tenochtitlan, this time with substantially larger armies and a navy of thirteen ships.

The day the war began, our battalion and many others went to fight by Tepepolco Island, where the enemy had just murdered our warriors on a hill. By the time the invaders had boarded their ships, we were ready to assault them, but the wind favored them. They rammed into us, and many of us fell; I hit my head on the side of the boat. It hurt.

"Everyone, quickly, get up, and assume your stances. There is no time to treat any injuries. Now! This includes you, Flower. Hurry! I said move, now! Be ready if they shoot at us!"

But they did not attack us; they just departed.

Cuauhtémoc ordered us to wait on shore in a safe area for further instruction, and by early evening, he ordered us to the Xoloc battle site. Although we were exhausted, the fighting did not pause until early the next morning.

We continued to dig ditches on the bridges and causeways the enemy had repaired and to assail them with swords, lances, stones, arrows, clubs, and sticks. The enemy would not stop burning buildings.

About three weeks later, the enemy took control of the Iztapalapa Causeway, allowing them to proceed to the main square. There, they killed a large number of our warriors with their weapons that shot fire.

That night again, on my pallet at barracks, I thought about Teputzitoloc, the day we escaped, and how we held each other and kissed in the forest. In the morning, I risked being yelled at again by my captain, but I had to know if he was safe.

"My job is not to keep you informed about Teputzitoloc. We all have loved ones who are fighting. We don't know if they are dead or alive. So what makes you think you have the right to know about him?

"I'm . . . I'm sorry, Captain."

She sighed. "I haven't heard he's dead."

I smiled, thanked her, and walked away.

Cuauhtémoc ordered several women's battalions to the Iztapalapa Causeway, and we succeeded in murdering a substantial number of the invaders and their allies. They withdrew. Our captain then led us to a base nearby, where we waited for our next orders. My stomach grumbled, as all we had to eat were nuts and sometimes flat corn cakes and beans. I was thirsty because water was scarce and rationed.

Our next command was near the Tlacolpan Causeway, where we surrounded and attacked two enemy ships in a canal, captured fifteen foreigners, and delivered them to Cuauhtémoc's men at a nearby camp.

We were hungrier and still thirsty, but we did not scale back our fighting. The next weeks were grueling because we dug breast-works and hidden pits on the causeways. Our warriors modified their lances with blades they had seized from the foreigners and flung javelins at them.

Our captain assigned us to different tasks each day and night. With little sleep, I dug ditches on the causeways and bridges after the Tlaxcalans had repaired them. I continued to kill enemies with arrows or stones.

Chapter Thirty-one

THE SPANIARDS:
CORTÉS

The War for Tenochtitlan began at sunrise on 1 June 1521. Our Tezcocan ally, Ixtlilxochitl, commanded a fleet of sixteen thousand canoes, which followed our brigantines. The first sighting of the enemy was on Tepepolco Island, where they were sending smoke signals. I led 150 men to climb the main hill to kill all the men but spare the women and children.

As we walked back to shore, more than five hundred enemy canoes appeared. We ran to the water, swam, and boarded our ships. With a favorable wind, I relayed orders to all the captains.

"Every ship: ram into the Mexican canoes to prevent them from attacking us!"

We managed to stop them from taking action against us, and we departed at a fast speed.

About two hours later, a good number of the rebel craft surrounded our flagship, captained by Rodríguez de Villafuerte, on which I, of course, was present. Had it not been for the heroic acts of Martín Lopez that day, I probably would have lost my life, in addition to twenty-five Spaniards. Villafuerte had let the brigantine ground, and numerous Mexican warriors swam toward us and climbed aboard our vessel.

"Abandon the ship," Villafuerte ordered.

"No, we can still save it and gain an advantage," Lopez replied.

"I'm the captain here. You have no right to disobey my command," Villafuerte said.

Lopez ignored Villafuerte and spoke to the sailors.

"All crossbowmen, follow me, now! Move! Shoot all Mexicans on board. Spare no one."

Lopez joined our men and chased and stabbed several enemy natives. He and the crossbowmen killed about fifty Mexicans and kicked them off the ship. The survivors fled, leaping off and swimming back to their canoes. We pursued.

"Shoot every Mexican on each boat and those who escape into the water," I commanded.

After we murdered many, the remainder retreated, and we asserted control of that part of the lake.

I took thirty men to the Mexican fortress of Xoloc, where we disembarked and seized temples. We stayed there and used it as a post because its location made it possible to launch assaults on Tenochtitlan.

My scouts reported the Mexicans were on the northern causeway from Tlatelolco to Tepeyac, bringing in food and supplies. "Sandoval, go there with a force and choke the main entrance to the capital and remove the insurgents' escape route."

By the Main Temple, we killed a significant number and damaged buildings, but the adversary fought back, driving us out of a nearby courtyard and from the square so fast we could not carry a cannon. The Indians seized it; not knowing how to operate it, they later threw it into the lake.

That evening, I sent horsemen to recapture the courtyard, but late that night they had to withdraw because rebels stationed on roofs pelted them with arrows and stones. By the middle of the second week of June 1521, we had surrounded Tenochtitlan.

We rested that night, and by the following morning, the insurgents had refreshed their troops by adding a significant number of fighters, including women, so I sent a rebel to deliver a message to Cuauhtémoc that if he did not submit I would completely demolish the city. Cuauhtémoc's reply was that he had ordered his military to refuse offers for peace and under no circumstance would he surrender.

"Set fire to the Palace of Axayacatl, the House of Birds, and Montezuma's animal park, and burn each structure on every street in the capital," I ordered.

We suffered a reversal when the enemy grounded two brigantines on a canal and the Mexicans attacked and seized fifteen Castilians. I ordered captains to secure the route west to Tlacolpan and boarded a brigantine to inspect Alvarado's progress. It was considerable.

My assessment was that we had subjugated at least half of Tenochtitlan and destroyed most farms within the city. As there was no food coming in or water from the aqueduct and the brigantines prevented the residents from fishing, I expected Cuauhtémoc now would contact me to arrange the terms of his surrender.

It was not he who approached me, however, but two sons of Montezuma, Axayaca and Xoxopehualoc, enemies of Cuauhtémoc. I refused to speak with them, as the only one who had power to submit was the emperor himself. Cuauhtémoc executed those traitors.

Cuauhtémoc moved his headquarters, military, and most of Tenochtitlan's population to Tlatelolco, and was obtaining food, water, and other supplies from there, so I set 30 June as the date for an offensive.

We went forward with the action at the central Tlatelolco marketplace. As we marched, my battalion captured two bridges before entering the city, but once there, we had to move slowly, as we did not know the streets, which were narrower than those in the capital.

Then, we halted, because a large Mexican contingent blocked the path at a location ahead of us.

"Reverse! The vanguard will now act as the rear guard," I commanded.

One troop had gone over a bridge, where the Mexicans had dug a breach twelve paces wide that rapidly filled with about eight feet of water. The enemy in front and behind us attacked, but because the street was congested, a problem we had faced multiple times in Tenochtitlan, we did not have sufficient space to aim and shoot. Another impediment was that we could not use our cannon effectively, as we sometimes inadvertently hit our allies who were mixed in with the thick crowds of the enemy.

Some Castilians jumped into the lake, attempting to flee, falling into the hands of the rebels, who seized or killed them. I fought two Mexicans, and as they were about to capture me, a swordsman, Cristóbal de Olea, sliced off their hands. They beheaded and hacked Olea into pieces.

We retreated and returned to our base with skirmishes along the route, counting twenty lost Castilians, and fifty-five taken captive, and that day, more than two thousand allies perished. As Alvarado and Sandoval marched, the insurgents threw at them the heads of the Spaniards, and the Mexicans sacrificed my men and allies on their altar.

Two weeks later, we observed that Cuauhtémoc had not recently launched any campaign of importance, other than a minor assault on Alvarado's camp that Alvarado had quashed, and that Cuauhtémoc's people had almost no food or water. I now had eight remaining brigantines, and we still controlled the lake, meaning that no one could enter or exit Tenochtitlan without our permission.

Chapter Thirty-two

THE SPANIARDS: CORTÉS

The Mexicans continued to defend themselves well, but by the middle of July, they had ended the practice of creating gaps on the causeways. Around that time, Alvarado found a spring that had been providing the enemy with sweet water and destroyed it, forcing them to turn to the lake. The fetid liquid sickened and killed a substantial number of inhabitants.

We, however, were fortunate, as a ship that had been in Ponce de León's second journey to La Florida arrived at Villa Rica, and the Castilians sent us food, additional gunpowder, soldiers, and crossbows.

Even so, we did not have sufficient gunpowder, but Francisco de Montano, one of the men who had come with Narváez, after the allies said it was possible because the natives had done it, offered to climb to the edge of Popocatepetl's crater to get us sulfur. One of the Spaniards who joined Montano on the adventure described what happened when they climbed to the rim of the volcano.

"The smell is like rotten eggs, and there are many huge and steep, rugged cliffs in the crater that look like latticework. And there's smoke, thick gray smoke everywhere that stings our eyes. Montano covers his face with a large handkerchief and secures it in the back of his head. He carries a big wooden bowl and a large canvas basket.

"We tie him to a heavy chain, and we hold it tight! Then, we slowly lower him down the crater. We hear him cough; we stop lowering him, but he yells at us to keep lowering him until we extend the entire chain. He is covered with ashes and surrounded by smoke, so for a few moments we can't see him. 'Montano, Montano,' I scream, 'how are you?' 'Just don't let go,' he says.

"Then, we see he is scooping sulfur. He fills the basket, drops the bowl into the abyss, and yells. 'Pull me up!' He rubs his eyes. As we lift him, and he is close to the rim, we see his eyes are bright red. He now has a raspy cough. When he is near, we take the basket and hand him a canteen with water, and he drinks. We pull him, he stands on the rim with us, and we take off the chain. We descend immediately."

The daily living of the Mexicans continued to deteriorate; we observed emaciated people on the roads pulling grass or scooping mud to eat. The following day, we seized three Mexican lords and sent them to Cuauhtémoc.

"Tell him that he should speak with me, that I respect him, and that I wished to avoid having to destroy the city. Also, tell him I will pardon everyone who surrenders."

He did not respond, but I discovered the Mexicans had significantly fewer warriors and appeared to be using more women and children in battle. On 23 July, at sunrise, we murdered about three hundred residents who were trying to flee Tlatelolco, but we saved two hundred for enslavement. On 24 July, we burned Cuauhtémoc's vacant palace in Tenochtitlan.

On 28 July, I climbed the steps of the Main Temple at Tlatelolco and there saw the dried heads of thirty Castilians but observed we were in charge of about seven-eighths of Tenochtitlan and Tlatelolco.

On 29 July, Mexican lords said that Cuauhtémoc wanted to speak with me, but from across a canal, so I went there. Shortly thereafter, an envoy from him arrived.

"He will not meet you because you will kill him."

"That is not true. In fact, I offer him a bond of safe passage."

They left. I waited two hours for the agent to return.

"The Supreme Ruler will not meet with you. And he said your word is worth nothing to him!"

"Tell your lord that, if he submits without further war and pledges to become a vassal of my king, he can continue to govern as all his predecessors. And tell him I will give him several days to respond," I said.

Cuauhtémoc ended all communication regarding peace, even though everywhere we saw ragged and hollow-cheeked people, but still the Mexicans launched a fierce assault with stones, arrows, and lances that challenged us, because we had little remaining gunpowder.

I moved my headquarters to the roof of a palace in the Amaxac area of Tlatelolco in a tent covered by a red canopy and from there directed Alvarado to advance into the district below, one of the last Mexican strongholds of Tlatelolco.

He killed many and took prisoners, among whom was a Tezcocan prince who was an ally of Cuauhtémoc's. I sent the prince back to Cuauhtémoc with a message to surrender, but Cuauhtémoc's reply was additional offensive action.

In the beginning of August, I asked for a meeting with Cuauhtémoc to negotiate his surrender. He replied he would come the following afternoon. I instructed our allies to construct a platform nearby on which to pile food and beverages and, the next day, five envoys presented themselves, without Cuauhtémoc.

"The Supreme Ruler is ill," one said.

"I am sorry to hear that, but I hope he will come when he is better. Please assure him that I guarantee his safety. Please stay to dine."

They ate well and left. They returned several hours later with Cuauhtémoc's reply.

"The Supreme Ruler said: 'I will never discuss a compromise with you, and you should cease asking. The only way to obtain peace is for you and your dog allies to leave our lands.'"

I refused to concede and tried one more time. They said Cuauhtémoc would be at the Tlatelolco marketplace the following day in the late morning. I waited there for four hours, but he did not appear. It was time to end the war. I addressed all the Spanish and allied captains and issued my orders.

"Beginning at dawn tomorrow, I want a simultaneous onslaught by the Spanish navy and armies and the allied forces, on water and land, and, in one day, kill everyone you see—first the Mexican forces; then turn to civilians, but only those on the streets.

"I want to see the lake red and the streets filled with blood. And the only bodies on the ground should be corpses of the enemy."

Two days later, after having murdered more than forty thousand people, we continued to secure all locations previously controlled by the Mexicans. Cuauhtémoc's envoys approached me across the lines.

"The Supreme Ruler is interested in negotiating peace and asks you to cease fire. If you do so, he will arrive here at sunset."

"I agree to these terms. Tell him I expect him promptly at sunset."

I ordered the armies to halt. We waited for the emperor, but shortly thereafter the enemy assailed us with arrows, spears, and stones. We fought and captured prisoners, three of whom I sent to Cuauhtémoc with another proposal to end the war. Still, there was no response from him, so we continued hostilities. I found out that Cuauhtémoc had executed all his prisoners of war, including the Castilians.

The following morning, before we initiated a new campaign, Cuauhtémoc's officials arrived to announce his message.

"We never surrender! We always fight to the death."

"Tell him this, then: you will soon die," I said.

When the emissaries had departed, I shot harquebuses into the air to signal the allied militaries to recommence fighting, and as I observed from my base on the roof, Alvarado and Olid moved against the Mexicans, who did not resist, forcing them to the lakefront, and prevented civilians from escaping by thrusting them into the water, where they drowned.

That afternoon, I learned that Cuauhtémoc was planning to go to one of his bases on the mainland to restructure his defenses and return to attack us. I called eight captains.

"You have two hours to search for Cuauhtémoc and bring him to me alive. I repeat: I need him alive!"

Olid stayed on land to secure our gains, while Sandoval took command of the eight remaining brigantines to join the hunt for Cuauhtémoc on the lake, where they saw well-attired Mexican families embarking vessels.

One of my captains noticed a group in a large boat with a canopy that appeared to be of high-ranking persons and chased it. When he was near them, he ordered them to stop or he would shoot.

Someone held up his hands, and my captain approached and recognized the emperor. A warrior stood in front of Cuauhtémoc to protect him. The captain shot and killed the bodyguard, and Cuauhtémoc and the others submitted.

The war formally ended 13 August 1521, when my men took Cuauhtémoc and the other rulers with him to stand before me at my base on the roof. Tenochtitlan was quiet. There, I observed all proper protocol due Cuauhtémoc.

"Emperor, I guarantee you will continue to rule as you and your predecessors did before we defeated you. Tell me, sir: Where is your wife?"

He glared at me as I approached him. Cuauhtémoc had married two of Montezuma's daughters, but I had taken one of them as my mistress.

"She is in the lodgings where we have been living in Tlatelolco," Cuauhtémoc said.

I sent Spaniards to guard her. The next day, I convened a ceremony to mark the end of war and the emperor's official surrender. Cuauhtémoc wore a dirty cloak made of quetzal feathers. He and other lords submitted and pledged to become vassals of my Majesty.

"Now that you are subjects of my king, you owe him your obedience," I said to Cuauhtémoc.

He silently stared at me.

"Produce whatever gold and other valuables you were taking when you were trying to flee. I understand you stored them in your quarters in the house we set aside for you."

He ordered a lord to retrieve the items. The man returned with a few gold armbands and discs.

"I need more, much more than that paltry quantity."

"But I thought you had taken all the gold that night we forced you to run from our city."

I ignored Cuauhtémoc's impertinence.

"Yes, but because of your aggression, we were forced to drop it in the water. And now we expect you to replace it. You will bring me two hundred pieces of gold, and each one must be this size." Marina, as I had instructed her, made a large circle with her hands.

"Montezuma owned all the gold of the Mexicans and gave it to you. What I have given you was my personal property. That's all I have," Cuauhtémoc said.

"We will see about that."

When Cuauhtémoc and the others returned to their lodgings, I called a meeting with my captains to plan how we would begin reconstruction of the city. The rotting dead lay in the open, and almost all the edifices were smoldering.

Indian women were disguising their wealth by dressing in rags and covering themselves in mud and hiding gold inside their bodies and clothing. I ordered all soldiers to search them, even the corpses, and to bring me all valuables they found. I then commanded the Castilians to supervise the branding of survivors so we could make a count of the number of slaves at our disposal for rebuilding.

Chapter Thirty-three

THE SPANIARDS: CORTÉS

I made Cuauhtémoc the formal ruler of Tenochtitlan but imprisoned him in Coyoacán with other lords. The day after the war ended, I moved to Coyoacán, in the former palace of a lord, and held a celebration for the Spaniards who had performed well in the conquest.

We had music and ample food and drink, including wine and pork from Santo Domingo, because another ship had recently arrived at Villa Rica, and the captains and I made speeches, and we even danced, as some Castilian ladies were present.

The following morning, the friars held a mass and led a procession that followed an image of the Virgin Mother to the top of a hill, where we saw the lake and the smoking wreckage of the city.

That week, because Cuauhtémoc and Tetlepanquetzatzin, king of Tlacolpan, continued to refuse to provide any gold or precious stones of significance, I ordered four captains to tie them to poles and torture them by oiling their hands and feet and separately setting each body part on fire; neither one ever revealed where he had hidden the valuable goods. Cuauhtémoc became permanently crippled from the injuries he sustained during the interrogation, and Tetlepanquetzatzin died.

We drafted plans to restore Tenochtitlan, but initially I did not want civilians living there and intended to construct only a fortress and military buildings. By the end of 1521, however, I had designed the city to house the Castilians in the center and the outskirts for Indians, to make it even more spectacular than it had been, and to make it resemble a Spanish city. Construction began the winter of 1521–22.

I instructed Cuauhtémoc to command the Indians to return to the city in the areas that were less damaged and ordered him and other noblemen, with the assistance of a wealthy black freedman named Juan Garrido, my friend from Cuba who had arrived at Villa Rica on a ship from Ponce de León's second voyage to La Florida and fought admirably with us in the war, to reconstruct both pipes of the aqueduct from Chapultepec to the city.

I appointed Mexican lords, including Montezuma's son Don Pedro Montezuma, in charge of rebuilding and repopulating Indian areas, reopening the marketplaces, and repairing the canal dividing Tlatelolco from Tenochtitlan. The location I used for my palace in Tenochtitlan was on the site of Montezuma's.

Cuauhtémoc never paused, not even as a prisoner, his quest to reconquer his empire. My spies reported he was making progress inciting rebellion. Then, because I did not want to leave him without my supervision in Tenochtitlan when I went to Honduras to deal with Olid, who had tried to install himself as governor of that territory, I hanged Cuauhtémoc in 1525.

Cuauhtémoc, by his first wife, Montezuma's daughter Xuchimatzatzin, had left an infant son, and after Xuchimatzatzin converted to Catholicism and was christened Doña María, I had her son baptized Diego Mendoza Austria y Montezuma and granted him towns and Indians.

By decree dated 11 October 1522, Emperor Carlos appointed me commander-in-chief, distributor of Indians, and captain general of New Spain, but even before I received documentation of my titles, I had granted land and slaves to my captains, certain noble-born Mexicans, and others, including Juan Garrido, to reward them for their services.

I took Coyoacán, Ecatepec, Chalco, and Otumba, territories that had 1.5 million inhabitants, and I granted Xochimilco to Alvarado, Teotihuacan to Francisco de Verdugo, Tula to Don Pedro Montezuma, and Tlacolpan, surrounding villages, and twelve farms to Doña Isabel, Montezuma's daughter who bore my child.

By 1524, I had prepared to develop the economy of New Spain and ordered all Spaniards to whom I granted land and Indians to oversee the establishment of churches, conversions of the Indians to Catholicism, construction of farms, and importing of European domestic animals. We planted mulberries for silkworms, grape vineyards, and olive groves, and Juan Garrido planted the first wheat fields in New Spain. We also began manufacturing weapons and gunpowder, using sulfur we obtained from the Popocatepetl volcano.

In late June 1522, my wife Catalina Suarez unexpectedly arrived at Villa Rica from Cuba with her sister and their brother Juan Suarez and his wife. At the time, I had multiple mistresses, including Marina, who was carrying my child, and Mexican and Castilian women living with me at my palace at Coyoacán.

Catalina complained about my domestic arrangements and became angry when Marina gave birth to my first son, whom I christened Martín, after my father. About a month later, after a banquet at my home, we had a ball, during which Catalina was enjoying herself but then argued with someone about slave ownership.

"I will do something with my Indians no one will understand," she said.

I asked her, in a loud voice, "What do you mean with *your* Indians?"

Her face and ears turned red, and she fled the hall, but I remained with our guests and invited them to stay and enjoy themselves. About midnight I went to her quarters and found the candles around the room still were lit. Spaniards inside and in the courtyard continued to entertain themselves with music, singing, and guitar playing, and I heard laughing and loud conversations. Catalina was in bed, but awake and crying.

"Go to sleep, and cease behaving like a child. And stop conducting yourself as if you were in command."

She yelled at me, "You are a whoremonger, and you sleep with filthy Indian savages. I despise you, you dirty man!"

"Be quiet, and be careful what you say."

She did not obey.

"You are a cruel man, and I wish you would go to hell."

I was standing next to her and grabbed her by the throat, choking her. She could not speak; her eyes bulged, her face became bloated, and her skin formed large red blotches. I removed my hands, she coughed, and I let her calm herself. When her breathing was normal again, she spoke.

"I'm not afraid of you. My family will protect me from you. I'm going to write a letter and send it to Spain, to the Council of the Indies, and I'm going to report how you have mistreated me and all the Spaniards, and how you sleep with dirty Indian savages and ignore your wife."

"You're a fool if you think anyone in Spain cares about you or any of that or any stupid thing you say. And I'm warning you again: Be careful what accusations you make against me."

She laughed. "Well, then, here's something they *will* care about. I am also going to tell them that you stole gold and other treasures from the king."

I slapped her and used both hands to strangle her, and, as I pressed both thumbs into her windpipe, her necklace broke and beads scattered on the floor. Her lips turned blue, eyes bulged, and nostrils flared, and I smelled a stench of feces and urine; then she became still.

When I realized what I had done, I called my majordomo Isidro Moreno to inform him Catalina was dead and ordered him to deliver a note to her family saying they should see me the next day, as I had bad news for them.

As I instructed him, Moreno sent for chambermaids to prepare Catalina for interment and for Father Olmedo, who went to Catalina's room to confirm she was deceased and prayed for her soul. I instructed Moreno to have a coffin made that night, put Catalina's body in it, and nail it shut. At sunrise, before her people arrived, we buried her in the courtyard behind the chapel next to my palace.

Don Hernándo Cortés
Marques del Valle

Dated: The City of Seville, Spain
The 27th day of January, in
the year of our Lord, 1547

Chapter Thirty-four

THE XOCHIMILCA: FLOWER

I fought under Captain Cipactli on the lake, where we ambushed several of the invaders' vessels by hiding our ships in thick reed beds and surprising their crews, killing a number of them with arrows. Another of our ships, I heard, lured two of theirs to a location that had a hidden sandbar, where their vessels ran aground.

We also were victorious against the foreigners and their allies by using a tactic where we shot them and jumped into the water to resurface at another area to attack. I kept dried tubular reeds on the boat and always took one when I jumped in the water so I could breathe and stay under for long periods of time.

The overwhelming impact on our senses is what I remember most from the final days in Tenochtitlan and Tlatelolco. Everywhere bodies were piled one on top of the other; heads were blown open, exposing their brains; ragged and emaciated people moved aimlessly.

As the invaders and their allies incinerated buildings, bricks and stones fell to the ground; people screamed when shot or lanced or when objects hit them; the foreigners' weapons made popping noises and released a stench like rotten eggs; their war animals made high-pitched sounds; dogs growled; burning flesh let off an acrid stink; gray ashes fell like snowflakes; blood covering the soil released a metallic odor; and dense dust and black smoke forced us to rub our closed eyes.

Toward the end, when Cuauhtémoc realized we could not beat them and the invaders controlled almost all of Tenochtitlan and Tlatelolco, he decided to withdraw to the mainland and plan another strategy to return and reconquer the empire. He ordered people, noble and commoner alike, disguised in rags, mud on their faces and bodies, hiding bundles of gold and precious stones and jewels, to hide in the mountains.

Teputzitoloc sent a command from Cuauhtémoc to Captain Cipactli that ten women warriors in my battalion, including me, should take eight noble families and their servants from Tlatelolco to towns in the mountains, and our payment for that service would be sacks we each carried containing items made of gold, precious stones, and silver.

I never saw Teputzitoloc after the day on the balcony when I shot Moctezoma. My love earned the highest rank as Cuauhtémoc's personal guard and military advisor, but I was just a soldier who did not even reach the status of Jaguar Warrior, so there was no opportunity for us to fight together. I missed him terribly and always asked messengers and others for any word about his well-being.

The nine women warriors and I obeyed, and we departed at night by ship to the western shore of Lake Tezcoco. From there we went inland and up into the mountains and northeast. Travel was difficult and slow, as the noble people had to walk because litters would have been conspicuous; they often needed to rest, and we had to hunt to feed them. Six of the families decided to stay at a village that had farms and was near a small lake.

The rest continued until we reached another area that had access to water and fertile land, and the remaining families and four fighters stayed. The other warriors went on, and it would take us more than a year to go north and around Lake Zumpango, then east, and back south, avoiding populated areas, to reach my ancestral village, Ixhuatepec, where my surviving family and many others had fled the war. I began writing this chronicle my first year in Ixhuatepec.

Mama, I was grieved to find out, had died from an illness when they were walking from Xochimilco. I sat on the ground when I heard Mama had died and cried for some time, thinking about how, once a week, even though it was a lot of work, she made my favorite meal of turkey stew and vegetables. I smiled briefly when I remembered how she laughed when Papa cut flowers from our field and tied them with a string.

"Here, wife—look at what I bought for you at the market in Tlatelolco!"

My sisters who were married, Blossom, Dahlia, Sage, and Jade, and their families had stayed in other villages along the way, but the little ones, my darlings Rose, Calliandra, and Turquoise, whom I helped Papa finish raising, brought me joy.

In those days, our people generally did not express emotion, so when I first saw Papa after our long separation, I did not embrace him. But we both shed tears.

"Papa, oh, Papa—I know everything you did to rescue me, Papa. I even know you tried to prevent Moctezoma from taking me away. I will be forever grateful that you are my papa. If it hadn't been for you, I would be dead."

"You are my girl. Aaah, I had to try to save you. Our family wouldn't have survived if we had lost you for good.

"But aaah, Daughter, even though your mother is gone, the rest of us are still here. We will do our best to take care of the little ones, as your mother asked me to do before she passed."

Papa never remarried, although he spent time with a widowed woman in our village. Ixhuatepec was a vibrant region, and the women warriors blended in with the residents, and each established her own farm, I with Papa, using the wealth I had earned transporting the noble families.

One day, about a year after I had arrived in Ixhuatepec, when Papa and I were working in the field, I became angry. I threw down the shovel I was using and knelt. I pounded the dirt with a fist.

"Daughter, Daughter, what's wrong?"

"I haven't heard anything from Teputzitoloc. Where is he? Why isn't he here?"

"Aaah, Daughter, please be patient a little longer; he's probably still trying to make his way here."

That night, in bed, I was still angry, but in the morning, I cried. Then I remembered Yaretzi and felt guilty that I had not thought about her in a while. I wept for the next four days. I told Papa I was sick so I would not have to go to the field. I am sure he knew the truth. Eventually I went back to work and did my best to pretend that I was not devastated. The sadness never ended.

I waited in my village for my love for five years before I finally accepted a proposal of marriage from a good man. My husband, who was a farmer, passed away fifteen years ago.

I have secluded myself in these mountains and never have gone back down, but, when my oldest child was about ten years old, native priests who belonged to the religion of the invaders came to my village. They wore long black clothing and white collars, their hair was short, and they were clean, yet I was afraid of them.

I refused to go outside my house at first when I heard they were there, but my husband and others, who sold our goods at the market in the town at the base of the mountain, said the clerics would not hurt us. The priests said it was the law that everyone had to learn the foreign tongue and convert to the government's religion.

I wanted nothing to do with them or their beliefs, but since they were the rulers and had a powerful military, I pretended to obey. They built a church and a school, which our children had to attend, but they did not force the adults who were farmers to go to church because we worked every day, and we said we were too old to learn their language.

At home, we continued to teach our children about our gods, but only the ones who made our land fertile and crops plentiful and the climate temperate. We grew vegetables, including corn, beans, onions, peppers, squash and, in the garden behind our house, herbs and flowers in brilliant colors.

I have never ceased loving or thinking about Teputzitoloc. I recently learned his fate from a young man who said he worked for the government and had been searching for me for years. This man found me and came to my home. He had on clothing my sons said was what the foreigners wore, a shirt underneath a jacket that had matching trousers.

He said he was the great-grandson of a warrior who had been one of Cuauhtémoc's bodyguards and had served with Teputzitoloc. The young man claimed I had become famous for killing Moctezoma and fighting valiantly, as he described it, in the battle when we defeated the foreigners and their allies and drove them out of the city that first time they invaded Tenochtitlan and then in the war.

He said his grandfather had told him stories about the wars of resistance and had wanted to find me to relay what had happened to Teputzitoloc, who had perished as a hero. Teputzitoloc, the young man said, had fought alongside Cuauhtémoc to the end, when the invaders seized Cuauhtémoc and his senior officials and generals as they were sailing to his base on the mainland to plan how to beat the foreigners a second time. Teputzitoloc was one of the Eagle Warriors who had tried to prevent Cuauhtémoc's capture, but the foreigners shot and killed him, and his body fell into the lake.

I am thin, and my body is weak, and so my children and grand-children let me sleep most of the day. We all know I soon will die, yet that is something I look forward to, as it means I will see Teputzitoloc in the Overworld, in the heaven reserved for warriors and, these days, I often cannot tell whether I already am there. This morning, I asked my daughters to walk with me to our farm, and, at the center of a mature field of corn, I stood next to my beautiful Teputzitoloc, who wore the same quilted cotton Eagle Warrior's uniform as the day I shot Moctezoma. A forceful wind blew, and my eyes watered.

AFTERWORD

In 1887, the Mexican government dedicated a monument to Cuauhtémoc, the last Mexican ruler, in what today is the most prestigious area in Mexico City. In August 1522, at the end of the War for the Mexican Empire, Cortés imprisoned Cuauhtémoc. In 1525, before he left on an expedition to Honduras to quash a coup by Cristóbal de Olid, Cortés hanged Cuauhtémoc because Cuauhtémoc continued to incite rebellion against the Spaniards.

Cuauhtémoc, as the reader will recall, had married two of Moctezoma's daughters, Xuchimatzatzin, with whom Cuauhtémoc had fathered a son, and Tecuichpo, with whom Cortés fathered a daughter.

After he killed Cuauhtémoc, Cortés named Cuauhtémoc's son Diego Mendoza Austria y Montezuma and granted him towns and slaves. Cuauhtémoc and Moctezoma have living descendants by the lineages of Melchor, Gaspar, and Baltasar, the sons of Diego Mendoza Austria y Montezuma.

Following the conquest, Cortés spent the remainder of his life defending himself in litigation, first in a lawsuit by the family of Catalina Suarez, Cortés's first wife, alleging that Cortés had murdered her, despite the earlier dismissal of criminal charges. Cortés denied killing Catalina Suarez and said she always had been sick, even when they lived in Cuba. Cortés's descendants paid compensation to the successors of Catalina Suarez's family for more than one hundred years.

In 1526, the Spanish Crown sent Judge Luis Ponce de León to Mexico City to commence a legal proceeding against Cortés called a Juicio de Residencia, consisting of a total of 101 allegations that Cortés had failed to pay the royal fifth and embezzled gold and other property, including enslaved people, belonging to the Crown. The accusations also asserted that Cortés had conducted massacres of native people at Cholula and other places, had allowed Pedro de Alvarado's massacre of the native people during the Feast of Toxcatl, had abused his power by beaching ships that did not belong to him, had criminally punished Spaniards who accused him of wrongdoing, had fought Pánfilo de Narváez, tortured Cuauhtémoc, and had taken for himself the best real property in Mexico City and other locations.

Judge de León died the day after dining at Cortés's house, and, soon after, arriving to take Judge Ponce de León's place, a second judge, Marcos de Aguilar, similarly died, probably by poison. Cortés faced public accusations, but the Crown did not prosecute him for the deaths of the judges.

In an attempt to repair his reputation with the monarchy, Cortés loaded gifts for the court, including jewels, gold, and live animals, and sailed to Spain in March 1528 with Gonzalo de Sandoval, Andrés de Tapia, three sons of Moctezoma—Don Martín, Don Pedro, and

Don Juan—and other native nobles. They arrived at Palos, Spain, in May 1528, where Sandoval became ill and died, and someone stole his treasure.

Cortés attended an audience with Carlos V, who granted him the titles Marques of the Valley of Oaxaca and governor "of the islands and territories he might discover in the Southern Sea," gave him one-twelfth of the profits of all his future conquests, and confirmed him as captain general but not governor of Mexico.

In Mexico, after the conquest, Cortés would marry his Cuban concubine Leonor Pizarro to one of his captains, Juan de Salcedo. In his will, Cortés provided well for Catalina Pizarro, his daughter with Leonor Pizarro, by granting her full income from some of his properties in Mexico. After Cortés's death, however, his wife, Juana de Zuniga, would strip Catalina Pizarro of her inheritance and force her to enter the Dominican convent at Sanlúcar de Barrameda in Cádiz, Spain.

The Crown also commenced a Juicio de Residencia against Pedro de Alvarado, but he suffered no punishment for his role in the massacre during the Feast of Toxcatl that led to the flight of the Spaniards and their allies the night of June 30–July 1, 1520, now referred to as the Noche Triste, or "Night of Sorrow."

Alvarado, who became the first governor of Guatemala, engaged in further massacres in Mexico and Central America. During a battle in 1541, indigenous people in Guadalajara, Mexico, killed him.

Cortés returned to Mexico with his wife, his mother, and four hundred others in the spring of 1530 and arrived in Villa Rica de la Vera Cruz on July 15, 1530. When he went to Mexico City, he found his house padlocked and guards posted outside, denying him entry because of the pending Juicio de Residencia.

Cortés took his family to Texcoco, where his mother died. He then went to Cuernavaca, where he built a hacienda, including farms, vineyards, and an olive grove, and brought in enslaved Africans as labor.

Cortés went on expeditions from Mexico on the Pacific with other conquerors, including the Black Spaniard Juan Garrido. While trying to find a strait linking that ocean to the Caribbean, they found and named California.

Cortés and his family returned to Spain in January 1540, but the emperor had turned against him and refused him an audience, chiefly because Mexico produced little wealth for the Crown. Cortés died on December 2, 1547, at Castilleja de la Cuesta, Spain, at the age of sixty-two, and was buried in the chapel of the monastery of San Isidro del Campo, near Seville, Spain, in the family vault of the Dukes of Medina Sidonia.

In May 1566, Cortés's bones were disinterred and moved to the Church of San Francisco in Texcoco, Mexico. In February 1629, the viceroy ordered Cortés's bones disinterred and reburied at the convent of the Church of San Francisco in Mexico City.

In 1794, the viceroy moved Cortés's bones yet again and reburied them in an elaborate mausoleum at the Church of the Immaculate Conception and Jesus of Nazareth, in Mexico City, where the annexed hospital, founded by Cortés, is the longest-running hospital in the Americas.

In 1823, two years after the Mexican War for Independence from Spain had ended, citizens threatened to remove Cortés's bones from the church and burn them in a bonfire to honor the fallen patriots of the War for Independence.

The minister of the interior, to deal with the threat, publicly claimed he had sent Cortés's bones to the Duke of Terranova, the

XIV Marques del Valle, in Italy, where some of Cortés's descendants lived, but actually he had hidden them underneath the hardwood floor at the altar of the Church of the Immaculate Conception and Jesus of Nazareth.

To ensure someone always would know where the bones were buried, the minister sent a letter, stating their location, to the embassy of Spain in Mexico, where it stayed in a vault for 123 years. In 1946, an official at the Spanish Embassy in Mexico City revealed the contents of the minister's 1823 letter.

The Mexican government directed the National Institute of Anthropology and History to exhume and rebury the bones. Cortés's final resting place, purportedly, is a small niche in an inside wall by the altar of the Church of the Immaculate Conception and Jesus of Nazareth marked by a plate that reads: "Hernan Cortes 1485–1547."

APPENDIX

I.
The Rise of Islam

Islam, the theocracy that would conquer territories from Spain to Asia, took root by 632 in what now is Saudi Arabia. The Last Prophet, Muhammad ibn Abdullah, who was born in 570 to a noble Meccan family of the Quraysh dynasty, founded Islam. At the time, polytheism predominated in Arabia, although some practiced Judaism and Christianity.

Muhammad's father, Abdullah, died before he was born. Muhammad's mother, Aminah, who was Jewish, and his grandfather, Abd al-Muttalib, noticed that he was an exceptional child.

As was customary among the prosperous families of Mecca, Aminah placed Muhammad in the care of a Bedouin woman and her husband, who lived in the desert. One afternoon, the couple's son told his parents that, when he and Muhammad were playing, two men had arrived, held down Muhammad, split open his chest, took out his heart, cleansed it, put it back in, and closed his chest.

The foster parents rushed to see Muhammad, still on the ground, pale and shaking. They returned him to Aminah, to whom they repeated what their son had reported.

"I am not surprised; I have seen signs that Muhammad is being prepared for an exceptional fate," Aminah said.

Muhammad and his mother lived in Mecca for two years. When he was six, she took him on a journey to visit her Jewish sisters at Yathrib, a city 200 miles north, founded in the first century by Jewish refugees fleeing Roman persecution. On the way, Aminah became ill and died; Barakah, her servant, delivered Muhammad to his grandfather, Abd al Muttalib. Two years later, Abd al Muttalib also died; Abu Talib, Muhammad's uncle, and his wife, became his guardians.

When Muhammad was twelve, he and Abu Talib went on a trading journey with a caravan going to Syria that stopped at Basra, where they met an influential Christian monk named Bahira, who said he saw a protective cloud around Muhammad. Bahira asked to examine Muhammad's back. He pointed out a skin growth.

"He has had it since birth," Abu Talib said.

"That marking, that marking is—it is the seal of a prophet—which means that Muhammad is destined to be a messenger of God!"

After that voyage, Muhammad, beginning in his teenage years, worked as a sheepherder in the hills by Mecca and, for three years, was a soldier in the Sacrilegious Wars.

He thereafter became a merchant and, by the time he was twenty, had acquired a reputation for trustworthiness. He drew the attention of a wealthy widow named Khadijah bint Khuwaylid, a trader and cousin of a well-known Christian named Waraquah ibn Nawfal. Khadijah asked Muhammad to sell a significant quantity of items for her in Syria and offered to double his commission if he sold all the goods at a high profit. Muhammad accepted and earned twice the amount of gains she had expected.

When Muhammad was twenty-five, Khadija, who was twenty-eight, asked a friend to arrange their marriage. After their families had negotiated a marital contract, they wed and settled in Mecca, where he became a prosperous businessman and politician. They had six children, two of whom died in childhood.

By the age of thirty-five, Muhammad was a spiritual man who regularly engaged in retreats and meditation. Among his favorite places to conduct these activities was at a cave in the hills, located at Hira, outside Mecca. Muhammad sometimes went there with food and water and stayed for a month; to reach it, he had to climb a mountain, cross an overpass, and walk to the other side.

One day, in 610, his fortieth year, Muhammad set out alone. He arrived as the sun was painting the rocky ground orange and red. He heard a voice but saw no one.

"Peace be upon you, Messenger of God!"

Muhammad ascended to the opening of a womb Allah had carved into the Earth. He entered; the cave smelled musty. Muhammad sneezed. After his vision had adjusted to the darkness, he chose a spot, knelt, lowered his head, and stretched out his arms in front of him, palms up.

He closed his eyes and inhaled for six seconds, held his breath in for another six, then exhaled, also for six, and he repeated this exercise hundreds of times, until he had cleared his mind of all distractions, his body was cool, and he had regulated the beating of his heart. He prayed, asking Allah for guidance and inspiration.

He stopped when a gentle, yet firm, force made him lower his arms and put his hands palms down on the ground, straighten his spine, and touch his forehead to the black soil. He heard a voice.

"Rise, and open your eyes."

He obeyed. The Archangel Gabriel was there, in human form, but with 600 wings.

"Read!"

"I do not know how to read."

"Read!"

"I do not know how to read."

The Archangel Gabriel held Muhammad by the shoulders and squeezed him; he squeezed him so hard Muhammad's entrails almost burst. The Archangel Gabriel released him and proclaimed the first Revelation.

"Read in the name of the Lord, who created humankind out of a clinging clot. Read; your Lord is the most bountiful, he who taught by means of the pen, taught humankind that which they did not know."

The Archangel Gabriel departed. The Prophet Muhammad was frightened, thinking he had gone insane, and, trembling, he left the cave and returned to Khadijah. He asked her to hold him; she covered him with a cloak and embraced him. When he was calm, he told her what had happened and said he was afraid; she comforted him until he went to sleep.

The next day, Khadijah consulted with her cousin Waraqah ibn Nawfal and relayed The Prophet Muhammad's experience. Waraqah replied that he had been waiting for The Archangel Gabriel to present himself and issue a Revelation from God to a prophet of the people. Waraqah met with The Prophet Muhammad and assured him he had been blessed by God's angel but warned him that many, including in his own community, would call him a liar and attack him.

After speaking with Waraqah, The Prophet Muhammad went back to the cave, but the Archangel Gabriel did not appear. He left. He returned once a week for a period of six months, but Allah still sent him no Revelation. The Prophet thought Allah had abandoned him. A number of times he left home and climbed to the top of a mountain intending to jump off, but on each occasion the Archangel Gabriel appeared.

"Do not take your own life! God rewards the faithful and the patient."

One evening, as The Prophet was alone in the cave, the Archangel Gabriel appeared and proclaimed another Revelation.

"Allah has not forsaken you. Rise! Go back to Mecca, and disseminate what you have learned, but first only to those closest to you. Allah will send further instructions on how to present His message to the larger community."

The Archangel Gabriel continued to deliver Revelations. In the first three years, after the first set of Revelations, however, only forty people accepted Islam, including Khadijah; but then the word of Allah spread, and more learned to recite the Expression of Faith: "I bear witness there is no god but Allah, and Muhammad is His messenger."

The Prophet approached the chiefs of his own tribe, the Quraysh, and invited them to a speech at the top of Mount as-Safa, where he castigated them for practicing polytheism. He told them to recognize and believe in God, the One. Many became angry, including his own uncle, and left, although the initial forty converts stayed with him.

The Quraysh afterwards said he was possessed, insane, and a sorcerer and taunted him by ordering him to perform miracles. The husbands of The Prophet's daughters divorced them, and his uncles' wives threw garbage on the street as he passed them, but The Prophet Muhammad continued to preach that people should abandon their false gods.

Most, especially the wealthy and powerful of Mecca, resented the criticism directed at them for being polytheistic. Hostility turned into violence and other persecution of The Prophet and his followers, now known as Muslims. Then, in an attempt to stop the spread of Islam, the Quraysh instituted a three-year ban against the Muslims, forbidding Arabic clans from trading with or marrying them.

The next important phase of The Prophet's life became known as the Year of Grief, 619, when his wife, Khadija, and then his uncle, Abu Talib, died. The Quraysh's opposition intensified. They called him pejorative names and even threw dirt and excrement at him.

The Night Journey and Ascension was the following critical experience in The Prophet's life. One evening, still in mourning, he dressed, covered his head, and went to the mosque to pray. He was alone. He entered the sanctuary and knelt, but, when he lowered his head to the floor, his thoughts became scrambled, until he thought only of light.

Illumination pierced The Prophet Muhammad's brain, and its brilliance pushed out all other images. He did not notice that six hours had elapsed, his back was stiff, or that the hard floor had broken the skin on his now-bloodied forehead, knees, and palms. He went outside, where the tomb of his ancestors Hagar and Ishmael was located, and fell asleep on the ground.

He woke when he heard a melodic voice.

"Rise and open your eyes, son of the Lord."

The Prophet obeyed. He saw different luminescence; now there were rays of red, orange, yellow, green, blue, indigo, and violet. The Archangel Gabriel and a winged horse appeared.

"The Lord, our God, has commanded me to take you on a journey," the Archangel Gabriel said.

The Archangel Gabriel mounted the horse, held the reins, and told The Prophet to sit behind him. They flew. As they rose, the Archangel Gabriel told him to look down at the glory of God's creations. The Prophet Muhammad felt sorrow to have to divert his attention from the wondrous universe above but was ecstatic to see the desert, fires people had lit, caravans of sleeping camels, the tops of palm, fruit, and pine trees, olive groves, and houses carved into mountaintops.

They crossed the Dead Sea, the lowest point on Earth, the Archangel Gabriel said, as he pointed out monasteries built into cliff walls. They reached the next body of water; The Prophet was astounded at the enormity of the Mediterranean, noting the white sand on its beaches.

They turned back in the direction of Jerusalem, which they surveyed at a slower speed. The Prophet never had seen such a large city. It had red clay roofs, palaces trimmed in gold, buildings constructed of off-white bricks, and churches with tall spires and crosses. They descended onto a quiet street. It was midnight. Some houses had open shutters; a woman kneaded bread, a man read the holy word by candlelight, and children and the elderly slept.

The Archangel Gabriel led him to the site of the ancient Jewish temple, today the Mosque of the Dome of the Rock. There, Adam, Jesus, John, Joseph, Enoch, Aaron, Abraham, and Moses greeted them. Together, they prayed, after which the Archangel Gabriel told The Prophet to stand straight, arms by his sides.

A vertical tube of platinum light surrounded them and propelled them upwards.

"Do not be afraid, my child. You have been obedient and have not questioned any part of this voyage. Our Lord is pleased, and He has commanded me to accompany you to His throne."

The Prophet gave a prayer of thanks, although he did not understand any part of what had transpired that night. He had never been outside Arabia and wondered if, as He had recently done to Khadijah and his uncle Abu Talib, Allah had taken possession of his soul and called him home, but that thought made him euphoric. He accepted his fate and surrendered himself to Allah.

The cylinder transported the Archangel Gabriel and The Prophet up, up through the seven stages of heaven, in what seemed to the mortal mere moments. They stopped, and the Archangel Gabriel told The Prophet that they had arrived at the Lotus of the Utmost Boundary, the farthest anyone could go, two bows' length from Allah.

The other Archangels, Michael, Raphael, Uriel, Raguel, Remiel, and Saraquel appeared. The Prophet Muhammad wept when he heard rapturous music and saw butterflies made of translucent sheets of gold.

All sound ceased. The Prophet lowered his head and closed his eyes until the Archangel Gabriel told him to open them and look up. Before him was an infinite number of colorful rays: the shield of Allah. The Prophet knelt. He bent his back, stretched out his arms, hands palm down, and lowered his forehead. He heard a mellifluous and comforting voice.

"We have called you to stand in Our presence because We heard your pleas and have chosen you to deliver Our word to more of Our creations and continue to guide them to the straight path.

"You must continue to listen carefully and memorize everything the Archangel Gabriel tells you and ensure it is thereafter set in writing.

"You have Our blessings, and We grant you relief from your grief. We are all-knowing, and will continue to guard and protect you, at all times. Rise."

The Archangels, except for Gabriel, had disappeared. He directed The Prophet not to a cylinder, but to the winged horse, and they departed. When he next saw Earth, from above, it was a black sphere encircled by blue light. They returned to Mecca.

After the Night Journey and Ascension, as people learned that the Archangel Gabriel had taken The Prophet to the presence of

Allah, his message attracted numerous converts but also the attention of nonbelievers, who mocked him. Even some of his own supporters were skeptical.

Although Jews founded Yathrib and were the second major population there, polytheistic Arabic tribes, the Banu Qaylah and Banu al-Khazraj, controlled the city. The main Jewish tribes in Yathrib were the Banu Qurayzah, the Banu Qaynuqa, and the Banu Nadir.

The Arabs of Yathrib were among the first to support The Prophet and accept his beliefs, when they met him on a pilgrimage in 622 and invited him to establish a community in their territory. The Prophet accepted their offer but first returned home to Mecca, from where he sent many of his followers ahead to Yathrib.

The Quraysh of Mecca, however, did not cease to oppose him, because he continued to convert people to Islam, and, when they threatened to assassinate him and stole his property, he fled with a few supporters to Yathrib. After his escape, almost all of the remaining Muslims left Mecca and joined him in Yathrib, which would become known as Madinat al-Nabi (the City of The Prophet) and, later, Medina.

At Medina, The Prophet agreed to serve as a judge for the residents, including Jewish and other non-Muslim people. Most of the Arabs would accept Islam, but the Jews, although they initially permitted him to preach to them, rejected him because his teachings conflicted with Jewish scripture. The Prophet, for example, preached that Abraham and Ishmael, Abraham's son by the Egyptian Hagar, were the fathers of Islam.

The Muslims started amassing resources for holy war against the Meccans by engaging in armed raids, known as *jihad*, on the trade route to and from Mecca. A seminal event in the history of Islam, the Battle of Badr, took place in the Muslims' second year in Medina. The Battle at Badr initially was planned as a *jihad* on a Meccan caravan carrying booty along the coast after trading in Syria.

When The Prophet's scouts reported that the Meccan caravan was near Badr, where the roads from the Red Sea to Mecca, Medina, and Syria converged, he ordered 628 Muslims to seize the merchants' property by force. Abu Sufyan, leader of the Meccan caravan, when his spies told him about the impending attack, sent an envoy to Mecca for military assistance.

A force of 950 departed Mecca and, when they arrived outside Badr, evaded the Muslims by going around the city. Abu Sufyan communicated to Abu Jahl, commander of the Meccan army, that the caravan was safe.

When the Meccan soldiers heard that their traders were on the way home, 350 of them also decided to leave Badr, but Abu Jahl resolved still to go to war against the Muslims with the remaining warriors to discourage them from conducting future *jihads*. The Muslims, in the meantime, did not know the caravan had escaped. They continued to Badr.

The Meccans arrived, and warfare started, after which the Muslims claimed victory. The Muslims killed fifty Meccans, including Abu Jahl, whom The Prophet beheaded, and they seized forty-three prisoners; the Meccans murdered fourteen Muslim soldiers. Badr unified the Muslims, raised The Prophet's standing, and drew polytheistic Arabs to convert to Islam.

After Badr, The Prophet turned to cementing his power in Medina, starting with assassinations of Jewish proselytes. He ordered his followers to kill Abu Afak, an old man who had written a poem criticizing The Prophet, and Asma bint Marwan for protesting Afak's murder.

The Prophet then focused on the Qaynuqa, the smallest of the three Jewish tribes of Medina. He sent for all members of the Qaynuqa to assemble in their marketplace square. There, he commanded them to convert to Islam or he would go to war against them. The Qaynuqa refused to accept him as a prophet or convert to Islam, so he imprisoned them in their fort for fifteen days, until they surrendered.

Then, he ordered them taken out, hands bound behind their backs, to have them executed, but Ibn Salul, a powerful Arabic friend of the Qaynuqa, persuaded him to expel them from Medina. After The Prophet had banished the Qaynuqa, he seized their marketplace, and the Muslims divided the booty, with The Prophet getting one-fifth.

The Prophet then turned to the Nadir, a wealthy Jewish tribe with extensive landholdings. Ka'bb b. al-Asraf, a Jewish leader, whose father was an Arab and his mother a member of the Nadir, sought assistance from the Meccans and told them that The Prophet had boasted about his victory at Badr.

When The Prophet heard this, he had Ka'bb assassinated and his head delivered to him. He then commanded the Muslims to seize the property of the Nadir and conduct a siege against them, which ended when they surrendered, on the condition they be allowed to emigrate to Syria. Many of them went there, although a good number fled north, to Khaybar, another Jewish community. After the Muslim attacks on the Qaynuqa and Nadir, the third Jewish tribe, Qurayza, rescinded an existing treaty with The Prophet.

In 625, when the Muslims had cut off all Meccan trading routes to Syria, the Meccans declared war on the Muslims. A Meccan army of 3,000 marched to Uhud, where they camped.

The Prophet left for Uhud with 1,000 warriors after his uncle, Ibn Assas, had provided him intelligence about the Meccan army's strategic plans. When the Muslims arrived, battle was joined. At first, the Muslims killed a significant number of Meccans, but then Muslims looted the undefended Meccan camp, providing an opportunity for a Meccan captain to assault the Muslims from the rear flank.

The Meccans gained control over the Muslims, who now fled haphazardly, and they hit The Prophet in the head with an arrow, smashing his face, breaking a tooth, and making him fall. His soldiers lifted him as they ran to a hill. The Meccans, however, withdrew without attacking Medina.

After losing at Uhud, The Prophet Muhammad proclaimed that, going forward, there would be two armies: one, Allah's, and the other composed of all nonbelievers who opposed Allah, including the Meccans, Jews, and Christians.

After Uhud, The Prophet heard about new Meccan plans to assault the Muslims, so he ordered a trench built around the exposed areas of Medina. The Meccans arrived near Medina in early February 627. The trench, which was more than a mile long, prevented them from penetrating Medina. After twenty-seven days of skirmishes, they retreated.

The Prophet next attacked the third Jewish tribe of Medina, the Qurayza. He held them in siege for twenty-five days, until their leaders sent a message to The Prophet asking permission to consult with a Muslim ally, Abu Lubaba. Abu Lubaba entered the Qurayza's fortress and said that The Prophet was planning to kill them; he advised them to surrender, on the condition they be allowed to depart.

The Qurayza agreed to be banished, but The Prophet replied that he had appointed Sa'd b. Mu'adh to decide their sentence.

When another Muslim sympathetic to the Qurayza heard this, he pled with The Prophet to allow them to depart without further punishment, but The Prophet maintained that Sa'd b. Mu'adh would render judgment. Sa'd b. Mu'adh decreed all Qurayza men killed, their property divided among the Muslims, and the women and children taken as captives.

Sa'd b. Mu'adh ordered the male prisoners escorted to the market, where the Muslim army had dug trenches. There, Muslim soldiers led the Jewish men, bound in iron chains at the wrist with their arms behind their backs, and forced them to the ditches. The Prophet and Sa'd b. Mu'adh beheaded each one and threw him in a trough. All Jewish boys had to display their pubic areas; anyone who had pubic hair similarly was murdered.

After executing 650 Qurayza men and boys who had reached puberty, The Prophet distributed the women and children to his soldiers. He proposed marriage to Raihana bint Amr b. Khunafa, daughter of a wealthy leader of the Banu Qurayza, but she refused to convert to Islam, so he raped her and made her his concubine.

After the massacre of the Qurayza, The Prophet launched a strategy to make peace with the Meccans. He devised the first part of a campaign in which he led a battalion of soldiers, all dressed as pilgrims, that marched to the outskirts of Mecca. From there he sent an envoy to discuss peace with Quraysh leaders. He negotiated a treaty to last ten years, with the condition that Muslims not enter Mecca that time and return to Medina, but they could begin annual pilgrimages to Mecca the following year.

The Muslims returned to Medina and remained there for the lesser pilgrimages, after which The Prophet initiated a plan for subjugating the Jews of Khaybar, where some of the Jews had fled when he had expelled them from Medina.

First, the Muslims went to a city called al-Hudaybiya and killed Abu Rafi, an important Jewish leader; then they departed and marched three days to Khaybar. When the Jewish men of a nearby town named Ghatafan heard the Muslims were on their way to massacre their brethren in Khaybar, they left to defend them, but an agent reported the Muslims were about to attack Ghatafan, and they returned home.

The Muslims, who had arrived close to Khaybar, slept in the outskirts that night. At dawn, as most Jews slept, they entered and killed many of the men and older boys. Afterwards, they plundered the city and captured the Governor, Kinana b. al-Rabi b. Abul-Huqayq, and his wife, Safiya d. Huyayy b. Akhtab.

The Prophet learned that Kinana had the treasure of the Nadir, so he tortured him with a heated block of iron, until he revealed the location of the valuable goods. The Prophet then beheaded Kinana and proposed marriage to Safiya, if she became a Muslim; she consented. The Prophet did not kill all the Jews but enslaved the survivors and distributed some of the women and children to his soldiers as booty.

After the Khaybar massacre, The Prophet went to Mecca for a pilgrimage, and, this time, according to the treaty of the prior year, the Meccans let the Muslims have access to the city undisturbed for three days before going back to Medina. There, The Prophet formulated a strategy to further ingratiate himself with the Quraysh, at the Battle of Hunayn. The Battle of Hunayn had started as a conflict between the Meccans and their foes, the Hawazin and the Thaqif, who lived in the walled city Al-Ta'if.

The Prophet volunteered to fight alongside the Meccans when Malik b. Awf, leader of the Hawazin, threatened them. Fighting began in January 630. The Hawazin at first dominated, but the Meccans and Muslims rallied and beat the Hawazin.

The Hawazin thereafter joined the Muslims and converted to Islam. By the end of 630, after The Prophet Muhammad had finalized his conquest of Al-Ta'if, the Thaqif also converted to Islam.

By 632, almost all of Arabia had converted to Islam. That year, in June, The Prophet Muhammad died, after having suffered a three-year illness which had begun when he ate a meal prepared by Jewish women, immediately after his massacre of the Jewish people at Khaybar. He died in the home of his favorite wife, Aisha, whom he had married when she was nine years old.

Abu Bakr, Umar, Uthman, and Ali, jointly known as the Rightly Guided Caliphs, were the first four successors to The Prophet Muhammad.

There was strife within the Muslim community after The Prophet's death because one group, known as the Shi'is, believed that his descendants, beginning with Ali, should have succeeded The Prophet.

Another faction, the Umayyads, who would play an important part in the conquest of Spain, considered themselves the traditional wing of the faith. The Umayyads rose after Ali as the first political dynasty of the Sunnis, now the main branch of Islam.

II.

The Muslim Conquest of Spain

Turning to Spain, now in 710, a group of Visigothic nobles elected Roderick as their monarch, instead of Akhila, son of the late King Witiza. Akhila went to the northeast, where he launched war against Roderick, who, at the time, was preoccupied fighting the Hispano-Romans. Roderick's vulnerability was the main cause of the next significant period in Spain's history, in July 710, when four hundred Muslims from North Africa sailed there to explore.

In early 711, as no one had objected to their presence the prior year, Tariq ibn Ziyad, governor of Tangier, led 12,000 men to Spain, where they built a base camp near Gibraltar. By the time Roderick knew about the invasion and arrived with a small army to defend his lands, the Muslims were entrenched, defeated his force, and killed him, after which Tariq sent troops to Córdoba. Communities in that city that had been repressed by the Visigoths, including a large Jewish population, pledged their support to Tariq, who captured Córdoba and Toledo.

Tariq's overlord, Masa ibn Nasayr, governor of North Africa, thereafter landed in Spain with an army of 18,000 to subjugate Carmona, Seville, and Mérida; then Tariq and Masa met in Toledo. The following year, Tariq moved north and captured Narbonne.

Once established, the Muslims engaged in mass enslavement and sent 30,000 Christians to the Caliph in Damascus as the royal fifth in booty. In 716, after the Muslims had conquered most of Spain, they renamed it Al-Andalus.

Pelayo, a Visigothic noble, was the first leader of the Christian resistance, who, in 718, defeated a Muslim army. When Pelayo died, in 737, Alfonso I, "the Catholic," proclaimed that the war against the Muslims was a religious one.

Alfonso I died in 757, but Alfonso II inherited a robust Crown and successfully repelled three Muslim attacks. By the mid-ninth century, the northern section of Spain was Christian.

Alfonso VI in 1085 triggered consequential events by conquering the important Muslim city, Toledo, and folding it into Castile. The Muslim ruler of Seville, in turn, called upon the Almoravids of Morocco for help against the Christian kings.

In response, Yusuf ibn-Tashufin crossed the strait with a large army in 1086 to rout the Christians near Badajoz, after which he went back home. Four years later, with a larger army, Yusuf returned and trounced Alfonso. He united Morocco and Muslim Spain under Berber rule.

Yusuf's successors maintained that power for fifty years, until the beginning of the era that became known as the *Reconquista*, when foreign Catholic monarchies and the papacy sent armies to Spain, bringing with them advanced military tactics, weaponry, new techniques in naval warfare, and financial support for campaigns against Muslims.

The Almohads of Morocco invaded the Iberian Peninsula in 1172 and conquered a large section of al-Andalus. In 1195, the Almohads defeated Alfonso VIII of Castile, causing Pope Innocent III to direct

Christian kingdoms across Europe to join forces against them, but it would not be until July 1212 that Catholic armies won a decisive battle against the Muslims at Las Navas de Toloso.

By the end of the thirteenth century, the Christians had retaken most of Spain, leaving only Granada in Muslim control.

III.

The Fall of Constantinople and New Muslim Threats to Conquer Spain Force Isabella and Fernando to Seek a Western Trade Route to Asia

By 1492, war against Portugal and a twelve-year war against the Muslims of Granada had depleted the Spanish treasury, but Spain could not raise income because it did not have access to valuable trade routes to Asia, as they had been long been blocked by the Turkish Empire.

The menace from the Turkish Empire had its roots in 1421, when the Ottoman Murad II ascended the throne. In 1430 Murad won Thessaloniki, the principal center of the Venetian Republic's trade route in the Levant. In response to the Turkish aggression, Pope Eugenius IV called for holy war against the Ottomans, but, because of a schism between the western and eastern churches and political conflicts among the Christian rulers, only the Holy See acted against the Muslims.

Murad's youngest son, Mehmed II, later known as Mehmed the Conqueror, was born in 1432 to a Jewish mother who was a concubine in Murad's harem. Mehmed, who became his father's favorite son, lived with his mother in the palace harem in his early years, where scholars educated the young boy.

Murad died in 1451. As Mehmed was consoling his father's highest-ranking wife, one of his henchmen, as Mehmed had ordered, strangled her infant son in another part of the palace.

Emperor Constantine XI sent envoys to deliver condolences for Murad's death and ask for affirmation of their peace treaties. Mehmed promised never to interfere with Constantine or any of the Byzantine emperors and, to seal the contract, Mehmed granted Constantine an allowance for the maintenance of an Ottoman prince named Orhan, Mehmed's cousin, who was living at the Byzantine court.

As Mehmed was traveling, however, Constantine's messengers arrived at Mehmed's camp and said that Mehmed had not paid Orhan's allowance and, unless he doubled it, Orhan would make a claim to the Turkish throne. Mehmed departed for his capital, Edirne.

When Mehmed reached the Bosporus Straits, however, they had been blocked by Byzantine ships, and he had to take a different route to Edirne. There, he commanded his governor to build a fortress on the shore of the Bosporus and a Byzantine deserter to build a cannon that could shatter Constantinople's walls. That news rapidly reached Constantine and other western rulers, including the Spaniards.

Once he controlled the Bosporus straits, Mehmed attacked Constantine's brothers to prevent them from going to Constantinople to assist him.

The conquest of Constantinople began on April 2, 1453. Mehmed had about 80,000 soldiers, while Constantine's forces numbered only 7,000. When Mehmed arrived outside Constantinople, his advance team put heavy artillery at strategic locations. Mehmed made his base camp on a hill facing the St. Romanus Gate.

The morning of April 6, the front column of soldiers marched, until they were about a mile from Constantinople. Later that day, Constantine and 3,000 men took their positions at St. Romanus Gate. The Ottomans and the Byzantines exchanged cannon fire; fighting continued throughout that day and night.

The Turks, however, could not make progress against the double wall, even with the massive cannon. Mehmed ordered his generals to attack, but the Byzantines won that first battle, killing about 12,000 Ottoman soldiers. Mehmed's cannon still could not breach the wall, so he tried to take Constantinople in a surprise raid, but Constantine's warriors forced back the Turks.

It was not until April 21 that the Ottomans finally succeeded in breaking down a portion of St. Romanus Gate, using an ingenious technique that prevented Constantine's naval crews from providing support to his soldiers in the city. Mehmed's armies moved part of his fleet overland by clearing a route, covering it in planking, and greasing the planking with sheep and ox tallow. Men placed rollers on the planking and pushed seventy-two ships from the Bosporus to the waters of the Golden Horn, where the Turks assaulted the Byzantine fleet.

Mehmed commanded the Ottomans to continue cannon fire upon the city, until groups of Constantine's soldiers deserted. Mehmed sent envoys to advise Constantine to surrender, but Constantine refused, saying everyone was prepared to defend Constantinople until they died.

On May 29, just before sunrise, the Turkish armies charged Constantinople, but, first, Mehmed sent his weakest troops into battle, after ordering his upper rank to disarm them and beat them with whips and iron rods, solely so the Byzantines would wear themselves out killing entire battalions of these abused men.

The war reached its apex when Turks climbed over the double wall at various locations, until they had outnumbered the Byzantine soldiers inside the city. The Ottomans killed a sizeable number of fighters, including Constantine.

The Ottoman army, as Mehmed remained outside the wall, plundered the city, forcing civilians to seek sanctuary in the Hagia Sophia. The Turks followed them to enter the cathedral, assault people, wreck statues of saints, and seize booty.

In the meantime, across the city, the Turks repeated similar acts at churches and palaces, while Mehmed remained outside the city at his camp, facing the now-demolished St. Romanus Gate. When his generals told Mehmed that Constantine was dead, he commanded his troops to find the emperor's body, which they did, under a pile of corpses, identified by his purple shoes. As Mehmed had instructed, soldiers cut off Constantine's head and spiked it on a tall pole, where it was displayed until nightfall. It was never known where, or if, his head and body were buried.

Mehmed entered Constantinople the afternoon of May 29; his first stop was the Hagia Sophia, where he declared: "There is only one God, and Muhammad is his Prophet."

The Ottoman military pillaged the city for three days, until Mehmed ordered his forces to retreat. He renamed the city Istanbul and departed June 4 with additions for his harem, Byzantine women and girls, and royal captives, including two of Constantine's nephews. Not long after, he transferred Jewish families from Thessaloniki and other places to repopulate Istanbul.

Venice was the first of the western powers to learn about the conquest of Constantinople, and, as other western European rulers learned that the Ottoman Empire had annihilated the center of the Byzantine Empire, fear spread about who would be Mehmed's next target.

In 1454 and 1455, Mehmed attacked Serbia and Hungary. Next, he invaded Athens and Corinth in 1456, causing further unease among the Spaniards, who had close ties with the Greeks. By 1459, Mehmed had conquered all of Serbia and, by 1462, all the Black Sea coast of Anatolia.

In 1469, Isabella heard a report that the Turks had massacred more than 20,000 near Vienna and that Mehmed was planning war against western Europe, beginning with the kingdoms along the southern Mediterranean coastline.

Mehmed invaded Scutari, on the Adriatic coast, with more than 80,000 troops, but the Albanians prevailed. The Ottomans returned there in 1479, at which time the Albanians surrendered.

In 1481 the Turks invaded Italy, at Otranto, where they killed 800 people and forced 8,000 onto ships and into slavery in Albania. In early 1481, Mehmed announced another attack on western Europe, without divulging where he was going to land his enormous fleet, but the Spanish Crown feared he was going to North Africa and then Spain.

Isabella concluded that it was time to begin the *Reconquista* of Granada. During Christmas week, however, Muslim forces were the first to strike, at Zahara, killing many residents and securing the town. The war against the Muslims of Granada would last almost twelve years, after substantial casualties and financial losses on both sides, forcing Isabella to consider Columbus' proposal to find a route to Asia through the west.

Mehmed would not achieve his goal of conquering all of Europe and did not invade Spain. He died in 1481, leading to a succession fight between his sons Bayezid II and Cem Sultan; Bayezid II won.

IV.
Isabella and Fernando

Isabella of Castile was the daughter of King Juan II of Castile and his second wife, Isabel. King Juan's first wife had been María, who resented the influence that Alvaro de Luna, her husband's close friend and advisor, had on him, so she ordered Luna out of the court. Shortly thereafter, María developed swollen purple sores over her body and face and died. Luna swiftly arranged King Juan's second marriage, to Isabel of Portugal.

A descendant of Pelayo, the Visigothic rebel, Isabella had his fair complexion, with reddish-blond hair and blue eyes. She was born in April 1451, when her older brother, Enrique, King Juan's son with María, was twenty-six and married to his cousin Blanca. Isabel's second child after Isabella was named Alfonso, born in 1453.

King Juan died in 1454, when Isabella was three, and his will provided Isabel custody of her two children, but only if she remained chaste. He left Isabella and Alfonso substantial income and property. When Enrique assumed the throne, however, he disregarded King Juan's testament concerning Isabella and Alfonso by giving away the properties and income their father had bequeathed to his second family.

In 1455, Enrique declared war on the Muslims of Granada. That year, Enrique divorced his wife, Blanca, claiming they had not had a child because they never consummated their marriage, as she had bewitched him and made him unable to get an erection. At the legal proceedings, Enrique arranged for two women to testify that he had paid them to have sex. When the legal action had concluded, he promptly wed Juana of Portugal, but he could not have sex with her, either, disappointing court officials.

In 1457, Enrique arranged a marriage for Isabella, then six years old, to their cousin Fernando, the younger son of King Juan II of Aragon. In 1461, when Isabella was ten, Enrique, still childless, ordered Isabella and Alfonso sent to him at his court in Córdoba.

Queen Juana, Enrique's wife, at the time was having sexual intercourse with Beltrán de la Cueva, a member of Enrique's inner circle, who also was Enrique's lover, and she finally became pregnant and had a girl named Juana. A few days after little Juana's birth, Enrique granted Beltrán de la Cueva the title Count of Ledesma; soon thereafter, Enrique's enemies questioned Juana's legitimacy, calling her "La Beltráneja."

Enrique became increasingly unpopular, and the Castilian nobles publicly announced that they no longer supported him. They issued a document demanding that Enrique dismiss his Moorish bodyguard, who, according to them, had raped men and women, discharge his lover Beltrán de la Cueva, rescind his title, and proclaim little Juana legitimate.

A significant number of aristocrats rebelled, and, on June 5, 1465, a faction in Ávila publicly dethroned Enrique in effigy and put a crown on the head of his twelve-year-old brother Alfonso. Enrique moved Isabella to Segovia to be with him, while Alfonso remained in custody of the nobles, who continued Alfonso's claim to the throne and engaged in battles against Enrique, culminating in war August 1467.

Alfonso led his own troops and forced Enrique to flee the field of battle. Alfonso entered Segovia to take custody of Isabella, who pledged her allegiance to him and accompanied his army for the next three months, after which they retreated to their mother's castle.

The aristocrats, however, subsequently turned against Alfonso and back to Enrique, partly because Alfonso opposed an attack in Toledo against Jewish people known as *conversos* who had converted to Christianity, whereas Enrique encouraged violence against them. Alfonso and Isabella immediately left to fight when they heard hostilities had begun in Toledo.

Alfonso went to sleep early one evening, after dinner, but did not rise the following morning at his usual time; he had a swollen tongue and a blackened mouth, and Isabella called a physician, who was unable to treat him. Alfonso died that afternoon; Isabella wrote officials throughout Castile that he had died of the plague but did not state she suspected Enrique had had him poisoned.

Isabella publicly circulated a letter asking for peace and stating that Enrique would be king of Castile and León, if he ruled properly and restored order, and that she was his successor to the throne of Castile and León.

Enrique sent envoys to negotiate with Isabella, and they reached agreement that she was his heir, she would own certain towns, she would not be forced to marry against her wishes, and he promised to divorce his wife.

Isabella, however, was making plans to marry seventeen-year-old Fernando, king of Sicily, whose mother was born Jewish and who was destined to rule Aragon. But there was a major obstacle to the wedding: Isabella and Fernando needed dispensation from the pope to marry, as they were cousins. Unable to get the waiver from Rome, King Juan pressured the papal legate in Spain to forge one. They were married on October 19, 1469, at the home of an aristocratic Jewish family in Valladolid.

Isabella attempted to persuade Enrique to reconcile with her, but when she did not succeed, she worked against Enrique, and more of the nobility transferred their support to her because she promised them land grants when she became queen.

Isabella tried again, after four years, to meet with Enrique and persuaded him to visit her in Segovia. The reunion initially went well, but after dinner Enrique became sick and claimed Isabella had poisoned him; he left for Madrid. Enrique never recovered from the illness that began at Segovia, and he died in Madrid on December 11, 1474.

Isabella was in Segovia when she learned of her brother's death. She ordered immediate transfer of the treasury to her control; then she announced Enrique was deceased. She put on white serge mourning clothes to attend a funeral mass with a procession at the Church of San Martín. Later she returned to the palace and changed into opulent dress and gold jewelry with precious stones; then she returned to the same church, where she crowned herself queen.

In Portugal, King Afonso V had won consequential victories in North Africa. Afterward, he turned his attention to Castile and León. He engaged himself to little Juana, who now, according to Afonso V, claimed that Isabella and Fernando had poisoned her father and illegally seized his throne. Isabella ignored Afonso V's demands, and he started war against Castile and León in May 1475.

Isabella and Afonso V battled for nine months, but the most important conflict was the Battle of Toro. On March 1, 1476, about a thousand died, forcing Afonso V to flee and Fernando's troops to capture the Portuguese royal standard.

Afonso V, who had married his niece, little Juana, deserted her after the Battle of Toro and abandoned war against Isabella. Hostilities between the nations did not end, however, and skirmishes continued until 1479. Isabella insisted the terms of the truce provide that little Juana would enter a convent, and she conceded to Portuguese dominion of any newly discovered lands on the west coast of Africa.

V.

Columbus and the Conquest of La Española and Puerto Rico

Christopher Columbus, who had experience with the Portuguese kidnapping and enslaving people from West Africa, approached the Spanish monarchs. By 1492, Columbus had been following their peripatetic court for seven years, petitioning them to fund a voyage across the Atlantic, which then was called the Ocean Sea, to India and Japan, after having been rejected by the Portuguese.

Isabella and Fernando, even as they were at war against Portugal and the Muslims of Granada, still paid attention to Henry the Navigator's explorations and discussed Spain's critical need to launch expeditions west for new sources of wealth that bypassed the Ottoman Empire, which controlled access to valuable trade routes to the east.

In April 1492, the monarchs and Columbus entered into a contract, the main terms of which were generous because they believed he would not succeed. Isabella and Fernando gave Columbus a revocable grant to explore passage to the Indies by route of the Ocean Sea, and he became Admiral of the Ocean Sea, a hereditary title.

When the parties finalized the agreement, Columbus went to the port of Palos, near La Rábida, to prepare. Palos merchants provided two ships, the *Pinta* and the *Niña*, and Columbus leased the *Santa María*, the largest, with funds he had raised. Each vessel had enough food and supplies for one year.

The voyage began on August 3, 1492, on the Río Tinto and stopped at Gran Canaria, where the ships stayed almost a month while Columbus consulted with mariners who had experience sailing the Ocean Sea and understood its trade-wind patterns.

The expedition left La Gomera September 6, but by September 24 some sailors plotted to murder Columbus. He promptly suppressed the plot, as well as a second one. On October 10, Columbus and others saw birds, an indication that land was near.

On October 11, they saw land, and on October 12, the ships disembarked at Guanahaní, now known as Watling Island in the Bahamas. Columbus named it San Salvador and asserted possession of it in the name of the Spanish monarchs.

They traded glass beads and hats in exchange for parrots and javelins with the first people they met. Some of the indigenous people wore nose rings made of gold; using sign language, Columbus and his men asked where they had obtained that metal, and a Guanahaní pointed south, across the water.

The Europeans returned to their vessels and sailed south along the coast, disembarking at several villages. One night, at the second place they stopped, when the townspeople were asleep, they kidnapped seven men from their huts at knifepoint, two of whom escaped the following morning, so they seized four more at other villages in the following three weeks, shooting at least one inhabitant at each place before capturing the prisoners. Columbus named one indigenous man they abducted after his son, Diego Colón.

They went to several other islands, still in the Bahamas, where he and the people exchanged gifts, and they searched for, but found no signs of, gold. They again asked for it at the next place they went, and a chief gestured to the south, across the sea, and said, "Colba." Columbus's ships departed for Cuba, thinking he was going to Japan and, when they arrived there, named it "Juana."

On November 1, Columbus kidnapped ten people and sent two Castilians inland with a Guanahaní and one of the seized Cubans. When they returned after four days, the Castilians said they had found a village with fifty wooden houses and the people known as Taínos, who smoked a leaf called tobacco and made fabric from the cotton of the ceiba tree.

On November 21, Captain Martín Alonso Pinzón, on the *Pinta*, surreptitiously sailed away with his crew to look for gold, and Columbus departed Cuba with the *Santa María* and the *Niña* and landed at Haiti, as the indigenous people, also Taínos, called it, and named it La Española. For the first time on the voyage, he noted gold in river sands.

On Christmas Eve, the *Santa María* wrecked in the coral reef off the northern shore of La Española, near what now is Cap-Haïtien, where the residents helped Columbus unload the goods from the ship. With only one ship left now, the *Niña*, he knew he could not take all his crew back to Spain and ordered forty of his men to remain and build the first European settlement, named La Navidad, and collect gold samples until the next expedition arrived.

Columbus began his return journey to Spain on January 4, 1493. He encountered the *Pinta* on the sea, and the ships approached so Columbus and Pinzón could speak. Pinzón said he also was going back to Spain.

Columbus resumed his voyage but then stopped to capture more people to enslave, so he attacked the Taínos, who fought back with arrow points coated with poison. Columbus retreated and reembarked, but on February 17, 1493, the ship met difficult weather and had to land in the Azores. The *Pinta* had disappeared.

Columbus continued but stopped to visit King João in Portugal to relate details about his voyage. João, who after the meeting rejected his courtiers' advice to murder Columbus so Portugal could claim the new lands, sent a fleet to search for Columbus's discoveries. When Isabella and Fernando received Columbus's letters about his success, they summoned him to their court in Barcelona.

Isabella and Fernando received Columbus in Barcelona on April 21, 1493. They held a parade for him, and he joined them at Mass in their private chapel at the palace, after which Columbus presented them with gifts from the New World in the throne room: six indigenous men wearing gold jewelry, *hutias* (wild rats), chili peppers, sweet potatoes, monkeys, parrots, and a small quantity of gold. Royal priests baptized the Taínos, with the monarchs serving as godparents, and they named one of the new Christians Juan de Castilla. He died a month later.

The Portuguese informed Spain that they considered Columbus's discoveries their own, and Isabella and Fernando lodged a formal complaint with Pope Alexander VI, sent him samples of the New World gold, and asked for bulls confirming the Indies belonged to Spain.

The pope complied, and on April 4, 1493, he issued the Bull *Inter Caetera Divinae,* ordering that all land Columbus had discovered belonged to Spain, unless it was already occupied by another European country, and that all "newly found barbarous nations" were to be made Christian.

The Spanish monarchs commanded Columbus to prepare a second expedition, and Columbus left September 25, 1493, with the *Niña* and four other large vessels and fifteen hundred people, including twenty knights, ten women, two physicians, thirty enslaved Africans, and three Taínos whom Columbus had taken to Spain as exhibits.

In early November they disembarked on islands Columbus named Guadalupe, Santa María de Montserrat, Santa María de Antigua, and San Martín, where the Europeans killed twenty-five people and captured nine men, although the indigenous people murdered a Spaniard.

The conquerors left San Martín and passed an island Columbus called Santa Cruz (Saint Croix) but did not go ashore; then they went to Boriquen (Puerto Rico), where they executed four Taíno men and kidnapped twenty women and a boy, before passing and naming other islands: Nuestra Señora de las Nieves (Nevis), Santa Anastasia (Saint Eustatius), and San Cristóbal (Saba).

They arrived back at La Española November 14, 1493, to find that the indigenous people had killed all forty Europeans and burned down La Navidad. Columbus bartered for gold with Guacanagri, a chief, who said they had gone to war against Columbus's men because they had kidnapped their women.

On March 12, 1494, Columbus went to Puerto Cibao and found signs of gold there, so he built another village, San Tomás, but soon a group of Castilians tried to overthrow him. He cut off their ears and noses and went to La Isabela on March 29. On April 1, Columbus sent soldiers to San Tomás because a messenger informed him that the ruler there, Caonabo, had been responsible for the killing of the forty Spaniards at La Navidad, had been waging war against them at Cibao, and was preparing to launch another attack.

When the Europeans reached San Tomás, they could not find King Caonabo, whose military strategy was to assault the Spaniards and retreat to the forests until the next battle, forcing Columbus to send an army who murdered fifty Taínos and captured Caonabo and three members of his family, including a prince whom they chained in public at the square, after slicing off his ears.

Columbus sent Caonabo to Spain, but the ship he was on capsized, and he drowned. After learning of their ruler's fate, all Taínos stopped providing the Europeans with food.

In Spain, the monarchs, who were disappointed with the small amount of gold they had received, dispatched Columbus's brother Bartolomeo to the Indies. Bartolomeo Colón arrived June 24, 1494, to replace Diego Colón, but members of Columbus's second expedition seized three of Bartolomeo's ships and sailed to Spain to report to the monarchs that there was little wealth in the Indies.

The Castilians who stayed behind at San Tomás murdered and raped Taínos and stole their property; the Taínos retaliated by killing ten Spaniards and burning a hut in which forty of them were recuperating from illness.

In the Indies, Columbus was sailing along the coast of Cuba but had to return to La Isabela September 29, 1494, for medical treatment, as he had gout, with severe inflammation and pain in his legs, and his skin had bubbling sores from sunburn. He was too ill to deal with his men, who continued to engage in violence against the Taíno population.

Another battle took place between the conquerors and the indigenous people, who killed twelve Castilians. Not finding much gold, Columbus increased his kidnapping of Taínos for the Spanish slave markets and sent a ship with 550 of them, two hundred of whom died on board.

Still eager to find gold, however, he decided to conquer all of La Española. On March 25, 1495, with an indigenous ally, Chief Guacanagari, he fought and defeated a Taíno army. After the victory, Columbus forced the Taíno chiefs to pay him an annual tribute.

Dissatisfied with Columbus, the monarchs sent Juan de Aguado to La Española to carry out a legal proceeding against him, but a hurricane destroyed Aguado's ships as soon as he arrived there. Columbus departed to Spain with thirty Taíno slaves and 225 disgruntled Castilians, but before he left, the Europeans found a new area with gold that he named San Cristóbal.

He installed his brothers Bartolomeo as governor of the island and Diego Colón as second-in-command. On his way to Spain, at Guadalupe, he killed twenty people and kidnapped fifty to enslave and take on the trip.

He arrived in Spain on June 11, 1496, and had an audience with the queen and king, where he gave them gold and "Diego," a Taíno who wore a gold collar and was the brother of the late King Caonabo, and he told them about the new source for gold. They were pleased and told him to return to La Española with eight ships and reaffirmed the privileges they had granted him in 1492.

While Columbus was in Spain, his brothers built seven forts and captured and imprisoned the Taíno leaders Mayobenix and Guarionex, and shipped them to Spain.

On May 30, 1498, Columbus left Spain on his third voyage to the Indies, with five ships, two hundred men, and twenty women. Before going to La Española, however, he went south to the mouth of the Orinoco River, where he anchored and met indigenous people who wore pearls and gold. On August 1, he landed at Paria, marking the European discovery of what would become South America.

Columbus arrived back at La Española August 31, 1498, just as Santo Domingo had been completed. Isabella and Fernando appointed Francisco de Bobadilla to go to La Española, investigate who had usurped their power, and conduct legal proceedings.

Pedro Alvares Cabral departed Belem, Portugal, with fifteen hundred men and thirteen vessels to go to India; after stopping at the Cape Verde Islands to load additional provisions, on April 22, 1500, they landed in what would become Brazil. He sent men back to announce the discovery, frightening Spain, so Bobadilla left Seville and reached Santo Domingo on August 25, 1500.

Bobadilla ordered Columbus and his brothers immediately arrested and jailed in a dungeon until he sent them in chains to Spain with an order that they should remain so for the duration of the trip. When they arrived in Spain, the queen commanded their chains removed and for Columbus to see her in Granada.

Isabella stressed the importance of obtaining gold, but because Bobadilla, like Columbus, continued to send only enslaved people, the monarchs also dismissed Bobadilla, and assigned Fray Nicolás de Ovando to assume control of La Española.

Ovando left Spain February 13, 1502, with the largest fleet to date, twenty-seven vessels and twenty-five hundred settlers, including women. On February 21, 1502, one of Ovando's ships sank in a storm, and 120 passengers died. Ovando arrived in Santo Domingo April 15, 1502, and began proceedings against Bobadilla.

Columbus, around that time, had left Spain and was supposed to be exploring South America and finding straits to Asia. Instead, he stopped at La Española, contrary to Isabella's instructions. On June 29, 1502, he reached Santo Domingo and sent Ovando a message stating that he needed to land and obtain a lighter ship in exchange for one of his and that Ovando should not allow anyone to leave for Spain because of an impending tempest. Ovando denied Columbus's requests and ordered his ships to depart.

Columbus was sailing along the shore when a hurricane struck. It spared his vessels, but the ship carrying Bobadilla, Guarionex, 200,000 *pesos de oro*, and the documents pertaining to Bobadilla's legal proceeding against Columbus perished. The tempest wrecked Santo Domingo.

Ovando rebuilt the settlement at its current location on the west bank of Río Ozama. Ovando continued his investigation of gold sources and sent an expedition to the eastern end of the island, but his men stationed there set one of their dogs to kill a Taíno chief, and the Taínos, in turn, murdered eight Castilians. When Ovando learned about these events, he sent a captain named Juan de Esquivel, future conqueror of Jamaica, to lead a battalion of four hundred to suppress the rebellion.

The Taínos, including women, fought back, but the Castilians killed a significant number and enslaved the rest. A native ruler, Cotubanama, surrendered to prevent additional attacks on his subjects and became a tributary to the Castilians.

By autumn 1503, with the eastern end of La Española under Spanish domination, Ovando turned to the western sector, Xaragua, the territory of Queen Anacaona, widow of King Caonabo, where Anacaona's subjects had refused to submit to the Castilians and constantly fought them in battles, preventing Ovando from planting sugarcane and mulberry fields in that region.

As war took a toll on her people, Anacaona tried to enter into a peace treaty with Ovando and agreed to his request for a meeting. When it was scheduled, he led an army to Xaragua.

Anacaona held festivities for the Castilians and, as Ovando had asked, invited her noblemen and many others to participate. On the third day, as he had arranged with his army, Ovando signaled.

Horsemen surrounded a large house where one hundred native nobles had gathered, as Spanish foot soldiers guarded its exits.

The Spaniards set the building on fire, killing everyone inside. Anacaona and her people attacked the conquistadors with arrows and murdered forty-five, after which she and others fled, but the conquerors captured her and took her to Santo Domingo, where Ovando hanged her and enslaved her subjects. The Castilians now controlled the island.

Isabella's death from venereal disease, on November 26, 1504, led to a crisis of royal succession. In her will, Isabella had removed Fernando as king of Castile and named as heir to the Crown her daughter Juana, who was married to Philip of Habsburg, the son of the Austrian Emperor Maximilian. Fernando remained on the throne to contest Juana's succession. Juana and Philip had two sons, the eldest of whom, Carlos, had been raised in Flanders and would inherit Spain and the Habsburg possessions and be installed as the Holy Roman Emperor.

After Isabella's death, Philip of Habsburg proclaimed he was entitled to the Crown of Castile and León and departed Flanders with Juana, and, when they arrived in Spain, he granted Fernando's request for a meeting. Fernando agreed that Philip would rule exclusively and Philip and Juana's six-year-old son Carlos was heir to the throne.

Later that day, Fernando publicly reneged and went to Barcelona and, on September 4, 1506, to Naples. Philip died September 25, 1506; the stated cause of his demise was that he drank cold water after playing ball.

Fernando waited in Italy as his agents in Spain resolved the crisis of succession while the legislature governed.

Fernando returned to Spain on August 21, 1507, and imprisoned Juana, claiming she was mentally ill and unable to rule and
proclaiming himself king of Castile and León.

Back in the New World, Columbus's final voyages took place
from 1502 to 1504, when he traveled to islands west of La Española
and off the coast of Central America, including the Bay Islands,
Honduras. Columbus, now an invalid who suffered from gout and
other illnesses, returned to Spain on September 12, 1504.

Columbus, who would spend the rest of his life asking Fernando
for money, died May 20, 1506, at the age of fifty-seven. He was
buried in Valladolid, disinterred in 1509, reburied in Seville, disinterred and reburied in Santo Domingo, disinterred and reburied
in Havana, and disinterred and purportedly reburied in a golden
tomb in the Cathedral at Seville.

At La Española, the population had gone from three hundred
Castilians to more than three thousand, and Ovando had stimu-
lated the economy of the island. The Taínos, however, had rebelled
again, in the east near Higuey, setting fire to a Spanish fortress and
killing ten Castilians.

To deal with the insurrection, Ovando sent a military force led
by Juan Ponce de León. The Spaniards killed hundreds of Taínos and
seized the rebel Chief Cotubanama, hanging him in Santo Domingo.
Some Taíno women committed suicide rather than be captured, and
people fled to the mountains. The Castilians enslaved all survivors.

The Crown sent Ovando the first large group, one hundred,
of enslaved Africans to be sent to the New World, but he issued
a decree that no more could be taken to the Indies directly from
Africa because many of those were Muslims who were rebellious
and had joined the native people, particularly a chief named Hatuey,
in attacks against the colonists.

Hatuey encouraged enslaved Africans to escape to the mountains, where he trained them to fight the Castilians. Ovando still failed to supply Fernando with the quantity of gold he wanted, and Ovando was unpopular with the colonists, who wrote the Council of the Indies in Seville to complain about his practice of appointing his relatives to important posts. One such family member was Cortés, Ovando's cousin, who had recently arrived at La Española from Spain in October 1506.

On October 29, 1508, Fernando concluded that Ovando had exceeded his authority and recalled him to Spain, appointing instead Diego, elder legitimate son of Columbus, new governor of La Española.

On August 12, 1508, Juan Ponce de León left La Española for Boriquen, the Taíno name for what became Puerto Rico, and landed on Guanica, on the southwestern shore, with forty-two Castilians, including the Black conqueror Juan Garrido and Ponce de León's son, Juan González, who had learned the Taíno language in La Española.

When they landed in Boriquen, the conquerors went west, where they founded Aguadilla. Initially, the Taínos were cooperative, but then they lured a Castilian to an area they said had gold, where they drowned him in a stream.

The Taínos subsequently wrecked a post at Aguadilla and killed almost all the Castilians there; González escaped with thirty arrow wounds. War was joined and lasted for one year and ended when González captured seventeen Taíno chiefs.

To reward Ponce de León, the Crown named him governor, after which he built a plantation near San Juan, but Diego preferred another conquistador in that post, Julio Ceron. Ceron then forced out Ponce de León, but Ponce de León obtained proof that he was the legitimate governor and arrested Ceron and sent him to Spain. He then appointed Cristóbal de Sotomayor as Puerto Rico's first chief magistrate.

In January 1511, a local chief led a rebellion of three thousand, burned Sotomayor's plantation, and killed him and his nephew. In retaliation, the Castilians massacred ten thousand indigenous people. The Crown blamed Ponce de León for the insurrections and named Ceron as governor. Ponce de León conceded power and departed to explore Florida in 1514.

Ponce de León returned to Puerto Rico from Florida in 1515, and King Fernando again made him governor. Late that year, the two surviving Taíno leaders, Humaco and Daguao, tried to oust the invaders, and the conquerors killed them. The Castilians finally completed subjugation of Boriquen after they had murdered or enslaved all Taínos who had not fled into the forests or mountains.

VI.
The Córdoba and Grijalva Expeditions

Diego Velázquez, the governor of Cuba, initiated a voyage in 1516 to explore the Yucatán, to the west. He financed an expedition commanded by Francisco Fernandez de Córdoba and 110 men. The Córdoba expedition left Santiago de Cuba on February 8, 1517, and after six days, they saw an island that had statues of goddesses.

As five large canoes approached from the island, the Castilians waved white cloths to signal they were there in peace. The indigenous people, Maya, boarded Córdoba's ship, where the conquerors gave them goods, after which the Maya returned to their boats and departed.

The following afternoon, a Maya chief arrived with twelve canoes and, using hand signs, invited the foreigners to disembark, and they did, armed with swords, crossbows, and harquebuses.

The Maya led them into the forest, where warriors wearing cotton armor shot them with arrows and darts and launched stones from slingshots and wounded fifteen Castilians, but the invaders murdered twenty Maya before escaping through the woods to a Maya city that had streets, marketplaces, stone houses, and temples.

The Spanish called it El Gran Cairo and stayed three days as guests of the king, who held feasts in their honor, but when the Castilians demanded gold, the Maya told them to leave and gave them a few objects and two enslaved men, whom Córdoba named Melchor and Julian.

They departed and sailed along the coastline, during which time six soldiers died from wounds they had sustained in battle. They disembarked at a beach they thought was uninhabited.

While they filled their casks with drinking water, fifty Maya arrived, invited them to tour their land, and led them to a temple, outside of which there was piled firewood. They walked in. Dead snakes hung from an altar covered in blood, and warriors stood nearby as Maya priests fumigated the Castilians with incense and then signaled they should go; the Spanish fled to the beach.

The conquistadors sailed and landed by a town called Champotón that had stone houses and maize fields. While the chief visited them, armed Maya wearing black-and-white face paint and feathered crests approached to stare at them. They left, and, that night, the Spaniards camped by the water but could not sleep because they heard the incessant beating of drums. The Maya attacked them at dawn and, using obsidian-edged swords, copper-headed axes, stones shot from slings, and arrows, killed thirty Castilians, captured two, and wounded the rest.

Córdoba himself received thirty-three injuries. He managed to get all his men onto only two of his ships, as he had to abandon the third because it was damaged. He went to Florida. There, as they were filling their casks, indigenous warriors charged them, wounding four Castilians and capturing one, but the invaders murdered twenty. They left for Cuba and, after two months, landed at Puerto de Carenas.

Córdoba and his captains went to Santiago de Cuba, where they reported to Velázquez that they had seen well-built towns with stone houses and prosperous farms. The people had given them gold objects, and the warriors wore thick, quilted-cotton armor that arrows could not penetrate.

Using signs, Velázquez questioned Julian and Melchor, and he understood them to mean the gold had come from the region where they lived and that there were people who looked like the Spaniards being held captive near their town.

Intrigued by these accounts, Velázquez prepared to send a different expedition to the Yucatán, but when he did not choose him as commander, Córdoba announced he was going to Spain to lodge a complaint. Córdoba died two weeks later.

Velázquez financed another fleet with a new commander, his young nephew Juan de Grijalva. Grijalva took Julian as an interpreter.

The soldiers on Grijalva's voyage had quilted-cotton armor that Cuban Taínas had made, similar to what Córdoba had reported the Maya warriors had worn; they also had better weapons than Córdoba's. Grijalva also had culverins that fired twenty-pound balls about four hundred yards, lighter guns, and fighting dogs.

The fleet departed Cuban waters on April 30, 1518, and saw an island called Ah-Cuzamil-Peten ten days later. Two canoes, each carrying two Maya, drew close but left without communicating, and the next day, when a chief arrived, he went onto Grijalva's ship accompanied by eight warriors. Using Julian as an interpreter, Grijalva and the native leader greeted each other, and the Castilian gave him shirts and wine from Spain. The chief disembarked and returned to land.

The following day, Grijalva and one hundred men went ashore at Cozumel and found only ten people, who said that the other residents had fled inland. He gave a woman glass beads and persuaded her to go to the chiefs and tell them to come back to town, but she returned alone two days later.

Grijalva and his men climbed to the top of a pyramid, where they saw human bones and statues. Three Maya leaders arrived afterward, and, ignoring the foreigners, one held a bucket of liquid balsam he offered to the gods.

Grijalva ordered his chaplain to hold a mass, and after both ceremonies had ended, the Maya offered the conquerors turkeys, honey, and maize, but Grijalva declined to take the goods, saying he wanted gold. The Maya did not respond to that request but invited them to a feast in town.

On May 7, 1518, the Castilians left and sailed along the coast of Yucatán and back to Cozumel, where they filled their casks with water and captured rats for food.

On May 26, 1518, they anchored three miles away from Champotón. Half the soldiers, taking three cannon and three harquebuses, went on boats to the shore, where they met Maya who invited them to enter.

"We are looking for gold. Will you give us some?"

"We have no gold here, so if that is what you seek, like your men who came last year and were soundly beaten at Champotón, you should leave. But we will let you fill your casks with water."

"Well, we also need food, and, really, are you sure you don't have gold?"

"We will give you food, but if you continue asking for gold, we will fight you and force you to leave the same way your brethren did last year."

The Spaniards stayed, but, in the morning, Grijalva asked for gold again. A chieftain offered them a mask of gilded wood and two gold plates if they agreed to leave. They again refused. That night, Maya warriors beat drums and blew conch trumpets. Grijalva did not take action.

At daybreak, the chief led three thousand Maya, wearing black, red, and white war paint and carrying bows and arrows, lances, single- and doubled-handed swords, slingshots, and stones, to the invaders' camp. The chief put a lit torch between him and Grijalva and ordered Julian to interpret.

"If you do not go before this light finishes burning, we will kill you."

Battle was joined. Grijalva ordered his men to put the cannon in a tower of the temple, and the Spaniards killed most of the Maya; then they drove the rest into swampland. The Maya murdered ten Castilians and wounded sixty, including Grijalva, whom the Maya shot with arrows three times and who lost two teeth. The combatants called a cease-fire for the night, and the conquerors treated their injured, buried their dead, and sent three captured native men to the chief with green beads as peace offerings.

The following morning, a large group of Maya arrived at the camp, and Grijalva addressed them. "We don't want to fight anymore. Would you please just allow us more water before we leave?"

The Maya gave them a mask of gilded wood and allowed them access to a well; then the Spaniards departed.

Their next stop was at a port leading to a large lagoon they named Puerto Deseado, where they saw temples and fishermen but few other people, as most had fled to the interior. They captured four men, including one they named Pedro Barba, and, on June 8, 1518, they sailed to the Tabasco River and renamed it the Grijalva River.

There, most of the expedition went up in boats and two of the smaller ships, while the others, including Grijalva's, remained on the larger vessels at sea. A group of armed Maya approached Grijalva on canoes and asked him what he wanted.

Grijalva spoke to Julian in Castilian, and Julian spoke in Yucatec Mayan to Pedro Barba, who spoke to their chief in Chontal of Tabasco Mayan. Grijalva replied that he wanted to trade and invited them on board. The chief and four armed warriors embarked, and the chief put on Grijalva a golden breastplate, gold bracelets, a crown designed in golden leaves, and fabric shoes decorated in gold.

Grijalva gave him green beads and mirrors, and told two of his men to dress the chief in Spanish clothing, a green velvet doublet, socks and shoes, and a velvet cap. Grijalva asked for more gold, but the chief said there was none and invited him and his men to a banquet. Grijalva asked if he could go inland to search for gold. The chief denied his request and disembarked.

The Castilians on the smaller vessels returned from exploring, and the expedition departed to spend the next five days in the Tabasco region, known for its valuable cacao bean, jaguar skins, and greenstone the Maya traded with Moctezoma, who in turn supplied them with gold, copper, obsidian, and enslaved people.

The Spaniards thereafter sailed along the coast and, on June 17, 1518, landed on a small island and went inside one of two stone temples. There, in front of the statue of a god, lay four dead people, two adults and two children, and there was blood on the walls and, on the ground, forty skulls and human bones.

The Spaniards ran out and went to the beach, where they boarded their ships and left. The next day, they saw men waving banners, so Grijalva sent a captain and fifty armed men with the interpreters. On land, the people greeted them and gave them cotton cloaks. The Spaniards asked them for gold, and the chief replied he would bring it for them in the evening. The conquerors returned to their ship, and, that night, the Maya went to them by canoe with more clothing but no gold.

The following morning, as the expedition moved on, they saw men on a beach gesturing to them. Grijalva and three captains landed, and, once they were there, a well-dressed man invited them to dine at his home. The people were the Totonacs, tributaries of Moctezoma's, who had to make significant remittances of semiannual payments of valuable goods to him.

Grijalva and his expedition spent ten days with them, although, at night, they returned to their ships. The Totonacs delivered to the Spaniards cooked food three times a day and smoked tobacco with them, although the conquerors continued to ask for gold, even after the Totonacs had given them gold masks, gold figurines, and a gold headband.

The Totonac ruler responded to Grijalva's query about the source of their gold.

"There is an emperor named Moctezoma who is immensely wealthy and powerful. His great capital inland is called Tenochtitlan, and his territories extend to this area and even beyond, to the lowlands. If you want gold and other riches, he is the one you should visit."

"But you say he is inland? How does one get there? Is it possible to go by river?"

"No, you would have to walk or be carried by litter."

The Castilians thanked their hosts, departed, and continued along the coast.

Moctezoma's vast intelligence system had been reporting to him about the foreigners, a few of whom had been shipwrecked off the eastern coast south of his empire, and when he learned the details of their time with the Totonacs, he sent an emissary to approach Grijalva at sea.

Grijalva granted permission to Moctezoma's envoy to board with his men, and the Mexican gave Grijalva cotton cloaks with elaborate designs and beaded necklaces and shared with the Spaniards a meal of turkey stew, maize cakes, and chocolate. The Castilians provided red wine. After dining, Moctezoma's agent departed for Tenochtitlan to report about the strangers and deliver hard biscuits Grijalva had sent him, which Moctezoma refused to touch.

Grijalva thereafter discussed with his captains what they should do next, but he opposed a faction that wanted to found a colony because the expedition was low on supplies. He decided they would not establish a settlement and return to Cuba after additional exploration.

They went on land, kidnapped a boy, and claimed the area for the Crown, naming it San Juan de Ulúa. Most of the Castilians proceeded north along the coast, but Grijalva sent Pedro Alvarado and others back to Cuba with the gold and other goods, and a written report about a wealthy empire located in the interior of Yucatán. When Alvarado arrived in Cuba, he gave Velázquez Grijalva's letter and the treasure, and said the land was rich.

Velázquez was pleased and began planning for a third expedition, but as he did not have permission to explore inland or colonize without a royal commission, he concocted, as a stated purpose for the next voyage, a search for Grijalva. He sent a petition with the gold objects to the king.

Back in Yucatán, while the Castilians were at sea, a people called the Huaxtecs attacked them and cut a ship's cables; Grijalva ordered his men to fire cannon, killing four and sinking one of their canoes. The Spaniards fled. The pilot and crew wanted to return to Cuba because the rainy season had begun and sailing conditions were difficult, but the ship was leaking, and it took two weeks to repair the vessel. They departed again, but then Grijalva's ship was damaged and had to be fixed before they could resume their travels. Grijalva reached Matanzas on October 5.

Velázquez had made progress on preparations for the third expedition even before Grijalva was back and had concluded that he needed someone bold for the venture, a man who could contribute funds and was capable of attracting the requisite number of captains, pilots, and crew to join him. The Cuban conquistador Velázquez had in mind, however, had no experience commanding a military and a proclivity for insubordination and failure to adhere to the chain of command. He was the chief magistrate of Santiago de Cuba, and he had made a substantial fortune: Cortés.

Velázquez offered Cortés the position as commander and gave him a report of the Córdoba and Grijalva voyages, including the Totonac statement about a great city in the interior and a wealthy emperor and read him the list of gold items Alvarado had brought from the Yucatán.

VII.

Hernán Cortés and the Conquest of Cuba

Hernán Cortés was born on July 31, 1484, into a noble family in Medellín, Castile. Cortés's father, Martín Cortés, was the illegitimate son of Rodrigo de Monroy, whose own father, Fernando Rodriguez de Monroy, had been a conqueror of the Muslims on behalf of the Crown, and Martín had fought in the war to reconquer Granada. Catalina Altamirano Pizarro, Cortés's mother, was an aunt to Francisco Pizarro, the future conqueror of Peru.

When Cortés was twelve, in 1496, his parents sent him to live in Salamanca, with Martín's sister and her husband, a business lawyer, to begin an apprenticeship. When Cortés was fifteen, he entered the University of Salamanca and graduated in 1501 with a Bachelor of Law.

He decided to join the military and was wavering between going to fight in Italy and joining an expedition to La Española when the Crown appointed his cousin Nicolás Ovando governor general of the Indies. Cortés intended to join Ovando on his voyage but instead traveled around Spain and lived in Valladolid for a year, worked as a business lawyer, and then went to Seville in 1504. At the age of twenty, he finally departed for La Española.

When he arrived in Santo Domingo on April 6, 1504, Ovando made him a soldier to participate in suppression of indigenous rebellions in Baoruco and Higuey, and Cortés performed so well in massacres of the insurgent Taíno villages that Ovando appointed him to manage Azua de Compostela and serve there as a business lawyer.

Diego Velázquez, then deputy governor in La Española, in 1511 obtained approval from Diego Colón to conquer Cuba and find and kill an indigenous ruler named Hatuey and his rebel ally, Caguax, who had fled there. Velázquez financed a fleet and recruited three hundred Spaniards, including Cortés, for an expedition. Cortés by that time had amassed riches from gold mining, cattle breeding, enslavement, and agriculture.

When they landed in Cuba, the conquerors founded the island's first capital, Villa de Nuestra Señora Asunción de Baracoa, where they annihilated the entire village, who had refused to submit and had fought back with arrows. Velázquez, with Cortés's participation, located Hatuey and captured and executed him by burning at the stake, after he refused a Christian baptism that would have made him eligible for beheading.

The conquest of Cuba continued. At Bayamo, the conquerors massacred a hundred Taínos, forcing the town to surrender, and pursued those who fled toward Camaguey, where they seized and murdered other people, including Caguax.

At Caonao, Pánfilo de Narváez sent a friar named Bartolomé de las Casas ahead with a Taíno interpreter from La Española to ask the native people for food, and they prepared significant quantities of meat, fish, and bread and served the invaders outdoors. More than three thousand Taíno adults and children gathered in one of their town squares to observe the strangers as they ate, and more than five hundred nobles watched from inside a nearby mansion.

The Castilians, after they had dined, sent de las Casas and two hundred soldiers to the house, where the cleric announced they wanted to enter, but the leaders refused to admit them. The Europeans broke down the door and murdered everyone there, even as Narváez and the rest of the Spanish Army beheaded and dismembered the people in the square. When the mass homicide was complete, the conquerors met at the square and departed as one force, and as word spread of the massacre, Taínos in their path yielded without the threat of violence.

In 1512, at Cuvanacan, Cortés successfully panned for gold with enslaved Taínos and built a hacienda. He made a Taína his concubine and christened her Leonor Pizarro. He fathered a daughter with her he named Catalina Pizarro.

Velázquez had trouble managing his colonists who, led by Cortés, publicly complained that Velázquez was not providing them sufficient Taínos as slaves. Velázquez arrested Cortés for insubordination and was about to send him in chains to Santo Domingo, but Cortés asked for a pardon. Velázquez granted it on the condition he marry Catalina Suarez, sister of Juan Suarez, Cortés's friend.

Cortés, however, after Velázquez freed him, refused to go forward with the wedding, and Velázquez again seized him, on the charge that he had seduced Catalina Suarez, and put him in jail, but Cortés's friends broke in, released him, and hid him in a church.

The town constable, on Velázquez's orders, made the priests force Cortés outside, and, when they did so, he put him in leg and wrist irons and took him back into custody. But Cortés's allies paid the warden to exchange clothes with Cortés and allow him to walk out of the jail.

Cortés sent a message, purportedly from detention, to Velázquez asking him for another pardon and promising to marry Catalina Suarez. Velázquez forgave Cortés on the condition he lead the conquest of Taíno villages in the western territories before his wedding. Cortés obeyed and suppressed rebellions in the region. When he returned to town, he married Catalina Suarez, with Velázquez as a witness.

On July 25, 1515, Velázquez made Cortés chief magistrate of Santiago de Cuba. The Castilians now controlled all the areas they wanted in Cuba, and that year Velázquez and Cortés founded its main cities: San Salvador de Bayamo, Trinidad, Sancti Spíritus, Puerto Principe, and the Port of San Cristóbal de La Habana, the original site of the current capital.

ACKNOWLEDGMENTS

Many thanks to my husband, Timothy Rogers, for his enduring support!

The following primary and secondary sources were invaluable in helping me to understand the worlds of the First Nations and the Spanish conquerors. In particular, I am deeply grateful to Michael V. Wilcox for providing me a lens with which to view the materials I read and to Hugh Thomas for his prodigious research and writing.

I thank the Instituto Nacional de Antropología e Historia de México for its extraordinary work. I also thank the New York Public Library for giving me my first borrowing card when I was ten and for its wonderful collection and staff in the Rare Books Division.

FURTHER READING

Babinger, Franz. 1978. *Mehmed the Conqueror and His Time*. Princeton: Princeton University Press.

Carimokam, Sahaja, 2010. *Muhammad and The People of The Book*.

Carrasco, David. 1999. *City of Sacrifice: The Aztec Empire and the Role of Violence in Civilization*. Boston: Beacon Press.

Carrasco, David and Scott Sessions. 1998. *Daily Life of the Aztecs: People of the Sun and Earth*. Westport, London: Greenwood Press.

Cortés, Hernando. 1939. *The Last Will and Testament of Hernando Cortés, Marqués Del Valle*. Edited by GRG Conway. Mexico City: Gante Press.

Cortés, Hernán. 1986. *Letters from Mexico*. Translated and edited by Anthony Pagden. New Haven: Yale University Press.

Díaz del Castillo, Bernal. 1963. *The Conquest of New Spain*. Translated by John M. Cohen. London: Penguin Books.

Downey, Kristin. 2014. *Isabella The Warrior Queen*. New York: Nan A. Talese/Doubleday Edition.

Gardiner, C. Harvey. 1956. *Naval Power in the Conquest of Mexico*. Austin: University of Texas Press.

Homza, Lu Ann. 2006. *The Spanish Inquisition 1478–1614*. Indianapolis: Hackett Publishing Company.

Martínez, José Luis. 1990. *Documentos Cortesianos I: 1518–1528, Secciones I a III (Arte)*. Tlalpan, Ciudad de México: Fondo de Cultura Económica.

———. 1991. *Documentos Cortesianos II: 1526–1545, Sección IV: Juicio de Residencia (Seccion de Obras de Historia)*. Tlalpan: Ciudad de México Fondo de Cultura Económica.

Smith, Michael E. 2012. *The Aztecs, Third Edition*. Chichester, Sussex: John Wiley & Sons.

Sugiyama, Saburo. 2005. *Human Sacrifice, Militarism, and Rulership: Materialization of State Ideology at the Feathered Serpent Pyramid, Teotihuacan*. Cambridge, UK: Cambridge University Press.

Thomas, Hugh. 1993. *Conquest: Cortes, Montezuma, and the Fall of Old Mexico*. New York: Simon & Schuster.

———. 2010. *The Golden Empire: Spain, Charles V, and the Creation of America*. New York: Random House.

———. 2003. *Rivers of Gold: The Rise of the Spanish Empire, from Columbus to Magellan*. New York: Random House.

———. 1997. *The Slave Trade: The Story of the Atlantic Slave Trade: 1440–1870*. New York: Touchstone, Simon & Schuster.

Wilcox, Michael V. 2009. *The Pueblo Revolt and the Mythology of Conquest, An Indigenous Archaeology of Contact*. Berkeley: University of California Press.

For additional resources, please visit my
website at: www.marlenbodden.com

CPSIA information can be obtained
at www.ICGtesting.com
Printed in the USA
LVHW090611051019
633306LV00002B/6/P